Georgia's Kitchen

G

GALLERY BOOKS

New York   London   Toronto   Sydney

Georgia's Kitchen

jenny nelson

G℡

Gallery Books
A Division of Simon & Schuster, Inc.
1230 Avenue of the Americas
New York, NY 10020

First Gallery Books trade paperback edition August 2010

GALLERY BOOKS and colophon are trademarks of Simon & Schuster, Inc.

For information about special discounts for bulk purchases, please contact Simon & Schuster Special Sales at 1-866-506-1949 or business@simonandschuster.com.

The Simon & Schuster Speakers Bureau can bring authors to your live event. For more information or to book an event contact the Simon & Schuster Speakers Bureau at 1-866-248-3049 or visit our website at www.simonspeakers.com.

Designed by Joy O'Meara

Manufactured in the United States of America

10 9 8 7 6 5 4 3 2 1

Library of Congress Cataloging-in-Publication Data

Nelson, Jenny.
  Georgia's kitchen / Jenny Nelson.—1st Gallery Books trade pbk. ed.
     p.   cm.
  1. Women cooks—Fiction. 2. Cookery—Fiction. 3. Restaurateurs—Fiction.
4. Manhattan (New York, N.Y.)—Fiction. 5. Italy—Fiction. I. Title.
PS3614.E44575G46 2010
813'.6—dc22

                                                          2009052442

ISBN 978-1-4391-7333-6
ISBN 978-1-4391-7334-3 (ebook)

For Ava, Flora and, of course, Warren

Chapter One

Georgia turned onto a tree-lined street of brick town houses and brownstones, stopping when she reached a gunmetal-gray low-rise that shared none of its neighbors' quiet charm. Strips of smoky glass sliced through the facade, and a row of porthole windows ran under the roofline: the restaurant. An architectural travesty or triumph, depending on which side of the design camp you fell, but it got people talking, which was, after all, the point. MARCO was discreetly stamped in a cement block over the door, though as far as Georgia knew, no one had ever noticed this so-called sign. If you had to ask, you didn't deserve to eat there.

Heaving open the vaultlike door, she walked through the steel-blue dining room, past the polished nickel tables and chairs and the white, ultrasuede banquettes, her heels clicking across the terrazzo floor. The floral designer freshened a mammoth arrangement on the lacquered bar, replacing spent stems with Casablanca lilies, irises, and peonies—all white, a Marco dictum.

The daily staff meal and meeting began promptly at three, and Bernard, the restaurant's laser-tongued general manager, had zero patience for latecomers. Six four-tops shoved together created a makeshift communal table, and seating was first come, first served. As waiters, cooks, and busboys rushed in, Georgia took her seat, instinctively turning her engagement ring—a cushion-cut diamond on a platinum band—to the underside of her hand, subway-style. Unpolished nails and nicked-up hands, unfortunate but unavoidable occupational hazards of chefs everywhere, were hardly the ideal backdrop for such a splendid ring. But Glenn wanted her to wear it, and not on a chain around her neck as she'd prefer. He wanted it on her left ring finger as on every other bride-to-be.

He was still sleeping when she'd left their apartment early that morning to head to the fish market with Ricky, her sous-chef. She kissed Glenn good-bye, first on his forehead, then on his lips, hoping he'd wake up and kiss her back, which he did for a second before rolling over and mumbling something she couldn't understand. Their conflicting work schedules had never allowed for a ton of snuggling time, but lately sleepy kisses and barely intelligible *See you later*s were as good as it got.

"Hey, Chef, long time no see." Ricky slid into the seat next to her, tossing his yellow hair out of his eyes. Wearing baggy shorts down to his knees and tube socks pulled so high they could have been tights, he looked more clown-school grad than classically trained chef. He wrinkled his nose and sniffed the air. "Did you forget to shower after our fishing trip? Or is it me who smells like a salty dog?"

"Definitely you, Rick," said Georgia. "I've Purelled my fingers to shreds."

She and Ricky had met years earlier while working for a tyrannical boss whose idea of a good time was throwing knives at a corkboard decorated with Polaroid pictures of his staff. Since then, they'd cooked side by side in cramped kitchens all over Manhattan, and when Georgia was promoted to head chef at Marco, she'd insisted on hiring Ricky as her second-in-command. Not only was he a culinary savant who could tick off twenty-nine different kinds of basil and the best uses for each, but he was one of the few people who told her exactly what he thought. About everything.

Bernard strode to the table, trademark red clipboard tucked under his arm, wire-rim specs perched on his nose. "Good afternoon, everyone. It's Friday and we have a big night." He tapped his pencil on the clipboard. "Socialites, B-list actors, even a low-ranking politician."

No one was better at building buzz than Marco, former chef and current proprietor of his eponymous restaurant, and the faux foodies couldn't eat it up fast enough. Though his menu was uninspired and his decor was as slick as his demeanor, his restaurant was booked months in advance, and even the five-and-dimes, the least desirable time slots, were reserved weeks out.

"And," Bernard continued, "rumor has it Mercedes Sante from the *Daily* may be dropping in. You know what that means. If anyone spots the old bag, punch it into the computer ASAP. We fucked up the *Herald*, let's not fuck this one up too."

Rumors of wig-wearing reviewers flooded the restaurant, but unless an actual source was named, everyone rightly assumed they came from Marco, who had somehow graduated elementary school without learning the story of the boy who cried wolf.

Three busboys brought out the staff's "family meal": a bowl of soupy spinach, a platter of spaghetti doused in a watery red sauce, and a plate of mini-meatballs directly from Costco's frozen-food section. As usual, this family meal would never be served to an actual member of Marco's family, not even his wicked stepmother.

Georgia listened as Bernard rattled off her daily specials for the servers, then allowed them small tastes of the samples the prep team had prepared. There was a beautiful branzino they'd picked up at Hunts Point; a house-made taglierini with peas and ramps from the Greenmarket, slivers of bresaola, and shaved pecorino; polenta with wild-mushroom ragout; risotto with baby artichoke, asparagus and mint; sautéed periwinkles; and herb-stuffed leg of lamb.

Having inherited the regular menu directly from Marco, who balked at even the tiniest change, Georgia's opportunity to cook the way she wanted was showcased in the nightly specials. There was no way she'd leave their fate in the hands of the waiters until they were completely schooled on the preparation details. Nor would she ever serve anything less than first-rate.

"Do you guys have any questions?" she asked after they popped their first tastes.

"Is there butter in this branzino al sala?" asked a ruddy-cheeked guy who was the latest addition to the team, his mouth full of fish.

"First, *sala* is a room. It's *sale*—as in 'salt.' But only tell people that if they specifically ask, otherwise they'll assume it's too salty. And tell them the salt, which dries into a hard crust that's cracked open at the end, preserves the fish's natural flavors and juices as it cooks so it's moist and tender. And no butter, just olive oil, fresh thyme, chervil, and lemon."

"Push this one, guys. We're selling it at thirty-three bucks a pop," Bernard said without looking up from his clipboard.

"Really?" Georgia said. "A little high for my taste, but almost worth it."

"So, it's rich and flavorful?" the new guy continued hopefully.

She shook her head. "Subtle and delicate. Tell them we only serve this when the branzino is really top-notch. Say that and it'll fly."

Georgia had waited tables while getting her degree at the Culinary Institute of America and knew exactly what to say to make a dish sell out. She also knew how to guarantee it'd be on the next day's lunch menu in a slightly different, and likely chopped, form.

"Uh, okay," he said, popping another bite into his mouth.

She ran through the rest of the specials, going over their selling points until the waiters knew them cold. When conversation turned to the new Zac Posen–designed wait uniforms, she rocked back her chair and stared up at the glossy blue ceiling, wondering how much longer she could stand working at Marco, or rather for Marco. Granted, there was the generous paycheck. And the exposure. Without it, she'd never be able to open her own place. Having seared her skin in some of the city's top kitchens, she was ready, really ready, to run her own restaurant. But planning a marriage and planning a business was way too much planning, even for an überplanner like Georgia. Though she hated to admit it, her engagement was sapping her energy.

It didn't help that Glenn was so busy defending his clients at the entertainment law firm where he worked that he barely had time for anyone else. When they'd first met, he spoke of becoming a public interest lawyer, but law school, his parents, and the promise of a fat paycheck killed his idealism fairly quickly, or at least put it on hold. Now the plan was to cash out at forty-five and work for an NGO, but until then, work/client schmoozing/partying took precedence over just about everything. Last week he'd had Georgia reserve at Marco for his biggest client, hip-hop star Diamond Tee. Apparently a huge Tee fan, Marco made sure the Cristal was flowing all night long. When it came to celebs, A-, B-, or even C-list, Marco was the best kiss-ass in the business.

"Yes, Georgia, even you." Georgia's chair fell forward with a thud. Bernard, who'd removed his tiny specs, stared at her.

"What was that, Bernard?"

"I said Marco doesn't give us free gym memberships for nothing. He wants everyone to look good—even those of you in the kitchen. And we're putting together a team for the Corporate 5K, if anyone's interested."

"Are you saying I'm fat?" Georgia sucked in her stomach the way she'd been trained to do by her whippet-thin mother back when she was a pudgy six-year-old.

"Fat? No. But remember: working out is as good for the mind"—Bernard touched his glasses to his forehead—"as it is for the middle. That's it, everyone. Have a good night." He nodded to Georgia, straightened his tie, and marched out to the floor, a picture of competence. Even the way he walked, as if an invisible cord were holding his carriage perfectly erect, was efficient.

"Now Marco's making us work out too? As a team? What's next—group therapy? A sweat lodge? Or maybe just a drum circle?" Ricky didn't bother concealing his contempt. Several months back, his parents had flown in from California for a visit. Aging hippies, they'd arrived at Marco smelling of patchouli and home-spun yarn and were ignored, made to spell their last name—Smith—a half-dozen times, and at last shunted off to a doily-size table in Siberia, all thanks to Marco, who'd checked them out from the tops of their multicolor caps down to their ergonomic shoes. While Georgia had her own reasons for disliking her boss, Ricky would never forget the slight to his mom and dad.

While he went outside to smoke, Georgia headed to the locker room, eager to get the night started. The minuscule room was empty. A couple of lockers lined one wall, and a flimsy mirror hung behind the door. During her first week on the job Marco had ripped down the mirror, emptied a bindle of coke on it, and chopped it up with his maxed-out credit card while Georgia stood by, pretending it was no big deal that her brand-new boss was doing lines in front of her. He offered her one, and she smiled politely and mumbled something about needing to get back to the kitchen. Of course she'd known the restaurant industry could get crazy, but it wasn't until Marco that she'd seen it in full-blown action. When she told Glenn the story, he barely raised an eyebrow. "In the restaurant?" was all he had to say.

Before anyone could barge in, Georgia slipped out of her street clothes and into her work uniform. Wearing shapeless khakis, white chef coat, and black clogs, she probably wouldn't turn any heads. But at thirty-three, she was tall and trim, any pudginess long gone thanks to her thrice-weekly runs at the Reservoir. Her eyes were green and catlike, her skin fair and clear, the type that pinkened from the slightest exertion, and her nose, long and thin, would have cast an aristocratic air were it not for the slight bump on the bridge, a remnant from a childhood roller-skating accident. As a college boyfriend once remarked, she looked as if she'd stepped out of the pages of a Victorian novel, a proper English lady, sun parasol and all. Except the hair. Unruly curls on a good day, a downright frizz fest in the summer and in a hot kitchen. Which is why at that very moment she was assiduously twisting her dark-chocolate-colored mass into submission. Two bobby pins dangled from her lips, and her eyes were narrowed with concentration.

"Georgia. I was looking for you." Georgia stared up into the slickly handsome face of Marco, boss, restaurateur, onetime chef, one-night stand. He had the jutting cheekbones, pillow lips, and perma-tanned skin of a daytime-soap star.

"Oh, hey, Marco." The bobby pins dropped to the floor with a barely audible ping.

"How's it going? Planning the wedding?"

If there was one thing Georgia couldn't stand, it was talking to guys she had slept with—particularly her boss—about her upcoming nuptials.

"Yup. Going smoothly. Very smoothly." She bent down to pick up the pins.

"That's great, Georgia." He held her gaze for a second too long. "So, Bernard told you about Mercedes Sante."

"He sure did. Exciting." She tried to force her hair behind her ears and felt it instantly spring back. "I'm sure everyone will do great."

"I wanted to talk to you about that." He looked down, put his hands behind his back, and cleared his throat like a high school football coach psyching up the team for the homecoming game. Georgia noticed his hair was thinning.

"A good review from the *Daily*, as you know, can bring in un-precedented business." He smirked. "Not like we really need it, but you never know."

She obliged him with a tight smile.

"But it can also make or break a chef. Especially an attrac-tive Food Network–worthy chef like yourself. You know what I'm saying?"

Georgia tried to remember why she had slept with him in the first place. Was it the devastating news that Glenn had cheated on her? The lobotomizing trio of bone-dry Sapphire martinis downed in response to said news? The fateful decision to play "Crazy" on the jukebox right before last call?

"Sure thing, Marco. Don't worry. It'll be great. I better run." She stepped around him carefully, so as not to brush even one button on his custom-made Borrelli shirt.

By nine o'clock, Georgia felt as if her clogs had been Krazy Glued to the floor. They must have done 150 covers, almost all of them seafood. As she'd predicted, the branzino special was a hit and was eighty-sixed an hour and a half after open. Despite the crush, the kitchen was holding its own, and most of the dishes were coming up on time. She'd replated more than usual, but at least everything had been at the window when she'd needed it.

"Did we get a write-up in the *Junior League Digest* or something? What's with all the salmon, sauce-on-the-side requests?" she asked Ricky.

"Close. *Tell* magazine. The 'Shit Girl' issue."

"You mean 'It Girl'?"

"*It, shit,* what's the dif? If you're blond, were born on Park Avenue, and are married to an investment banker, chances are you're at Marco tonight."

"Hence the disproportionately large number of arugula salads. Got it. Speaking of Park Avenue princesses, are you coming to see Lo tonight?" Lo was one of Georgia's two best friends and, at the moment, a folksy singer-songwriter. This followed stints as a film production assistant, a junior copywriter, and an apprentice herbalist; there was no telling how much longer her Joni Mitchell phase would last. The house phone rang before Ricky could answer.

"Chef! Glenn!" yelled a dishwasher from across the kitchen.

"Take over, Rick." She picked up the extension as he began expediting, calling out orders to the line cooks. "Hey, sweetie. How are you?"

"I miss you."

"Me too. What are you doing?"

"I had to meet Diamond Tee up at Piece in Harlem. He wouldn't take no for an answer."

"Please tell me you're not bailing on Lo's show." Last-minute cancellations had become part of Glenn's MO lately.

"I'm not bailing. I'll be there."

"Good. I feel like I haven't seen you in forever."

"You mean that wasn't you who kissed me good-bye this morning?"

"No, it must have been your other fiancée."

"Her again. If I don't make it to the restaurant, I'll definitely make it to the show. The Rumpus?"

"The Rumpus."

"Okay, George. I'll see you there. Promise."

"Great. And give my regards to Mr. T. Oh, wait, that's the guy who kicked Rocky's ass, right?"

"Funny," Glenn said before she hung up.

Ricky looked over. "Your dude coming tonight?"

"He is," Georgia said. "He promised."

"Awesome." Ricky held up his hand for a high five.

Georgia swatted it away. "I'm not sure having my fiancé agree to meet me at a dive bar on the Lower East Side is worth a high five."

"I guess a high five is a little excessive." He dropped his hand. "Low five?"

She laughed. Sometimes Ricky and she got along so well it seemed a shame they couldn't just get it over with and fall in love. But he'd never made her belly ping or her neck tingle or distracted her so much she couldn't think of anything other than how sexy his *forearm* was. Glenn did.

Bernard burst through the swinging door and into the kitchen. "Table fifteen. She's here."

Georgia and Ricky looked at each other blankly.

"None other than Mercedes Sante herself. She's disguised as a fat carpetbagger," Bernard said. "On second thought, I don't think she's disguised at all. Check out her order—you better make that guinea hen sing like a canary." He turned to the rest of the staff. "People of the kitchen, the vippiest of VIPs is in our midst. Let's make everything perfect. And if anyone has some spare ecstasy to slip into her, er, hen, that wouldn't hurt either."

Ricky pulled up the order. "Holy shit, Chef. In addition to the hen, she wants the grouper—when's the last time we served that? The venison, ditto, the special risotto, ravioli, the lamb, that rabbit no one but Marco likes, Oysters Marco, the beet salad, and the three special apps." He looked at Georgia. "We're screwed. Aside from the specials, she ordered the worst things on the entire menu."

"It's Marco's funeral, not ours," Georgia said, knowing full well that if the famed food critic wasn't happy, it was Georgia's future that would swoosh straight down the toilet. But a great Mercedes Sante review would catapult her into the top echelon of New York City chefs, Food Network–ready, as Marco put it. Even more important, it would enable her to open her own restaurant. With a glowing review, financing would be a cinch; she'd have investors lining up outside her apartment, fat check-books in tow. Taking a few deep breaths, she mumbled a quick prayer to Ganesh. Two and a half, she begged the Hindu god and remover of obstacles, just two and a half forks. Please. She set to work.

Word of Mercedes's arrival spread as fast as the latest starlet-in-rehab rumor, and the kitchen sprang into high-alert reviewer mode. This was slightly different from high-alert celebrity mode, in that the food mattered more than the booze, and at night's end not even a smidgen of the check would be comped. The goal was for Mercedes to eat like a queen, and to assume every other no-name diner did too.

Georgia walked from station to station, staring over the shoulders of the line cooks, scrutinizing the dishes they pre-pared, sampling sauces, poking meats, stirring pots, sticking her nose everywhere, her spoon everywhere. Her manner was steady and calm despite the oppressive heat and cacophony of clanking pans, clashing blades, grinding machinery, and doors heaving open and closed. Only her hair betrayed her frazzled nerves, poking out like bunches of past-its-prime frisée. The two parallel lines etched between her eyebrows, the "elevens" as Glenn's mom referred to them, deepened with concentration. Her skin flushed pink, then rose, finally settling somewhere around unripe strawberry.

She dipped her spoon into the special risotto. "Not bad. A tad more butter to finish."

The cook nodded. "Yes, Chef."

Georgia looked around. "Where's my grill guy?"

No one answered. Leaving the station during service was not tolerated. During a review was unthinkable. She turned to the line cooks. "All hands on deck. Got it? Tell him if he doesn't get his fucking ass back now, he's fired. I mean it."

The kitchen stopped for a split second. Georgia was known as one of the coolest chefs around. She rarely cursed (mostly because she wasn't very good at it), wasn't above plucking a chicken, and made everyone from the new guy washing dishes right on up to Ricky feel appreciated. Sure, she was a bit of a control freak, but compared to the pot-slamming, dish-dumping antics of some of her peers, this was easily overlooked. In return, she demanded full accountability from her kitchen.

"Sure thing, Chef," said the cook.

Georgia grabbed a board of basil chiffonade from the garde-manger, who was in charge of cold apps, and slipped it into the garbage. "Try again. And make it pretty. Please."

He pulled out another bunch of basil, rolled the leaves into a fat joint, then gracefully sliced the roll into thin ribbons.

"Lovely," Georgia said. She'd worked in too many kitchens

where the head chef berated his cooks into creating what he wanted without offering a word of thanks or the tiniest smidge of a compliment. Never, no matter who was sitting in the dining room, would she become That Chef.

After wiping up the last drop of misplaced sauce, she green-lighted the appetizers. The servers came to pick up, and a doe-eyed girl who looked like Bambi and talked like a trucker gave her a thumbs-up.

"She's drinking like a mother-fucking fish," she whispered. "That's gotta be a good sign."

Georgia nodded. Drinking was good. It meant Mercedes was thoroughly enjoying herself, and if she wasn't, whatever she didn't like might be a little hazy when it came time to put pen to paper.

When the app plates came back to the kitchen with nary a scrap in sight, Georgia allowed the smallest of smiles to escape her lips. The cooks had prepared three versions of each entrée, and she chose the best-looking for Mercedes's table, waiting until the last minute to sauce and garnish. She eyeballed the entrées one final time before their tableside debut, drizzling extra green-peppercorn sauce on the venison and rearranging the sprigs of spiny rosemary on the lamb. An old boss had dubbed her Chef Georgia O'Keeffe, and she still considered presentation one of the most important elements of restaurant food. The waiters whisked away the entrées, so beautifully plated it seemed almost a shame to eat them, and she watched them go, then took a step back and stretched her hands to the tin ceiling.

"Nice job, Chef." Ricky patted her back. "You done good."

"You too, Rick. Whatever happens . . ." She left her thoughts unsaid. Whatever happened would set the course for the rest of her life. It was that simple.

Chapter Two

Two and a half hours later, Bernard finally poked his head into the kitchen. "She just finished her third caffè corretto. She's gone."

The kitchen burst into applause, whooping and hollering. The grill guy let loose an earsplitting whistle. According to industry lore, the number of grappa-laced espressos Mercedes drank equaled the number of forks she intended to bestow upon the restaurant. Busboys knew not to clear her espresso cup until a manager had checked to see if it was empty or half full, a full or half fork respectively. Three forks were more than anyone had hoped for, including Georgia, who could practically taste her own restaurant. Even Marco always said he'd be happy with two.

"She must have a wooden leg, and a bottomless expense account. She and her four friends polished off a round of gimlets at the bar, a bottle of Dom, a Ribolla Gialla, and two Barolos." Bernard chuckled. "Whatever it takes, sister." He looked around the room, pausing on Georgia.

A waiter burst through the kitchen door pushing a trolley laden with champagne flutes. The drinking portion of the evening had officially begun.

Bernard continued, "Cheers to all of you on a job well done. On behalf of our boss, Marco, and yours truly, you all were magnificent. And you, Georgia, especially." He picked up a glass and raised it in her direction.

She smiled, feeling her face grow hot.

Ricky handed her a glass of champagne. "Good news, Chef."

"Three forks is better than good news, Rick. It's—"

"No, I mean Glenn's here. In the dining room."

"He is? He's here?" She took a sip of champagne and stepped through the swinging door to greet her fiancé, feeling lighter than she had in a long time.

"There she is," Glenn said in a loud voice, a smile spreading across his face, his pale blue eyes fixed on Georgia. "My favorite three-fork chef." He stood at the bar, drink in hand, surrounded, as he usually was in social settings, by a group of people. He was not the kind of guy who'd ever lack for someone to talk to at a cocktail party.

"I'm so glad you're here." Georgia reached up to push his hair behind his ear. She loved his hair. Black, straight, shiny, not even the teensiest bit of frizz, so unlike her own.

"So am I. Three forks? This is incredible, George!"

"I know. Can you believe it?"

"Of course I can." He put his empty glass on the bar and pulled her into him, placing a long, soft kiss on her mouth. No sooner had they stopped kissing than he drew her into his chest and kissed her again.

"Wow," she said, pulling back slightly. "I should get a three-fork review every day." She glanced around to see if anyone had noticed, but her coworkers were too busy basking in their glory and in the free-flowing booze to notice much of anything.

"You should," Glenn said. "More champagne?"

"Did someone say champagne?" Marco walked over with a bottle of Cristal and refilled their glasses.

"We made it into your Cristal club," Georgia said, raising her flute. "I'm flattered."

In Marco's champagne hierarchy, he and his fabulous friends drank Cristal, cooks and servers drank Veuve Clicquot, and busboys and dishwashers drank prosecco.

"You're always in, Georgia, you know that." He turned to Glenn. "How's it going, chief?" He threw out his hand for the half-high-five/half-handshake that was the universal greeting of thirtysomething metro men.

"Pretty good, man. You?" Despite professing to hate Marco's guts for having slept with Georgia, Glenn acted cordial, even chummy, with him. A little chilliness would have been fine with her.

"All good. You heard your fiancée got us three forks?"

"I did." Glenn rested his hand on the small of Georgia's back.

"So what's the plan? We gotta celebrate these forks." Marco took a quick survey of the room. "All of us. Together."

"Actually, we have to go to the Rumpus," Georgia said. "It's a small bar on Rivington. My best friend is playing there and we promised we'd go, so—"

"Cool. I love the Rumpus. We'll all go," Marco interrupted.

"Oh," said Georgia. "Great." Lo, who was used to singing and strumming for single-digit crowds, would probably fall off her barstool when they entered.

"Hey, chief, you're a lawyer, right?" Marco asked Glenn.

"Attorney, yeah. Entertainment law."

"Want to do me a solid?" Marco didn't wait for an answer. "I have this new lease I need someone to eyeball. You mind?"

"It's not really my thing, but sure, I'll check it out."

"It's in my office. Don't worry, Georgia, I'll bring him right back." Glenn squeezed her hand and set off behind Marco.

"Where are those two going?" Bernard walked over as they slipped into the crowd. "Locker room?"

"Marco's office. He has some lease he wants Glenn to look at."

Bernard watched them for a second. "So, good work tonight, Georgia. Really great. Marco is damn lucky to have you."

"You too, Bernard. This place would run about as smoothly as a FEMA rescue operation without you. I've never worked in such a tightly run place."

"Then it seems a toast is in order." Bernard lifted his glass. "To us. A good team."

"Good? Three forks and we don't even rank great?"

"You're right. To us, a great team."

They touched glasses just as Ricky, sipping his trademark tequila sunrise, popped over. Despite the drink, he didn't seem to be in a festive mood.

"I don't mean to spoil your moment, guys, but do you really buy this three-espresso, three-fork crap?" He looked from Georgia to Bernard. "I mean, I know Mercedes is no Bruni, but doesn't it seem sort of JV?"

" 'Jay' what?" Bernard asked.

"Junior varsity, *amateur,* for her to announce the rating before the review comes out? And the whole theory comes from a blog written by a guy who bused at like five restaurants she reviewed in six months. Do we trust a guy who worked five places in six months?"

"A blogging busboy came up with the theory?" Georgia said. "I hope he's at least been promoted."

"It's more than five places, Ricky. I'd say nine, maybe even double digits." Bernard shrugged. "Besides, Mercedes looked pleased as punch when she left tonight. Or drunk as punch. Now if our esteemed boss can keep his hands off her daughter, we'll be on our way."

"What daughter?" Georgia asked.

"The very pretty, very nineteen-year-old NYU girl Marco's been salivating over since meeting her at Lilly last week," said Bernard.

"How do you know she's Mercedes's daughter?"

"Well, for starters her last name is Sante. Also, she told us."

"Us?" Georgia said. "You and Marco?"

"A bunch of us went out after close. Marco was buying." Bernard shrugged again.

"Even he couldn't be so dumb," Georgia said. "Even Marco couldn't ruin his shot at three forks by doing something stupid with Mercedes's daughter." She looked across the room, spotting Glenn and Marco leaving Marco's office. They were engrossed in conversation, trading hand slaps and chest pokes like a couple of old drinking buddies. She turned back to Bernard. "Right, Bernard?"

"Right," he agreed. "Even Marco couldn't."

A caravan of cabs turned onto Rivington, lining up in front of a storefront bar with blacked-out windows. A sign over the door spelled out THE RUMPUS in Day-Glo graffiti. In case there was any question as to how the bar derived its name, a mural of Sendak-style monsters hanging from trees, gnashing their teeth, and letting "the wild rumpus start" covered the entry. It was a fitting venue for the Marco staff, who tumbled out of the cabs and onto the sidewalk, gathering in front of a bouncer half sitting on a barstool parked outside the door. He held a roll of cash in one hand and a heavy-duty flashlight in the other and didn't bother looking up as the group descended on him. Georgia had been sandwiched between Ricky and Bernard on the bumpy ride across town, and she jumped out of the taxi behind Ricky while Glenn, who'd insisted on taking the front seat, paid the cabbie.

Music from the bar spilled onto the street each time a new patron passed through the door. Georgia got a text from Clem, her other best friend, who had arrived and was waiting inside.

"Ready?" Glenn said as the cab sped off with a new fare in the backseat. He'd barely spoken to Georgia since leaving Marco's office and had spent the entire taxi ride pounding out e-mails on his BlackBerry, leaving her to wonder what could possibly be so important at Smith, Standish and Lockton that it couldn't wait until morning.

She nodded. "Is everything okay? You seem a little jumpy."

"I'm fine," he said, running his fingers through his hair. "Let's go in."

He peeled out a ten for their covers and handed it to the bouncer. "For both of us," he said, continuing in without stopping.

"ID?" the bouncer said. He had little eyes and protruding lips and wore a puffy jacket, which made him look even beefier than he was. He propped his foot against the door just as Glenn's hand reached the knob.

"I'm thirty-four, man. Give me a break."

"ID?" the bouncer repeated, shining his flashlight in Glenn's eyes.

"Jesus Christ." Glenn pulled his wallet from his pocket, turned his back on Georgia, and began thumbing through it. "Here."

The bouncer took his driver's license and stared at it for a few seconds. "What sign are you?"

"Are you kidding me?"

The bouncer shook his head.

"I'm a fucking Gemini. Now get that flashlight out of my face and let me in." Glenn raised his hands, and for a second Georgia thought he was going to shove the guy.

The bouncer dropped Glenn's license to the ground. "Whoops."

Glenn stared at him, then at the license, then back at him. His hand curled into a fist. Before it could go anywhere, Georgia grabbed his arm and stooped down to pick up his license.

"Here," she said, handing it to Glenn. "And here's my ID." She held it in front of the bouncer.

He didn't take his eyes off Glenn, not even to glance at her birth date. "Have a good night, sweetheart."

She steered Glenn through the door and into the bar, not stopping until they were safely camouflaged behind a bunch of the line cooks.

"What the hell was that? You were about to hit that guy! You don't hit people!" The music was so loud she had to shout, but she was so mad she'd have shouted anyway.

"That guy was a tool," Glenn yelled back.

"He's a bouncer, Glenn. Of course he's a tool. Since when do you pick fights with bouncers?"

In the seven years they'd been together, she'd never seen him so much as elbow someone for getting too close on the subway. Now that he was a thirty-four-year-old attorney about to get married, it didn't seem the best time to start punching people out.

"I didn't start with him, he started with me," Glenn said. "Did you see the way he—"

"It doesn't matter who started what, Glenn. It was stupid. And since when do you even care if someone starts with you?" She glared at him. "You could have been hurt."

He rolled his eyes.

"Or sued."

That got his attention. It wouldn't do for a soon-to-be-partner at Standish to be implicated in something so street. An illicit affair, maybe, but a barroom brawl? Not so much.

One of the cooks turned around, holding a shot glass in his hand. Georgia immediately pivoted in the other direction, but it was too late. "Chef! Chef!" he yelled. "Come do a shot with us!" The others followed his lead, motioning for her to join them.

She waved to them over Glenn's shoulder, smiling and nodding and pretending not to hear what they were saying. Fortunately, the charade worked, and they downed their shots without her.

"You're right," Glenn said after a moment. His face had softened but his voice still had an edge. "It was stupid. I don't know what I was thinking."

"Is everything okay with you?" She reached out and touched his cheek.

"Everything's fine. But I have to hit the head. I'll be back in a minute." He squeezed her hand and disappeared into the crowd. The Glenn who'd known it was important to show up when she asked, who'd kissed her like he meant it, was gone.

Sneaking by the line cooks, who held a fresh round of shots, Georgia scoped out the room for Clem. Even in the low lighting, Clem's ginger bob beckoned from the bar, and Georgia rushed over to join her.

"Do you think this bartender will be able to make a good mint julep?" Clem asked, studying a drink menu. "The Derby's coming up, and I'm trying to get in the mood." A Kentucky girl through and through, Clem believed the Derby was not only the two most exciting minutes in sports, but in life.

"Order a Hendrick's and tonic like a normal person. Please. Or have some bubbles." Georgia gestured to a bottle of Mumm sitting in an ice bucket, one of many now scattered around the club courtesy of Marco, who was nothing if not a big spender. With its faux-wood paneling and low-slung black leather sofas, the place looked like a messier version of her parents' rec room in Wellesley circa 1984.

"Oh, guess what? I think I found our dress." Clem and Lo were Georgia's co–maids of honor and had been searching for their dresses for weeks.

"Can we not talk about weddings right now? At least not mine?" Georgia poured two glasses of champagne and handed one to Clem. "Cheers."

"You're the bride. Whatever you say." Clem sipped her drink. "Is something wrong, George? I thought we were supposed to be celebrating."

"Glenn almost got into a fight with the bouncer."

"*Your* Glenn?"

Georgia nodded.

"Ouch."

Georgia relayed the entire story, beginning with the Mercedes Sante review and ending with Glenn being seconds away from ramming his fist into the bouncer's heavily padded belly. By the time she'd finished, Clem was halfway through her second glass of champagne, and the band onstage was making its exit. Lo was up next. Georgia rushed to the bathroom to ensure that both she and Clem would be front and center when Lo went on. Not exactly brimming with confidence, Lo needed all the support she could get.

Georgia took her place at the end of the short line for the lone unisex stall, which gave her a good view of the bar. She spotted Ricky, Bernard, and a bunch of the waitstaff, but no Glenn. After what seemed like ages, the restroom door opened and Marco staggered out. She considered slipping away before he saw her, but after all that excitement, and all that champagne, she really had to pee.

"Hey, star chef." Marco flashed a wobbly smile, and his eyes closed for a few seconds before a head bob snapped them open.

"Hey, yourself."

"I didn't have a chance to congratulate you."

"Sure you did. You poured me a glass of Cristal, remember? Right before you stole my fiancé?"

"Oh, that's right," he mumbled.

"But I don't think I've congratulated you, Marco. This will be great for the restaurant." She took a step back. He smelled as if he'd spent the last few hours soaking in a gin bath. Or maybe it was just his pheromones.

"And great for you." He tried to focus on her eyes but got lost somewhere around the hollow of her throat. "I hope you don't have any plans to leave us."

"Nope, no plans." She turned her head and watched a hipster sporting muttonchops walk out of the bathroom. A guy in skinny jeans and a Unabomber beard took his place.

"You should take tomorrow off. Yeah, take it off. You deserve it."

"Really? Saturday? You sure about that, Marco?" Head chefs did not take off Fridays or Saturdays, unless they really were star chefs with the cookbooks and TV shows to prove it.

"Yeah, take it off. I'm the boss, remember?"

"Okay, if you say so, boss." A whole day together could be just what she and Glenn needed. "Thanks, Marco."

"You know, I have contacts at the Food Network. I'd love to hook you up with them. You'd be awesome. Pretty, tall, sexy." He dropped his chin and stared up at her.

"Sure, that'd be great."

"I still think about that night we had together. Do you remember?"

"Just the hangover. Nothing else." She wished it were true.

"Then you'll have to trust me. It was incredible. You loved it. You know, if you weren't engaged—" He lunged forward, one hand grabbing her waist and the other landing way too close to her breast.

She turned her head, and his large, wet lips caught a mouthful of hair.

"Wait," he said, steadying himself. "I don't—"

The bathroom door swung open and Georgia slid in, leaving him standing with his mouth agape.

"Georgia! Over here!" Clem waved her hands over her head. She, Ricky, and a bunch of Marco people had commandeered a table in front of the stage, which looked as if someone had pieced together a dozen or so milk crates and then stapled a sheet of plywood on top. The last act had walked off with their limbs intact, so Lo would be fine, especially since she'd just finished a ten-day master cleanse and was even waifier than usual.

Georgia started making her way to the table, but her eyes scanned the room for Glenn, the one person she really wanted to see after that mess with Marco. Please, she thought, please let him still be here.

"George!" Glenn stood at the end of the bar with a group of guys he'd never met before and would probably never see again. They were laughing. Holding up his hand, he mimed tipping back a drink, then pointed to Georgia.

Relief washed over her, and she smiled for the first time since arriving at the Rumpus. She walked over to join him, and before he could say anything, she slipped her arms around his waist and squeezed, resting her head against his chest and closing her eyes.

"Does this mean you're not mad at me?" he asked after a minute.

"No. But this does." Standing on tiptoe, she kissed him, knowing she'd catch flack from the line cooks, who were almost certainly watching, and not caring. "Although, even if I were still mad, I wouldn't tell you. You might punch me out."

"Funny, George." He leaned down to kiss the top of her head. "Real funny."

Chapter Three

The apartment door slammed shut behind her, and Georgia reached down to unclick Sally's leash and collar, dropping them to the floor with a clank. It was eleven o'clock. An hour earlier and she might more carefully have closed the door, placed the leash and collar on the table. But it was eleven, the first Saturday in a long while that she and Glenn would be able to spend together, and he had slept long enough.

She walked into her living room, flopping down on the sofa. A sea-grass carpet stretched across the cheap parquet floor, and a large glass coffee table was stacked with books and magazines. The walls were painted a warm khaki and lined with vintage prints of Italian and Spanish food products. For an unremarkable Upper East Side rental, it felt like home. The fifty-inch flat-screen, dominating an entire wall, had arrived via special delivery the day Glenn moved in.

She left a voice mail for Bernard in case Marco forgot he'd given her the day off, which seemed likely considering the shit-faced shape he was in by evening's end. When last she saw her boss, he was draped across a girl who looked as if she'd gone to the Rumpus straight from an SAT prep course. Not one to moon, Marco either didn't care or didn't remember that minutes earlier he'd been trying to make out with his head chef. As long as her surname wasn't Sante, he could sleep with whomever he wanted. Between Marco's meandering mouth and Mercedes's review, Georgia felt she'd more than earned a three-day weekend. "See you Tuesday, Bernard," she said before hanging up.

En route to the kitchen, she cocked her head and pressed her ear to the bedroom door. Nothing. She continued into the kitchen and Sally followed, watching as Georgia scooped up coffee beans from the silver tin and dumped them into the fancy grind-and-brew Glenn had bought for Christmas.

"Whaddaya think, Sals? Do I tell him about Marco?" She purposefully hadn't told him at the Rumpus or in the cab ride home. After the bouncer incident there was no telling how he'd react, but chances were he'd be much more levelheaded when he didn't have five or six drinks sloshing around his stomach.

"You need a clip, my friend," Georgia said, scratching the yellow Lab mix behind the ears. "And as usual, you're right. Of course I should tell him." Coffee in hand, she walked to the living room and took a seat at the dining table pressed against the wall. She nibbled a croissant she'd picked up from Via Quadronno and flipped through the *Times Magazine*, wondering what the Ethicist would think of her conundrum.

It wasn't as if Glenn had always been Boy Scout honest with her. Like when he cheated on her. Had the girl—Tammy was her name—not called him, and had he not been too busy opening a bottle of Brunello to take the call, and had Georgia not been standing directly next to the answering machine as the call came, she might never have known. But she did, he was, and she was, which left Georgia no choice but to flee his apartment—though not before throwing a glass of the ruby red wine all over his camel cashmere sweater.

But things were different now, and not being totally honest was not an option. In just nine weeks the cute guitar-strumming guy with the outsize dreams and the swishy black bangs she'd fallen for all those summers ago would become her *husband*. Things had to be different.

She finished off her coffee and stood up, tired of waiting. Knowing the kind of night Glenn had had, he'd easily sleep past noon. After dropping Georgia at home, he'd continued uptown to meet his client Diamond Tee. Business, he'd said, and, no, it couldn't really wait. Too drained to protest, she'd kissed him good-bye. He crept into bed sometime around four.

A shopping bag stuffed with dry cleaning sat in the front closet, and she grabbed it, adding a pair of Glenn's pants she picked off the floor. At least he'd managed to peel them off before falling into bed. Sally followed her to the door and Georgia leaned down, clicking on her collar. "Of course you're coming."

A black-haired girl stood behind a computer, her hot-pink nails poised at the keyboard. "Name?" she asked without looking up.

Georgia spelled her name, last and first, and started sorting through the pile of clothing. A week's worth of Glenn's shirts, a couple black sweaters, a top she'd worn to a party. She picked up the pants he'd worn the night before, folding them at the seat and then waist to cuff. A white paper square, no bigger than a packet of dental floss, fell to the counter.

The girl looked up. "Is that yours?"

Georgia stared at the packet, then at the girl, then swept her hand across the counter, scooping it up and placing it in her pocket in one fluid motion. "Just have them delivered, okay? Come on, Sal." The door jingled closed behind her.

It wasn't such a big deal. Marco did it. Probably lots of the line cooks too, and definitely some of the waitstaff. Practically everyone in the restaurant industry did a little blow now and again. But she didn't. And Glenn wasn't in the restaurant industry. He was a lawyer.

She paced up and down the little living room, her anger mounting. To think she'd been feeling bad about Marco trying to kiss her while Glenn had probably been snorting coke in bathrooms all over the city. This was no longer a question for the Ethicist, it was a question for a couples counselor.

The bedroom door creaked open, and Georgia's shoulders reflexively shot up.

"Morning," Glenn said from the hallway.

"Morning. How are you feeling?"

"All things considered, not too bad." He smiled sleepily, too fuzzy to detect her frostiness. "When's the last time I got to spend a leisurely Saturday morning with my fiancée?" He walked over, wearing the bottom half of the red pinstripe pajamas she'd given him for his birthday, and bent down to give her a kiss.

She turned so that his kiss caught her cheek. Even after a coke-and-champagne-filled rager, he looked good. Maybe his eyes were a little pouchier, his belly slightly softer, but if she squinted her eyes just so, she still saw the handsome launch-boat driver she met while serving gin and tonics at the Newport Yacht Club. That summer he lived in Levi's and flip-flops, blasted Phish on his earbuds, and carried his guitar everywhere. That they would get together was a given for him and the realization of a fantasy for her.

"Is everything okay, George?"

"I got you a croissant when I was out with Sally. It's in the kitchen."

He walked into the galley kitchen, which Georgia had painted an unfortunate tangerine orange after taking a feng shui class at the Learning Annex. Instead of stimulating healthy appetite, as intended, it stimulated claustrophobia. She took a deep breath and followed him.

He raised his coffee mug. "Cheers to New York's newest three-fork chef."

"Thanks." She poured herself a glass of orange juice and took a swig. "So I brought your dry cleaning in."

"Yeah? Great."

"Including the pants you wore last night."

"They probably needed it after the night I had."

"Something fell out of the pocket." She pulled the bindle from her back pocket, holding it out in her open palm. "This fell out of the pocket."

"What the fuck? How'd that get there?"

"Please don't pretend it's not yours."

He exhaled loudly, looked down, then back at her. "Okay, George. I won't lie to you. It is mine. So I do a line of coke every once in a while. It's not that big a deal."

"Oh, it's not?" She threw the coke on the counter. "Maybe not to you. To me, doing a line of coke once in a while is a big deal, especially because I don't believe it's once in a while."

"Believe what you want. I'm telling you it's once a month, once every few weeks, max. And I didn't tell you because I knew you'd overreact like you are right now. You look like you're about to burst."

"Maybe that's because I am! Is this why you got into a fight with that bouncer?"

"This has nothing to do with that, and I *didn't* get into a fight with him. Besides, he was a prick and you know it."

"He was, Glenn, but that's not the point. You never would have done that before."

"Before what?"

"Before you started working all the time, hanging out with Diamond Tee—" She paused midsentence. "Is this why you had to meet him last night? To get coke?"

"Of course not. It was business, George." He folded his arms across his chest. "You know if it weren't for Tee, you wouldn't be wearing that rock on your finger."

"What are you talking about?"

"I told him I wanted to propose and he hooked me up with his jeweler. He did Tee a favor and gave me a sick deal on a sick stone. You think I just took a stroll down Forty-seventh Street and bought that?" He pointed to her left ring finger.

"He did Tee a favor? And Tee did you a favor? Well, he didn't do me a favor." Georgia tried to slide the ring off her finger, but it got stuck on her knuckle. "I didn't even want this ring, Glenn. How much more explicit could I have been? Chefs don't wear rings!"

Glenn's eyes, which were planted firmly on the kitchen's terra-cotta tile floor, snapped up at this revelation. "You didn't? They don't? You mean, you didn't want a ring?" He paused. "Did you want to get engaged, Georgia? Do you want to get married?"

"Is this your way of avoiding talking about your coke problem?"

"I don't have a fucking coke problem!" He stared at her, hands on hips, before storming into the bedroom, where he cursed at the kilim carpet he constantly caught his toe on. Seconds later he flew through the living room before the apartment door slammed shut.

Georgia stood frozen in her tangerine kitchen, feeling as if the walls would swallow her up and wishing they would. What should have been one of the happier days of her life was registering red-alert disaster. In nine weeks she'd be the wife of a cocaine-snorting attorney who bought her engagement ring—the one she never even wanted—from some gangster diamond dealer. She dialed Clem on her cell, relayed the crucial details, and left the apartment as quickly as she could to meet her.

More sprawling French château than tony Central Park West co-op, the Dakota would forever be known as the place where John Lennon was shot. It was also the superluxe home of Clem's current charge: an oversize pug with an attitude problem. Georgia arrived at the fabled building, cheeks slightly damp from the persistent spring drizzle, and gave her name to one of four uniformed doormen manning the entrance. Clem lived in a tiny studio in Hell's Kitchen and offered her dog-sitting services to anyone and everyone, so long as the deal included park views and an elevator operator. She poked her head into the marble-floored hallway as Georgia made her way from the elevator.

"Sit down, Petal. Sit. Come on in, Georgia. Hurry!" Clem hissed. Her hair was pulled back in a stumpy pigtail, and her freckled face was makeup free. She wore a red hoodie and matching yoga pants and was the only redhead Georgia knew who wore red almost every day.

Georgia sneaked past the dog and whistled as she took in the Bordeaux-colored walls, egg-and-dart moldings, and cast plaster medallions on the ceiling. "So this is a classic eight, huh? Not bad for a pug." She took a seat on a zebra-print-covered ottoman and jiggled her foot impatiently. "What's our plan?"

"Bloodies at Lenny's? Mimosas at Mars? Or maybe just a stroll through the park with my new horse?" Clem gestured to Petal, who eyeballed her from his crushed-velvet bed. "Although"—she gestured to Georgia's haloed hair, frizz factor at least eight—"I guess it's still raining."

"Whatever you want to do. I don't care. My fiancé is a coke-head. Even worse is that he lied to me about it. How do you lie to the woman you're about to marry?"

"I knew there was something up with him last night. At least you found out before the wedding."

"Are you saying I shouldn't marry him? Because of the coke?"

"I'm not going to tell you what to do, Georgia. But even without the coke, things haven't seemed so great between the two of you. Ever since he proposed, you've seemed, I don't know, anxious."

Georgia stood and walked to the window. "Glenn's a great guy," she said slowly. "He is. He's smart, successful, funny—he's everything any girl would want. It's just been hard to see lately."

"But is he what *this* girl wants?" Clem pointed at Georgia.

"Yes. At least I think so. I don't know." Georgia stared at the treetops dotting Central Park, full and verdant after the barren winter. The rain had stopped and the sky filled with a dim light. "Maybe I'm just suffering from a severe case of cold feet."

"Maybe," Clem said doubtfully.

"Where's the kitchen?" Georgia asked. "I'm starving."

Clem directed her to the kitchen, easily the size of her entire apartment, and she took stock of her ingredients. Some people smoked when they were upset, some did yoga, or drank, or paced, or picked fights, or counted to one hundred. Georgia cooked.

As a small girl growing up in Massachusetts, she'd spent most of her time in her grandmother's kitchen, watching wide-eyed as Grammy kneaded the dough for her famous pumpernickel bread, sliced up parsnips and turnips for her world-class pot roast, or, if she was feeling exotic, butterflied shrimp for her

delicious Thai basil seafood. A big-boned woman of solid peas-
ant stock, as she herself used to say, Grammy moved around the
cramped kitchen with grace and efficiency, her curly gray hair
twisted into a low bun. Humming pop songs from the forties,
her cheeks a pleasing pink, she turned out dish after fabulous
dish from the cranky Tappan stove she refused to replace. Those
times with Grammy were the happiest Georgia could remember.
It had been almost a year since she died, and not a day passed
that Georgia didn't miss her.

She pulled out half a dozen eggs, sliced supermarket Swiss
and some bacon from the double-width Sub-Zero. A quick scan
of the spice rack yielded a lifetime supply of Old Bay season-
ing, three different kinds of peppercorns, and *sel de mer* from
France's Brittany coast. People's pantries were as perplexing
as their lives. Whisking the eggs, Georgia considered Clem's
words. Marriage *was* a huge step. Had she accepted Glenn's
proposal because she wanted to marry him or because she
wanted what came with marriage: a baby, a family, security? Or
maybe she was scared of what would happen if she didn't marry
him. But how could she build a life and family with someone
she couldn't trust? She turned on the stove and listened for the
whish that signaled the burner was on.

The eggs sizzled in the sauté pan. Her brow moistened and
she preemptively twisted her hair into a bun, knotting it at
her neck. During her yearlong break from Glenn, Georgia had
dated a dozen men, sleeping with four. There was Marco. And
that truffle purveyor who had always flirted with her. And Jim,
the singer-songwriter Lo was friends with, the one who lived in
corduroy suits. And Paul, the really cute guy who, it had turned
out, had a really scary girlfriend.

The thing was, Georgia loved being half of a couple. Waiting in line for overpriced brunches, soaking up sun in Sheep

Meadow, late-night flicks at the Angelika—she felt her best when part of a pair. And in that whole year, she hadn't met anyone, not anyone, she could pair up with. So when Glenn came knocking on her door a year after she walked out of his, bearing a bouquet of out-of-season ranunculus, she welcomed him back with cautiously open arms, sick of hoping to meet *him,* ready to be an *us* again.

The smell of crackling bacon lured Petal into the kitchen, where she licked imaginary food drippings from Georgia's sneakers. Ignoring her, Georgia flipped the omelet, trying to recall the last time she and Glenn had sex. With their equally grueling but opposite schedules, they barely had time for a kiss let alone a romp. Every girl who'd read *Cosmo* even once knew that once the sex is gone, you may as well kiss the relationship good-bye.

Their first time was that summer in Newport on *Mysterious Ways,* a sixty-five-foot burled-wood beauty that looked as if it belonged in a Bond movie and was docked at the Yacht Club where they both worked. Easy access to unattended boats was a perk of being the head launch driver. Save for the waves of nausea rippling through Georgia's belly with each pitch of the boat, it was amazing. After, he sang the Beatles' "Julia" only semi-ironically, replacing the title name with hers. Somehow she managed to smile serenely as bile danced in her belly, never letting on how close she was to spewing her guts all over her unsuspecting lover. By summer's end they had inaugurated nearly every boat in the harbor—plowing through three albums' worth of Beatles songs—and she hadn't thrown up even once.

Clem walked into the kitchen and pulled up a stool at the center island. "Are you okay?"

"Yeah. Just trying to figure out if it's really possible that I haven't had sex with my fiancé in five weeks. And I'm part of the problem too, so I can't blame it all on the coke. What is happening to us? And why am I just noticing it now? Here"—Georgia slipped the omelet onto a plate—"have an omelet."

"You know, sometimes nothing happens," Clem said with her mouth full. "Sometimes you just grow apart. Happened to me, happens to everyone. There's probably even a Hallmark card for it." She popped another bite into her mouth and rubbed her tummy. "Now this is good. Even with these lame ingredients, this is good. Open up Georgia's Joint, and it'll be a huge hit, no question. Just make the kind of food you like to eat, and they will come." Clem was the food and wine editor for *Happenings,* a weekly magazine about the city, and even more obsessed with the restaurant scene than Georgia.

"That's the plan, minus the Georgia's Joint part. The Mercedes review definitely doesn't suck as far as financing is concerned, but first I need to figure out my life. I have a date with a white dress and a judge in nine weeks, with a guy I'm neither sleeping with nor, as it turns out, talking to."

Clem put her arm over her friend's shoulder. "Cheer up, George. Everything will work out the way you want it to. You just have to figure out which way that is."

Georgia ate her omelet and left the Dakota, turning down Clem's invitations for a shopping trip on Columbus or a bad teen movie on Vudu. Walking through Central Park, she settled in front of the William Shakespeare statue on Poets' Walk. The crocuses had come and gone, grape hyacinths and daffodils pushed through the dirt, the tulips would soon follow. Anything could happen in springtime in New York.

Fishing through her bag, she pulled out a red leather Smythson journal, a Valentine's gift from Glenn. Thanks to his mother, who basically shopped for a living, Glenn was privy to all the finer things a girl could want, and generous as well. As Mrs. Tavert said, almost everything worth buying could be purchased at the four Bees: Bergdorfs, Barneys, and Bendels, in that order. Bloomingdale's, the last of the Bees, was a distant fourth, unless you happened to be on the hunt for an electric toothbrush.

She scrawled *Pros* and *Cons* across the top of a page and drew a line down the middle. When in doubt, her father, the physics professor, always said, make a list. This was one of the few points on which she wholeheartedly agreed with him.

Under *Pros* she wrote:

Smart
Sexy
Good hair
Good in bed

She crossed out *Good* before *in bed* and wrote *Great,* then added an arrow indicating it should sit before *Good hair.* Still not satisfied, she added, (*when available/in the mood, i.e., never*). Which was actually a con. She crossed it all out, rewrote *Good in bed,* and moved on.

Successful
Funny
Plays guitar
Athletic
Good taste (gifts)
Makes great burger (and steak)
Loves good wine

And cocaine, she thought. Which brought her to *Cons:*

Cokehead
Not trustworthy
Workaholic
Sketchy clients
Doesn't like my hair/offered to pay for crazy expensive Japanese
  straightening.

She stopped writing. He sounded like a white-collar criminal who might or might not knock her socks off in bed, feed her a postcoital steak au poivre, then take off for a game of pickup basketball, but not before strumming a ditty on his gee-tar, snorting cocaine from the glass coffee table in her living room, and leaving behind a wad of cash for an overpriced beauty treatment. So much for lists.

Maybe the coke was just a passing phase. Maybe, as he said, it really wasn't a big deal. She'd get home and he'd be waiting, and before she could even ask him to stop, he'd say he already had. Then they'd kiss and he'd tell her she was way more important than the coke, or his clients or even his career. She'd believe him . . . wouldn't she?

A sax player wearing dark shades and a tweed newsboy cap played "From This Moment On" and Georgia looked up, taking note of all the happy-looking couples strolling and laughing. Euro tourists, she thought, eyeing one especially stylish couple. Lousy with love, the pockets of their his-and-her Helmut Lang jeans lined with euros just waiting to be spent on fabulous clothes, meals, and shows. She was suddenly desperate for a trip to the Italian countryside she loved, for the rolling, green vistas, the quaint hill towns, the alfresco meals. In between her two years at the Culinary Institute, she'd done an externship in Florence with Claudia Cavalli, the famous chef, unearthing a love of all things Italy. Her last visit there was with Glenn, to the wedding of American friends who were married at the former villa of Dante Alighieri. The couple recited their vows in a garden overlooking the Duomo, and she and Glenn had squeezed hands thinking, next time, maybe us.

Her eyes grew heavy and she felt a knot in her throat. Do not cry, she told herself. Do not do it. She stared at the elm trees looming overhead, having once read it was impossible to cry while looking up. Only when she was certain her tears wouldn't fall did she pick herself up and begin the walk home.

Sally greeted Georgia as she stepped into her apartment, tail wagging, pink tongue lolling happily out of her mouth. Georgia wrapped her arms around Sally's head, pressing her nose against her dog's wet, black snout; she had never felt so glad to see anyone. There was no sign of Glenn, no message, no note. Sally nudged her hand and Georgia sank down next to her on the floor. The phone rang.

"Hello?" She didn't bother checking caller ID.

"Hey." It was Glenn.

"Glenn. Where are you?" She was ready to forget everything: his coke, her doubts, their problems.

"I'm over at Ray's. I think I'm gonna crash here tonight." Ray was Glenn's hedge-funder cousin who shared a multimillion-dollar, four-thousand-square-foot Tribeca loft with a tank of exotic fish. Georgia and Glenn had toured the space with him before he made his all-cash offer, and she was quite sure she had visibly salivated over the kitchen: six-burner Wolf range, twin Miele dishwashers, double wall ovens, marble countertops honed from a quarry in England. All this for a guy whose Sub-Zero would never hold more than a bottle of Dom Pérignon and a six-pack of Bud.

"Are you serious? You're not coming home?"

"Yeah. I went back to the apartment while you were out and grabbed some stuff. I need a break, Georgia."

For the second time that day, Georgia pointed her chin to the ceiling, willing herself not to shed even one tear. "Hold on. You mean, you're not coming back?"

"Not right now."

"Because of the coke?"

"It's not just the coke, Georgia. I need some time."

She swallowed. "Then take it."

Georgia replaced the phone on the receiver. She looked into the kitchen, her eyes falling on the pricey Vita-Mix blender Glenn had given her as a makeup gift after their year break. That night they whipped up fresh-mango margaritas and strolled clumsily up Madison Avenue for gelato. It was a balmy spring evening, one of the first of the season, and they had just decided Glenn would move into her apartment. Or rather Glenn had decided and Georgia agreed.

She frowned. Was that how it was between them? He made the decisions and she went along with whatever he decided?

Sally rolled over on her back, nudging Georgia's hand with her paw. "Time," she said as she reached down to scratch her pooch's belly. "He says he needs time." For what, she didn't know. As far as she could tell, he'd already decided. And maybe she had too.

Chapter Four

Ginger Rogers and Fred Astaire danced across the screen while Georgia lay on the couch waiting for the delivery guy. As far as thirties musicals went, it didn't get more glamorous than *Top Hat*. She and Grammy had watched it together a million times, a bowl of popcorn propped on the sofa between them, swooning over debonair Fred and gorgeous Ginger. That night, popcorn wouldn't cut it. The doorbell rang and Georgia went to answer it, picking up a twenty from the dining-room table.

Ice cream in hand, she shuffled into the kitchen, swung open the oven door, and pulled out the second sheet of Toll House cookies, baked to back-of-the-package specifications. Sally had followed her in and now looked up expectantly.

"I'm afraid you're out on this one, Sals. No chocolate allowed. You know the rules." She pried off the top of the Ben & Jerry's Chubby Hubby and stuck in her spoon. " 'Heaven,' " she sang à la Fred Astaire as she took her first bite. " 'I'm in heaven.' " She'd tried convincing Glenn that "Cheek to Cheek" should be their wedding song, but he vetoed it as too cheesy. They still hadn't agreed on a song for their first dance.

After scooping nearly all of the ice cream into a mixing bowl, she popped it into the microwave to get it sufficiently slushy. She stuck half a dozen cookies into a Ziploc, smashed a frying pan on top of the bag, then mashed the cookie bits into the ice cream, topping it off with a generous pour of U-bet chocolate syrup. For a classically trained chef, Georgia's tastes, at least in crisis mode, tended to the plebeian.

The phone rang and she picked it up without checking caller ID, sure it'd be Glenn. "Hi."

"Georgia. I've been leaving messages for a week. Didn't you get them?" It was her mother, Dorothy. After years of twice-monthly phone calls, she'd taken to calling two, sometimes three times a week. Georgia blamed the ring on her finger for her mother's ringing on the phone.

"Oh, hi. I've been really busy lately." Georgia scooped up a bite of the magical Chubby Chippie concoction. "Sorry," she said, her mouth full.

"What are you eating?"

"Chubby Hubby ice cream and chocolate chip cookies."

"With the wedding just weeks away? Not to mention that our family has a history of diabetes." Dorothy paused. "Although with my mother in the bakery business you'd never know we had issues with sugar."

Georgia refused to take the bait, well aware that Dorothy's relationship with Grammy had been less than perfect. Based on Georgia's own relationship with Dorothy, she was pretty sure she knew why—and it had nothing to do with Grammy.

"Are you trying to get sick, Georgia?"

"Nope." She took another bite. "Just fat."

Dorothy sighed. Georgia's rejection of her mother's bone-jutting body ideal had been a point of contention between them since Georgia turned three, which was the age, Dorothy believed, when baby fat was no longer adorable.

"Mom, please try to remember I'm a chef. It's practically illegal for me to be skinny. And I'm not even fat."

"I know, I know. Anyway, I'm calling to remind you about tomorrow and to check on the wedding planning. I haven't heard an update lately." For some inexplicable reason Georgia couldn't figure out, Dorothy cared more about this one day in her daughter's life than she had about her entire thirty-three years put together.

"We already have the space, the caterer, the florist, the band, the judge. There's no more updating to do."

"The invitations?"

"We're going to see the proof next week."

"Good. How's Glenn?"

"Glenn is great." It would never occur to Georgia to tell Dorothy the truth. "Remind me about what?"

"Tell him we're looking forward to seeing him."

"I will. Oh, it looks like we're getting a three-fork review."

"A what?"

"The restaurant. We're getting a three-fork review."

Dorothy was silent.

"Marco? Where I work? A really important reviewer came in last night, and she's giving us a fantastic review."

"That's great, Georgia. I'm glad that cooking is finally working out for you, since it's obviously what you like to do."

"Oh, is it that obvious?"

Dorothy charged on, as seemingly oblivious of her daughter's sarcastic tone as she was of everything else about her. "I was wondering if you thought I could wear a sort of rosy-red dress to the wedding. I know red is traditionally very Republican, but it's more magenta actually, a floor-length tunic with hand embroidery around the neck."

"Sounds like Mrs. Roper from *Three's Company*." Considering Dorothy's obsession with skinniness, you'd think she'd have at least a vague clue about fashion. Instead, she was stuck in the era of Earth shoes, muumuus, and rust-colored pantsuits.

"Mrs. Who? Is Glenn's mom wearing something similar?"

"I doubt it, Mom. Wear whatever you'd like."

"Great. Then I'll see you tomorrow. The party's at one."

"Party?"

"You haven't forgotten, I hope? Dad and I are driving down tomorrow and spending the night in Millbrook at Uncle Paul's. I have the environmental summit in New York on Monday, remember? Paul invited us all to a lunch he's having at the farm. All four of us. You said you were coming."

Georgia put down the Chubby Chippie and tried to remember when Dorothy had mentioned the luncheon. Paul was her dad's younger, only, and extremely successful brother. He owned a co-op on Sutton Place and a horse farm upstate and had recently gotten engaged—for the third time.

"Georgia, you said you and Glenn would come, and we've already told Paul to expect us all. It's an easy train ride from Grand Central, and Dad will pick you up at the station in Dover Plains."

Now Georgia remembered. She had accepted the invite in the hopes that a yes to Millbrook would get her off the hook with Dorothy for the duration of her city stay. As general counsel of a small environmental nonprofit, Dorothy had been attending the summit for years. It ran for three days, and with her mother a mere cab ride away, this was three days too many.

"Of course I didn't forget," said Georgia. "I'll be there."

"What about Glenn?"

"I mean we'll be there." Explaining Glenn's absence would be easy, and she already knew what she'd say: working on an important case, couldn't get away. Dorothy would be suitably impressed and wouldn't ask more.

She hung up the phone and went back to the couch. The Chubby Chippie was almost gone; conversations with her mother had a funny way of driving her to eat. If Grammy hadn't been around during her childhood, she'd be big as a house. And without Grammy's intervention, she might not have become a chef.

At the tail end of Georgia's college graduation dinner, a mediocre meal at the second-best restaurant in town, Grammy announced that she had something to say. Georgia closed her eyes, praying Grammy wasn't about to reveal that she had some horrible, fatal disease. Instead, she said she'd set up a trust that would allow Georgia to go to any grad school she pleased, plus have a little something left over for a rainy day. The way Grammy saw it, Georgia would either get the money when Grammy was dead, her ashes sprinkled over Silver Lake, or while she was still kicking and could watch her enjoy it. A stunned Dorothy dropped her spoon into her lemon Pavlova, where it quickly sank into a cloud of meringue, while Hal launched into a fit of throat clearing.

She'd paid for Dorothy's schooling, Grammy explained, so of course she'd do it for Georgia—after all, she was practically her daughter. Sniffling a little, Georgia told her family exactly what she wanted to do: go to culinary school and become a chef. Grammy was pleased, Georgia's parents—having just lost any influence they'd hoped to exert over her choice of grad school or career—dead silent.

Top Hat's final credits started rolling, and Georgia headed into the bathroom for a shower. A day in the country sounded grand; a day in the country with Dorothy and Hal, less so. But at least her uncle Paul was cool and could usually be relied on to pull some fairly impressive bottles from his wine cellar.

She sloughed off the dead skin on her arms, legs, and back with a sea sponge and grainy body wash that smelled like mint. After, she stood in front of the bathroom mirror, her mouth fixed into a discerning *o*. Could everyone see those little hairs above her upper lip, or was it just the lighting? She searched the medicine cabinet for the facial mask Lo had given her, the one that erased pimples, though not, sadly, girlstaches. A pill canister rolled out from behind a tub of Glenn's shaving foam and she picked it up from the sink. Affixed to the side was a yellow-and-black warning label: "Do not operate heavy machinery or drive a car after taking this medication. Do not drink alcohol with this medication." She flipped the canister over in her hand. It was a well-known sleeping pill, prescribed to Glenn by his family doctor. Frowning, she shook the canister. A handful of pink pills rattled at the bottom, and she poured them into her palm. She paused for a second, then popped one in her mouth, swallowing it with a gulp of water from the sink. Just what the doctor ordered.

A loose-jowled woman behind the ticket counter looked down through the drugstore reading glasses perched on her nose and exhaled heavily. "Yes?"

"Dover Plains," Georgia said. "Round-trip, please. Off-peak."

She turned around while her ticket printed and stared up at the domed, blue-green ceiling sky dotted with constellations that loomed over Grand Central. The balcony restaurants on either end of the massive hall were empty, and travelers took their time climbing the double staircases that would deliver them to the city streets. A group of teenagers wearing huge backpacks and knee-length shorts, despite the cool spring morning, met another, identically clad group at the clock in the center of the terminal. They exchanged hugs and grins, and a girl with two thick braids hanging down her chest pointed to the famous four-sided clock and said something that made them all laugh. Georgia paid for her ticket and headed down to the lower level to catch her train. The food court, a United Nations of culinary offerings, was bustling even on this sleepy Sunday morning, and she surveyed her options, settling on a very American coffee, banana muffin, and *New York* magazine.

Despite logging nine hours of sleep (that little pink pill kept its promise), she felt the same jittery way she did after a triple espresso on an empty stomach. She boarded the train and turned into the first empty row available, planting herself next to the window and placing her handbag on the seat next to her. The last time she'd seen her parents was in Wellesley, when she and Glenn had broken the news of their engagement over Vietnamese takeout. They spent the night at the split-level ranch where she'd grown up, she and Glenn in her old room (where, despite her parents' unspoken blessing, they couldn't bring themselves to have sex), and had left the next morning after bacon and blueberry pancakes. Her parents stood at the end of the driveway and waved good-bye, their breath turning to smoke in the frosty morning air. Georgia turned for one last glimpse of her childhood and caught them kissing. They were always kissing.

The navy blue Saab was parked at the curb, and Georgia spotted it as soon as she exited onto the platform. DOVER PLAINS the sign said. Her dad climbed out of the front seat and waved.

"Georgia!" he shouted.

"Hi, Dad!"

Hal was tall and bearlike, burly but not fat. His hair was the color of strong black tea, with shiny silver-gray threads woven throughout. He wore beige pants, a windowpane-checked sport coat of muddy browns and greens, and thick-soled leather shoes. Tortoiseshell glasses framed his eyes. He would have looked at home with a pipe dangling from his mouth, a leather-bound volume of classic literature under his arm, and a knotty walking stick in his hand. It always surprised people to learn he was a physics professor since he had none of that mad-scientist aura that everyone believed all scientists should.

They hugged, and Hal patted his daughter's back a few times before climbing into the car. Georgia sat in the passenger seat, smoothing her swingy black dress underneath her and wishing she'd worn tights. It was colder than in the city.

"So how are you, George?"

"Great, Dad."

He turned to look at her. "You look great. Well rested. I guess this marriage business agrees with you."

"I'm not married yet."

"I know, but just in general. You look content."

Georgia didn't say anything.

Hal turned on the radio. "I can't seem to find NPR."

"It's probably *Car Talk* anyway. So, did Mom tell you about the review?"

"Review?"

"The restaurant? We should be getting a three-fork re-view. That's really good." She'd been through it before with her mother and couldn't expect her father to know more than his wife about the *Daily*'s rating system or, for that matter, his daughter's career.

"That's great, Georgia. We'll have to come in for dinner sometime."

"Anytime. Are you coming to the city with Mom tomorrow?"

"No, I have classes tomorrow afternoon. I'm just here for the night. Mom will take the train in tomorrow." He turned to her. "Hey, I just realized, where's that fiancé of yours?"

"Oh, he's working on a really important case. He's sorry he couldn't get away, but it's sort of down-to-the-wire." She looked down at her hands.

"Really." Hal kept his eyes on the road but stole a sideways glance at his daughter.

The road grew steep and winding, and Hal hunched over the wheel, his hands firm at ten and two. Georgia was relieved not to have to talk and concentrated on the scenery instead. Trees lining the road were starting to leaf, the grass shone green; the sleeping landscape was coming alive. In another week or so the majestic brick and shingled houses hiding out behind stone walls and tree perimeters would be camouflaged by leaves. They'd remain hidden through the summer and fall until the cycle began anew.

"Here we are." Hal pulled up to a wrought-iron gate flanked by stout brick columns. A call box stood on the left, and he punched a button, shouted his name, and the gates swung open. They drove through an allée of maples, past a pond where a small gazebo rested on a bank. A large stretch of wild grasses morphed into a manicured carpet of emerald green lawn, which sprawled uphill to a white Greek Revival with black shutters and stately columns. Behind the house, layers of smoky hilltops streaked the sky.

"Wow," said Georgia. "This place is even nicer than I remembered. Talk about Tara." *Gone With the Wind* was another Grammy/Georgia favorite.

"We'll have to go for a walk on the grounds later." Hal parked the car in the circular, brick-paved driveway, next to a fleet of Range Rovers.

WINTERBERRY FARM a small sign announced. Outside the front door were six iron hitching posts from the days when people traveled by horse, which, luxury SUVs aside, didn't feel all that long ago at Winterberry Farm. It wouldn't have surprised Georgia to see a party on horseback hacking up the drive.

"Come on around this way," Hal said, leading Georgia to a staircase at the side of the house. When they reached the top, he stopped. "Georgia."

"Yes?" She turned and faced him.

"Thanks for making the effort to come out and see us. It means a lot to me, and it means a lot to Mom, especially with the anniversary of Grammy's death just around the corner. I know you have a lot going on with the wedding and with the, uh, review, and I'm glad you came." Hal took off his glasses and cleared his throat.

"Me too, Dad." She squeezed his arm, touched by his sensitivity. Hal was a physicist of the old school; he'd devoted himself to a life filled with scientific data, backed up by still more data. This left little room for emotion, and what little he had seemed to be reserved for Dorothy. Her parents were like two teenagers in love, even after almost thirty-five years of marriage.

"Georgia!" Her mother, a pin-thin woman wearing jade-green raw-silk pants, tapered at the ankle, and a matching Nehru-style jacket, walked to the door. Her pewter hair was flat and straight—so unlike Georgia's and Grammy's—stopping at her shoulder blades. A multicolored scarf twisted into a thick headband held it back, revealing a dramatic widow's peak and an unlined forehead. Earrings of stacked wooden disks floated under her ears, and a matching necklace hung outside her jacket.

"Hi, Mom," said Georgia.

"Come in," Dorothy said, her arms opened wide in preparation for the trademark Gray family hug. Georgia complied with her own back pats, then followed her mother into the house.

"We're in the drawing room," Dorothy said over her shoulder. "And where's Glenn?"

Georgia pretended not to hear her, feigning active interest in the party. Two dozen or so people filled the room, milling about with mimosas and other afternoon-appropriate drinks in their hands.

A server stopped before Georgia. "Champagne or mimosa? Screwdriver or Bloody Mary?" He recited this without a smile.

"Bloody Mary," Georgia said. "Thanks."

The waiter returned with her drink, and Dorothy with Uncle Paul and his new fiancée, Holly, their hosts. They exchanged hellos and hugs, and Holly asked to see Georgia's engagement ring, making her wish she'd got a manicure or at least filed her nails.

"So, Georgia, where's your fiancé hiding?" asked Paul.

"Yes, Georgia, where *is* Glenn?" Dorothy asked.

The pianist playing Gershwin tunes on the baby grand in the corner chose that moment to need new sheet music, and the room was suddenly quiet.

"Um, he has an important case," Georgia stuttered. "You know, he's working. At the office. He couldn't pull away. He's really sorry."

"There'll be other parties," Paul said. "You'll meet him before the wedding, Holly."

"Definitely," said Georgia, wondering if he meant theirs or hers.

"Your father tells us you met at Newport?" Holly said.

"We worked together at the Yacht Club. We fell out of touch for years and ran into each other randomly in the city." Georgia smiled sweetly, wondering what they'd think if they heard the uncensored version. She'd spotted Glenn at a dive-y East Village bar where he was ordering a round of shots for his pals and the girls they'd acquired for the evening. Ever the charmer even after multiple Cuervos, he ordered two sex-on-the-beach shooters, sent one Georgia's way, and insisted he'd been searching for her since that fabled summer. She knew he was lying, but that didn't stop her from going home with him.

"Kismet," said Holly. "You must be made for each other," she added before gliding off to greet some guests.

"It's really too bad he couldn't come," Dorothy said. "We were looking forward to seeing him."

Georgia shrugged.

"And unfortunately I'll be so busy with the summit I doubt I'll even be able to see him in New York."

"That is too bad." Georgia bit off a piece of the celery stalk garnishing her drink. "But he'll understand."

"How's that Bloody Mary?" Dorothy asked.

"Good," Georgia said, looking around the oak-paneled, octagonal room. Rows of oil paintings grouped according to subject—some landscapes, mostly horses—lined the walls. The dark-wood furniture was upholstered in silk damasks and tonal stripes. None of it looked particularly sturdy or comfortable. Georgia watched as one of the guests, a heavy woman with a cane, heaved herself into a tiny slipper chair that looked as if it were designed for a child. The chair groaned slightly but stood fast on its own four feet.

Dorothy summoned the waiter. "I'd like a Bloody Mary too, please."

"Are you sure, Mom?" Dorothy barely drank, and never anything stronger than chardonnay.

"Why not? It isn't every day I get to see my engaged daughter, minus her fiancé, of course."

"Of course," said Georgia.

The waiter brought the drink and Dorothy held it up. "To Glenn."

Hal walked over. "Are we toasting the affianced couple?"

"Nope," Georgia said. "Just Glenn."

"We can easily remedy that." Hal raised his glass. "To our daughter, Georgia, and her imminent two-spoon review. Congratulations, Georgia."

Her mother knocked back a quarter of her drink. "This drink certainly packs a punch," she said hoarsely.

"And while we're toasting, I'd like to raise a glass to your late grandmother," Hal nodded at Georgia, "and my mother-in-law. A wonderful woman, fabulous grandmother, terrific baker, astute business owner, and a great friend." His eyes grew shiny. "Things just haven't been the same without you, Mary. We miss you."

"To Grammy." Georgia sipped from her glass. "I can't believe it's been almost a year."

"I still wonder if the doctors couldn't have done more," Dorothy said. "At least she died doing something she loved."

Georgia stared at her mother. "No, she didn't." Grammy had suffered a massive stroke while practicing tai chi at her local Y. The ambulance whisked her away and meds were administered, but it was too late. Hours later she was dead. "She didn't love tai chi. She only did it because she saw it on *Oprah*."

Watching a little television and sharing a homemade snack—usually a muffin, sometimes maple-walnut, sometimes banana-chocolate-chip—had been a Grammy/Georgia after-school tradition. With Grammy living around the corner and up the street from the Grays, and Dorothy and Hal working nonstop, Grammy was like a substitute mother and father rolled into one. It was Grammy who taught Georgia how to play T-ball, who was "class grandma" of her second- *and* sixth-grade classes, who taught her the secret to a perfect soufflé.

Before Dorothy could respond, a white-haired man and his much younger date approached her parents, and her father and the man exchanged a hearty handshake. The four of them were soon engaged in a spirited conversation about low-VOC house paints.

Georgia smiled benignly at the back of her mother's head, wondering how much longer she'd have to stay at her uncle's party. In true high-WASP style, the hors d'oeuvres were limited to sandwiches—chicken, turkey, and roast beef—cut into triangles, and a lame cheese-and-cracker plate where a Vermont cheddar was the standout. She contemplated ordering a dirty martini just so she could nosh on the olives.

"Let's take a walk in the garden," Hal said when the couple finally moved on.

"Good idea," Georgia agreed.

"Let me refresh my drink," said Dorothy, putting down her near empty glass and picking up a white wine from a tray. "And get my purse."

They walked through French doors onto a wide terrace surrounded by rhododendrons, hydrangeas, and other flowering shrubs, nowhere near blooming, but slowly awakening from their long winter slumber. Teak furniture, weathered to a silvery gray, was dressed for the season in snappy white-and-green stripes.

"These shoes aren't the best for walking," Dorothy said, eyeing the plump cushions on the sofa. "How about we sit for a spell?"

Her parents sank into the sofa, facing the rolling hills in the distance. Hal put his arm around Dorothy, and she rested her hand on his knee. Georgia pulled up an armchair next to them, and they sat in silence until a waiter balancing a tray of drinks walked through the doors. Each took a glass of wine, even Dorothy, whose glass was practically full. "In case he doesn't come back," she said to no one in particular. Another waiter appeared with a platter of chicken skewers, and Georgia and Hal each took one, gobbling them up immediately. Dorothy passed.

"So," Hal said, wiping his mouth with a cocktail napkin, "Paul just told me a funny story. Apparently this is where Timothy Leary did his acid tests."

"Here?" Georgia asked. "As in this house?"

"No, not this house. But in Millbrook in some house nearby."

"Reminds me of how we met, Hal," said Dorothy. She was feeling no pain on a record one and a half glasses of wine, plus the Bloody Mary. "The acid part."

Georgia chuckled. "I wonder how many other offspring of lawyers and physics professors can say they were conceived at a Dead show while their parents were tripping their faces off?"

"At least you got a beautiful name out of it, honey." Her father pressed his palm into his slacks, smoothing an imaginary wrinkle. He'd never been all that comfortable with the conception chapter of the Gray family bio.

Dorothy and Hal had met in a parking lot on a steamy summer night in Atlanta while waiting to see the Grateful Dead and drinking lukewarm beer that had been—unbeknownst to them—dosed with acid. They passed a dreamy night together dancing, laughing, and staring in wide-eyed wonder at breathing walls and shifting floors, and ended up sleeping in the two-person tent Hal had erected in the parking lot earlier in the day. Nine months later Baby Girl Gray was born.

"Give us some credit," Dorothy said. "It was the seventies after all—everyone was getting blotto on blotter."

"I'm sure they were," Georgia said, laughing, "but still."

Her parents had a subscription to the Boston Symphony, were regulars at Tanglewood, and traveled to New York three times a year for opera. Despite having heard the story so many times she could recite it by heart—down to her mother's buffalo-sandal-bedecked feet—Georgia couldn't picture even a young Dorothy and Hal at a Dead show. *Tripping* at a Dead show was inconceivable.

"I'll never forget the look on my mother's face when I told her I was pregnant and getting married. You'd have thought I was joining a polygamist cult." Dorothy plucked a cigarette from a crumpled pack of American Spirits that had mysteriously materialized from her purse. "She didn't speak to me for two weeks."

Georgia was so transfixed by the cigarette in her mother's hand that she barely registered her words. "You *smoke*, Mom?"

"Only when I'm drinking," she said, ashing in her wineglass.

Georgia looked at Hal, who shrugged. "Don't ask me."

"Remember when I told my mother I wasn't going back to law school, Hal? That I was going to stay home with the baby, maybe open an art gallery?" Dorothy dragged on her cigarette. "That didn't sit well. She said she hadn't worked her fingers to the bone in that bakery so I could throw my life away. She said I owed it to her and I owed it to my late father's memory to graduate and practice law. 'I'm terribly disappointed in you, Dorothy.' I can still hear her in my head."

Georgia frowned. This picture of Grammy didn't jibe with Georgia's image of her loving, accepting, always-there-for-her grandmother.

"Is that how you felt when I decided to become a chef?" she asked.

"We're not disappointed in you, honey," Hal said quickly.

Dorothy squinted her eye against a stream of smoke slowly

curling upward. "Maybe a little bit, Georgia. Yes, I suppose something like that."

She'd always known her parents, Dorothy in particular, weren't thrilled with her choice of career, but neither had ever come out and said it. In a way it was a relief to finally have it out in the open, but it was also maddening.

"I'm the head chef at a well-known New York City restaurant—it's not like I'm running the cafeteria at Rikers Island. What's wrong with being a chef? I'm not fighting pollution, keeping the rivers clean like you do, Mom? Or maybe you'd prefer if I were an entertainment lawyer like Glenn, getting my sketchy clients off on concealed-weapon charges?"

"Of course not, Georgia. You're not cut out for law. But it's not too late to change course. You can still do something with regular hours, something a little more family friendly, a little more . . . intellectual. You've always been a smart girl, Georgia. We never had to worry about your grades."

"You never worried about me at all, Mom. You left that to Grammy."

"I didn't have the chance to," Dorothy said. "Grammy hired someone to run her business the day you were born so that she could raise you and I could be an attorney, just like my dad, just like she'd planned."

"Lunch should be served soon," Hal said, standing up. "Why don't we all go inside and have something to eat."

"Just so you know," Georgia said, "cooking *is* intellectual. It's not all slicing, dicing, and deep-frying. If you'd ever let me prepare a meal for you, you'd see that."

"Let you? I don't recall a recent invitation." Dorothy stubbed out her cigarette on the bottom of her shoe and laid it on the floor.

"I've given up! You guys make so many excuses about why

you can't come for dinner—even when you're already in the city for opera or whatever—I finally stopped asking."

"The next time we're in," Hal said, "we would love to come for dinner. I know I would and so would your mother. Right, Dorothy?" He stared pointedly at her.

She nodded.

Paul popped his head out onto the patio, his face brightening when he saw them. "There you Grays are. Lunch is served in the dining room."

"We were just coming in," said Hal.

Dorothy picked up her cigarette, wrapped the butt in a tissue, and slipped it into her purse so she could dispose of it later. "Perfect timing," she said, rising from the couch and walking to the door. "I'm starving."

Chapter Five

Sally charged down the street, pulling Georgia behind her, sloshing through puddles, bypassing all her favorite trees until she caught up with the object of her affection: a Wheaten terrier whose twentysomething owner looked styled for a *Vogue* fashion shoot no matter the time of day. Georgia glanced down at her own black windbreaker, faded jeans, and Merrell mocs; a killer outfit it wasn't, but it was Monday morning and the rest of the world was safely working. The two dogs chased each other in circles, rolled on the sidewalk, and got in a few good sniffs before their owners pulled them apart and continued on their ways.

Yesterday's visit with her parents had left Georgia woozy, and she headed to the bakery for a sweet treat, Grammy's prescription for just about everything. Not only had Dorothy finally admitted that Georgia's job wasn't quite white-collar enough for her taste (the white chef's coat apparently didn't count), but she'd blamed Grammy for making her choose career over motherhood. As if anybody could make her mother do anything she didn't want to.

The rain stopped and it settled into one of those gray mornings that seem to occur every couple days during early spring. Georgia leashed Sally to a ginkgo tree outside Pain Quotidien and headed into the bakery, placing her order for a sugar waffle with a side of praline spread and a large café au lait. A teenage boy with nose-skimming bangs stopped to pet Sally, and Georgia watched through the window as her dog's tail swished from side to side, ready to run out if the boy went anywhere near her collar. A friend at the dog run knew someone whose field spaniel had been dognapped while she waited on line for an iced mochachino, and the story had freaked Georgia out. The boy moved on, and Sally sat back on her haunches. The woman on line behind her cleared her throat.

"Excuse me. Are you Georgia Gray, the chef at Marco?" Her ash-blond hair was swept into a chignon, and her skin was smooth and a little pink, as if she'd just had a chemical peel. She wore black trousers, those Belgian shoes with the tiny bows, and she carried a pebbled-leather satchel. A lady who lunched, a well-kept sixty-five, sixty-eight tops.

Georgia smiled. "Yes, I am. Have we met?"

"No, we haven't. But I believe I saw you yesterday at Paul Gray's farm in Millbrook."

"Oh, right, Paul is my uncle."

"I was hoping to meet you, but you disappeared suddenly."

"I hadn't seen my parents in a while," Georgia said. "We had a lot to talk about."

"I saw your picture in that *Big Apple Business* magazine. '35 under 35,' I think the article was called. That's how I recognized you."

The editor of *BAB* was a friend of Clem's who'd been looking for a young chef to spice up an article about bland business types. That Georgia was a woman—and attractive—had ensured not only a nice blurb and pull quote, but a flattering photo as well.

"Have you had a chance to come into the restaurant?" Georgia asked.

"As a matter of fact, yes. I had the distinct pleasure of dining at your establishment once, just a few weeks ago." The woman spoke in an expensive voice, sounding like a cross between Lauren Bacall and Madonna, after she'd decided to become British.

"Well, I hope you enjoyed your meal."

"It was lovely. The scallops were fantastic, the tuna divine, but the venison was a tad too salty for my tastes." The woman whispered this last bit under a cupped hand, then laughed. Georgia liked her immediately.

"I hope you'll come in again. We always appreciate discriminating palates." Georgia bent her head toward the woman. "And I promise to go easy on the salt this time."

A pair of doctors in matching green hospital scrubs and black clogs descended the stairs and joined the line. One of them checked her beeper, said something to her friend, and charged back up the stairs.

"Wonderful. As a matter of fact"—the woman pulled a Louis Vuitton day planner from her bag and flipped through its pages—"I'd love to come in tomorrow night at eight." She looked at Georgia and waited, clearly a woman accustomed to getting what she wanted.

"I'll take care of it. And for whom shall I make the reservation?"

"Henderson. Barbara Henderson. Dinner for four. Here's my card." She handed Georgia an eggshell-colored calling card engraved with her name and phone numbers. Georgia noted the card's heft and subtle sheen, trademarks of Dempsey & Carroll stationery, before sliding it into her back pocket. Glenn's mom had wanted the posh stationer to do their wedding invites, but the cost made Georgia's eyes bug out of her head. There was no way she would have paid that much for paper.

"See you tomorrow, Mrs. Henderson." Georgia scooped up the little brown bag waiting on the counter and turned toward the door. "Thanks," she said to the heavily pierced barista. The girl looked at her blankly, and Georgia wondered which had hurt more: the silver hoop in her nose or the pair through her eyebrow.

"Please. Mrs. Henderson is my mother-in-law. Call me Huggy. Everyone does."

"Well then, see you tomorrow, Huggy."

Georgia untied Sally, then called the restaurant on her cell and left a message for the reservationist. Marco got annoyed with last-minute reservations from the staff, but after the Mercedes Sante review she didn't think he'd care. VIP, she said on the message. Table nine if it's available, and at least table sixteen. She had a feeling Huggy was worth it.

The next afternoon Georgia flew into the restaurant, her navy trench flapping behind her as she blasted by the busboys setting up for dinner. Despite her most timely intentions, she was late. It had been nearly impossible to rouse herself out of bed, and she wondered if the little pink pill she'd swallowed was somehow to blame.

On top of that, she had had to wait forever for the F train. When it finally came, it looked as if it'd been stuffed by the white-gloved people packers who work the Tokyo subway during rush hour. The thought of squeezing into some sweaty straphanger's armpit was as appetizing as a mug of hot-dog water, so she waited for the next one.

Bernard stopped talking when she arrived, pushing back

his shirtsleeve and peering at the Roman numerals on his wristwatch. His sandy hair was parted on the side with just enough product to hold it in place without making it too shiny or crunchy. He always looked perfectly put together, his face freshly shaved, Windsor knot expertly tied, and today was no exception.

"Seventeen minutes late, Georgia. May I remind you that we expect you, as we do everyone, to arrive on time. Not"—he stared down his long nose at her—"seventeen minutes late."

She smiled coolly and took the seat next to Ricky, annoyed that the review wasn't acting as the get-out-of-jail-free card she thought it would. Good thing her staff liked her, otherwise after that rebuke they'd pounce on her like stockbrokers on steak.

"Bad timing, Chef," Ricky whispered.

Georgia swung her bag from her shoulder and hung it over the back of a chair. "What?" she mouthed.

He shook his head. "Later."

"As I was saying," Bernard continued. "Basic crowd: a few front-row fashion-show fixtures whose outfits cost more than our weekly salaries combined, Greenwich soccer moms toting fat husbands with even fatter wallets, uptown slums downtown, and a handful of overstuffed gourmands who fancy themselves foodies." He wrinkled his nose. "God, I hate that word." He flipped through the reservation list on his clipboard. "We do have one legitimate VIP: megamillionaire Huggy Henderson, philanthropist extraordinaire. Once again, the review will be out tomorrow." He tucked the red clipboard under his arm. "God help us all."

"What happened to 'keep the champagne flowing, we've just hit the restaurant-review jackpot'?" Georgia asked. "Bernard?"

He whizzed by without answering, either ignoring or not

hearing her. While the meeting devolved into an eating and gossip fest, Georgia followed him to the front of the restaurant, catching up with him at the hostess stand.

"Bernard," she said loudly. "What is going on?"

When he turned to her, the smile on his face was so meager, so pitiful, so the opposite of what a smile should be, that she knew the news was going to be very, very bad.

"I hate to be the one to tell you this, Georgia."

"Just tell me."

"It looks like the three-fork isn't happening."

Her stomach dropped. "What happened? What did Marco do?"

"Exactly what you think."

"Bernard, please tell me."

"Okay," he said, glancing over his shoulder. "Saturday night, the night you were off, there was a very pretty, very young girl sitting at the bar. As is his wont, Marco was only too happy to flirt with her and ply her with free booze. Once he'd gotten her sufficiently sauced, he did what any self-respecting scumbag would do. He took her home. The next night, when she was seated on the very same stool, he was a little less happy. I think his words were something along the lines of 'What the fuck are you doing here?'" Bernard paused. "Anyway, the girl stayed, drank a couple drinks, full fare this time, and broke down when Marco left with a *different* drunk girl on his arm. One of the waitresses spent half an hour consoling her in the bathroom, and we finally got her in a cab home. I'm sure you already know the punch line, but just in case: she was Mercedes's daughter. Mercedes's only daughter."

Georgia closed her eyes. "What's the damage, Bernard? Did we lose a fork?"

"If only. Looks like we're down to one."

"One fork? From three to one? You can't cut a review by two forks because of the restaurant's scumbag owner!"

"I'm afraid you can. Especially when said scumbag groped and pawed your nubile daughter, all nineteen years and ninety-nine pounds of her, and then cast her out like yesterday's coffee grounds. I'm afraid you can."

"I can't believe this. I cannot fucking believe this." Georgia needed the review. Especially with everything else going on, she needed the review.

Bernard cleared his throat. "Speak of the scumbag devil."

Marco stood in the doorway, white motorcycle helmet in hand, black wraparound sunglasses shading his eyes. With his cosmetically enhanced grin and tight T-shirt, he looked like the grown-up member of a long-defunct boy band.

She turned around and walked back to the locker room, passing Ricky, who held up a piece of wan broccoli to his mouth before inspecting it and returning it to his plate. The one thing helping her keep her shit together amid all the crap with Glenn, the proverbial light at the end of the tunnel, had just gone Alaskan-oil-spill black. A one-fork review was a career breaker. A fire-the-chef, scrap-the-name, change-the-decor, if-you-even-stay-open kind of review. She was screwed. And all because of Marco and his fucking libido.

Dressed and ready for dinner prep, Georgia went outside to nurse her nerves before service. Ricky stood smoking with the garde-manger, who spoke little English and cleared his phlegmy throat frequently as if to make up for it. Ricky blew a smoke ring Georgia's way and joined her on the step.

"You okay?"

"Jesus, Ricky, this is going to be really bad."

"Remember what you said that night. It's not our funeral, it's Marco's. You said it, Chef."

"The thing is, Ricky, I was lying when I said that. It's not Marco's funeral, it's not your funeral, it's my funeral. One hundred percent." She looked down at the butts littering the ground. "Can I have a cigarette?"

"You don't smoke, Georgia. You know, it may not be as bad as we all think. Maybe she'll surprise us and give us two forks. That's more than respectable." He stomped out his cigarette. "Come on. Let's grab some joe."

The Juilliard-trained-cellist-cum-waitress who had been Mercedes's server made them two cappuccinos. "Georgia, don't sweat the review. Everyone knows what happened. No one will blame you. Here," she said, handing over the coffees. "Extra foam."

"Thanks," Georgia said, amazed at how quickly bad news spread. She slugged down her cappuccino, her inner strength dissipating faster than her career prospects.

Ricky motioned toward the doorway, where Marco stood, legs wide, hands behind his back. At least he'd lost the shades.

"Guys." Marco strutted toward the group, his hands palming the air, his eyes resting on the waitress's well-endowed chest.

Scumbag, Georgia thought for the millionth time that day. And he wasn't even good in bed.

"So how's it going?" He flicked an imaginary piece of lint from his T-shirt and ran his hand through his hair several times. "Everyone feeling good?" His leather-soled shoes tapped the floor, and he jingled the keys in his pocket. "Big night tonight. Huggy Henderson's coming in. You guys know who she is?"

Georgia opened her mouth, then shut it.

"A big-deal socialite. A friend of mine. I made the reserva-

tion for her myself, so make sure you do her right. Table nine."
He squeezed the waitress's shoulder and winked, then walked
away.

He hadn't looked at Georgia once. When the review hit, he
would fire her. She was sure of it.

Georgia attacked her dinner prep more aggressively than usual.
As she saw it, there were two kinds of chefs. First, there were
the cerebral types, who cooked with an intellectual, almost aca-
demic, bent. They cooked with precision and accuracy, studying a particular ingredient's effects in multiple settings before
introducing it into their kitchen. These chefs loved the science
of food. Fastidious in their pre-prep prep, they knew with 99
percent accuracy that a dish would turn out well. Then there
were the chefs who worked from the heart. Who were furious
when a dish fizzled, chopped angrily at the food as if it were
their enemy, but on a good day could coax such sensuous, sublime flavors from a paltry potato and a handful of herbs that no
diner would suspect its humble origins. When they hit, they hit
big. But when they fell, it was like a sequoia cracking open in
the redwood forest.

Georgia belonged to the former (she was, after all, her father's daughter), but that night she let her anger at Glenn, at
Marco, at Mercedes, and even at Mercedes's presumably unsuspecting daughter give way to a fervor she normally kept in close
check. The line cooks fed off her intensity, each station playing
its part in the unspoken choreography that defines a stellar
night. Miraculously, no one was in the weeds; the roundsman,
who stepped in wherever he was needed, did his job seamlessly;
orders came up on time; the front and back of the house were
perfectly in sync. The dining room—diners, servers, bartenders,
hostess, even the coat-check girl—sparkled with energy.

Georgia placed four small plates on the pass-through and called over her favorite waitress. "Send these to Huggy Henderson, table nine, with my compliments."

"Wow. The potato-and-caviar treatment," the waitress said, checking out the plates. "She really must be important."

If sitting on a handful of the city's most prestigious boards and routinely appearing in the party pages meant she was important, then, yes, Huggy was important. Beyond that, Georgia liked her. Meeting the imperious woman with the *Preppy Handbook*–style nickname had been the highlight of a couple of low days. As if on cue the new pimple on Georgia's chin started tingling, a pesky reminder of her Chubby Chippie binge.

Bernard walked back into the kitchen and tapped her shoulder. "Georgia. What are you guys doing back here? That dining room is on fire."

"I had to do something."

Ricky stretched his head around the door to catch a glimpse of the dining room. "He's not kidding, Chef. You gotta check it out. Table eight's about to go at it on the table."

"Must be the oysters," Georgia said.

That night, she unilaterally struck Oysters Marco, her least favorite dish, from the menu. Instead she served what she jokingly called Oysters Roc-a-fella, a slight twist on the famous Antoine's Restaurant original, subbing cress for spinach and adding chopped fennel and a splash of (now legal) absinthe. The recipe was a tip-top secret, but Georgia had known it for years, thanks to a former colleague who'd once worked at Antoine's and who'd recited it to her as if it were a Shakespearean sonnet. After, he'd professed his undying love and devotion to her, and after that he'd face-planted into a bowl of remoulade. She hadn't seen the cook in ages, but the recipe she remembered.

A waitress walked to the pass-through. "The very important

Huggy Henderson is requesting your company. I know Marco doesn't go for this, but I thought maybe this one time."

"Go for it, Georgia." Bernard gave her a polite shove. They both knew her fate at Marco was as good as sealed.

Huggy Henderson held court at table nine, a corner banquette bathed in a soft glow. Far enough from the bar and the server station to seem almost intimate, yet central enough so fellow diners couldn't help but crane their necks to see who graced the table at which they'd never be seated, it was the undisputed best table in the house. Huggy wore a South Sea pearl-coral-and-diamond necklace that hit directly above her collarbones, and a creamy cashmere cardigan with scalloped edges. Her hair was pulled back into a loose bun, and her ears were festooned with quarter-size pearls rimmed with pavé diamonds that matched her necklace. She was, as Glenn's mom would say, the original Mrs. Got Rocks.

Georgia smoothed her hair, slicked some gloss across her lips, and straightened her white chef's jacket. There wasn't a whole lot she could do to improve her appearance. She marched through the dining room, eyes straight ahead, hoping she didn't look like a girl heading for the guillotine, which was how she felt. She wouldn't miss these at-table appearances, rare though they were. Some chefs loved them, basking in the spotlight, beaming as they sauntered through the crowd of adoring diners. Not Georgia. She was delighted when Marco told her he believed the chef belonged in the kitchen and the front of the house was his and the managers' domain. Marco didn't go much for anything that took the limelight from where he felt it rightfully belonged: on himself. In this case, Georgia happily agreed with him.

Placing her hand on the back of Huggy's polished nickel

chair, Georgia smiled at her two companions, noting an empty place setting. "Hello, I'm Georgia Gray. I hope you're all enjoying your meal."

"Georgia. How lovely to see you." Huggy held out her hand. "Don't you look wonderful in your smart white chef coat. I was just telling my family how we met yesterday at the bakery. What a fortuitous encounter."

"Wasn't it," said Georgia.

"Tell me, dear, a friend of mine at the *Daily* says you'll be reviewed tomorrow. Is that so?"

Georgia bit her lip. "I'm afraid so, Huggy. We believe Mercedes Sante was in last week, so the review should be out tomorrow."

"Afraid? Afraid of what?" said a dapper man with thinning salt-and-pepper hair and thick black eyebrows. "That was the best soft-shell crab I've ever had."

"I'm glad you liked it. It's one of my favorites too." The crab was a seasonal special, and a big crowd-pleaser.

"Lawrence Henderson. Her worse half." He motioned in Huggy's direction and chuckled. "Good to meet you, Georgia. Allow me to introduce my son, Andrew."

Andrew's face was chiseled and sharp, but his espresso-brown eyes were soft, sort of like Sally's. "Nice to meet you, Georgia. The food is delicious. Everything is." His voice was mellow and rich, and his ripe mouth turned up at the corners. He gestured to the table with an open palm, his eyes crinkling. Georgia was smitten.

"Now, Georgia, you needn't be afraid of this review. The food is simply heavenly, although all this lacquer and mirror"—Huggy gestured to the white lacquer bar, which was backed by mirrored shelving holding multihued bottles—"is a bit much. But trust me, dear. It will be a good review and you'll be even more of a star than you already are." Huggy beamed as if Georgia were her very own creation.

"Gee, thanks, Huggy. But I'm not so sure of that. We'll see what happens."

Huggy pulled out a calling card from her quilted Chanel clutch. "In case you lost my other card. Please, dear, should you ever need anything, don't hesitate to call."

Georgia accepted the card. "Thanks, Huggy, I will. It was nice to meet you all." She looked at Andrew for just a second longer than necessary, then left the table, grinning at a waiter as she passed.

Despite her doomed career and disastrous relationship, Georgia felt a flicker of joy. Marco was firing her. The entire city would soon read a terrible review that would likely mention her name half a dozen times. And yet, Andrew's eyes were so . . . nice. And that voice. Maybe she could do the single-girl thing after all. Feeling almost giddy, she sailed toward the kitchen, stopping shy of the door. She turned for one last look at the table, just in time to catch a stunning brunette in a strapless dress rush over. Andrew's sister? After blowing kisses to Huggy and her husband, the woman half bent, half stooped next to Andrew, planting a kiss squarely on his mouth. Not a chance.

Georgia looked down at the hand clenching Huggy's card and was momentarily blinded by the glittering diamond on her left ring finger. The reality of her life settled in like a bad summer cold. Of course a guy like Andrew had a girlfriend, maybe even a wife. Besides, she was still engaged to Glenn. Though their breakup seemed more a matter of when than if, they were still engaged and she had the hardware to prove it.

"What's up with you, Chef? Is everything okay?" Ricky asked. When Georgia didn't respond, he continued, "I guess having a big night will do that. The waitrons said their tips are insane and they want to take us out for drinks after close."

"That's sweet of them, Ricky. But I think I'll make it an early night and go home. I don't really feel like going out." Her emotions were pogo-ing all over the place and she could barely make sense of them. Andrew's soulful gaze and sexy mouth had triggered such instant elation it made her wonder. One smile from some random, taken guy and she's running and dancing for joy? She raked her fingers through her pouffy hair, a cardinal sin for both chefs and curly girls, but sometimes impossible to resist.

At midnight Georgia was at last able to call it a night. The restaurant had its most successful night ever, hitting 256 covers, and an average ticket well over a hundred bucks. How ironic that it would soon be over. Seventies disco blasted through the kitchen as the crew drank their shift drink and readied themselves for more at the bar next door.

Ricky danced over to Georgia, hip-checking her as the song ended. "You sure I can't convince you to come out? It'll do you good."

"Don't think so, Ricky, but thanks. I have a much needed date with my second-to-last sleeping pill." She wouldn't be able to sleep without it. She swung her bag over her shoulder and started walking out. "Talk to you tomorrow."

"Have fun on your date," he called after her.

Halfway through the dining room she bent down to smell the flowers spilling onto the bar, cupping a particularly perfect peony in her hand. When she reached the door, she paused, turning for a last look at the restaurant. "*Arrivederci, amici,*" she said to no one. She pushed open the door and exited into the cool night.

Chapter Six

The digital clock shouted 6:03 like a tabloid headline. Georgia sat up and stretched, rubbed her eyes. Judgment Day, aka The Day Georgia Got Forked, arrived earlier than most, and she cursed her internal clock for being so punctual.

Her feet touched down on the kilim carpet her parents had bought for her on a trip to Turkey, a culinary school graduation gift. Georgia had been surprised by how much she liked it and had decorated her slightly ethnic room around its faded blues, reds, and greens. The bed and bedside tables were ebonized bamboo, the walls were painted a deep eggplant, and an etched-glass lantern hung from the ceiling. The bookshelf was stuffed with cookbooks, novels, and Glenn's beloved biographies and history books, spillover from the shelves lining the living room.

Two photographs sat on her dresser. One was of Grammy sitting on the dock at Silver Lake, her curly hair hidden by a flowered bathing cap, her legs crossed in front of her like Esther Williams. The other was of Georgia and Glenn at his sister's wedding, in a sterling Tiffany frame the couple gave to the wedding party. His arm was thrown over Georgia's shoulder, his smile open and off-center, as if he'd just heard a funny joke. Togged out in his tux, he looked Rat-Packer suave. Georgia wore Lo's diamond drop earrings, a strapless black dress, and had treated herself to a blowout, so her hair fell down her back in smooth waves. Her smile was genuine, but her eyes looked just beyond the photographer. She didn't recall having the picture taken, and when Glenn had asked what she was looking at, she couldn't honestly remember.

She pulled up the shades and watched the sun begin its slow ascent over the East River, a sliver of which was visible from her bedroom and living-room windows. Water views, the ad for her apartment had boasted, and she had laughed when the Realtor pointed to the swish of muddled army-green water all but hidden between two towering buildings. Because she had spent childhood summers at Grammy's cabin on Silver Lake, even that tiny slice of water offered comfort in the then still unfamiliar city, and she rented the apartment on the spot.

On weekday mornings she liked to watch the mammoth barges—what little she could see of them—traverse the river, wondering where they had come from and where they were going. Such an unlikely Manhattan scene, she had remarked to Glenn on one of only a handful of weekdays she could remember waking up next to him. He was home, sick with the flu, and wasn't interested in boats or their stories, or how easy it was to forget the city was an island.

She slipped into sweats and flip-flops, chugged the glass of water on her bedside table, and left her apartment. With unbrushed teeth and hair, and five bucks in her pocket, she padded down the silent city streets, Sally plodding faithfully by her side. Turning in to the twenty-four-hour bodega, she braced herself for the worst. The *Daily* sat right next to the *New York Times*, a place of honor it didn't deserve. But Mercedes's restaurant reviews were, if not the most respected reviews, then at least the most read and were single-handedly responsible for more failed restaurants than the citywide smoking ban years back.

"Good morning, miss." The young Indian owner smiled at her as she held up the newspaper and handed over a bill. "You're up early today," he said in a charmingly clipped accent, recalling her face from occasional late-night ice cream outings. He gave her the change. "Have a good day."

"Thanks. I'll try."

Back at her apartment, Georgia sat down at the repro Chippendale dining table, scarred by decades of Gray family use, and rifled through the newspaper until she hit the lifestyle section. There it was, for all the world to see: half a fork. In case anyone might mistake it for a full fork, the art department had added the fraction ½ in front of the tiny half-fork graphic. It couldn't be any clearer. She bit her lip to stop it from trembling. "No fucking way," she whispered before folding back the page.

If you, like the rest of this city, have been desperately trying to score a coveted reservation at Marco, the latest and inexplicable darling of the downtown restaurant scene, you may want to reconsider. Your time could be better spent slurping a tallow milk shake and a plate of wiggly fries at the corner diner. (And given the restaurant's astronomical prices, the bill, and possibly even the food, will be a lot more palatable.) From the ticky-tacky décor to the haughty service to the largely subpar food, Marco is a must miss that the fickle see-and-be-seen crowd will surely vacate for hotter (or perhaps cooler) pastures soon.

One redeeming quality of this velvet-roped-nightclub-cum-restaurant is a marginally interesting wine list, but with sky-high prices and markups upwards of 400%, it clearly caters to the flat-out loaded social and Hollywood-by-way-of-SoHo set who care not that a mediocre bottle of wine could easily set them back a Benjamin (or two or three).

Georgia felt like throwing up. This was worse than anything anyone expected.

As for the food, will someone please tell chef Georgia Gray salt is not a flavor unto itself but a flavor enhancer? Assertive salting is one thing, but Gray takes it to another level entirely. Some of her dishes taste as if they've been dunked in the cold Atlantic Ocean and then hung out to dry in a curing shack. Others are simply inedible, as in the venison, the texture of which recalls leather shoes that have been tap-dancing in the rain a little too long. Guinea hen, an iffy proposition even in more capable hands, fails to impress, floating as it does in a pool of glassy beurre blanc and lifeless baby root vegetables. Oysters Marco, the specialty of the house, according to our uppity, unsmiling waitress, resembles a slippery mass of Silly Putty flavored with cheap, overly acidic balsamic vinegar and the ubiquitous fistful of salt. My four companions and I egged each other on à la *Fear Factor* to suck down the esophagus-obliterating concoction, and none of us were successful.

The menu is not entirely without merit, and daily specials ably showcase Gray's mastery of cooking simple rustic fare, particularly in the pasta department. A bresaola and pecorino taglierini, decorated with spring peas and ramps, is tasty and satisfying, and the special risotto, purple asparagus and artichoke with a healthy dose of Asiago cheese and crunchy caramelized shallots, offers a palate-pleasing meld of flavor and texture. Polenta with wild-mushroom ragout, updated favorably with tangy sheep's milk cheese, is earthy, velvety and downright good. Gray is clearly in her element with these peasant-inspired dishes, and my advice to her is to stick with them. Desserts are across-the-board insipid, bland and boring. If you must satisfy a sweet tooth, go for the house-made gelato.

Unfortunately, with 85% of the menu missing its mark, a blindly inattentive waitstaff, ambience that recalls a past-its-prime Atlantic City casino, and prices that surpass those at the city's genuine culinary treasures, I cannot in clear conscience bestow even one full fork on Marco. Perhaps owner and former chef Marco Giado should scamper off, tail between his legs, and hone his skills in a less competitive market before attempting to play with the big boys of the Big Apple.

Georgia reread the review three times before crumpling it up and throwing it on the floor. From that moment on she would forever be known as the half-fork chef, inextricably linked with the most seething review written in the history of restaurant reviews.

"Fuck," she said, loud enough to rouse Sally from her nap. Georgia stared at the balled-up newspaper, wishing she could make it burst into flames, then walked into the bedroom and changed into running gear. On her way out, she kicked the newspaper ball, then snatched it up, holding it between her thumb and index finger like a bag of doggy poop. "Come on, Sals," she called. "Let's get out of here."

While they waited for the elevator, she tossed the review down the garbage chute. It wasn't worth recycling.

A few hours later, naked, Georgia stood under the showerhead letting the hot water wash over her body and missing Glenn from the top of her tangled head to her polished toes. Any traces of her sweaty run around Central Park's upper loop were long gone, but she couldn't bear to leave the shower. Not with the phone incessantly ringing and not with nine messages waiting on the answering machine, and especially not with that review. Her anger had given way to a resigned exhaustion. Another quarter-size squirt of conditioner, worked into the ends, another round of soap, everywhere but the face. Sally, who had parked herself on the bath mat, poked her nose through the curtain and stared at Georgia for a second before returning to the floor.

"Okay, okay," she muttered, turning off the water with wrinkled fingertips. She stepped over her dog and wrapped a towel around her torso and another around her head. When the phone rang, she took a deep breath before walking into the living room to pick it up.

"Georgia." It was Lo.

"Hey," Georgia said flatly.

"Oh my God. I'm so sorry."

"Yeah." Georgia didn't feel like talking, even to her best friend.

"Can I buy you breakfast? Lunch? Treat you to a facial?"

"Thanks, Lo, but I have to deal with this. I'll call you when the shit really hits the fan after I get axed."

"Maybe you won't—"

Georgia cut her off. "Please don't even go there. I'm getting fired and we both know it. Anyone who reads the *Daily* knows it."

"Sorry, George. I just can't believe how spiteful that woman is. That was the meanest review I've ever read."

"Yeah. Anyway, my call waiting is going nuts. I gotta go."

"Dinner or drinks tonight? On me, okay?"

"Maybe. I'm sure I'll need a stiffie or six by the end of this day."

She hung up and clicked over.

"Georgia, it's Bernard."

"Not so good, huh?"

"No, not so good at all I'm afraid." He cleared his throat.

"When am I getting fired?"

Bernard paused. "Let me buy you breakfast and we'll talk then."

"You don't want to just get it over with now?"

"Balthazar in an hour. Can you make it?"

"If I'm cabbing all the way downtown to get fired, Marco better at least pick up the cab. I'll be unemployed soon, remember."

"The cab's on me, Georgia. Breakfast is on Marco."

"In that case, I'll see you there. And I'm feeling mighty hungry."

Sitting at a corner table at Balthazar, once one of the city's trendiest restaurants and now a New York institution, Georgia silently prayed not to see anyone she had ever worked with or who knew her even remotely. She wore cropped white jeans, a shrunken black cardigan, and black ballet slippers, which covered her coral toes. She had chosen her outfit carefully, going for a Jackie O in Capri look. Everyone knew that when getting fired or dumped, the ever-dignified Jackie was the icon to channel. Her hair was miraculously devoid of frizz, thanks to the eighty-five different products holding it down and the flat iron her hairdresser claimed would change her life. No way was she getting fired with frizzy hair.

Taking stock of the Balthazar scene, she did a quick scan for familiar faces, famous or otherwise. The last time she was there she'd seen a radiant Uma Thurman dining near Anderson Cooper. Her eyes paused on a two-top against the far wall, a desirable table under the gigantic antique mirror upon which all eyes fell when entering the restaurant. A porcine man used stubby fingers to scoop up something from his plate, while his lady friend, who bore an uncanny resemblance to Donatella Versace, pretended not to notice. Georgia looked closer. Please no, she thought. The man lifted his nearly bald head and she sank back into the red banquette, clutching the sleeves of her sweater like a security blanket. It was Pierre du Mont, her former boss. With any luck he hadn't seen her. She'd left his bistro to work at Brit bad boy Stanley Quinn's first stateside venture, and when she last saw Pierre, he razzed her nonstop. Though he was half joking, she knew he was steamed. Pierre went back to his finger food, seeming not to notice her. For the moment anyway, she was safe.

Wearing a tan raincoat, an umbrella tucked under his arm, Bernard hurried over to the hostess stand, where he cased the room for his breakfast companion. Georgia let him find her, not wanting to draw attention to herself with Pierre just a few tables away.

"Georgia, good to see you." Bernard took the seat across from her.

"You're such a liar, Bernard. And a bad one too." She sipped a glass of Pellegrino. "Unless you're genuinely psyched to fire me, which wouldn't make you a very nice person." She smiled, letting him know he was off the hook.

"Listen, you're right that I'm firing you. And I'm not happy about it. We all know the review had nothing to do with the food, or even the shitty decor or the overpriced wine list or the waitstaff's bad attitude or anything that"—he paused, trying to find the right word—"that *woman* wrote. It's all because of Marco and his inability to keep his dick in his pants." Bernard looked around for the waiter, who materialized instantly.

"Two Bloodies with Ketel One. Right?" Bernard glanced at Georgia for confirmation.

"Actually, I'm more in the mood for champagne. What do you have?"

"By the glass we have Pol Roger, Veuve—"

Georgia cut him off. "I think we'll have a bottle, actually. What do you have that's really good? Krug?"

The waiter nodded. "Of course. Be right back."

"Great, Georgia. Just because you're getting fired doesn't mean you have to get me fired too."

"Come on, B. You know Marco won't be able to say shit about the cost of this meal. Plus, look at how happy we made our waiter."

"True." Bernard looked down at his hands. "So, as I was saying, you're right I'm firing you. No need to beat around the bush. You can clear out your locker, I can messenger your stuff home, give it to Ricky, whatever you like. You've cooked your last meal at Marco."

No matter how ready Georgia thought she was, nothing had prepared her for the severity of that killer sentence. She swallowed hard. For a second she felt like the heroine in a film noir after she's learned her husband has been killed—and that he'd been carrying on an affair with his secretary for years. In the film version, she'd dramatically crumple into the private dick's arms, and he'd offer her smelling salts or something strong, and likely brown, to drink. Instead, the waiter returned to the table, holding out the champagne for her inspection.

"Thanks," she said, wasting no time in swilling her first sip.

"What a fucking mess." Bernard exhaled. "Here I am, firing a damn good chef, the kind of chef Marco never was and never will be, and all because that dirtbag thinks the nineteen-year-old daughter of the woman who's reviewing his restaurant is fair game. Of course he was so fucked-up at the time he probably didn't even realize she was barely out of high school." Bernard finished his Bloody and poured himself a glass of champagne. "Scratch that. I'm sure he knew exactly how old she was. Now the bastard can't own up to it, and someone has to take the fall. 'Heads will roll,' he told me this morning. 'Ax the chef-ette.' Who does he think he is, Henry the Eighth?"

"Or Gargamel," Georgia said. "He really called me the chef-ette?"

Bernard was way too worked up for questions. "His restaurant is a sinking ship. It's the fucking *Titanic*, for Christ's sake." He poured the champagne down his throat and immediately refilled his glass.

"Wow, Bernard. You'd think you'd been called chef-ette."

Ignoring her attempt at levity, he steamrolled on. "He's going to have to deal with the consequences at some point. Even though no one can see it, it's his name on the goddamn door. Doesn't he realize?"

The waiter walked over and Bernard paused long enough so

he and Georgia could place their identical orders: eggs Norwegian and croissants. He started up again the moment the waiter turned his back.

Georgia refilled his glass for the third time and turned the bottle neck-side down in the ice bucket. They hadn't started breakfast and had already killed a bottle of champagne. It wasn't yet eleven o'clock.

"So do you have any plans, Georgia?" Having finished his diatribe, Bernard reverted back to his all-business self.

"Plans? No, I have no plans. I just realized I was getting fired yesterday. The day before that I thought I was heading for a major raise and some Food Network show Marco kept talking about. No, I have no plans."

The truth was, she felt lost without a plan. She always had a plan. She stabbed her fork into an egg, watching the yolk spill onto the plate. "And lest you think my life isn't a total and complete wreck, my fiancé walked out on me last week and may never return. So not only am I unemployed, but I'm probably about to be unengaged too. Things are not looking up."

"Oh, Jesus, Georgia. I'm sorry." He looked around for the waiter, who again miraculously appeared. "Let's get some oysters." Like most restaurant people, Bernard thought the right dish could cure just about anything.

"Six Malpeques, six . . . ?" He looked at Georgia.

"Kumamotos," she said.

After their first shipboard rendezvous, she and Glenn had shared a dozen Kumamotos and a couple pints of Stella Artois at Scales & Shells, her favorite restaurant in Newport. Then they went back to his place, kicked his roommate out of the tiny bungalow, and had sex on the screened-in porch as the sun sank into the ocean. Glenn made some joke about oysters and aphrodisiacs that at the time was wildly funny and which they repeated often throughout the summer. She couldn't remember it for the life of her.

"You know, if you're desperate, I could hook you up with a friend of mine uptown," Bernard said.

"Glenn's been gone a week, Bernard. I'm far from desperate, but thanks anyway."

"I'm not talking about that kind of desperate, Georgia. I meant if you're desperate for a job. My friend owns Lagoon on the Upper West. Though not exactly Per Se, it's not the worst place either. He's looking for sauté."

"Really, Bernard? Do you seriously think I'm going to have to accept sauté at a third-rate restaurant on the Upper West? Is that what it's come to?" Though the highest station on the line, right below sous, sauté was a far, far cry from head chef at a white-hot restaurant. She hadn't considered accepting anything less than sous, and only at a reputable and popular spot, and even that made her cringe. Maybe some place intimate and innovative, some place chef-owned. Not, she thought, sauté at a yuppie dump Zagat rated high teens.

"You have to face facts, Georgia. It isn't going to be easy to get hired after this review. You need to consider your options."

"I know, I know. But it's too depressing to think about it now. Can't we talk about it later—like next year?" Drunk and suddenly tired, Georgia felt as deflated as the tires on the mountain bike Glenn never rode yet insisted remain in the living room should the urge ever strike.

The waiter walked over with a tray and two orangey-pink drinks. He placed them on the table. "Georgia Peaches. Peach schnapps, brandy, cranberry juice—the first request the bartender's ever had for one of these. From the gentleman over there, who says a Georgia Peach for a Georgia peach." He pointed to Pierre. "Or something like that."

Georgia held up her drink in acknowledgment, smiling tightly at her former boss's glowing head.

"Is that Pierre du Mont?" Bernard asked.

Georgia nodded.

"That's what I thought," the waiter said. "And the bartender was wondering if you're the Georgia who got slammed in that Mercedes Sante review." He pointed to the drinks on the table. "Hence the Georgia Peach drinks."

"Yes, I am, and, yes, I get the Georgia Peach reference, thanks."

Apparently reading her gesture as an invitation to chat, Pierre pushed back his chair and walked toward Georgia, his bleached-blond friend in tow.

"Georgia," he boomed. His voice was almost as big as his body.

"Why, hello, Pierre. Thanks so much for the drink." She stood and they exchanged air kisses.

"Terrible break for you, Georgia. Just terrible. That Mercedes Sante is a real killer." He chuckled, shaking his head.

"Yes, well, I'll get over it, I'm sure."

"This too shall pass," offered his girlfriend with a nasal twang. "I'm just amazed you're out in public today. I mean, after what she said about you, I don't think I'd show my face for like a year. You got chutzpah, honey." She folded her arms across her ample chest and tapped a stiletto-clad foot.

"Well," Georgia said, sitting down, "what can you do."

"And to come here of all places. Everybody knows this is like the in place for restaurant people. I'm sure half the place is talking about you." The girlfriend looked around as if to prove her point.

Georgia's mouth dropped open. "You're right," she said quickly. "I hadn't thought about it, but thanks for pointing it out."

"I insisted she meet me," Bernard interjected. "I'm Bernard

Lambert, the GM at Marco." He offered his hand. "I've been fielding calls from restaurateurs across the country who are dying to snap her up." He dropped his voice. "On the DL, a certain Chicago restaurant with a three-letter name is very interested."

"Is that so?" Pierre patted Georgia's back. "And to think I was about to offer you sous at my Boston place opening this fall. If you change your mind, let me know."

"You should think about it," the girlfriend said. "No one in Beantown will know who you are, or that you got a half fork from the *Daily*. You can leave your rep behind." She winked a clumpily lashed eye. "Y'know, I didn't even realize they could give a half fork. I think you might be the first to get one." She paused to adjust the strap of her leopard-print cami. "One-half, I mean."

"You've got lipstick on your teeth," Bernard said, pointing a finger to the slash of magenta across her tooth. "Wouldn't want you to embarrass yourself"—he gestured to the room—"here, of all places."

She tongued her tooth and shot Bernard a dirty look. Pierre excused them, but not before offering Georgia his card. "I'm serious about Boston. Think about it."

Georgia nodded. "I will."

"Jesus," Bernard said when the two were safely out of earshot. "Who was that woman? I didn't realize people like her actually existed."

Georgia laughed. She threw back her head, closed her eyes, and laughed like an only child who has just realized that every last present under the Christmas tree belongs to her. She laughed so hard her shoulders shook and a salty tear rolled down her cheek and onto her tongue. When she was done laughing, she dabbed at her eyes with a napkin and put on her oversize tortoiseshell sunglasses before walking out into the gray afternoon. It's what Jackie would do.

Chapter Seven

$\mathcal{S}$pring Street teemed with pretty young things, crisply dressed gray-haired men with long-legged girls in skinny jeans, skate rats from the badlands of Westchester, and well-heeled couples who shopped at Dean & Deluca, where even tilapia cost twenty bucks a pound. The only remnant of the starving artists who'd once roamed the SoHo streets were at a few sidewalk tables displaying photos and paintings. In New York, especially, today's street artist could be tomorrow's Basquiat and was at least worth a peek. Georgia stopped at a table covered with small watercolors, bending down for a closer look at a hazy landscape of rolling hills, cypress trees, and a field of poppies.

"Did you do this?" she asked the high-school-looking boy standing behind the table. He wore a hooded, gray sweatshirt and kept his hands dug into the front pouch.

"I did," he said with more confidence than she expected.

"It reminds me of Tuscany."

"It is. It's in Fiesole, outside of—"

"Florence," she finished for him. "It's really pretty."

"You've been?"

"Yeah, but not for a long time. I keep saying I'll get there but things keep getting in the way."

"I know what you mean. So do you want it?"

"How much?" Georgia asked.

"For you, twenty bucks."

"Sold."

He sandwiched the landscape between two pages of an old *New Yorker* and gave her the magazine. "The magazine's free. For you."

She tucked it into her bag and continued walking, pausing outside a trendy boutique where she knew she could score something pricey and pretty. Lo claimed that retail therapy was the panacea for just about whatever ailed you, and Georgia was tempted to test out her theory. If Lo had lived through Georgia's morning, there'd be a citywide shortage of size 4, black pants, which Lo snatched up with reckless abandon even when she was happy as a hummingbird. As Georgia contemplated blowing her entire two-week severance pay, two model-skinny, madly texting girls walked out of the boutique, hot-pink bags swinging over their shoulders. Georgia felt for the rolled-up magazine in her bag and continued walking. One treasure in a day was enough.

Standing in the hallway outside her apartment, Georgia fished for her keys. Sally's leash wasn't on the doorknob, and she worried that the dog walker had forgotten her lunchtime loop. "Coming, Sals," she said under her breath.

"Hey, Sally girl," she called, tossing the keys onto the desk and dropping her bags on the floor. She picked up the magazine and flattened it out on the desk, using the Harney tea tin that served as a pencil cup and a paperweight to hold it down. Sally barked, which she only did to announce someone's arrival, and only when someone else was already in the apartment. Georgia slipped off her trench and placed it on the chair. Her eyes widened as she noticed a jacket thrown across the chair, a navy blue, zip fleece. *Glenn's* navy blue, zip fleece. Before she could gather herself, Glenn walked out of the bedroom.

"Georgia." He walked toward her, a duffel bag printed with the Smith, Standish and Lockton logo in his hand, a short stack of books under his arm. Sally barked behind him.

"Glenn. What are you doing here? Why aren't you working?" She stared at him. He looked good. Tired, but good. The circles under his eyes were deeper than usual, making his blue eyes even bluer. He wore a thin, white T-shirt emblazoned with the name of his alma mater, his lucky shirt.

"I decided to take the day off. A mental health day, I guess. And I, well, I came back to grab some more stuff. Some clothes, some reading material." He held the books up for inspection. "And I was hoping we could talk."

"Sure." Georgia felt her stomach tighten. The "when" part of the breakup had been answered. "Guess you thought you'd need some help today?" she said, pointing to the T-shirt.

"Oh, yeah, no, actually, just a coincidence." He laughed nervously.

"So how are you?"

"Fine. Good, I guess. Staying with Ray, working a lot, you know. Same old stuff."

She nodded. "So what's going on, Glenn? What are we doing here?"

"The thing is, I'm not really sure." He looked down, puffed out his cheeks, and exhaled a slow stream of air.

"Could you be a little more specific? That's not giving me much."

"This isn't easy for me, Georgia." He placed the bag and the books on the phone table. "I know I wanted to marry you. Two weeks ago I wanted to marry you. And I don't know if it was that fight, or being away from you, or not doing any blow for the past few days, or all of the above, but I don't know if I feel the same way anymore."

"You don't know if you want to marry me?"

He nodded his head without looking at her. The air grew heavy with silence.

"Why?" she said at last.

"It doesn't feel perfect, or at least the way I want it to feel. Something's out of whack. I'm partying too much, working too much, doing too much coke so I can work and party so much, and I think it's because of us. Because of our commitment."

"Don't blame your coke problem on me, Glenn."

"That's not what I mean. I mean something is at the root of my, my"—he waved his hand in the air, searching for the right word—"my behavior of the past, I don't know, couple of weeks."

"Couple of months, Glenn, months."

"Okay, months. Something is making me act this way, and I think it might be us. Or me." He crossed the room to the sofa and sat down. "The thing is, I don't know if I'm ready to get married."

"You don't know if you're ready to get married." She sat in the tight-backed chair next to the sofa, folding her legs underneath her. "Then let's call it off."

He looked at her. "Call it off?"

"Yes, Glenn, call it off. Don't act so surprised. That's what you came over here to do, isn't it?" She felt weary, unable to get as mad as she felt was her right.

"I guess it is, Georgia."

"Did you see the *Daily* today, by any chance?"

"You know I don't read that junk. Why?"

"The review was today."

"Oh, hey, that's right. I forgot. With everything that's been going on, I forgot about the review. Congratulations, George. You deserve it."

"We got half a fork."

"What? I thought you were getting three."

"We were supposed to, but we got half. When I walked in, I was walking in from getting fired, thanks to your pal Marco." She stared at him. "And now I've been dumped too."

"Georgia, I had no idea. I swear, I would never have done this today." He reached out his hand to touch her and then withdrew it. "I'm so sorry."

"I know you wouldn't have. I just can't believe it—no fiancé, no job, all in a mere"—she checked her watch—"six hours."

"Marco's an asshole, George. He snorts so much coke he makes me look like Opie. You're better off without that job. And you're probably better off without me too." His leg jiggled up and down as he considered his words.

"I knew you were doing coke with Marco the night of the review."

He looked down at his hands, his silence confirming what he couldn't say. A few days earlier this would have infuriated her, now it just made her sad.

"I took almost all of your sleeping pills," she said.

"What?"

"The sleeping pills. The ones Dr. Androse prescribed. I took all but one."

He raised his eyebrows.

"Not at once, Glenn. Don't worry, I'm not that despondent."

"I didn't think you were."

"I hope you deal with the coke. I mean really deal with it. Therapy or something."

"I know. I will."

Sally nudged Georgia's hand with her wet nose, and Georgia stroked her dog's head. The realization that Glenn's coke problem would not be her problem made her feel suddenly lighter.

"I guess you'll want this back." She twisted the engagement ring off her finger, yanking it past her knuckle, and held it out to him. He plucked it from her outstretched hand, brushing his fingertips against her palm.

"You know, I really did think you'd like it."

"I know. But it makes it easier to give back." She smiled thinly.

"I'll miss you, George. I know it's a cliché, but I hope we can be friends."

"Maybe at some point. But not right now."

He nodded. "If you need me to take Sally or anything, let me know. Ray said I could stay with him as long as I want, rent-free too. Guess he's lonely in that big old loft with no one to share it with."

"Honestly, I have no idea what I'm going to do next. But I'll figure it out." She stood up. She was done being dumped.

Glenn stared out the window. "Check that out." He gestured to the mammoth barge stealing up the river. "Wonder where it's going."

Georgia looked at the boat, then at him. "Now you notice?"

"What are you talking about?"

"Nothing," she said. "It's nothing."

There was something vaguely glamorous about taking a sleeping pill at four in the afternoon. There was also something that reeked of an aging ingenue on a slow, downward spiral. Regardless, Georgia needed sleep. She turned off her cell and home phones and called down to Danny the doorman to let him know she was officially not home. For anyone.

The bedroom was dark as a cave, thanks to the heavy-duty blackout shades Glenn had special-ordered, and acoustical windows muffled the sounds from the street below. She swallowed the last pill with a gulp of water from the glass on her bedside table, then slipped into bed, pulled the covers up to her nose, and closed her eyes.

Comfort food. She needed comfort food. But what to eat after being jilted right after being fired right after being publicly humiliated in the city's most popular newspaper? Even for a seasoned chef, this was a stumper. Still groggy from her late-afternoon nap, even though it was after ten, Georgia poked around her fridge and freezer, scanned her kitchen cabinets, and hastily assembled the ingredients for an easy meal that would feed her head, heart, and, most important, her stomach. She decided on soup, a simple zuppa di ceci she'd learned to make in Florence; bread, because carbs were good and because the last time she baked Grammy's sourdough she froze half a loaf; cheese, because she'd yet to meet an occasion—happy or sad—that cheese didn't make better; and wine, no explanation necessary.

One bowl of zuppa, two quince-paste-and-Manchego-slathered pieces of bread, and three glasses of Sancerre later, Georgia threw on an old pair of ill-fitting jeans and a light jacket and walked out the door, Sally at her side.

"See you later, Danny," she said to the doorman on her way out. The mirror in the lobby showed her frizz factor registering an eight and a half, but she didn't care.

Danny nodded. "Your friends came by. I told them you weren't home."

"Thanks." Clem and Lo, along with her parents and anyone else who'd read the review, would have to wait.

Georgia and Sally strolled to Park Avenue, a favorite spot for late-night walks. The avenue's famously broad medians were dressed with tulips, their rounded tips barely visible from the sidewalk. It was after midnight, and traffic, foot and motor, was light, save for the occasional hedge-funder yammering into an iPhone or white-gloved doorman getting a breath of air. She walked quickly, her head tucked down, hoping speed would keep her from remembering all the things the little pink pill had helped her forget. Without looking up, she stepped off the curb at Eighty-first Street.

First, she heard the revved-up engine. Then she saw it, the emerald green convertible tearing across the avenue, straight toward her and Sally. She froze in the middle of the crosswalk, getting a way-too-close look at the miniature-yet-menacing jaguar atop the car's hood, before it slammed on its brakes and screeched to a stop inches from Sally. Georgia's heart pole-vaulted straight into her esophagus. "Oh my God," she whispered.

The driver, a mustachioed man with windswept hair, pumped his fist at Georgia. "Where's your head!" he shouted before peeling out.

"It's too cold to have the top down!" she yelled after him. It was the best she could come up with.

Safely on the sidewalk, she stooped down and threw her arms around Sally, who seemed blissfully unaware of how close she'd been to becoming urban roadkill. She nuzzled Georgia's shoulder, and Georgia did what she'd been trying so hard not to. She cried. Tears pooled in her eyes and she let them fall, watching them disappear in Sally's fur. A wet spot formed in the middle of Sally's head, then spread to her ears, and Georgia knew she was nowhere near done.

She walked down the street trying to steady her breath, her brain hopscotching through a minefield of images from the day that had passed. For once, she was grateful for her mass of hair, and she walked with her eyes firmly on the sidewalk, her curls an impenetrable curtain around her face. Eighteen long blocks and months of festering dissatisfaction later, she reached her building, her tears just beginning.

Chapter Eight

The buzzer rang. And rang again. Georgia cursed Danny for not leaving a do-not-disturb note for the day doorman. She could easily have spent the day in bed, especially after last night's sob fest. Exhausted though she was, she felt relieved to have run out of pink pills. Suffering through a few sleepless nights was definitely better than developing a pill problem. Too Anna Nicole.

Before she could drag herself to the buzzer there was a knock at the door. And another, this time followed by the doorbell in short, annoying bursts. She pulled on a pair of yoga pants balled at the foot of her bed and walked to the door, peering through the peephole.

"We're here to kidnap you," Lo yelled through the closed door. "We know you're there."

Georgia opened the door and Lo stepped around her and into the apartment. As usual, she looked like a poster child for the high-low look the fashion magazines always touted: Chanel sunglasses pushed back on disheveled black hair, gigantic It Bag in hand, black beat-style turtleneck, skinny black jeans, and Chuck Taylor high-tops.

"Jesus, George, are you still sleeping?" Clem asked.

"I *was* sleeping," Georgia mumbled. "Why? What time is it?"

"It's almost three," Lo said.

"Seriously? I don't think I've slept this late since you made me go to that after-hours club in Williamsburg." Georgia walked into the kitchen and pulled out the illy coffee beans.

"Coffee?" she asked her friends, patting her matted hair.

"On it," Clem said, handing her a to-go coffee cup. "Triple-shot macchiato, one sugar. We came here to rescue you. You blew us off all night and the damn doorman almost didn't let us up."

"He shouldn't have," Georgia muttered, taking the cup. "And shouldn't you be working? What is it with everyone not working? I'm the one who's unemployed."

"I'm at an ad sales meeting that's going to run really long, all afternoon actually. And you're coming with us," Clem said. "Now."

Georgia stared at the floor. "I really don't want to go out. I feel like shit. I don't think I can handle lunch at some trend pit."

"We're not going to lunch. We're going to the Bamboo Baths, Lo's treat. We have massages and facials in forty-five minutes, and then we'll sit in the steam and flog ourselves with olive branches. Grab your flip-flops and your bathing suit, and let's go," Clem said as Lo charged into the bedroom.

Georgia didn't move. "That's really nice of you guys, but I think I'd rather stay home and figure out—"

"Now," Clem said, pushing her toward the bedroom. "There'll be plenty of time for figuring things out later."

"I've already got them right here," Lo said, holding pink flip-flops triumphantly in one hand and a green bikini in the other. "And we need an outfit too. We'll be going for dinner after. Nothing too trendy, don't worry." She slid open the closet door and rifled through the hangers. "Oh my God. How many pairs of jeans do you have?"

"I don't know," Georgia lied. "A lot."

Clem and Lo looked at each other and then at her.

"What can I say? I like jeans."

"How about this?" Lo asked, pulling out the black dress Georgia had worn to Millbrook. She tossed it into her bag without waiting for an answer.

"Fine. I'll come with you, but please don't ask me any questions. I'm not ready to talk about anything yet."

The girls nodded solemnly. "No questions, Scout's honor," said Clem. "I'll take Sally out while you doll yourself up."

Despite herself, Georgia sniffled. She walked to the bathroom and splashed cool water on her face and around her eyes, determined not to cry. Last night's meltdown was enough. She brushed her teeth, threw on a long-sleeved T-shirt and jeans, and joined her friends, her eyes puffy but dry.

True to their word, the girls didn't ask a single question on the cab ride down to the Bamboo, as Lo called it. Not until they had checked in with the spa's stony-faced receptionist ("Why do spa and salon receptionists always have attitude?" Clem whispered loudly), had changed into their robes, and were drinking green tea in the lounge did Lo break.

"I can't stand it anymore! Are you okay? Can we please talk about this now?"

Georgia placed her mug on the wood-slab coffee table and folded her arms across her chest. "If we have to." She spotted a statue of Ganesh on a table in the far corner and sat up a little straighter. "Let's see. First, I had breakfast at Balthazar, where

I ate oysters, drank champagne, and got fired. Then I got home and Glenn was there." She paused. "And he broke up with me." She held out her ringless left hand. "See? No more dazzle."

"No way," said Clem. "That bastard. After that review he dumped you?"

"He said he didn't read it, and I believe him. But even if he did, who cares. The point is I don't know what I'm going to do." Georgia wrapped both hands around the mug and let the heat seep into her skin. "I'm all alone. I have no career to speak of and I'm all alone." It was the first time she had said this aloud.

"But you're not alone," Lo said. "You have us. And Ricky. And your family. And—"

"I know I have you guys, for which I am eternally grateful. But my parents? Please." Clem had her folks and a bundle of brothers back in Kentucky, and even poor little rich girl Lo had her sister, her dad, and whichever Spence schoolmate of hers he was dating at the moment. They'd never get what it felt like to grow up in a household where you were a third wheel to your parents.

"You know what really sucks? Aside from the fact I'm essentially unemployable unless I want to move to Boston?" Georgia took a sip from her mug and wrinkled her nose. "This tea is really bad."

"Isn't it disgusting? What is it?" Clem finally spoke up.

"It's good for you, Clem." Lo shot Clem a dirty look. "Go on, George."

"The worst part is discovering what I dreamed about having my entire life—a career, a handsome, successful fiancé, the possibility of a family soon—even that didn't make me happy. Even before I found out about the coke I wasn't happy. And if being on the verge of getting everything I wanted didn't make me happy, then what will?"

"You'll find another job, George. And another guy," Lo said.

"Or open your own place," Clem interjected.

"I know I will. Eventually. But who's to say I'll be any happier than I was with Glenn or at Marco? What if the real problem isn't with either of them, but with me?" Georgia stood up and walked to the ceramic Ganesh idol, painted blue, orange, and red—fiesta colors. She ran her hand over the glaze, crackled with age, stopping at the spots that had been rubbed bare.

"Wait a second. Just because you weren't happy with your cokehead fiancé and at your job with your asshole boss doesn't mean you'll never be happy again. Glenn has a drug problem, George, and maybe it's not the sole reason he didn't make you happy, but it certainly has something to do with it," said Clem.

"She's right, George," Lo said. "And the job wasn't all that. Sure you were head chef at a superhot restaurant, but you weren't even allowed to change the menu. What's so great about that?"

Georgia shook her head. "Nothing."

"You know, no one knows what will make them truly happy until they find it. Think of it as finding the right pair of jeans— we all know you're good at that. The J Brand's may be too low, the Earnest Sewns too saggy in the butt, the Citizens too tight in the tummy, but the Rogan's, now those make your legs look a mile long, your belly flat as a Frisbee, and your tush like a juicy Georgia peach." Clem sat back and smiled, pleased with her metaphor.

"But you have to go for it, George, or try on the jeans, in Clem-speak," Lo added.

"I hear what you guys are saying. I really do. But I have a zillion pairs of jeans in my closet. I buy jeans like other people buy toilet paper. And you know what the problem is? I still haven't found the perfect pair."

A birdlike woman dressed in a black T-shirt and shapeless

cargo pants, who looked way too frail to be a massage therapist, walked into the lounge. "Georgia?"

"Hi." Georgia wrapped her robe tightly around her waist and smiled at the woman. "See you guys," she said over her shoulder.

Her friends were right. Her two exes—fiancé and job—weren't right for her, but finding the ones that were would be like finding truffles in Central Park. She wasn't even sure it was possible to have the great job *and* the great guy. One or the other, maybe. As easy as finding the right pair of jeans, Clem had said. Only Georgia had spent half her life searching for the perfect pair and still come up short.

"Totally mortifying," Clem said. "I couldn't help it. It was that green tea. I knew it tasted funny." She patted her belly for good measure.

Fresh from their spa treatments, the girls nestled in comfy club chairs at Grasslands, a low-key spot a few blocks from the Bamboo, drinking Pimm's Cups and nibbling grilled calamari, country pâté, and sliders. Too far off the radar to register with the cognoscenti, the place was blissfully empty, which was all the better as far as Georgia was concerned. Clem relayed her story about her mousy massage therapist and a bodily function she couldn't control.

"Clem, green tea is good for your stomach," Lo said. "It doesn't give you gas. It gets rid of it."

"Oh, believe me, I know," Clem said. "I tooted at least five times, and while the massage therapist was working my hamstrings too."

"You're lying," Lo said.

"I was like a machine gun. Not silent, but very deadly indeed." Clem held up her drink as if it were a cross. "All true; swear."

Clem was queen of the Story. She would sacrifice nearly everything to tell a good one, even if what actually happened bore little, if any, resemblance to the tale she told. For as long as Georgia and Lo had known her, she'd signed off each story with her signature "all true; swear" tag, which meant absolutely nothing. Regardless, she made for a great dinner partner and went on more second dates than anyone else. It was the third date she had trouble with.

"So I hope you don't mind we told some people to come by," Lo slipped in between bites of pâté.

"Some people? And who would those people be?"

"Oh, you know, Ricky, your friends from the restaurant. They said they'd drop by after their shift."

"You're kidding, Loreen. *Marco* people?" Georgia polished off the rest of her drink and stood. "I'm bailing." But it was too late. She spotted Ricky's Angels cap bobbing in the distance, getting closer and closer. "Shit."

Lo stared at the table. "But we thought you'd want to see Ricky—"

"Ricky's fine. But everyone else after I just got fired? You guys are killing me."

"Killing you? The plan isn't to kill you, Chef, the plan is to get you stinking drunk, maybe sell off one of your kidneys, and let you wake up in a tub of cold water with a note next to you that says to call 911." Ricky swung his arm around her shoulders.

"Funny, Ricky."

"I knew three forks was too good to be true," he said. "But half a fucking fork? That's just cold. Not that Marco doesn't deserve it, but you don't."

"Thanks."

"Seriously, Chef, I'm so pissed off I don't even know what to say." He tossed his head, and his bangs rested on his temple for a split second before sliding right back into his eyes. "Yeah, I do. Want a drink?"

"Sure. Whatever you're having, as long as it's not a tequila sunrise."

"Hey. Don't knock the mighty TS."

"Friends! Frenemies! Chefs! Former chefs!" All heads turned as one of the Marco bartenders, whose claim to fame was a walk-on role on *Law & Order: Criminal Intent,* made his entrance. Relishing the attention, he scuffled with a dining chair that got in his way, knocking it to the floor before arriving at the table. "Good to see everyone." He winked at Georgia. "Especially you, Georgie Girl."

Trying to recall if she had ever spoken to him, Georgia offered a halfhearted smile.

"Georgia," Bernard said, walking toward her, "it's only been two days and we already miss you." Even in after-hours mode—collar unbuttoned, shirtsleeves rolled up, necktie nowhere to be found—he looked country-club polished.

"So says the axman himself!" Clem snorted. She was well on her way to being shit-faced, had already shared her green-tea gas story with an unsuspecting waiter, and was just waiting for her next victim.

"I was merely the messenger, Clem." Bernard turned to Georgia. "Thought you'd like to know, we were dead last night, and tonight was even worse. Twenty-six covers and"—he looked at his watch—"shut down at nine thirty. This is not Scranton, Pennsylvania. I was practically recruiting people from the street."

"Is that supposed to make me feel better?" Georgia asked. "Because it sort of does."

She excused herself from the growing-bigger-by-the-minute

party and walked to the bathroom, joining the wannabe actor-slash-bartender who stood in the vestibule between two unisex stalls.

"Hey," she said.

"Are you following me, Georgie Girl?"

"No."

"So tell me, is it true that your fiancé dumped you?"

She stared at him. "Tactful, Mr. Whatever Your Name Is."

"Fred." He squinted his eyes and gave her a once-over, appraising her like a horse he might buy. "I've been keeping tabs on you, Georgie Girl."

"Can you please stop? My name is Georgia. And since we've never spoken, I'm not sure why you're even here."

"Feisty." He cocked an eyebrow. "I like that in a girl."

A wobbly guy walked out of the bathroom, grazing his hands against the walls to steady himself.

"After you," Fred said, motioning to the bathroom.

Georgia slid in, leaning her back against the door. Please, she thought, please let my prospects be better than him. She pulled down her jeans and squatted over the toilet; she'd never dream of sitting on it, even over a layer of toilet paper the way Clem did. No matter how clean it looked, or how many doctors said you couldn't catch anything from a toilet seat, she'd spent the last ten years working in restaurants. She knew better.

By the time she returned to the dining room, a portion of the floor had been transformed into a makeshift disco with college-boy waiters doing the white-man overbite, beefy line cooks exhibiting surprisingly graceful footwork, and trained ballerinas-slash-hostesses doing their best Hustle. The sound track from *Fame* blared in the background.

"Chef, you gotta dance with me," Ricky said, grabbing her waist.

"If you were anyone else, I'd say no. And by the way, thanks for that drink."

"Oh, shit. That was for you. I was wondering why I was double-fisting."

She laughed. "Nice, Ricky."

"Did I tell you a friend of mine is opening a place in Brentwood? He's still looking for a chef." He twirled her under his arm. "You always said you liked L.A."

"Brentwood? Isn't that where O.J. killed his wife?"

"Just giving you an option."

"I know. But I really hope I don't need to traverse the country to find a job."

"Maybe that's the problem. Maybe you need to *leave* the country." Ricky dipped her to the floor as the song ended. "You know, go to Barcelona or Vienna or something."

"Wiener schnitzel's not really my thing, Rick. But it is an interesting idea. Definitely an interesting idea." She headed back to the table, but Bernard intercepted her before she could sit down.

"Tell me, Georgia, how is it that whenever we go out, we end up looking like the cast of *Dance Party USA*? Shouldn't we be scarfing down plates of cow balls and headcheese like all the other hardworking restaurant folk?"

"You may be hardworking restaurant folk, Bernard. I, as it turns out, don't work at all." She grinned. "Just giving you shit."

"Yes, and thanks for that." He took a sip of his drink. "So, I don't mean to harp on this, but have you given any more thought to what you're going to do?"

Georgia placed her hands over his shoulders and pretended to shake him. "Can you cut me some slack, please? I've been unemployed for exactly"—she checked her watch—"thirty-six hours, and I'm drunk. Please stop pestering me."

She continued to the table and picked up her bag, catching Clem's eye over the hulking frame of the garde-manger who barely spoke English and was grinding his crotch into Clem's in time to "Hot Lunch." She broke from his grasp and rushed over to Georgia.

"What are you doing?"

"I'm going home. I'm drunk and I'm tired. Tell Lo I said good night."

"You won't stay for just one more drink?"

"I've already had just one more several times over. Call me tomorrow." Georgia kissed Clem's cheek and walked out the door. "Ciao," she shouted over her shoulder.

Pulling out the huge file marked "Italy" from the desk drawer, Georgia plopped down on the floor and placed the brown accordion file on her lap. Sally lay down next to her, resting her head on Georgia's knee. Georgia rifled through the file, tossing aside newspaper articles, glossy magazine pages, maps, restaurant cards, felted drink coasters, directions to the Prada outlet, matchbooks, wine labels, numbers scrawled on napkins, a drink ticket from a club, everything but what she was looking for. Then, finally, there it was, a piece of paper torn from a notepad. IL BORGHETTO it said in navy block letters, then underneath in careful Euro script:

Claudia Cavalli
039-55-5555
claudial@borghetto.it

Claudia had been Georgia's boss the summer between her first and second years at the Culinary Institute, when she apprenticed in Florence at Claudia's restaurant, La Farfalla. She was one of Italy's finest female chefs, finest chefs period. Her influence on Georgia had been huge. Hadn't Mercedes Sante said Georgia did rustic Italian food well (or at least not terribly)? For that, she had Claudia to thank.

They had connected here and there over the years, and anytime Georgia made a significant move, she'd let her mentor know. Now she was hoping Claudia would know someone who needed a chef. Fuck Brentwood, Boston, *and* Barcelona. Georgia was going to Italy.

She sat down at the desk, powered up her Mac, and punched in Claudia's e-mail address and then the subject— *Greetings from New York!*—friendly, upbeat, *not* desperate. *"Cara Claudia,"* she began, speaking aloud as she typed, *"Ciao, bellissima . . ."*

Chapter Nine

It had been four days. Four agonizing days during which Georgia waited to hear from Claudia and, while waiting, began canceling her future. She peeked at her watch; seven minutes since her last e-mail check. Seven was okay; anything less made her feel too desperate. She put her iced coffee on the desk and took a seat in the swivel chair she'd had since college. It squeaked its disapproval as she bellied up to her computer; the chair had seen more action in the past ninety-six hours than it had in its entire life. Her in-box was filled with the usual deletable junk: a one-day sale at some shoe store, a chain letter about a sick kid in Saskatchewan, an unfunny joke Clem forwarded from her brother, nothing from Claudia.

The wedding vendors were surprisingly understanding about her predicament. Apparently, canceled weddings were a lot more common than one would think. Besides, they retained their fat deposits, unless they were supercool, which they weren't. Except for the caterer, who immediately told her how glad she was Georgia wouldn't be walking the walk with Glenn. She knew it should have made her feel better, but it only made her question herself, yet again. Why had she stayed with him for so long when even *the caterer* knew he wasn't the right guy for her?

She sold her Monique Lhuillier wedding dress on eBay to a Beverly Hills bride on a budget. Brandie the bride cared not about the potentially bad karma and even e-mailed Georgia to ask if she was interested in selling her wedding band too "since it's obvs you've got amaaazing taste." Georgia didn't bother responding. If she'd had a wedding ring, which she didn't (the engagement ring had been bad enough), she'd pawn it. The biggest financial loss was the deposit on the space, a loft in Chelsea with a wraparound terrace and views of the Hudson. Glenn could eat that one.

The phone rang, and Georgia glanced at the caller ID. It was her parents, again. She'd broken the news of her broken engagement in a quick phone call, refusing to answer any but the most basic questions, and they'd incessantly been calling ever since. The machine picked up.

The landscape she'd bought the day she was fired hung on the wall behind the desk in the same tortoise frame that had, until a week earlier, held the program from Glenn's college graduation. Mrs. Tavert was into commemorating life's big events, especially when said event concerned her son and an Ivy. Every member of his family had a copy.

Georgia checked her watch and, noting another seven minutes had passed, crossed her fingers. "Please, Claudia," she said under her breath. She stared at the picture, then closed her eyes, imagining herself walking through the field of Tuscan poppies, sort of like Judy Garland in *The Wizard of Oz,* only she didn't fall asleep. Those TV gurus claimed visualizing yourself where you wanted to be was the key to getting what you wanted, and it was certainly worth a shot. Then, for good measure, and because it seemed like the right thing to do, she whispered, "*Per favore. Per favore.*" She clicked. There it was, in her in-box. Sender: *Claudia Cavalli;* subject: *Georgia!* Double click.

Cara Georgia,

Sì! Sì! I am opening a trattoria in San Casciano and I need a cook. There are several rooms in the villa—you can have one! I need you at the end of May to prep for the open, and you will stay through the high season until the end of September.
    Okay?

Baci!!
Claudia

Okay? If she were wearing a hat, Georgia would have tossed it into the air. Instead she leaped from her chair and promptly tripped over Sally, who had planted herself at Georgia's feet. She grabbed Sally's snout and gave her a huge kiss. "I can't believe it, Sals. I'm really going to Italy!"

"You're what?"

"I'm going to Italy," Georgia repeated into her cell phone as she walked down Broadway to ABC Carpet, where she was meeting Clem and Lo. "Not on vacation, not to join an ashram or a cult, but for a job." She'd vowed not to talk to her parents until she had an airtight, infallible plan in place, one in which even Dorothy, with her razor-sharp, unpolished nails, couldn't poke a hole. Thanks to Claudia, Clem, and, much as she hated to say it, Glenn, she now had such a plan. "It's just for the summer, Mom. I'll be back in New York in the fall."

"This is just terrible," Dorothy said. Georgia could picture her pacing through her all-white kitchen, running her hand over the seamless Corian counters. "Losing the job you'll get over. But Glenn? He's so wonderful. I still can't believe it. What happened?"

"Let's see. I put up with him cheating on me once, and I even might have put up with his doing coke once in a while, but when he said he no longer wanted to marry me, I decided not to try to convince him otherwise. Okay?"

"She didn't mean that, Georgia. She means that she's sorry you're going through this," Hal said, having picked up the extension in the den.

Dorothy was silent. Sorry my foot, Georgia thought, sidestepping a large pile of poop, smack in the middle of the sidewalk. New York was more like Paris than people realized.

"Maybe the chef life isn't for you," Dorothy said. "Maybe it's time for a career change. I never thought you were cut out to wear an apron and a silly hat."

"It's called a toque, Mom. And for the record, I don't wear either."

"Your mother has a point, Georgia. It's not too late for grad school. You could get a great in-state rate and live with us back in your old bedroom."

"Did I hear you correctly, Georgia? Did you say Glenn uses cocaine?" Dorothy interjected.

"Yes, you heard me correctly. Dad, thanks for the offer, but I already went to grad school and I told you, I'm going to Tuscany to work at a restaurant Claudia's opening."

"Who?" Dorothy asked, inhaling deeply.

"You're *smoking* again, Mom?"

"Only when I'm upset."

"Or drinking," Hal reminded her.

"Anyway," Georgia continued, "Claudia Cavalli is the woman I did my externship with in Florence. One of the greatest chefs in Italy. She's been very important to me, to my career. I'm surprised you don't recognize her name."

"Oh," Dorothy said. "*That* Claudia."

By the time Georgia hung up, she had resolved not to call her parents again until she was safely in San Casciano. The farther away they were, the better.

She pulled open the glass doors and walked into ABC, which was like entering a souk, Manhattan-style. Glass chandeliers dripping with beaded fruit hung from the ceiling, jewel-colored satin pillows littered the ground, brass incense burners and candleholders shared space with fancy linen tablecloths. Georgia pried herself away from the expensive eye candy and headed to the fifth floor, where she found Clem and Lo sprawled across a leather sofa that looked like a NASA launchpad. Lo was exchanging the pair of gilded Louis XV love seats her father had gifted her (only after they failed to sell at the Christie's home sale) for something more mod and had recruited Georgia and Clem as test sitters.

"Shove over," Georgia said, flopping down next to Lo and almost bouncing off the seat. "This is your new sofa? I hope you don't plan to actually sit on it." She flipped over the price tag dangling above her shoulder. "Or eat for the rest of your life."

"I can't believe you're really leaving us," Lo said, ignoring Georgia's comment. "Are you sure you have to go all the way to Italy to be happy?"

"Ugh. You sound like my mother. No, I don't *have* to go to Italy. I *want* to go to Italy. It's mecca for chefs. The food, the wine—"

"The men," Clem pointed out.

"But what about us?" Lo said. "What are we going to do without you, George? We're a trio. We're—"

"Please don't say it," Clem said. "Please."

"The three musketeers!" Lo said, shooting Clem a dirty look. "We are."

"No," Clem said. "We're not. We are so not the three musketeers."

The elevator dinged and a pert girl with shiny hair and knee-high boots got off, dragging a guy behind her. She skipped over to a George Nelson marshmallow sofa, above which arched an Arco lamp. The guy shuffled along behind her, his hands shoved in his pockets, his eyes glued to the floor. Most guys didn't have the shopping gene. Despite all his faults, Glenn could shop.

"I'll be back in a few months. You won't even notice I'm gone," Georgia said, turning back to her friends. "But between you guys and Sally—"

"I still can't believe you're letting Glenn take Sally," Clem said.

"I didn't hear you volunteering for the job, Clem, dog-sitter extraordinaire and alleged best friend."

"If you were west of Third I might have considered it," she said. "Seriously, if you hadn't sublet your apartment to my brother, I would have. You know I would have."

Before Georgia had to even contemplate a Craigslist posting for her sublet, Clem offered up her brother as the perfect candidate. He and his buddy had just graduated college and wanted to relocate their rockabilly band to the Big Apple, where they were sure they'd strike it big. After listening to their demo, Georgia was less sure, but they had jobs that would cover the rent, and that was all she cared about.

"I appreciate it, Clem. But Sally loves Glenn. And he loves her too. It'll be fine."

Glenn was due to pick up Sally first thing in the morning, just hours before a car service would whisk Georgia to JFK, final destination Amerigo Vespucci airport, Florence, Italy. She'd already planned not to be there when he arrived and would instead be enjoying a buttered bagel, a weak cup of coffee, and the *New York Times* at Silver Star diner, a few blocks from her apartment. There was no way she could watch him walk out that door again, especially with her best friend leashed to his side. Besides, she had already said everything she wanted to say to him; her brand-new ballistic-nylon suitcase was the only baggage she planned to bring with her to San Casciano.

"Italy is so far away," Lo said. "What if you fall in love with an Italian count and never come back?"

"Or maybe she won't fall in love at all," Clem said. "Get a taste of how the single half live for a change."

"All I'm doing is following your advice. I'm trying on the jeans." Georgia rolled her eyes. "I can't believe I just said that."

"But why go all the way across the globe when everyone knows Barneys has the best selection in the world?" The earnest expression on Lo's face almost made Georgia laugh.

"Because I'm looking for something a little different." And though Georgia didn't know exactly what it was, she thought that maybe, just maybe, she could find it in Italy.

Chapter Ten

"*Scusi, signora. Vorrei un bicchiere di prosecco e tre tartufati per favore.*" Georgia sat at a small table at Procacci, a fashionable food store and café on via Tornabuoni, Florence's equivalent of Madison Avenue.

The Lilliputian store's two other tables were occupied by a chic mother-daughter duo and a handsome gray-haired couple in crisp button-downs, pressed jeans, and driving mocs, the unisex uniform of Florence's moneyed set. Before Georgia could blink, the waitress placed a flute on a scalloped-edged coaster.

"*Grazie,*" Georgia said, smiling broadly. She'd been smiling since her arrival in Italy a few days earlier, perma-grinning like a blissed-out hippie.

And why not? The sun was shining, the air was downright balmy. Even her hair looked good. She felt so cheerful it was almost spooky. If she were the paranoid sort, she'd be looking over her shoulder for Marco or Mercedes or her mother to pop out from behind some marble statue and ship her back to the half-fork, zero-ring reality she'd left behind in New York. Fortunately, she wasn't. America and all of its lousy M-people were far, far away. Maybe karma really was a boomerang, like that stupid bumper sticker said, and her happiness was simply payback for a really, really bad week.

Whatever it was, she'd take it, along with her third mouth-wateringly delectable truffle-spread mini-brioche. The waitress placed an artfully arranged cheese plate before the mother and daughter next to her, and they gleefully rubbed their hands together before digging in to a runny Robiola. Tempted though Georgia was to order a few selections, she didn't. She had too much money invested in her jean collection to start eating cheese plates for one on day two in Italy.

"Qualcos'altro?" The waitress shifted her attention to Georgia.

"Sì, un caffè macchiato," Georgia said, tearing her eyes from the oozing cheese. A police car whizzed by, its two-note siren sounding just like the ones in the classic movie *Roman Holiday*. Italians seemed to have the uncanny sense to not fix what wasn't broken.

The elementary school around the corner had let out for the afternoon, and young girls wearing pleated skirts and kneesocks charged down the street in groups of four and five. It was early enough in the tourist season that the streets still belonged to the Florentines. In a couple weeks the deluge would begin and the city's bars, cafés, churches, museums, and restaurants would be clogged with camera-wielding Americans, Germans, and Japanese. But for now the city was at rest, contented. Shopkeepers smiled, street sweepers whistled, even the carabinieri joked with their partners, tipping their caps to the old ladies walking the streets in pairs, their arms linked.

The waitress placed the espresso and a silver tray holding the check on the table. *"Faccia con comodo."*

Georgia unsnapped her wallet and counted out several crisp euro bills. She'd taken out a couple hundred from the airport

ATM, figuring it was enough to get her through the first few days but not enough to indulge her inner shopper, who was dying for a go at the Florentine shops. If Lo were here, she'd be up to her eyebrows in black pants and anything else that suited her fancy. Georgia rested a moment longer, drinking in Procacci's old-world elegance and watching the parade of smartly dressed Italians pass by. Then she placed the bills on the tray and walked outside to join them.

The Hotel Leo was located on viale Michelangelo, a winding road rich with grand villas that culminated in the Piazzale Michelangelo and one of the best views of Florence. Georgia had stumbled upon the hotel ten years earlier when she interned at Claudia's first restaurant and had returned a couple times since on vacation. Not much had changed since that first visit. Yellowing black-and-white photos of the Ponte Vecchio, the Uffizi, and other landmarks graced the walls, thready Persian carpets covered scuffed marble floors. Gabri and Cesca, the brother-and-sister owners, were from an old Florentine family and could trace their lineage back to the Medici—the poorer side, they always said, as if there were one. Family heirlooms, including swords and antique maps, decorated the hotel, giving it a slightly medieval-castle vibe. The Hotel Leo clientele fell into two distinct camps: tour groups and independent-minded (read: budget) travelers, all trying to find their very own room with a view.

On Georgia's first visit Gabri and Cesca took her under their collective wing, bringing her to swank palazzo parties, showing her where to get handmade paper and almond hand cream, teaching her Florentine slang over card games of *scopa,* the Italian version of spades. Though this was the first time she'd been back in years, the hotel and its small staff were as familiar as an old cardigan.

Mickey, who moonlighted as an opera singer when he wasn't manning the front desk, handed her the key to room 18 as she entered the lobby. Far from the street, with a queen-size bed and an actual bathtub, instead of the usual sliver of a shower, it was the best of the single rooms.

"*Buon giorno,* Mickey. Any messages?"

"No, signora, no messages." Mickey smiled regretfully, his lips drooping like those of a sad clown, and Georgia realized Gabri and Cesca must have filled him in on her story. "Have a seat, and I'll make you an aperitivo." He gestured to the lobby, where a young English couple drank red wine and flipped through a guidebook, discussing where to have dinner, between slurpy kisses.

Georgia sat down on the silk love seat directly across from them and offered a hopeful smile, eager for a little native-English-speaker chitchat. When they didn't look up, she cleared her throat. Nothing. Soon, the guy was running his hands through the girl's feathery blond hair, and Georgia was thumbing through a year-old *Vogue Italia*.

"Campari and soda, splash of orange," Mickey said, handing her a drink. "And delicious olives my mama cures herself." Though approaching forty and recently married, Mickey was an Italian mama's boy through and through. He placed a small bowl on the coffee table. "Gabri and Cesca want you to be their guest for dinner. I reserved at Benci for eight o'clock."

Osteria de' Benci was a casual and sometimes raucous trattoria run by the "Benci boys," a group of young, handsome guys who served tasty regional fare to a mixed crowd of locals and tourists. Meals at Benci were inevitably followed by house-made limoncello, a highly alcoholic concoction that had been known to sideline more than a few overzealous American tourists.

"Perfect," she said. Dinner with those two was always a boisterous affair, since they seemed to know just about everyone in Florence, locals and expats alike.

Georgia popped a half dozen of the briny olives into her mouth without even thinking, lining up the pits on her cocktail napkin. The English couple grew more amorous with each slug of their Chianti, and she wished she'd chosen to sit across the room; pretending not to notice their tongue twists was impossible from her front-row seat. The girl whispered something in her boyfriend's ear, and he wrapped her in his arms and kissed her. Their guidebook fell to the ground, where it sat, splayed, until she broke from his embrace and, giggling, picked it up. They kissed again; this time for what seemed like a whole afternoon. Georgia set down her nearly full drink and stood. If she hadn't before recognized how single, how *sola,* she really was, there was no avoiding it with these two.

"Tell Gabri I'll meet them down here at quarter of," she called over her shoulder to Mickey.

Though still deeply entangled, the couple broke their lip-lock and the girl made a halfhearted attempt to fix herself, smoothing her yellow hair and running a finger over each incongruously dark eyebrow. Georgia considered suggesting La Farfalla—she could probably even get them a last-minute reservation—but didn't. They were in love; food was unimportant. Even she could understand that. They'd likely opt for the lovers' diet of pizza margherita, a glass or two of Montepulciano, and a moonlit stroll to Vivoli, the city's best gelateria, followed by a leisurely walk back to the hotel, where they'd make mad love until morning.

Georgia and Glenn had once passed a similar evening at the Hotel Leo. That day they'd witnessed the wedding of American friends in a sprawling garden overlooking the Duomo. The air was heady with young love and promise, and never was Georgia more certain that Glenn was the man she wanted to spend her life with. Back at the hotel, they turned down Gabri's offer of a nightcap and rushed to their room, unbuttoning, unzipping, and diving into bed. The sex was fun and free, passionate and tender, the kind that happens when everything magically aligns and both partners are equally crazy about each other. After, they lay in bed drinking cans of *aranciata* from the minibar, laughing about nothing in the dazed and dopey afterglow.

How, Georgia wondered, as she trudged up the marble staircase to her room, had they lost it? How had they gone from ripping off each other's clothes to "forgetting" to have sex? The same way they'd gone from engaged to broken up: a slow but steady spiral that involved jobs and lives and indiscretions and an empty bindle of blow.

"*Scusi, signora,*" Mickey said, running up the stairs behind her two at a time. "A phone call for you. You take here?" He pointed to the guest phone at the bottom of the stairs. "Your mama and papa."

"Now? They're on the phone now?"

"*Sì*, now." He gestured to the phone again, more urgently this time.

She turned around to walk back down, then paused. "I'll call them back," she decided out loud. "Mickey, can you tell them I'm not here? That I just left?"

As promised, she'd called to let them know she'd arrived safely, and neither had been home. She didn't bother calling their cells since they never answered and she wasn't eager to talk to them anyway. While Dorothy's "Glenn-is-so-wonderful" shtick made her gag, it was her comments about Georgia's career that still bugged her.

Mickey looked shocked. He had obviously never lied to his mama and papa, and certainly not when they were calling from another *continent*. "Okay, signora," he said doubtfully.

"Thanks, Mickey. It's not as bad as it sounds, I promise." Georgia finished climbing the stairs and unlocked the door to room 18. The bed had been turned down, and she slipped off her flats, unbuttoned her jeans, and slid in between the sheets for a nap.

"You have to try this," Gabri said, pushing his zuppa inglese to Georgia and offering her a fresh spoon.

"I'm so stuffed I couldn't possibly." She leaned back and exhaled loudly while rubbing her belly. "But okay."

Georgia and Gabri were seated at a large round table at the bustling Osteria de' Benci with Cesca and Oscar, a boyhood friend of Gabri's who was something of an aristocrat, or so he had said at least a dozen times. Gabri had apologized in advance for the last-minute addition, explaining that Oscar was in from Milan and though he was a bit of a *cazzo* Gabri felt obliged to invite him. Georgia had a hard time keeping straight whether he was a Ferragamo or an Agnelli, neither, or possibly even both—and a harder time pretending she actually cared. As far as she could tell, he wasn't interested in the family business, be it shoes or cars, and instead concentrated on being a professional American-basher who dabbled in high-stakes poker.

"You Americans," Oscar said, swatting the air with the back of his hand. "You always eat too much."

Gabri dropped his spoon. "Oscar," he said sharply.

"What? At least she's not fat." Oscar cocked his head and eyeballed Georgia. "Not yet, anyway."

Earlier in the dinner, around the time she had been enjoying a magnificent ravioli ai broccoli di rapa, Georgia felt a hand on her knee. When it began crawling slowly upward, she flicked it with as much force as she could muster, hoping to hit a supersensitive nail bed. Bingo. Oscar's bloodshot eyes went wide and he bit his lip and glared at her. Since then, he'd grown more obnoxious with each sip of his wine.

"What did you say, Oscar?" Georgia asked, swatting the air as he had just done. "I've been having a hard time understanding you all night." She smiled through her lying teeth. His English was flawless.

"I went to boarding school in England." He folded his arms across his chest and looked down his aquiline nose at her. "My English is perfect."

She cupped her hand around her ear. "You went snowboarding in England? And your schussing is perfect? Interesting. I never think of England as big ski country."

Gabri and Cesca snickered. Sitting next to each other, they looked like identical twins. The only obvious difference was Cesca's black hair, which hung down her back in loose waves, and Gabri's, cropped close to his head. Otherwise, they shared the same soaring cheekbones, bee-stung lips, and creamy complexions of the genetically blessed. Though Georgia had never met their parents, she imagined they must look like Sophia Loren and Marcello Mastroianni.

Oscar threw up his hands. "This girl will never understand me. What can I expect from an American?"

"It's better not to expect much," Cesca said. "That way you won't be disappointed."

A slight man with a pom-pom of gray hair and a lopsided gait approached the table. "Georgia!" he boomed in a deep voice usually associated with larger men. "So it's true, eh? We heard rumors you'd be heading our way, and here you are. Wonderful to see you again."

Georgia stood and kissed the man's ruddy cheeks. "Vincenzo. It's great to see you. And, Katherine, you too." She turned to Vincenzo's wife, a tall Englishwoman with a pointy, foxlike face and the slightly concave posture of a woman who'd spent the last ten years married to a shorter man. Together they owned several restaurants in Florence, and both were close friends of Claudia's. Georgia had met them when she interned at La Farfalla. As Grammy would say, they were good eggs.

Georgia was about to introduce them to the rest of the party, but they already knew everyone except Oscar, who grunted hello.

"Drinking the good stuff, I see." Vincenzo picked up the empty bottle of wine in the center of the table and whistled through his teeth, a sound Georgia would forever link with Italy, and which she had never been able to master despite trying until she was—literally—blue in the face. She swore this would be the trip.

"Sì, too much," Gabri said, hanging his head forward in mock-drunkenness.

Oscar never traveled without a trove of wine because, in his words, "most of what these places serve is shit." Much as she disliked him, Georgia had no qualms drinking his sublime Serpico, and neither had anyone else. Things had grown slightly fuzzy at the first scrumptious bite of panna cotta, and she'd been gulping Pellegrino since.

"So, Georgia, we hear you'll be working with Claudia in San Casciano?" Katherine asked.

"Yup, I'm going there in a few days. I can't wait."

"I'll bet. Especially after all that business in New York," Katherine said.

Oscar's ears perked up. "What business in New York?"

"Wow, I guess good news really does travel fast," Georgia said. "Is there anyone who doesn't know what happened in New York?"

"I don't," said Oscar.

"I only heard because Gabri told me," Cesca chimed in.

"And I only because you told me," Gabri said to Georgia.

"And we only did because of Claudia," Vincenzo said.

"It's really not so terrible, Georgia. It's happened to the best of us." Katherine squeezed Georgia's shoulder.

"I know. It's just that it seems like when something bad happens, the word is all over town, make that all over the *world,* in a matter of minutes."

"What exactly happened?" Oscar asked again. Everyone ignored him.

"Meantime, I hope you can cheer up Claudia. I'm afraid she's a bit in the dumps," Katherine whispered to Georgia.

"Cheer her up? Why? What's going on?" Georgia's belly dropped. "Are the restaurants okay?"

"It's not the restaurants," Katherine said. "It's her boyfriend."

"Her *boyfriend*?" Women like Claudia didn't have boyfriend problems. "What's going on with Claudia's boyfriend?"

Katherine opened her mouth to speak and was promptly cut off by a belligerent Oscar. Unlike Georgia, he had not switched to water and was now working on his second grappa.

"Before you continue your conversation, I demand to know what happened to Georgia in New York. It's bad manners not to tell the only person at the table who doesn't know."

Georgia turned to him. "I was fired, okay, Oscar? From a real, live job. Now will you stop asking?"

He nodded smugly. "I've never been fired."

"You've never been hired," Gabri pointed out.

"As I was saying," Katherine continued, "they're going through some growing pains. I'm sure you'll hear about it, but please don't mention it unless she does. Wouldn't want her to think I was gossiping, just thought you should know."

Georgia thanked Katherine for clueing her in and promised

to help Claudia however she could, though she couldn't imagine how that might be. Not that she lacked experience with the opposite sex. Way back when she was stuffing her hair in scrunchies and smearing Clearasil across her T-zone, she had her first boyfriend, a bookish eighth-grader named Eddie who had a pink retainer and a silver bike. Since then, a parade of serious boyfriends had marched through her life—right up until Glenn, who was to have been the most serious at all. Clearly, experience wasn't everything.

Gabri requested *il conto,* which gave them at least fifteen minutes before the check was on the table. Knowing she couldn't stomach one more minute of Oscar's arrogance, Georgia walked her friends back to their table, promised to visit them at their farmhouse in Pistoia soon, and continued outside for some air.

The half dozen or so outdoor tables were filled with laughing locals, tipsy tourists, and an international brood of smokers. The air had cooled, yet still held the unmistakable promise of summer. A group of college-aged Americans ran down the street laughing and shouting, no doubt on their way to the Irish pub around the corner. Georgia walked down a few doors to a closed *farmacia.* Perusing fancy pharmacies was one of her favorite things to do in Italy, filled as they were with herbal remedies for everything from acne to weight loss, and white-coated salesclerks to assist customers in choosing precisely the right one. Transfixed by a life-size cutout of a bikini-clad woman with a tape measure wrapped around her waist and a bouquet of daisies seemingly sprouting from her head, she was startled by a voice behind her.

"Scusi, signora, ha del fuoco?" A late-thirtyish man with broad cheekbones and heavily lidded eyes stood before her, a cigarette dangling from his mouth. He wore a knee-length trench coat and looked bored. Handsome and bored.

"*Momento, signore,*" Georgia said. Though she hadn't lit a cigarette in years, she still collected matchbooks from restaurants and bars. She passed him a mini-matchbox and watched him slide it open and strike a match on its side.

He inhaled deeply and blew the smoke to the sky. Holding the matches up to the light from the streetlamp, he made out the name of the restaurant.

"*È americana?*" he asked, handing them back.

"*Sì. Sono di New York.*"

"I went to New York City once," he said in accented English. "The energy. The people, rushing here and there. Do they never stop?"

She laughed. "Not really."

"Not really here either anymore." Two Vespas charged down the street as if to prove his point. "We used to care more about family. Friends. Life. Now we care about success. Money."

"I think it's like that everywhere."

He shrugged his shoulders. "Maybe so." He gestured with his cigarette to the blurry glow of outdoor tables. "Did you have dinner over at Benci?"

"Yes, I did. Did you?"

"No, across the street. Da Gino. Much quieter, but they make delicious pasta bolognese. My favorite." He patted his belly with his nonsmoking hand and smiled, the memory of the meal momentarily erasing his distaste with his country's capitalistic ways. "Forgive me. I am so rude. Do you want one?" He held out a pack of Marlboro Reds.

She did. Watching his fingers graze his lips as he inhaled, the hand then coming to rest nonchalantly on his thigh, the thin trail of smoke escaping his lips as he spoke, the slight clench in his voice—yes, she wanted one. Her first cigarette in five years, and she wanted to smoke it with him.

"Sure," she said, plucking one from the pack. She held the skinny cigarette dumbly in her hand until she remembered he had returned her matches and unzipped her bag to find them.

He flicked a lighter, pulled from his pocket, and Georgia looked up into his face, lit by the flame. He had a thin, white vertical scar, the size of a sewing needle, under his left eye.

"I thought you needed a light," she said, removing the unlit cigarette from her mouth.

"I did."

"But why'd you ask me if you had one yourself?" He smelled like a mixture of oranges and olives. Oranges, olives, and smoke. If someone could bottle that scent, she'd buy it by the barrel.

"I don't know." He shrugged, his lips turning down slightly at the corners as he did. "I thought you looked nice, maybe someone to talk to. For a little conversation, I guess. I meant nothing by it."

This guy, who was handsome and real and looked sort of like Javier Bardem and loved pasta bolognese, had seen her and wanted to talk to her and she wanted to talk to him too.

She held out the cigarette, slightly sticky with lip gloss. "Do you want this back? I don't actually smoke anymore."

He shook his head and she tossed it into the garbage can a few feet away.

"You have a good arm," he said. "Isn't that what they say in America? A good arm?"

"They do." She tried to think of something clever to add, but all she could think was how much she liked the way he talked and smoked and smelled. And how he was one of the few guys she knew who could wear a trench without looking like a Wall Street warrior about to hop the 5:51 local to Larchmont.

"So what do you have planned for your vacation in Firenze?"

"Well, I only have a few more days here." She swallowed

hard, summoning her courage. "Maybe you could show me around? We could have lunch, maybe?"

The cherry of his cigarette froze on the way to his mouth, hanging there like a hazard signal, until he brought his hand back to his thigh. "I would love to, really, but I cannot. I am leaving the city in a few days myself. And I have a girl, I'm in a relationship. I'm sorry."

"Oh." Georgia's face burned. "That's fine, I mean, that's great. Don't be sorry. Like I said, I'm leaving soon anyway. I'm going to San Casciano. It's a small town, supposed to be really charming. I'm working there."

His eyes widened. "In San Casciano?"

"Have you heard of it?"

"*Sì, sì, sì, certo.* San Casciano is beautiful. You'll enjoy it, I'm sure." He held up the cigarette as if toasting with a glass of champagne and smiled. "Thank you for the fire. It was nice to meet you. Good night." He turned and walked down the street, in the opposite direction of Osteria de' Benci.

Georgia watched him for a few seconds, wondering where he'd go. But it was dark and the street was poorly lit. When her eyes could no longer make out his figure, she returned to the restaurant, the scent of oranges, olives, and smoke lingering in her mind.

Chapter Eleven

The Tuscan countryside whizzed by in a kaleidoscopic whirl of shapes and colors. Green grass and trees melded with blue sky, purple and yellow wildflowers, peachy-orange villas, brown-and-gray farmhouses, and the occasional red-and-white Autogrill, Italy's (delicious) answer to fast food. Georgia surveyed the scene from the backseat of a cramped Lancia driven by Richard, one-half of the all-over-each-other British couple from the Hotel Leo. That morning in the breakfast room, Cesca had steered Georgia to their table and introduced her as the famous American chef who was headed in the same direction they were and, as it happened, needed a ride. They didn't seem to buy the famous chef thing, nor had they looked thrilled about having a passenger, but Cesca wasn't the kind of person one said no to. So Georgia, her giant suitcase, L.L. Bean tote, and oversize handbag stuffed into the tiny red car's backseat, along with a handful of the couple's guidebooks and three neat black umbrellas. Apparently Richard and Hillary expected rain.

To maximize her sliver of space, Georgia aligned her left leg on top of her right and wedged herself into the crook of the car door, triple-checking to make sure it was locked. It wasn't the most comfortable way to travel, and certainly not the most stylish, but who was she to turn down a free ride. With her right butt cheek growing numb and visions of varicose veins dancing in her head, she started to wish she had.

Her stomach leaped with each turn of the steering wheel, and it wasn't only due to Richard's screechy driving. She'd phoned Claudia a few days earlier, and though their conversation had seemed perfectly friendly at the time, in hindsight it *had* been a little brief. What if Claudia—no kids, not married, fighting with her boyfriend—was not the same upbeat, ebullient restaurateur Georgia remembered? What if age and disappointment had changed her? And what if—and this was the question that kept Georgia up at night like a nasty case of food poisoning—what if Georgia was changing too? Unwittingly bypassing any chance at the guy and the baby and taking the shortcut straight to spinsterhood? At thirty-three she was no *giovincella*. Ten years ago, she'd assumed that by thirty she'd be married, the mother of two, maybe three, kids, the owner of two, maybe three, restaurants. Lofty goals, sure, but change two or three to one and not entirely unreasonable. Instead, she was sardined into the backseat of a second-rate Italian sports car, no closer to having the kids, the husband, or the restaurants than she was a decade ago, her fragile leg veins engorging with blood by the second.

"This must be it." Richard stepped on the brake and the Lancia slammed to a stop next to a silvery eucalyptus tree.

Hillary peered at the wrought-iron gate and stuck out her finger to buzz the intercom. COLLINA VERDE a white-and-green ceramic sign spelled out in thick script letters. Green Hill.

"Hey, hold the phone a sec," Georgia yelled from the backseat. "I'm not ready to go in yet."

"You can't bear to leave us?" Richard asked. "Or is it my driving you'll miss?" He climbed out of the car and began pulling Georgia's bags from the back.

"Your driving, for sure," she said. Despite having their hands all over each other the whole drive (had Georgia not been crammed in the backseat, there was no telling what might have gone down), the Brits were all right. She couldn't hate them just because they were in love.

The late-afternoon sky was hazy with heat, heavy with moisture, and she gingerly patted her hair. Without a mirror, she'd guess the frizz factor hovered around seven. She twisted the mass into a bun and secured it with a band. Claudia hadn't hired her for her hair anyway.

"Wish me luck, guys." Forgoing the intercom, she pushed on the gate and it swung open.

"You'll be brilliant, Georgia," Richard said, closing his door and throwing the car into reverse. "Positively brilliant."

"Toodle-loo, darling!" Hillary shouted.

"She means *buh-bye*," Richard yelled, sticking his head out the window. "Isn't that what you Yanks say?"

Georgia waved good-bye and watched the car grow smaller and smaller, until it looked like a dusty apple imprinted on the sky. She turned around slowly, taking in the surrounding green hills, the verdant vineyards, the cypress trees stretching to the sky—her home for the next four months. With her tote bag slung over one shoulder, her handbag over the other, her suitcase wheels chewing up chipped stone behind her, she made her way up the long brown path before her.

No one answered the door. After her third knock, an insistent *rat-a-tat-tat*, she followed the path to the back of the villa. Pressing her nose against one of the fan windows flanking the back door, she cupped her hands around her eyes to better see into the house. A pair of tall green Wellies stood next to a shorter pair of duck boots, next to a pair of old tennis shoes. A brown umbrella leaned against an empty umbrella stand, and a shiny rubber hat hung from its curved handle. The house was definitely inhabited, which was a relief; she was beginning to wonder if Claudia had forgotten her arrival and slipped out to Sicily or Sardinia or some other Mediterranean paradise. She raised her hand to knock on the door, but it jerked open before her knuckles could connect. A doughy-faced man with thinning brown hair and flinty eyes of an indeterminate color stood before her. He wore a white chef coat and khaki shorts. He did not smile.

"*Buon giorno,* I mean *buona sera. Sono Georgia,*" she said, flustered by his pursed lips and steely expression.

"*Buona sera.* You are the American," he answered after a long pause. "I speak English."

"Oh, great." Georgia chuckled. "So do I."

He still didn't smile. "Come in. We've been expecting you."

"Really? I was knocking on the door for a while. I guess you didn't hear me." She stepped into the house and was greeted with the scent of fresh, pungent olive oil, as rich as liquid gold.

"I heard you. I was busy. And we never use the front door."

"Oh." Georgia lined up her suitcase next to the tennis shoes and retracted the handle. She placed the tote bag on the floor, her handbag on top of it. "Is Claudia around?"

"She's over there. In the kitchen." He gestured with his thumb but didn't move his stocky frame from the door separating the mudroom from the rest of the house.

Georgia tried to look over his shoulder, but he was planted squarely in the door frame and she could make out only a large, pleated lampshade behind him.

"Are you planning on letting me in?"

"Of course. Excuse me." He turned on his heels and Georgia

followed him into a cozy sitting room with a sofa, two overstuffed armchairs, and a large fireplace. Bouquets of wildflowers, one propped in a ceramic pitcher, one in an old can of San Marzano tomatoes, and another in a mason jar, decorated the room.

"So, shall I go find her or are you going to tell her I'm here?" The guy was beginning to bug her.

"You go. She's expecting you."

"Okay. I guess I'll just leave my stuff there."

He grunted in response.

"I didn't catch your name," Georgia said in a last-ditch attempt to be friendly. If this guy ended up working for her, she couldn't afford to be on bad terms with him. Hostility was one ingredient to keep out of the kitchen at all costs.

"Bruno," he said, folding his arms across his chest.

After several wrong turns, Georgia finally discovered the kitchen. From the outside, the villa didn't look especially large. A passerby would never guess that its ocher-colored walls housed eight bedrooms, one less bathroom, and an assortment of public rooms that stretched across the endless first floor. By the time Georgia found the kitchen, she had also uncovered a marble-floored entry hall, a dining room with seating for twenty, and a book-lined library. Either Claudia had been born to nobility or the restaurants were doing even better than Georgia thought.

"Hello?" Georgia called, stepping into a room as big as her apartment. The kitchen was almost entirely stainless steel: an eight-burner range, twin refrigerators, a rotisserie oven, two dishwashers, two double wall ovens, miles of countertop—everything gleamed in cool silver-gray with the exception of the Carrara-topped pastry area, a rustic wooden table and matching chairs, and the herringboned brick floors. Georgia had never seen anything like it.

A slender figure stood over the range, her feet forming a *V*, a ballerina's first position. From the back, she could have been a high school cheerleader: her brown hair was pulled into a high ponytail, her hips nonexistent under black pedal pushers.

"Claudia?" Georgia tried again.

Claudia turned from the stove and wiped her hands on a dish towel tucked into her waistband, a smile spreading across her face. "Georgia! Ciao, bellissima!" Her hazel eyes sparkled and her bangs were cut into a pixie fringe. Were it not for the laugh lines etched like quotation marks on either side of her mouth, she could have passed for a decade younger than her forty-two years. She grabbed Georgia by the shoulders and kissed her cheeks. "You're here! *Brava!*"

With her tremendous talent and gamine looks, Claudia had been at the forefront of the revival of the Florentine dining scene, a spot she hadn't yet relinquished. Judging from the smells emanating from the oven, she wouldn't be doing so anytime soon.

"I'm so glad to see you," Georgia said. "I'm so happy to be here." Any fears she'd had about Claudia morphing into a bitter old maid disappeared. If she was going through a rough time, Georgia certainly couldn't tell by looking at her. She was as gorgeous and effervescent as ever.

Claudia took a step back and gave her apprentice the once-over. "So, you got a bad review. It's not the end of the world. You Americans care too much about reviews. I read it myself online. It was almost *too* bad." She smiled again. "But you're here now, so no matter."

"Yes. Here I am."

"And the boy? The fiancé?" Claudia picked up Georgia's bare left hand. "No ring?"

"No ring, no fiancé." Despite the touchy subject, Georgia beamed. Between the spellbinding scenery, the smells wafting through the kitchen, and Claudia's infectious enthusiasm, Georgia's perma-grin was starting to return. "What are you cooking? It smells amazing."

"Cinghiale with red wine and olives." Claudia studied Georgia's face. "No ring, no fiancé, and the biggest smile I've seen all day." She nodded her approval. "We'll eat later. Now, let me show you the room."

Georgia followed Claudia across the kitchen and up the back staircase to a pretty room with whitewashed beams, a dresser, a bed, and a writing table. The small bathroom had a shower stall and a window that overlooked the vineyard next door.

"It's perfect," Georgia said.

She heard sniffing outside the door, and a wiry, gray-haired dog butted its head into the room. A dog. Claudia had a dog!

"My son, Chien," Claudia said, scratching him between his ears. "He's very friendly. You're not afraid of dogs, are you?"

"Oh, no. I love dogs." Georgia stooped down to Chien's level. She'd been missing Sally since the minute she climbed aboard the plane. "Come here, Chien. I guess he doesn't speak English?"

"Not yet. But he's got the rest of the spring and the whole summer to learn." Claudia walked out the door, Chien at her heels. "I'll leave you to settle in. Come down when you're ready and we'll eat."

Georgia sprawled across the bed, placing her head on the lone lumpy pillow. The whole summer in San Casciano—she liked the way that sounded. And though she had no idea what would happen when she returned to New York, for once not having a plan didn't bother her. All that mattered was that she was in glorious, glorious San Casciano, and her new home came with a dog.

A bowl of frothy cappuccino steamed on the table. For the third time Georgia tried to slug a sip to placate her caffeine-starved brain; for the third time she couldn't lift the bowl without scorching her finger pads. Despite polishing off two helpings of cinghiale, a mound of polenta, and plenty of spinaci saltati at last night's dinner, she was starving. After her feast, she'd tossed and turned in her lumpy bed, envisioning Sally snuggled up next to Glenn in his cousin's bachelor pad, the two of them happily snoring. The made-up scene made her bluesy, and she tossed and turned some more before vowing not to think about Glenn in exchange for a few hours of sleep. Somehow, the trade-off had worked and she drifted into fitful slumber.

She eyed the five other people in the kitchen with her, feeling like a contestant on a culinary reality show. Of the five, the only face she recognized was Bruno's. He sat at the head of the table, his arms crossed, a snub-nosed girl with a Clara Bow mouth on his right. Seated on his left, Georgia had the misfortune of being eye level with an oozing pimple buried in his scraggly sideburn. At the stove, a girl in a plain white oxford and Bermuda shorts cooked the eggs Claudia had promised the group before sweeping out of the kitchen, her black tunic rippling behind her. The girl hummed something that sounded like the Cars' "Just What I Needed," occasionally blotting her shiny forehead with a dish towel.

The decaffeinated group sat in silence. Several champagne flutes sparkled in the center of the table, next to a basket filled with silverware and linen napkins. Georgia took one of each, arranging them around her coffee bowl. This kickoff breakfast, as Claudia called it, was a mandatory meeting for the core kitchen staff, who were not only colleagues but housemates. Through the high season most of them would bunk at the villa, which was large enough to accommodate them all in varying levels of comfort. Earlier that morning, Claudia had knocked on their doors, telling them to report downstairs by seven. It felt a little

like restaurant boot camp but was no worse than being repri-
manded about working out at a Marco staff meeting.

After several minutes, the girl turned off the burners and
set down a plate of fluffy eggs, finishing them off with a healthy
shaving of black truffles. Next, she placed a platter of buttered
toast and another of meats and cheeses on the table, her brown
braid swinging across her back. She smiled at Georgia, revealing two dime-size dimples. Taking this as an invitation to dig in,
Georgia smiled back, then scooped up some eggs and speared
a few slices of bresaola and prosciutto. A couple bites and one
scalding sip of cappuccino later, she felt enough herself to chat
up the guy next to her.

"Hi, I'm Georgia. What's your name?"

"Tonio. You're the American." His rusty hair stood in spikes
and splotchy orange freckles covered his arms.

"Is it that obvious?" Georgia said, then drank her coffee, which
had finally cooled. "Then I guess that makes you the Italian?"

"We are all Italian," he said, stone-faced. "Except you."

"Right." Georgia looked at his eyes. His translucent lashes
could use a tint job.

The girl with the braid took the empty seat across from
Georgia. "Hi, my name is Vanessa. You must be Georgia?"

"Yes. The lone non-Italian, as Tonio just pointed out."

"Don't mind him. He's just grumpy." She bent across the
table and lowered her voice. "Almost as bad as the boss."

"Claudia? She doesn't seem—"

"*Buon giorno,* everybody!" Claudia strode into the room, an
ear-to-ear grin lighting her face. "Welcome to Collina Verde and,
more importantly, to the future home of Trattoria Dia."

There was a smattering of applause, and even Bruno smiled.

"I have handpicked this team of chefs from my own restaurants in Florence, as well as the top tables in Rome, Bologna,

Milan, and"—Claudia turned to Georgia—"even New York City. I expect us all to work together, as a team, to create what will soon be known as the best trattoria in all of Tuscany." She popped open a bottle of Pol Roger and began filling everyone's glass. When she reached Tonio, she popped a second bottle. "I know it's early for champagne, but this morning we are celebrating."

As the group sipped from their flutes, Georgia wondered how anyone could say Claudia was grumpy. Like any successful restaurateur, she obviously demanded hard work and dedication, but grumpy? No way. With her easy smile and twinkling eyes, she was like a younger, hipper version of Mrs. Claus.

"And now," Claudia said, "I'd like to introduce the talented team that will build Trattoria Dia."

Georgia bowed her head slightly, trying to calm the flutters in her belly. There was no telling how the staff felt about having an American boss, but she'd soon find out.

"Our head chef," Claudia said, "needs no introduction. My former sous-chef at La Farfalla, Bruno Valchese has proven himself to be hardworking, talented . . ."

Blood pounded through Georgia's veins. Her face, then her neck and chest, grew hot and prickly, as if she'd buffed her skin with a Brillo pad soaked in rubbing alcohol. *Bruno* was head chef? *Bruno?* Hadn't Claudia said there was a spot for Georgia on the team? She closed her eyes and tried to string together the e-mail Claudia had sent. She must have read it a dozen times, and there'd never been a doubt in her mind that Claudia wanted her as head chef. Of course she wanted Georgia to be head chef—what else could she possibly be?

". . . all the way from New York City, our sous-chef, Georgia Gray, a former apprentice of mine and an incredibly skilled chef."

There was her answer. Sous-chef. Georgia somehow managed not to cry and not to throw up. She raised her glass and offered a slight nod, her lips squeezed together to suppress the scream shooting up her larynx. Replacing her glass on the table, she clenched her hands together until her fingertips turned red with blood, the words *sous, chef,* and *Georgia* bouncing across her brain. She was Bruno's fucking sous-chef.

Claudia worked her way around the table, introducing Tonio and Vanessa, grill and sauté respectively; Effie, a beanpole of a guy with bad skin and a teen 'stache, who was garde-manger; and finally, Elena, the diminutive girl sitting next to Bruno, who was the general manager. The rest of the staff would start closer to open. That the Mary Lou Retton–size GM could control a dining room and a kitchen seemed questionable, though sleeping with the head chef probably helped. Their smug smiles, mirrored body language, and not-so-veiled glances were proof enough that Elena and Bruno were involved in way more than a working relationship. The whole situation made Georgia jones for Bernard's red clipboard and verging-on-insufferable competence. Until she thought about the sleazy boss who came with him.

The champagne idled on the sideboard behind Vanessa, and Georgia was tempted to commandeer it for her personal consumption. But sauced was not the way to begin her career as an Italian sous-chef. For a split second she considered going back to New York, but quickly vetoed the idea. Jobless, penniless, and loveless in sweaty, sticky New York was no way to rebound. She joined in for the team toast to "the success of Trattoria Dia!" mentally counting the days until her time in San Casciano was done, careful not to empty her glass with one very large sip.

$\mathcal{B}$runo was killing her. It was day five of Georgia's life as a sous-chef, and her boss was driving her crazy. Everything about him irritated her: the beady eyes that tracked her every move, the hangnailed thumb he stuck into her sauces, the gurgly throat-clearing that followed his commands ("More fire, less salt!" was his favorite anti-Georgia admonition). Clearly, he felt the same way about her. Wrinkling his nose as if he'd just lost a sneeze, he tasted whatever she made, grunting if he didn't hate it, and fake-retching if he did. Then he'd remind her, as if he hadn't a thousand other times, that the only people who could cook Italian food were, naturally, Italians. Except him. His food was reliable, consistent, sometimes very good. But it lacked the flashes of brilliance she expected from the head chef at a Claudia Cavalli restaurant. That he was her boss and not the other way around was eating her up.

So with heavy head and heavier feet she walked into the kitchen that morning, once again the last to arrive. Bruno sat at the table with a laptop propped open in front of him, reading from the screen. The staff huddled around him, their heads cocked to better hear what he said. No one noticed when Georgia slipped in.

"*La carne di cervo, la cui consistenza richiama la pelle delle scarpe,*" Bruno read, "*le quali hanno ballato il tip-tap nella pioggia un po' troppo a lungo.*" He threw back his head and snorted. The group tittered, and someone—it sounded like Elena—said something that elicited more tittering.

Georgia crept closer, wishing her Italian were better.

"*La faraona, una proposta incerta perfino nelle mani più abili . . .*"

It was definitely about food.

"*. . . rassomiglia una scivolosa massa di plastilina . . .*"

It was definitely about *her* food. She knew these words so well she'd understand them in Mandarin. He was reading the Mercedes review, aloud, to a table of her brand-new coworkers. So much for her fresh start; thanks to Bruno she was drowning in a sea of salty venison and greasy guinea hen all over again. Even for him, this was low.

"Good morning, everyone," she said, forcing herself to smile. "It looks like you're all having fun."

Vanessa turned, her face ashen. "Georgia. We didn't hear you come in."

"No, I didn't think you did."

Bruno smirked. "We're reading a review." He didn't bother to close the screen.

"Really?" Georgia said. "And what review would that be?"

"Yours," he said, snickering. "The worst review I've ever read."

"At least she got reviewed," Effie, the young guy, said.

"It wasn't all bad," Vanessa added. "She said the pasta was good. And the risotto."

"Bah," Bruno scoffed. "Since when have you known an American who can make pasta?"

"Are you serious, Chef?" asked Effie. "What about your idol, Molto Mario?"

"He has Italian blood!" Bruno yelled, snapping shut the laptop. "Mario has Italian blood. That makes him Italian!" In homage to Mario Batali, Bruno wore orange rubber clogs and shorts 24-7. It was only a matter of time before he grew out his scraggly brown hair and started dyeing it orange. The staff called him Much Bruno behind his back.

Vanessa walked next to Georgia. "I'm sorry, Georgia. Bruno told us he had something interesting to share with us. If I'd known what it was, I would have ignored him."

"It's not like it's classified information," Georgia said. "But I was hoping to leave all that behind me."

"So leave it." Vanessa linked her arm through Georgia's. "Come, let's get a *caffè*."

"Good idea." Georgia passed by Bruno, refusing to meet his eye. At least until Claudia returned, she'd keep her mouth shut, her head down, and cook. If she clashed with Much Bruno one more time, she might snap.

Hours later, the kitchen was a beehive of activity, with Bruno barking orders, Effie zigzagging between the fridge and his station, Tonio cursing anyone who crossed his path, and Vanessa guarding her burners like a Secret Service agent on presidential patrol. Though huge by residential standards, the kitchen was not designed for professional use, and the staff couldn't wait to move into the restaurant, where they wouldn't risk committing hara-kiri each time they turned around with a Santoku knife in hand. Trattoria Dia was already way behind schedule; the latest issue was the final coat of the three-coat plaster walls, which hadn't dried properly. Even the unflappable Claudia was beginning to crack.

Georgia was making her *ragù,* her delicious *ragù,* if she did say so herself (and why not, since everyone else did), when she heard the squeak of Bruno's clogs. He planted himself a breath's width behind her.

"What are you making?"

"Ragù," she answered, the hairs on her neck standing up.

"Where's the jar?" he chortled, his belly jiggling like a fruited Jell-O mold. "Or did you already throw away the evidence? Or maybe I should look for a can. I hear you Americans use canned *ragù.*" He made a show of searching for the can, poking around pots and pans, flipping through trays and pulling out items in the pantry, all the while providing a running commentary of his actions for the rest of the staff. Vanessa rolled her eyes.

If it had been the first or second time he'd ragged on Georgia's cooking because she was American, she might have let it pass. But it was the fourth or fifth time, and she was fed up. While Bruno was busy tearing up the pantry, she dropped several ladles of sauce into a smaller pot, then quickly dumped in a scoop of ground cayenne, stirring until it wasn't visible. When she bent over to smell the new sauce, the lining of her nostrils burned.

"If you're so sure an American can't make a *ragù,* why don't you have a taste," Georgia said loudly. "I even have a spoon for you."

Bruno charged over, dismissing her spoon with a wave of his hand. "Which one?"

"Start with that one." She pointed to the bigger pot.

He skimmed his spoon across the surface. "Urgh," he said after swallowing. Then he dipped his spoon into the cayenne concoction, tipped back his head, and let it slide down his throat. "Fuck!" he screamed. Tears streamed down his face as he ran to the sink, spewing tomato chunks onto the floor. "Too much fucking heat!"

"There is? Sorry. You're always telling me 'more fire' so I thought it'd be right up your alley." Georgia filled a glass with water and handed it to him. "Have a drink."

Bruno glared at her through watery eyes, but did as he was told. Vanessa and Effie laughed out loud, and even Tonio snickered. Georgia turned her back on her boss, a small smile escaping her lips. It was a petty, stupid, childish prank. But, man, it felt good.

The kitchen was blissfully empty, the only sound the gurgling of the Faema espresso machine Georgia cranked up. Yawning so hard her jaw popped, she massaged it back into place before downing her drink. Thanks to the band of randy roosters camped outside her bedroom window, she'd awoken at daybreak. After a few tosses and turns she rolled out of bed and threw on her running shoes. Her belly was looking more and more marsupial since her arrival in Italy, and she couldn't afford to keep inhaling pasta and cheese without working out. So far, the most exercise she'd got was wrestling the top off a drum-size jar of preserved Meyer lemons. She slugged down her second espresso, cringing when she heard Bruno's signature squeak behind her.

"Buon giorno, Georgia," he said flatly, his voice lacking the melodious quality that made Italian such a feast for the ears. "Where are you going so early?" He packed the Faema with fresh grounds and fixed himself a *caffè.* Since the cayenne caper they'd stayed as far away from each other as possible, even in the kitchen, where it was as if an invisible wall kept them from locking eyes or—God forbid—bumping each other. This was their first real face-off.

"A run. Gotta get in shape." Georgia instinctively patted her belly. She eyeballed her boss's paunch, which hung over the top of his pleated khaki shorts, then looked away. Pleats weren't a good look for anyone, especially cooks with extra padding.

"We have a big day today. Don't be late."

"Of course, Bruno. It's only six thirty. I'll be back, dressed, and at your disposal in two hours." She flashed a fake smile.

"Fine." He slurped his coffee and a trickle ran down his chin. "Have you thought about the sig dish at all?"

"The what? Oh, yeah, the signature dish." She nodded her head as if it had totally slipped her mind and was just coming back to her. "Not so much, actually."

His face brightened. "Then you may as well forget it. I have three incredible dishes. All I have to do is figure out which one is best."

She gave him a thumbs-up, not trusting what might come out of her mouth if she opened it, and jogged out the back door, carefully dodging the cocks in the yard. According to Claudia, an amazing signature dish was a prerequisite for any new restaurant hoping to make a splash in trattoria-soaked Tuscany. Tourists, especially, would travel huge distances for the ultimate carciofi judaica, risotto ai funghi, or even a stracotto di manzo, plus it gave journalists something to write about. Despite what she'd told Bruno, Georgia had given plenty of thought to Dia's signature dish. Pretty much every minute of every hour that she wasn't thinking about not being head chef and not being engaged, she thought about the signature dish. It'd be a coup for any of the Dia staffers to create it, but Georgia, the half-star American, needed it most. And snatching the honor away from Bruno would almost make up for being his sous-chef.

A dust cloud formed in her wake as she ran through the gate, her legs churning underneath her. In the past, she'd managed to rise above tyrannical bosses, creepy investors, and customers who didn't know the difference between arugula and rugelach yet still complained that the food wasn't up to snuff. But a boss like Bruno—one who seemed hell-bent on destroying her credibility as a cook—was a new beast entirely.

Sprinting up the hill, she passed the hand-painted sign for the Etruscan tomb. The road dipped, then elbowed sharply, and she felt herself lose traction on the turn. She tried to slow down, but her feet skidded out from under her legs. Before she could catch herself, her right shoulder crashed into the dirt, followed by her head, hip, and knee. Her limbs bounced up slightly, then thudded back to the ground, her head turned awkwardly to the side. When she opened her eyes, she was staring at the bottom third of an olive grove—roots and trunks as far as she could see. In the sky above, a group of large birds circled, hoping they'd just discovered breakfast. She lay still for a moment, then stood up to assess the damage.

Her knee was mottled with dirt and shredded skin; her shoulder throbbed with each beat of her heart. After the one-two Marco/Glenn punch, plus the demotion to sous, what else was left to do but fall flat on her face? She brushed herself off and began the painful walk back to the villa, convinced that somehow Bruno was to blame.

Despite her mangled limbs, Georgia still managed to report for duty on time. No way would she let Bruno call her on tardiness. After she'd organized her *mise en place,* she started preparing branzino saltimbocca, a twist on the original veal preparation. Each slice of her knife sent shivers through her shoulder, and she waited for the four Motrins she'd swallowed to kick in.

"Are you okay?" Vanessa asked. "You look a little pale. And your cheek is swollen."

"I'm fine. I fell running, but I'm fine." Georgia threw a handful of kosher salt on the branzino.

"Easy on the salt, Georgia." Bruno stood behind her, hot-breathing her neck. "It's *salt*imbocca, the salt's already in there."

Georgia glared at him. Did *no one* understand aggressive salting? Between Bruno and Mercedes Sante, you'd think salt had been outlawed. She slammed down her sauté pan just as Claudia walked into the kitchen. Claudia's mouth, which had been half open, snapped shut. She stood in the doorway, her arms folded across her chest, unnoticed by the dueling cooks.

"As I always say," Bruno said, "more fire, less—"

"Bruno!" Georgia yelled. "Will you please back off? For just one second, please. I know you're my boss, but can you let me cook in peace for one second?" She slammed the sauté pan again in case he'd missed it the first time.

"Georgia!" Claudia said sharply. "What is going on in here?"

Georgia spun around to face her boss. "Nothing. Everything is fine." She felt her cheeks burn.

"Because in my kitchen we don't slam pots and pans. Or knives, or feet, or doors. And we don't yell. And this is, I trust you remember, my kitchen."

The kitchen stopped. So infrequently did Claudia raise her voice or appear anything less than delighted with her staff that no one would have been surprised if she had fired the American on the spot.

"Do you understand me?" Claudia asked. Her eyebrows shot up almost to her hairline.

Georgia nodded. The universe had come knocking. The road rash decorating her knees and shoulder was its none-too-subtle calling card, and she had slammed the door in its face.

"Then we're okay." Claudia walked out of the kitchen. "Cook," she said to the staff, twirling her hands over her head as she left.

Vanessa walked over to Georgia and squeezed her shoulder. Georgia grimaced.

"It's all right," Vanessa said. "She'll get over it."

"Not the shoulder, please." Georgia removed Vanessa's hand and shut her eyes. The truth was, it wasn't all right. She'd been acting like a mini-Marco in training. Though she'd sworn she never would, she had become That Chef. Worse, she had become That Sous-Chef.

Bruno walked up next to her and cleared his throat. "Claudia knows you're a good cook."

"I guess so." Georgia took a deep breath and closed her eyes for a second, dreading what she had to say. "I'm sorry I've been such a jerk. I—" She stopped, hoping he'd let her off the hook.

"You what?" No such luck.

"I'm used to being head chef. And I, for some reason, thought I was going to be head chef at Dia. And then I found out I wasn't, that you were. And I didn't handle it at all well, maybe because I was fired from my last job, or maybe because I'm used to being head chef, or maybe because you weren't all that nice to me." She held up her hand to stop herself. "Which is no excuse. Either way, Bruno, or, I guess, any way you look at it, I behaved badly. And I'm sorry."

Bruno nodded his head slowly. "Okay. I accept your apology. And I owe you one too. I'm sorry for all I said about you not being able to cook Italian food. You cook it quite well . . . for an American." He paused for a second. "I'm joking."

"I got that."

"Don't forget that this restaurant is important to both of us. We all need it to succeed, but maybe you and me a little bit more than everyone else."

"I know. I lost track of that for a while, but I won't again." It was true. If Dia was a success, it would make waves that would cross the Atlantic and reverberate all the way from Brooklyn to the Bronx. New Yorkers loved nothing more than a big, crashing fall from grace and a subsequent redemption. Dia would redeem her career. *Could* redeem her career. But only if she let it.

"We need to make some changes," Bruno continued. "We have to get along. We don't have to be best friends, but we have to get along."

"I can do that."

"Good. So can I. And you have to remember that I'm the boss."

She swallowed. "Okay, Bruno, I mean, um, Chef."

"And you have to hold the salt."

"I'll try," she said. "Chef."

He shrugged his shoulders and began to turn away.

"Okay, okay, from this moment forward, I'll lose the attitude and the right to salt. Anything more than a pinch of either, and I'll get permission first. But no more 'American' comments. If you don't like my food, tell me, but don't tell me it's because I'm American." She held out her hand. "Deal?"

He looked at her for a second before shaking it. "Deal."

That night, in the middle of dinner prep, Claudia asked Georgia to join her on the patio for an aperitivo.

"Sure, Claudia." Georgia removed her apron.

Vanessa offered her friend an encouraging smile. "Don't worry," she mouthed.

Georgia followed Claudia into the hall, through the French doors, and onto the patio, steeling herself for the worst. Two Camparis, a ficelle, a bowl of green olives, and a wedge of prima caciotta sat on a tray on a round table. The sun was poised to begin its descent into the ribbons of hills. A warm breeze filled the air.

"Please sit down." Claudia pulled up two chairs to face the sunset and sat back in one. Georgia did the same.

"Look at that sky," Claudia said. "It gets more beautiful each time I look at it."

"It's amazing." Georgia reached for her drink, changed her mind, and folded her hands in her lap.

Claudia turned to her. "I am sorry you have been unhappy. Especially because I don't understand what you have to be unhappy about."

Georgia opened her mouth to speak, but Claudia held up her hand.

"We all have things we wish were different in our lives. Problems, disappointments, frustrations—whatever you call them, we all have them." She cut a few pieces of cheese and took one for herself. "Take me, for example. I have a restaurant opening in a few weeks. The kitchen isn't done, the chairs are so uncomfortable no one will be able to sit through an entire meal, the floor is the wrong color. I still don't have a signature dish, and my staff"—she paused—"well, let's just say my staff needs a bit of fine-tuning."

The words *staff* plus *tuning* sent a shudder through Georgia's already throbbing shoulder. How, she wondered, would she ever recover from her second sacking in less than three months? That Brentwood job was starting to sound pretty good.

"On top of this," Claudia said, popping an olive into her mouth, "on top of this, my boyfriend hasn't set foot in my house in three weeks."

"Your boyfriend?" Vanessa had confirmed his existence, but almost a week into Georgia's stay at the villa there was still no sign of him, and Georgia assumed he was out of the picture for good.

Claudia sighed. "I'm forty-two years old. I have three successful restaurants. I'm about to open my fourth. I have two cookbooks, a cooking show. Sergio, he wants to get married."

"He—Sergio—wants to get married and you don't?"

"I tell him things are good as they are. We don't need to get married. But"—Claudia pulled on her drink—"he wants a child."

"And do you?"

Claudia looked off to the hills. "We tried for a long time, but the injections, the hormones, I can't do it anymore. Not now, with the restaurant opening. And later . . . well, later isn't an option."

Georgia considered Claudia's words. It was true. Sure, there was the odd celebrity who gave birth at forty-two, forty-three, but postforty births for regular folk weren't exactly the norm. Then again, Claudia wasn't exactly regular folk. "So what will happen with you and Sergio?"

"I don't know. He doesn't understand that my restaurants are my children. I love him. And I don't want to lose him, but—" She stopped short and drew her arms across her chest. A few seconds passed before she spoke, and her manner had become matter-of-fact, dispassionate.

"I'm not telling you this to burden you, but so you can see that you're not the only one with—how do you Americans call it? Issues. You lost your job, your fiancé, but here you have another chance. Stop looking for what you don't have, and start seeing what you do."

"I will. I mean, I do."

"I couldn't make you head chef. I considered it, but I couldn't do it. You know what people would say if I had an American running Trattoria Dia? *Pazza,* they'd say. She's crazy." She tapped her skull to demonstrate. "Bruno is a good chef. Not as creative as you, but consistent. You can learn from him. And he won't hold you back."

Georgia stared out at the open sky. It was purple and blue, soft, like a growing bruise.

"So we're okay?" Claudia stood. "We understand each other?"

"We do." What Georgia understood was that even people who looked as if they had it all had issues of their own. Relationships, children, work—Claudia grappled with the same problems Georgia did. But instead of focusing on what she didn't have, she focused on what she did. If it worked for Claudia, maybe it would work for Georgia. Or so she hoped.

Claudia patted Georgia's head like a puppy's. "Don't think too much. Overthinking anything—food, love—it spoils it." Claudia walked across the patio, pulled open the door, and stopped, her hand resting on the handle. "Georgia," she called out. "I have an idea."

"Yes?"

"The specials. How about if you run the daily specials?"

"The specials?" A smile spread across Georgia's face. "Really?"

"Really. Bruno is still head chef, but you're in charge of specials." With that, Claudia disappeared into the villa.

Georgia sat underneath the inky sky, her hand wrapped around her drink, slightly dazed by the turn of events. Instead of firing her, Claudia was giving her a chance. Maybe focusing on what she had wouldn't be so tough after all.

Chapter Thirteen

Georgia, Vanessa, and Effie walked single file, their eyes scanning the ground for a bunch of wild arugula, lavender, maybe some late-season morels. They wore chunky rubber boots and wide-brimmed hats pulled low on their foreheads. Neither offered protection from the hot Tuscan sun, and their feet and brows perspired profusely. June had been unseasonably warm and wet, and the black dirt beneath their feet was rich with vegetation.

"What about this?" Effie squeezed the head from a purple coneflower.

"Echinacea?" Georgia asked, turning to look at his upturned palm. "I don't think so, Ef. Unless Claudia's fighting a cold we don't know about."

"Have you ever tasted echinacea tea?" Vanessa interjected. Her hair was piled under her hat, and a few sweaty tendrils stuck to her forehead. "Or those pills that are supposed to keep you from getting sick?" She stuck out her tongue to catch a bead of sweat rolling toward her mouth.

Georgia had never met anyone, male or female, who sweat

more than Vanessa. After five minutes at the flattop, she was as slick as a tenth-round prizefighter.

Effie shrugged and put the coneflower in his front shirt pocket. The trio continued forward, making their way down the dusty dirt road. With their oversize utility pails and rubber boots they looked like fly fishermen off for a little catch-and-release instead of a bunch of cooks foraging for their supper.

Since arriving in San Casciano, the Dia staff had been camping out under the bright lights of a kitchen, first in the villa and with construction finally completed in the restaurant itself. They'd spent the last month creating, shaping, working, reworking, tweaking, and scrapping menu items, which could make even the sharpest chef a bit loopy. As Dia's grand opening grew nearer, they'd been leaving the kitchen only to sleep, shower, and shave (though, as Effie's amorphous facial hair attested, shaving was optional). They were a frazzled and pasty lot. Fearing either a mutiny or a collective nervous breakdown, Claudia decided that a sun-drenched scavenger hunt was the pick-me-up they all needed. She split them into two groups and instructed them to get out and find as many viable ingredients as they could for that night's dinner.

"Have fun!" Claudia called as they wandered outside, squinting beneath the dazzling sky, dazed expressions on their pale faces. With less than seventy-two hours before they'd serve their first customer, no one was worrying about his or her daily dose of vitamin D.

"Hey, guys, wait up," Effie called to Vanessa and Georgia. He stood over several bunches of silvery sage plants.

"Good one, Ef." Georgia knelt down next to the plants. She plucked a leaf and rubbed it between her fingers, then held them to her nose. "This sage is gorgeous."

"Speaking of gorgeous," Vanessa whispered.

"What's that, Vee?" Georgia looked up.

Vanessa gestured to a chestnut-haired guy pacing in front of a stone wall forty feet away. Behind him was a sign that read VIGNA DI VOLPE BIANCA in crimson letters superimposed over a drawing of a white fox with sharp teeth. The guy waved one hand in the air and held a cell phone in the other. Wearing close-cut jeans, an untucked white shirt, and chocolate loafers without socks, he had that elegantly disheveled Italian look down.

"Who is he?" Georgia asked.

Effie had finished pillaging the sage and was fingering some fronds sprouting from a gangly yellow plant. He sneaked a peek at the guy. "Gianni. He runs Volpe Bianca, the vineyard next door. They're doing Dia's house wines. They've got a great Chianti and a good Sylvaner, if you're inclined to whites." He wrinkled his nose.

"More importantly, is he single?" Vanessa asked.

"How would Effie know?" Georgia said.

"Actually I do, and, yes, he is. He's a huge playboy."

"Really," Georgia said as noncommittally as she could muster. Since the guy in Florence, the one she so totally and mortifyingly misread, she hadn't met anyone even remotely interesting. She'd dutifully been following her friends' advice to give single living a whirl, repeating her Claudia-inspired mantra so frequently she could hear it in her sleep: focus on what you have (Italy, new friends, the experience of a lifetime), forget what you don't (her own restaurant, a husband, a boyfriend, a guy to smooch). But this guy, she thought, was interesting. And really, seriously cute.

Gianni snapped shut his cell and slipped it in his pocket. He turned to the trio and flashed a dazzling smile. *"Buon giorno!"* he called out.

"Ciao, Gianni," Effie said, removing his hat and holding his hand in front of his eyes like a visor. It was approaching noon and the sun was beastly hot.

Gianni sauntered over, clearly relishing the attention of his audience. His curls bounced as he walked, and his olive skin gleamed. The two men shook hands and Effie introduced Georgia and Vanessa before wandering off to a purple patch a few yards away that he swore was the coveted and elusive wild asparagus.

"You must be the famous American," Gianni said, kissing Georgia's hand. "Enchanted to meet you."

Georgia smiled. "I don't know about famous. Infamous, perhaps."

He chuckled. "Beautiful, a master in the kitchen from what I hear, and a sense of humor too. You American girls truly have it all."

"Hey, Italian girls aren't so bad either," Vanessa chided.

"Italian girls are the best, of course. But there are a few exceptions." He looked pointedly at Georgia, who felt her face redden under her hat. She'd forgotten about her dopey hat.

"I'm glad you all had a chance to meet," Effie said, returning empty-handed from his foraging. "But we need to find some plants. We have enough cheese back in the kitchen."

Vanessa choked back a laugh.

"What are you doing out here?" Gianni asked, not catching Effie's cheese reference. "Shouldn't you be sweating over a hot stove?"

"Searching for our supper," Georgia said. "We're on the hunt for anything edible. Got any ideas?"

"A couple," Gianni said slyly. Pausing a beat, he pointed to the abandoned well midway between his vineyard and the villa. "I guess you could start there."

"Thanks. We'll check it out." Georgia crossed her clunky green boots.

"Guys," Effie said impatiently. "Plants."

"You are busy," Gianni said. "And I must get going too. It was nice to meet you, Vanessa, and to see you, Effie." He offered a slight bow. "And, Georgia, it was truly a pleasure."

"Yes, it was. So, since you're doing Dia's house wine, will you be at the friends-and-family party tomorrow night?" Georgia's voice sounded two octaves higher than normal.

"Of course. I wouldn't miss it for anything. Especially now." Gianni turned his palm inward and offered the signature Italian wave. "Ciao, bellissima."

"Ciao," Georgia said.

"Nice one, George," Vanessa said when he was out of ear-shot. "I didn't think you had it in you."

"I wasn't so sure I did either. But I'm glad I did."

He *was* cute. Cheesy, as Effie said, but Italians could get away with being cheesy in a way Americans couldn't. A little harmless flirting was always a good distraction, and if it led to something more, then why not? She was in *Italy*, for God's sake. Single and in Italy. The cute vineyard manager with the chiseled cheeks and the bouncy curls could be just the distraction she needed.

The two teams reconvened in the Dia kitchen to show off their scores. Georgia's group brought back the sage, dandelion greens, and wild fennel. Bruno's crew offered a bouquet of wildflowers Claudia proclaimed lovely to look at but likely poisonous, save for a mass of wild geraniums, and the echinacea the other group rejected. Since calling their truce, Georgia and Bruno had become, if not exactly best friends, then at least friendly. He still drove her crazy, but she no longer actively wished for his taste buds to implode.

"Well," Claudia said, clapping her hands together, "this is going to be even worse than I feared."

"It's my turn for music tonight," Tonio yelled as the crew assumed their stations. He stuck his iPod into the Bose sound system on top of the steel filing cabinet that, along with a child-size desk, functioned as the Dia cockpit. It held one of two computer screens, a phone, and the official cookbook, a thick, leatherbound volume in which Claudia and the crew kept notes on their favorite purveyors, seasonal ingredients, ideas for specials, and whatever else they couldn't risk forgetting.

"None of that trance shit, please, Tonio," Effie said.

Tonio scowled, scrolled down his playlists, and soon electronica pulsed through the kitchen. "Sorry, man. It's all I have."

Bruno pulled out bottles of Campari and sweet vermouth from the makeshift bar cabinet he'd created from a vintage milk crate. "Negroni?" he asked, not bothering to turn around. It was the staff's night to celebrate, before the friends-and-family party, before the grand opening. It was a rhetorical question.

An hour and a half later, the not-quite-delicious dinner had been prepared, set on the table, and (mostly) eaten. The highlight was the salad, composed of wild greens and baby vegetables from the organic garden, which would provide many of the herbs and vegetables on the Dia menu. Those that didn't come directly from the garden would come from nearby farms, whenever possible. Italians were still ahead of their American counterparts when it came to the local food movement.

Claudia raised her glass of Sassicaia, pulled from her personal cellar. "I'd like to say a few words, if I may. I promise I'll be brief."

The chattering stopped and all looked at their boss, who had stepped away from the table and stood in the center of the staff room, a snug little room tacked on to the Dia kitchen, where they had started taking meals and holding meetings. She wore skinny black pants, black ballet flats, and a crisp white button-down that hit midthigh.

"She looks like Audrey in *Funny Face,*" Vanessa whispered to Georgia.

"Exactly," Georgia agreed.

The two girls had discovered a shared love of old movies over a late-night, Italian-dubbed version of *How to Steal a Million,* complete with bowls of popcorn followed by Italiamerican sundaes with *nocciola* and *gianduia* gelato, grappa-soaked cherries, and canned whipped cream.

"This may not be the best meal any of us have cooked, or any of us have eaten." Claudia grinned. "But we had fun making it, and sometimes that's even more important than the end result. Though certainly not with a reviewer in the house." She smiled at Georgia, who shifted in her seat. "This meal is what being a team is all about. Overcoming obstacles, building on each other's strengths, collaborating. You've all come so far in such a short time. I'm so proud of each of you."

The wine had flowed all night, and the crew soaked up Claudia's words. This was clearly turning into the official preopening pep talk. Employees the world over fell into two camps: those who cringed at these rally-the-troops talks, and those who hung on every syllable. With their dreamy smiles and dewy eyes, the Dia staff was a sentence away from a group hug. They were a rapt, if woozy, audience.

"In three days, we open Trattoria Dia. Opening a restaurant is never easy. But we have a wonderful restaurant, and an even better team." Claudia raised her glass. "I wouldn't want to open Dia with anyone other than the people sitting at this table tonight. To all of you."

Effie whistled, and Bruno stood and thrust his glass in the

air, looking like a portly Statue of Liberty. "To Claudia!" he shouted.

"To Claudia!" the staff sang in unison. They polished off their glasses, and another bottle was passed, a downgrade from the Sassicaia, which, at close to $200 a bottle, was not a swilling sort of wine.

"And to Trattoria Dia!" yelled the usually composed Elena. Her cheeks flamed scarlet and her eyes were glassy.

"Tomorrow's going to be so ugly," Vanessa said to Georgia as the group continued toasting anything even remotely connected to the restaurant. "I'm already seeing one and a half of everything."

"Red wine's the worst," Georgia said, taking another sip.

"One more thing," Claudia shouted above the din. "We still don't have a signature dish. Of course we can let one evolve, but it's always better to open with one in place. As added incentive, a weekend off for whoever creates Dia's dish."

Amid whoops, whistles, and still more toasting, Georgia put down her almost full glass of Barbaresco. She'd been working on a signature dish for weeks and was so, so close to nailing it. The chance to salvage her reputation, plus spend two nights in Maremma—complete with a heavenly meal at La Pineta—was too good to let slip through her hands. While a solo sojourn would do just fine, there was always the option of inviting someone along, like, say, a certain vineyard owner. Georgia picked up her untouched water tumbler and chugged down its contents, then refilled her glass. She had work to do.

At 3:00 a.m. the alarm went off. Though not exactly refreshed, Georgia didn't feel totally terrible, thanks to the three glasses of water she'd slammed before her nap. She slipped into an old pair of Levi's she hadn't worn since college but stashed in her suitcase at the last minute thinking they could come in handy. No power-washing, deconstructing, sandblasting, whiskering, or any other treatment that quadrupled the price of an ordinary pair of jeans could come close to the comfort of an old pair of velvet-soft Levi's. They felt like home.

She walked across the winding stone path that stretched between the villa and the restaurant. Camouflaged by thorny rosebushes, it had carefully been plotted to allow for easy passage between the two buildings. It snaked by the southern tip of the gigantic garden, past the curing shack, at last arriving at an elegant brick patio that served as the unofficial staff smoking area. Framing the patio was a garden of cool blue and purple blooms intermixed with lacy ferns and shiny blue-green shrubs. Beyond the garden stretched a seemingly endless and somewhat overgrown meadow that created a striking counterpoint to the neat, gridlike vineyards and orchards surrounding it. Softly lit by a mix of unobtrusive lanterns and hidden spotlights, the setting was breathtaking, even in the thick of the night. Georgia stepped onto the patio and through an eggplant-colored door into the Dia kitchen.

Twenty aprons hung from an old-fashioned peg rack, and she grabbed hers and slipped it over her head. The kitchen stood empty, the dishes washed, the floor mopped, the stainless countertops polished and shiny. Everything was in place for tomorrow's friends-and-family party. She pulled her hair into a low, looped ponytail and scrubbed her ringless hands.

Overthinking food spoils it, Claudia had said. And that was exactly Georgia's problem when it came to the signature dish. She'd been so focused on creating the end-all, be-all whatever it was that she'd forgotten to look right in front of her, where every good dish begins: the basic ingredients. This wasn't New York City, where anything worth eating came from a great purveyor or a farm at least fifty miles away. This was Tuscany, where the biggest organic garden Georgia had ever seen lay right outside her bedroom window. She grabbed a pad and pen to write down the recipe. If all went well, she'd copy it into the cookbook so it could be replicated exactly as she'd made it.

She soaked, washed, and trimmed three artichokes, baby purple Romagnas, which would sadly lose their beautiful hue once they hit hot water, then washed and peeled a bunch of pencil-thin asparagus. She pulled out several small zucchini and sliced them into translucent moons. She washed three leeks, slicing them down their centers and peeling back each layer, carefully rinsing away any sand, then chopped the white, light green, and some of the darker parts into a fine dice. She shelled a couple handfuls of spring peas, collecting them in a ceramic bowl. She chopped a bulb of fennel and julienned one more, then washed and spun the fronds. She washed the basil and mint and spun them dry. Last, she chopped the shallots. With the vegetables prepped, she started on the risotto, the base layer for the torta a strati alla primavera, or spring layer cake, she'd been finessing since her arrival, and which she hoped would become Dia's dish. She'd make a total of six *torte*: three artichoke and three asparagus.

The trick was getting the risotto to the perfect consistency, which was considerably less creamy than usual. It had to be firm enough to keep its shape and support the layers that would be placed on top of it, but not gummy, the kiss of death for any risotto. She started with a *soffritto* of shallot, fennel, and leek, adding Carnaroli rice, which she preferred to arborio, pinot grigio, and, when the wine had plumped the rice, spring-vegetable stock, one ladle at a time. Once the risotto had absorbed all the liquid and cooked sufficiently, she divided it into six single-serving crescent molds, placed the molds in a glass baking dish, and popped them all in the oven, which made the risotto the consistency of a soft Rice Krispies treat. Keeping the molds in place, she added the next layer, steamed asparagus in one version, artichoke in the other. A layer of basil and crushed pignoli pesto followed, then the zucchini rounds, flash-sautéed, and the fennel matchsticks, cooked until soft, and finally, the spring-pea puree. She carefully removed the first mold and was rewarded with a near-perfect crescent tower, which she drizzled with red-pepper coulis. Finally, she placed a dollop of chilled basil-mint *sformato* alongside the crescent and radiated mint leaves around the *sformato* so that it looked like a sun. The sun and the moon, *sole e luna,* all anyone could hope for.

The dish was so beautiful to behold, with such lovely coloration, such perfect plate-to-food ratio, she almost couldn't bear to bite into it. But of course she did, because as much as she loved creating a gorgeous plate, she loved eating it even more. So she dug in, delighted when her fork slid through the layers without any help from a knife, and even more so when the cake traveled from tine to tongue without slipping. And the taste, the texture, it was, well, *sublime* was the word that crossed Georgia's mind. She hated getting all food-critic-y with herself, but it was true. It had to be Dia's dish.

She pulled out the cookbook and carefully transcribed the recipe in neat script. A wave of paranoia washed over her as she imagined Bruno or Tonio stealing her recipe and claiming it as his own. But they were all friends now, and especially after Claudia's teamwork pep talk, no one would dare. She closed the book. Really, no one would dare.

After a hasty cleanup, she hurried out the door and onto the rose-lined path back to the villa. The air was soft with summer, and a glittering array of stars illuminated the sky. She paused midway between the restaurant and the villa and trained her eye on the horizon. Though she couldn't make out the hills in the distance, knowing they were there was enough. Surrounded by the heady scent of roses and fresh green grass, she felt lucky and content. If life was really a bunch of tiny moments daisy-chained together, then this, she thought, was one of those moments.

She realized she'd left the *torte* out on the counter instead of in the walk-in and was considering going back to the kitchen when she heard a loud rustling. Claudia had warned her about a pack of coyotes who roamed the property, and Georgia wasn't interested in making their acquaintance anytime soon. Besides, the housekeeper would toss the *torte* in the morning. She high-tailed it back to the villa and fell into her bed, fully clothed, sated at last.

"Dude, no way. I'm not listening to that shit again!" Effie was in worse form than usual after the festivities of the night before. The object of his wrath, Tonio, had once again commandeered the iPod.

"Break it up, boys. We're all friends here, remember?" Georgia swatted the back of Effie's head. "Claudia's running the show tonight anyway, and she gave me her iPod. So back off." Georgia docked the iPod, and Louis Armstrong started singing about missing New Orleans. "You guys clean up nice, by the way. It's good to see everyone in something other than chef whites or playground clothes for a change."

Both Tonio and Effie were decked out in jackets and slacks, the one nice outfit they each owned. The rest of the staff was similarly attired in their best party duds.

"How come you're so chipper?" Effie growled. "I feel like an ice pick is slowly scooping out my left eye and shooting it into my right, and you look fresh as a turnip. Weren't you drinking grapes with the rest of us?"

"Some of us opted out early, Ef. Some of us had cooking to do." She cuffed him on the shoulder. Always ripe for a little ribbing, Effie was turning into the younger brother she never had.

"You too, Georgia?" Bruno walked into the kitchen. "I was also in the kitchen very late last night, the sun was almost up, and I made a really interesting vegetable dish. What'd you make?"

Georgia swallowed hard. "You made what?"

"A vegetable layer cake, with herbs and vegetables from the garden. I just fixed a fresh batch and gave it to Claudia. Would you like a taste?"

The rustling she'd heard! He'd scooped the dish from under her nose. She clenched her fists together.

"Is everything okay, Georgia?" Bruno asked with mock concern. "Suddenly you look pale."

She didn't answer. She couldn't. So this was her lot in life. Forced to play second string to a succession of no-talent, no-good bosses, each one worse than the last.

"The thing is," Bruno continued, "the recipe's not really mine, or all mine. I went to the kitchen thinking I'd do some work on the signature dish. When I got there, these beautiful crescent towers were just sitting there, and the recipe was right there in the cookbook." Bruno paused, allowing Georgia to savor his words.

"I thought they'd make the perfect signature dish. The ingredients come straight from the garden, there's nothing too complex or expensive, and it's a plate even the least sophisticated palate would like." He crossed his arms over his chest. "The only problem is, the ingredients are seasonal. We can't have a seasonal signature dish."

Georgia exhaled, puffing out her cheeks. Bruno was right. Much as it killed her to admit it, he was right. Claudia's entire food philosophy was built on eating locally and eating seasonally. How could she have overlooked her dish's fatal flaw?

"So I decided to come up with a cold-weather version using eggplant, wild mushrooms, stewed tomatoes, you get the idea. It's delicious." He kissed his fingers to prove his point. "Now I'm looking for the person who created the original."

"Bruno," Georgia said as calmly as she could, "do you seriously not know whose recipe it is, or are you effing with me?"

His face fell blank before erupting into a gigantic grin. "Effing with you, whatever that means. Of course I know it's yours."

"Are you guys talking about me again?" Effie said. "I keep hearing my name."

"Georgia," Bruno said, ignoring Effie, "I think this is the one. I think you did it."

"I did—" She paused for a second. "I did some of it, Bruno. And you did the rest."

"I was only joking, Georgia. It's your dish."

"Didn't you hear what Claudia said last night? It's all about teamwork. And collaboration. My *torta* wouldn't have a shot without yours to back it up. Teamwork, Bruno." She couldn't believe the words coming from her mouth.

"Then in that case," Bruno said, "the artichoke is better."

She nodded. "I know."

"And there is one thing it needed."

Georgia frowned. "Really? Because I thought it was pretty perfect as is." Her willingness to share the credit didn't mean her ego had entirely been snuffed out. "What'd you add?"

"Salt. It needed salt."

"You've got to be kidding me."

"No." He shook his head. "It really did."

Claudia walked into the kitchen, dressed for the party in a swishy black skirt, a white silk shirt, and large gold hoops. "*At-*

tenzione!" she shouted. "I need to speak with whoever made what used to be on this plate." She held up her plate, which was bare save for a slick of pesto. "Right away!"

Bruno and Georgia looked at each other. "That would be us," Georgia said.

"You two?"

"Us two," Georgia said.

Claudia looked from one to the other. "Then congratulations, Georgia and Bruno. It looks like you've created Dia's signature dish!"

Bruno threw his arms around Georgia's waist and he half lifted, half tilted her off the ground in a bear hug. Her strappy sandals dangled above the floor.

"Put me down," Georgia said. He didn't move a muscle. "Bruno, put me down now!"

He pulled his hands away and she landed with a thud. "Whoops," he said.

She straightened the bodice on her green shift, which was the same color as her eyes, and which Lo had insisted she buy despite its hefty price tag. "Don't ever pick me up again," she said with the slightest hint of a smile. "Just because we scored the signature dish together doesn't mean you can pick me up." But she burst out laughing, and so did Bruno.

"And what do you call your delicious dish?" Claudia asked when they had stopped laughing.

Georgia glanced at Bruno, who nodded. *"Sole e luna,"* she said. "The sun and the moon."

"Wonderful." Claudia clapped. "So, could this mean that the two of you might consider spending your holiday weekend together?" She threw an arm around each of them and kissed their cheeks, leaving shiny lipstick smudges behind. Air kissing was so not her style.

Georgia smiled. "Bruno and I are finally friends, Claudia. Let's not push it."

"You're right," Claudia said. "Besides, Bruno seems to have his hands full these days."

Bruno turned pink. Though everyone knew they were an item, he and Elena tried to keep their relationship under wraps. Or had, until the previous night when in a meandering monologue directed at Claudia, Elena mentioned him and his measurable assets at least ten times. The salami was officially out of its casing.

"Anyway," Claudia continued, "friends are so underrated these days." She gave Bruno and Georgia each a little shove. "Now go enjoy the party. It could be the last one for a very long time."

The dining room was beginning to fill with fashionable Italians, expats, and industry people, none of whom Georgia knew, all eager to check out Claudia's latest venture. Amazingly, after weeks of running behind schedule, the restaurant was not only finished, but beautiful. The floors had been whitewashed to complement the pale pistachio plaster walls, the uncomfortable chairs replaced by graceful dove-gray armchairs upholstered in white-and-gray ticking. Tables covered in crisp white linen ringed the room. A fireplace of antique bricks held logs of white birch, and a spray of peonies in a large glass vase sat on the worn-walnut mantel. Claudia had created a space equally suited for an afternoon lunch on a sunny day or a late-night dinner on a stormy evening. If the food lived up to the decor, Trattoria Dia was sure to be a culinary coup.

A waiter with a tray of Bellini passed by, and Bruno grabbed two, handing one to Georgia. Before they could toast their victory, Vanessa rushed over, scooped a drink from the same tray, and almost knocked the poor waiter down.

"Oops, sorry," she said over her shoulder. "Heard about the sole e luna. Congratulations, guys." Though Vanessa had hoped to create the dish herself, she was glad for Georgia and half glad for Bruno. "This must be your night, Georgia."

"Well, it's not just mine, it's Bruno's too—"

"No, I mean because *he's* here. Gianni. And he asked about you."

Georgia scoped out the dining room as nonchalantly as possible, which was never as nonchalantly as one would like, then turned back to Vanessa. Bruno had been summoned to the patio by a pale, Panna-swilling Elena mumbling something about air.

"I don't see Gianni, Vee, but there's Gabri and Cesca." Georgia waved to her Florentine friends. Claudia had told the staff to invite whomever they wanted, and Gabri and Cesca topped Georgia's two-person list. Before she could make her way through the crowd to greet them, she felt a pinch on her waist. She turned and looked up into the long-lashed eyes of Gianni.

"*Buona sera*, Georgia." His hand brushed her hip bone. He wore a navy sport coat, a pink dress shirt unbuttoned at the neck, and pressed jeans. His curls framed his face in Botticelli corkscrews, and she resisted the urge to pull one down and watch it *boing* back into place. They greeted each other with double air kisses.

"Congratulations," he said, motioning to the dining room with his hand. "The restaurant is really beautiful. You must be very proud."

"Claudia is the one who should be proud. I just work here." But she beamed nonetheless.

"I thought Americans were so boastful, but you are so modest." He pushed a strand of her hair behind her ear. "And may I say, how lovely you are tonight."

Before she could respond, Gabri charged over. "Georgia," he said, pulling Cesca behind him, "this place looks amazing!"

"It really does," Cesca echoed. "We're so excited for you."

"It's so great to see you guys!" Georgia hugged her friends, who looked as if they'd arrived straight from the runway of an Armani fashion show. She started to make introductions, but it turned out Gianni already knew Gabri and Cesca, and in the way most Italians did, they had much to chat about. The room was packed, and waiters dressed in gray twill pants and starched white shirts passed trays of salvia fritta, polpetti, and crostini misti, while Paolo Conte's scratchy baritone rumbled through the room. The party was suddenly in full swing, having crossed that crucial line from small gathering of acquaintances making small talk to roomful of revelers eating and drinking way too much.

Holding a tall, clear glass of something that was not water, Vanessa beelined to Georgia and nudged her in the ribs.

"The mysterious Sergio is here. He's talking to Claudia on the patio. And he's *magnifico*." Vanessa flipped her thick brown hair, worn loose to her waist for the first time since Georgia had known her, into the face of an unsuspecting server, the same one she had almost knocked down earlier. "Excuse me. Is it hot in here or is it just me?" She wiped her sleeve across her forehead.

"Sergio's here?" It seemed odd that Claudia's estranged boyfriend would show for the party, but Georgia had more pressing issues to deal with. "I'll meet him later. I'm sort of busy right now." She gestured with her head to Gianni, who was laughing at something Gabri had said.

"Ohhh," Vanessa whispered. "How's it going?"

"So far, so good. I'll fill you in later." When Georgia turned back to her friends, Gianni was gone. She spotted him laughing

by the fireplace with a willowy blonde and cringed as his fingertips grazed her bare shoulder.

Cesca frowned at Gianni and shook her head. "That guy may
as well have a *W* tattooed on his forehead."

"A *W*?"

"For 'womanizer.' I'd say he's slept with at least a third of the
women here."

"Seriously?"

"Yes. He used to date a friend of mine. His idea of a relationship is three dates: on the first you establish the relationship,
on the second you consummate it, and on the third you end it."
Cesca patted Georgia's shoulder. "But he is cute."

"He is." Georgia grabbed a Bellini from a waiter passing by
and snuck another peek at Gianni. "Too bad about that three-
date thing."

Three Bellini, one Campari-tini, a truly noxious concoction
swilled from a martini glass, and half a *vin santo* later, three
dates sounded fine. In fact, Georgia thought, they might as well
skip the first date entirely and get right to the second. What was
wrong with fooling around a little? She'd just ended a seven-year
relationship. She was in Italy. It was time.

Vanessa, Effie, Tonio, Bruno, and some of the other staff
had taken over the outdoor patio and sat at a round table littered with empty glasses and crushed cigarette packs. Effie was
at last in charge of the music, and Tom Waits wailed across the
moonlit night. It was way past cocktail hour and the party was
over, the guests having moved on to dinner at neighboring trattorias or villas. As her friends drunkenly deconstructed the Italian
culinary canon (*Silver Spoon* for casual cooks, Pellegrino Artusi's
Science in the Kitchen and the Art of Eating Well for diehards),

Georgia rose on wobbly legs. She had to find Gianni. And, she thought, he better have eighty-sixed the blonde.

"Off to bed," she said to her friends, offering a lame wave. "G'night."

She pushed open the *melanzana*-colored door—so much prettier sounding than *eggplant*—and tiptoed into the kitchen like a high school girl sneaking in past curfew. The cleaning crew had done their job well, and the kitchen sparkled like a brand-new engagement ring. In two days, it would be a madhouse, but for now the subway tiles gleamed, the stainless steel shone, the rubber jigsaw-puzzle floor was so clean you could eat off it. The only sounds were the persistent hum of the walk-in and the even more persistent hum of the partyers outside.

A bunch of daisies in an illy coffee can sat on the desk, and Georgia absentmindedly fingered the white petals. Momentarily derailed from her Gianni-seeking mission, she contemplated the path that had led her to Dia. The breakup, the firing, the planning, the waiting—it had been a long journey with more twists and kinks than her hair after a hot summer day at the beach. If everything did really happen for a reason, then this—the kitchen, the restaurant, Claudia, her new friends, San Casciano—was the reason. Her eyes moistened. The booze was making her wistful, an emotion she avoided like canned olives.

She heard a whoosh of air and a handful of footsteps as someone passed through the swinging door from the dining room into the kitchen. Attempting to compose herself, she cleared her throat, forced her lips into a smile, and turned to face the interloper. Her smile disappeared as quickly as it had appeared. It was the smell she recognized first, and her eyes went wide at the first whiff.

"Hi. You're that guy I met in Florence." Her eyes traveled to the sewing-needle scar under his left eye.

"I knew it'd be you," he said, smiling. "I knew you were the American working for Claudia."

"Georgia!" Claudia walked into the kitchen. "You've been hiding all night. I'm so glad to see you." She placed her hand casually on the man's back, and in that one gesture Georgia understood everything. On that balmy spring night in Florence he'd lamented the loss of family and love in favor of career and success. He'd been talking about Claudia.

"Hi, Claudia," Georgia said.

"I see you've met Sergio?"

"No, not really. Hello, I'm Georgia." She stuck out her right hand, offering an awkward American greeting. There was no way she'd risk getting closer to that smell.

"Pleased to officially meet you, Georgia. I'm Sergio." He turned to Claudia. "Georgia and I crossed paths in Florence, outside of Benci. Only we didn't know who each other was." He chuckled. "Although I had a feeling."

They shook hands, and Claudia threw one arm around Georgia and the other around Sergio. "Oh, I love Benci. And I'm so happy you two have finally met. Officially."

"So am I," Georgia lied.

"I am too." Sergio held Georgia's gaze for a second longer than necessary.

Claudia opened a drawer in the filing cabinet and pulled out an old bottle of grappa with a yellowing label. "My lucky grappa. My first boss, my mentor who taught me everything, gave it to me twenty years ago. I only drink it on very special occasions, and only with very dear friends." She filled two cordials and handed one to Sergio and one to Georgia. "Tonight we have two wonderful things to celebrate." She glanced at Sergio, who was grinning. "To my husband-to-be, Sergio, and"—she patted her belly—"to our baby on the way."

Sergio and Claudia kissed while Georgia swallowed half her drink.

"Wow!" she said, coughing slightly. "That's fantastic!" She polished off the second half. "Claudia, I'm so happy for you. And you too!" Her voice was too loud, her smile too big. After she'd based her entire theory of happiness on Claudia's not needing a baby or a husband, after that stupid mantra she'd repeated day and night, this was not what she wanted to hear.

Claudia giggled. "Last night I pretended to drink so no one would suspect anything. I think Elena caught on, but she was too tipsy to remember. Anyway, it's still very early in the pregnancy, and we're not telling anyone, but I wanted you to know."

Georgia tried to smile serenely but suspected she looked more like a baby passing gas.

"So, Georgia, it turns out that I was wrong. Sometimes things do work out just as you want them to." Claudia interlaced her fingers with Sergio's and gave him a hip bump. He looked down at their locked hands.

"I guess sometimes they do," Georgia said. "Well, I'd love to stay and celebrate, but I'm really, really tired. I've got to go to bed." And this time she meant it.

Chapter Fourteen

Nursing a hangover as big as the Ritz, Georgia arrived at Bar Bodi, the Dia crew's local hangout, wearing Jackie O sunglasses, sweats, and flip-flops, perfect day-after attire. Her head was still reeling from the baby bomb Claudia had dropped at the end of the party. That the father/fiancé was the only guy Georgia had asked out in a decade didn't help her head—or her hangover—one bit.

Vanessa and Effie were already at the café, sitting at a small table flipping through *Corriere della Sera,* wearing shades. It was that kind of morning for everyone. Over *uovo,* taleggio, and pancetta panini (what Georgia would have done for a good old bacon, egg, and cheese), her friends dropped another bomb, though this one was more Katyusha rocket. Apparently, Gianni had left the party wearing the bodacious blonde.

"And I'm pretty sure they weren't going apple picking," Effie said, his mouth full of panini. "If you get my drift."

Georgia found the news more distressing than she'd like. For the first time in seven years, she was single. Up until that awkward moment in the kitchen when Claudia poured out her heart, along with those shots of grappa, she'd been fine with it. Not loving it, but definitely dealing. She'd even stopped worrying about the twin time bombs ticking away in her ovaries. Granted, after a handful of cocktails she'd wanted to jump Gianni's bones, but that was more boozy lust than a real desire to couple up. Then she learned about Claudia's baby and marriage, and all she could think about was how far she was from either, and how badly she wanted both. To make matters worse, she couldn't even score a lousy one-night stand with Gianni, the Italian Stallion.

"Is it possible," she wondered aloud, "that I could really be the only single American woman not to hook up in Italy? Is that even legal?"

"Don't tell me you're seriously upset about some greaseball who uses more hair products than you." Taleggio oozed down Effie's chin and he wiped it off with the back of his hand and then sucked it back up.

"It's not just Gianni. I mean, I almost smoked my first cigarette in five years for that guy!"

Vanessa looked at her quizzically. "Gianni doesn't smoke."

"You know what I always say," Effie interjected, pulling a pack of Camels from his front shirt pocket. "Smoke 'em if you got 'em!"

"Thanks anyway. But if getting dumped and axed in six short hours didn't make me start smoking again, I don't think a womanizing wino will either." Georgia sighed. "At least this time."

Effie and Vanessa walked outside, he to smoke, and she to inhale his secondhand smoke, since she was now "nine months off the Reds," as she frequently reminded her friends. Georgia gulped down the last sugary drops of her second double cappuccino. Being totally solo with zero prospects smarted more than she cared to admit. It smarted a whole lot.

With graying walls covered in beer posters, a chewed-up lino-
leum floor, and a handful of grubby Gateway computers parked
on one long simulated-wood table, the local Internet café was
more low-budget frat house than high-tech hot spot. Georgia
had been there once before, got weirded out by some greasy-
faced guy who kept staring at her, and avoided it ever since. She
probably had a thousand e-mails in her in-box.

Aside from the cashier, the place was empty. She sat down at
the computer closest to the door so she'd see Effie and Vanessa,
who'd gone in search of Happy Days, some over-the-counter all-
natural vitamins that were supposed to cure hangovers. No one
was feeling too swell after the friends-and-family party.

In a dozen e-mails, her friends back home reported on new
restaurant openings (Clem), and not-so-hot dates (Lo). Buried in e-mail number eleven from Lo, between lame dates at
Orsay (snooty banker) and Buddakan (sleazeball banker), was
a late-night Glenn spotting at 'inoteca. Seeing his name on the
screen made Georgia's belly flip, though it could have been
that Campari-tini coming back to haunt her. Lo said he looked
"tired."

"Tired?" Georgia muttered to herself. "That's all I get?"

Who was he with? she typed. *How late-night? What day was
it? How tired did he look? Tired or wired?* She reread her pathetic
queries and deleted every last one of them. These were not the
words of a girl *so over* her ex-fiancé. And she was. She really was.
She wouldn't have a crush on Gianni if she weren't over Glenn,
would she? So she typed the only thing that really mattered—
Did he say anything about Sals?—and forced herself to move on
to an e-mail from her dad.

She'd finally spoken with her parents after settling in at San Casciano. Though she was still annoyed with their Glenn-worshipping ways, she had to give her mother props for not mentioning him or Grammy in the entire twenty-seven minutes they spent on the phone. She even asked what Georgia had been cooking at Dia—the first time in her ten-plus years as a chef she could recall her mother asking a food-related question that didn't have to do with her daughter's weight. Since then, they'd had a couple of perfectly brief, perfectly benign conversations. Still, one never knew what scary news an e-mail from the 'rents might hold, and it was with more than a little trepidation that she opened her dad's.

Not scary, terrifying: Dorothy and Hal were planning a trip to Tuscany in September. As Hal wrote, they hadn't been to "the Continent" in decades. Now that Georgia was there, it gave them a great excuse to see their daughter and indulge their love of the Renaissance masters at the same time. The news smacked of a plot to whisk her back to Wellesley and enroll her in grad school (subject TK and TI—totally irrelevant) or maybe just lock her up in her childhood bedroom.

Great! she wrote back, amazed at the false enthusiasm one little exclamation point could convey. *Looking forward to it!* Then, for good measure, she added, *Keep in mind that it could still be insanely hot in September. You might want to come in October for the grape harvest. I probably won't be here, but will hook you up in Tuscany and Florence and wherever you want to go.* Though her parents had been fine on the phone, there was no telling what might happen in person. Georgia anticipated their visit as eagerly as she did a trip to the gynecologist.

Then she saw it, wedged between Daily Candy and Tasting Table NYC: Glenn Tavert, with an attachment. She took a sharp breath and clicked.

Hi Georgia,

Hope this email finds you eating pounds of pasta and drinking vats of Barolo in sunny Tuscany. Sals is great. She has become the neighborhood mascot and is best buds with everyone. We can't walk down the street without someone stopping to say hello.

Georgia paused, looking up at an ancient Spuds MacKenzie Bud Light poster tacked on the wall. Everyone knew dogs were total chick magnets—even Spuds. Sally had probably scored Glenn a dozen dates by now.

I'm doing well. Started therapy a few weeks ago. Get to talk about my favorite topic—myself—to someone who charges as much as a partner at Standish and nods a whole lot. Not a bad deal for either of us, I guess. Anyway, it seems to be working as I am being a good boy and not doing anything I shouldn't. Ha ha.

Attached is a pic of Sals at my folks out east. We've been going every weekend. The other dog is her new best friend, she just moved in to the house next door.

Email if you get a chance. Hope the friend part of our relationship can start now.

Glenn

In the photo, Sally sat on the beach with her back to the water, a cockapoo or some other hypoallergenic breed that cost a fortune by her side. Sally looked happy. Two lounge chairs draped with beach towels, a couple of magazines, and a mini-cooler were next to them. One of the towels was Glenn's—

Georgia recognized the navy-and-white Ralph Lauren stripe, which his mother bought for her beach house by the boatload. The other one obviously belonged to the poo's owner, who was decidedly female. No guy friend of Glenn's would stretch out on an orange-and-hot-pink paisley print.

Georgia deleted the entire e-mail, including the picture. Glenn knew her well enough to know she'd scrutinize it, which meant he wanted her to know he was dating the poo's owner or, at the very least, sleeping with her. This didn't make Georgia feel especially friendly toward him; it made her want to punt-kick him across Mecox Bay.

By the time she finished wading through the rest of her 457 e-mails, she had a fresh response from her father in her in-box. *Don't care about harvest,* he wrote, *care about daughter. See you in September, late September, per your advice re: insane heat.*

Georgia sunk down in her plastic chair. Glenn had a girl-friend, Sally had probably forgotten her, and Hal and Dorothy were coming to visit. Next she'd hear Sam Sifton had given Marco three stars.

Startled by a rap at the window, she turned, semi-expecting the greasy guy from last time to be staring at her with a pair of scissors in his hands. It was Effie, who pressed his nose into the smudgy glass and held a white pill bottle with a neon-yellow smiley face on its label, grinning like a junkie who'd just scored powdered Dilaudid. Georgia logged off and walked outside, palm outstretched, to join him and Vanessa.

"Please," Georgia said, "please tell me something in that bottle will cheer me up."

"Happy Days," Effie said, popping off the top of the pills. "Good for whatever ails you. It's got mega doses of herbs, algae, and every vitamin you've ever heard of. If this doesn't cheer you up, it'll—"

"Make you vomit?" Vanessa asked.

"I don't care. Just give me the bottle." Georgia pictured Glenn and his new girlfriend lubed up and lying side by side on their pricey towels, Sals and the poo sprawled next to them, all of them basking in the Bridgehampton sun. The friend part of their relationship, she thought, as she swallowed two grass-green pills with a slug of water, definitely did not start then. Not then, and not ever. She closed her eyes, willing the Happy Days to work their magic.

Trattoria Dia opened its doors to the public on the summer solstice, a bright and balmy evening without even a hint of humidity. Claudia's astrologer picked the date, claiming the alignment of the stars ensured a smash success. She was right. At half past four, groups of two, four, and the odd party of five began queuing outside the double doors for the six-o'clock seating. By five thirty, the parking lot was completely filled; by six a line of parked cars snaked past the villa, overflowing onto the road. With no advance notice to the press, a no-reservation policy, and no phone, Claudia had planned an under-the-radar open that would allow the staff to work out the kinks before the masses came. Despite her efforts, the masses came and they showed no interest in going anywhere else. They sat on the low brick wall lining the front courtyard, they gathered by the potted roses and hydrangeas, they spilled onto the grounds, over the back patio, and into the garden swilling tumblers of complimentary Chianti to ease the hour-long wait. They all wanted one thing: to eat a meal at Trattoria Dia. And when that was done, they wanted to do it all over again, but this time with a dozen of their closest friends.

From that day forward, Georgia barely had time to shave her legs, let alone worry about her parents' fall visit, Claudia and

Sergio, Gianni and the blonde, Glenn and the poo girl, or her own sorely single state. Besides, she'd come to Italy to cook, not to be consumed by what was happening in the Hamptons or rejected by guys she barely knew. So cook she did, forgetting, for a while anyway, about everything else.

Chapter Fifteen

$\mathcal{D}$id they really send dessert back?" Vanessa asked. Her face was slick with sweat, despite the red terry-cloth headband she'd taken to wearing around her forehead à la Björn Borg. It even had the little Fila *F* on it.

Georgia nodded. "I don't care who they're related to. Two bottles, one app, one entrée, plus a dessert?" She wiped her forehead with the back of her sleeve. Despite the late hour, the temperature hovered in the upper eighties, and the air in the kitchen was so thick you needed a scythe just to move from sink to stove. She was probably rocking a Jackson Five–style 'fro, frizz factor at least nine. "Who sends dessert back?"

The table in question was a twelve-person party of a certain age, several of whom were said to be distant relations of the deposed Italian monarchs. Socialites and social climbers might be snippy, thought Georgia, recalling her Marco days, but low-ranking royals were worse. The restaurant had been open for four excruciatingly busy but ultimately satisfying weeks, and until this group showed up, the number of sendbacks could be counted on one very small pinkie.

"Are they even allowed in the country these days?" she asked. "The king or prince or whoever it is?" She swiped her blade across her stone several times, then slipped it back into her knife roll.

"Yes," answered a male voice. "They are. As of a few years ago, they're allowed back in." Looking cool as a frulatte in an untucked white shirt and perfectly faded jeans, Gianni stood in the steamy kitchen. He held a bottle of *rosato* and two wine-glasses.

To Georgia, he may as well have been a mirage. The last time she'd seen him was at the friends-and-family party in June. It was now the end of July, and after what she'd heard about him and the blonde, she'd assumed there wouldn't be another time. His curls crept past his collar, but otherwise he looked exactly the same: all chiseled cheekbones, olive skin, and juicy lips. No wonder she'd wanted him.

"Hi, Gianni."

"Ciao, Georgia." He crossed the room and walked toward her. "I came to deliver my compliments to the chef. The dinner was spectacular, especially the *maiale*. Each time I eat here the food gets better." He looked at her slyly. "You really are as good as they say."

"Thanks." Feeling her face get hotter than it already was, she stared down at her clogs. "But it's really a group effort."

"Even the specials? Claudia tells me they're yours."

"The specials are, yes." Georgia would forever be indebted to Claudia for putting her in charge of specials, which attracted even more attention than the à la carte items. One day, one day very, very soon, she would create an entire menu *and* the specials.

"Then I delivered my compliments to the right person." He smiled. "Would you join me for a drink? I can fill you in on the Savoys, our answer to the Windsors."

She looked at him blankly. "The who?"

"The Italian royal family? The one you were just talking about?"

"Oh, right," she said in her best easy-breezy voice. "The Savoys. Let me finish up here and then"—she met his eyes—"I'd love to join you for a drink."

"I'll be waiting." He walked to the *melanzana* door. "Ciao, Vanessa," he called over his shoulder.

Vanessa, who'd fastidiously been cleaning her station, looked at Georgia from underneath her sweatband. "I thought you were working on being happily single these days?"

"I am. It's just a drink." And if it turned into something more, well, being single didn't mean being celibate. Banishing all thoughts of frazzled hair, sweaty skin, and bodacious blondes, she took off her apron and followed Gianni out the door and into the sultry night.

They sat at the same table where Claudia had delivered her pep talk to Georgia at the beginning of the summer. Gianni opened the bottle with a corkscrew on his key chain and poured two glasses. "To you," he said.

"Not sure why, but why not."

That night they sipped pink wine under white stars, and when they'd polished off the first bottle, he magically produced a second, which he'd stashed—in a cooler, no less—under the table.

"Guess you were pretty sure I'd join you for a drink."

"Actually," he said, uncorking the second bottle, "I was."

Halfway through, he invited her back to his place. She said yes. The last person she'd slept with was Glenn, and it was so long ago it felt as real as a cheesy sitcom dream segment. She was beyond overdue.

They walked back to the vineyard hip to hip, their shoulders and elbows occasionally meeting. His fingers grazed her leg as they climbed the stairs to his apartment, and seconds later they were entwined in a kiss that landed smack in her stomach. They stood in the hallway, kissing, and he cupped her face in his hands, then ran his fingers to the nape of her neck. He gently pushed her head forward and kissed the hollow just beneath and slightly behind her ear, instinctively zeroing in on her most sensitive spot. Her skin tingled, and she clenched her shoulder blades together.

"Finally," she murmured, her eyes half lidded, her lips turned into a lazy smile.

Then, without any warning, he stopped. Just like that, Gianni stopped kissing her.

Her eyes sprang open. "Gianni? Is everything okay?"

"I'm sorry, Georgia, but I don't think this is a good idea."

"You what?"

"It's not you, Georgia. I like you and I want to get to know you. But not like this." He bowed his head. "Please forgive me."

"Sure, Gianni. But it's okay, really. I *want* to do this." Was she begging the Italian Stallion to take her to bed? Because it sure sounded as if she was.

"I don't want it to be this way. Not with you." He held out his hand. "Come. Let me take you home."

Throwing herself out there—out of desperation or desire, it didn't matter which—and getting flat-out rejected was more mortification than she could handle. Without a word, she turned and walked out the door and down the stairs. Maybe, she thought, as she headed to the villa, it really wasn't her. Maybe he'd suddenly remembered he'd run out of condoms. Or Viagra. Or maybe he was having a herpes flare-up. Then again, maybe it *was* her. She walked faster.

Gianni followed behind, shouting for her to slow down, finally catching up when she reached the villa's back door. "Please don't be mad at me," he said breathlessly.

She spun around to face him, but before she could say anything, he reached out and touched her cheek. "You're beautiful,
Georgia. Even when you're mad, you're still beautiful."

"That's great, Gianni. Thanks. But if you don't mind, I think
I'll go inside now."

"Will you listen for one minute? You left so quickly I couldn't
explain."

"No explanation necessary. Good-bye, Gianni." She turned
back to the door.

"Come to Sicily with me," he blurted.

"What?"

"In two weeks, for Ferragosto, one of our biggest holidays. I
have business to do in Bologna and Milano, but then I am going
to Taormina, to the Palazzo Lazzaro, my most important client.
It's so romantic you can't imagine. The beach, a suite in the best
hotel in Sicily. A nice restaurant. Or better yet, room service.
Taormina in August is *perfetto*." He clutched his hands together
in mock prayer. "Come with me."

"You're crazy, Gianni. One minute you want me, the next you
don't, now you do again."

"No." He put his finger on her lips. "I've wanted you since
that day we met, even with that ugly hat on your head. But I
want it to be right."

He looked so genuinely earnest—and so insanely gorgeous—
there was no way to not consider his offer. Plus, he'd invited her
to Sicily. Sicily! Then there was the weekend Claudia owed her,
and the lack of anyone to share it with. Which led to her third
rationalization: if not Gianni, then who? There wasn't exactly
a cast of thousands (or even one) waiting in the wings. And
though it made her feel like an eighteen-year-old boy on spring
break in Cancún, there was the sex. She could have sex in Sicily.

"Okay," she said slowly. "You're on."

■ ■ ■

"Are you sure that's a good idea?" Vanessa asked. "Going away with Gianni?"

Georgia and Vanessa sat on the patio drinking glasses of icy *limonata* laced with fresh mint, relishing their only break of the day. The air was hot and heavy with humidity; swollen clouds hung, unmoving, in the gray sky above. Dinner rush would hit shortly, and neither Vanessa nor Georgia nor anyone else on the Dia staff would rest until the last customers walked out the door, their bloated bellies hanging over their belts, pledging their imminent return. The summer had seen a stretch of near flawless weather, and that, combined with near flawless reviews, meant a jam-packed restaurant each and every night. The crew was exhausted; rain was just what they needed.

"No," Georgia answered, "I'm not at all sure it's a good idea. But I'm going anyway."

"But you hardly know him! What if he's a series killer? And what about that blonde?"

"He's not a serial killer, Vanessa. A womanizer, yes. But a murderer? No way. And she's his cousin."

"Sure she is." Vanessa put down her glass and stretched her fingers to the splotchy sky. "As long as you know what you're doing."

"I'm giving it a chance. Isn't that what I'm supposed to do? Isn't that what we're all supposed to do?"

Fat raindrops began to fall, leaving leopard-print spots on the slate patio. Neither girl flinched.

"I guess so," Vanessa said finally, not sounding entirely convinced.

With a single clap of thunder, the sky broke open and an avalanche of water tumbled out, instantly drenching them both. Shrieking, they jumped from their seats and ran to the *melanzana* door, which was locked. They pummeled it with their palms, shouting for someone to open it.

Effie peered out at them through the window next to the door. "Oh, hi, guys. Did you want to come in?"

"Effie, open the door now!" Vanessa yelled.

Effie fumbled with the lock. "Whoops. Having some difficulty here, girls, stay with me."

"Open it now!" Georgia shouted as Effie pulled open the door.

Georgia and Vanessa jumped into the vestibule, laughing as water pooled at their feet.

"Is it raining? You guys look a little wet." Effie tossed them two dish towels.

"You," said Vanessa, "are a dead man, Effie."

That night it rained so much a flood warning was issued and drivers were advised to stay off the roads. Trattoria Dia shuttered its doors at 11:07 p.m., the first time in the restaurant's brief but bustling history it had closed before midnight. The staff celebrated by going to sleep.

For the next two weeks, Georgia tried to focus on work and nothing else—not on Gianni, who was away on business, and whose kiss she could still sort of feel when she closed her eyes and imagined his delicious, red lips, and not on their upcoming trip to one of the most romantic places in the world, where what she'd been hoping would happen since the friends-and-family party would almost definitely happen. Fortunately for her, the restaurant was jumping all day long, leaving little time for daydreaming or anything else.

At last, the eve of their departure arrived. Georgia packed her bag, did a homemade avocado hair mask in a futile attempt to tame her frizz, and fell into bed, where she promptly passed out. The next morning, she and Gianni sat in seats 3a and 3b, respectively, on Alitalia flight number 4144, final destination Taormina.

"Nice seats," Georgia said as the stewardess ushered them to their Magnifica-class seats. "They even come with choice of water." Georgia pointed to the small bottles of sparkling and flat waters tucked into the roomy armrests between seats.

"You deserve the best." Gianni placed his black Prada duffel bag into the overhead bin. "Is this yours?" he asked, pointing to the L.L. Bean tote sitting on the seat.

"Yes. My grandmother gave it to me."

He swung it into the bin next to his own bag.

Fifteen minutes into the flight, Georgia realized how difficult it was traveling with someone she barely knew and with whom, she was discovering, she had little in common. Once the industry chatter dried up (no, she didn't know Padma Lakshmi; no, she didn't know Gordon Ramsay; and, no, she hadn't been on *Iron Chef*), silence descended. Until she made the mistake of asking how he'd got into wine. Launching into a seventy-five-minute monologue that might as well have been entitled "Gianni: The Man and His Wine," he proceeded to lecture her on seemingly everything he'd learned about grapes including what, when, where, and sometimes why. At least she liked wine.

Despite the cloudless skies, unlimited Pellegrino, and the tastiest chocolate truffles she'd ever bit into, the flight was a bit of a letdown. If she'd followed her gut, she'd be nibbling gnocchi—alone—in Maremma. Instead, she'd got spooked by spinsterhood and seduced by Sicily and was now on a weekend jaunt with a womanizing wine wonk. She checked her watch: forty-seven hours to prove she'd made the right choice. Or not.

■ ■ ■

As Gianni promised, the hotel was magnificent. An eighteenth-century palace that was now an opulent five-star hotel, the Palazzo Lazzaro was the perfect place for an indulgent, romantic weekend. Georgia toured the junior suite, a sumptuously appointed bedroom, spacious sitting room, and an even larger bathroom, while Gianni unpacked his bag. A bellboy delivered a complimentary bottle of bubbly from the hotel's general manager, and Gianni pressed a twenty into his palm.

"Prosecco?" he sniffed, rolling the bottle in his hand. He put it back in the wine cooler.

Georgia kicked off her shoes and stretched out on the king-size bed. "I could get used to this," she said, clicking on the plasma TV.

"You should." He climbed on top of her and took the remote out of her hand, turning off the TV and turning on some ambient music with a few clicks. "Isn't it romantic?" he whispered. "You, me, Sicily. I've been dreaming about this since you agreed to come with me." He leaned down and kissed her forehead, her cheeks, her lips.

Georgia murmured something unintelligible and Gianni began unbuttoning her top, running his hands across her breasts, expertly unhooking her bra. She swept her hands under his shirt and ran them up his sides, pushing up the shirt and pulling it over his head.

The phone rang—a loud, old-fashioned *brrrring*. They stared at each other, amazed at the audacity of that ring. *"Merda,"* he said, climbing off her.

Georgia propped herself up on her elbows. "Don't get it."

On the third ring, Gianni's cell phone joined the booty-busting brigade. Scowling, he grabbed the hotel phone, almost jerking it off the night table.

Though she could only hear one side of the conversation,

she got the gist. They were due at dinner, downstairs, thirty minutes ago. Twenty minutes late was accepted practice in Italy, but thirty was pushing it.

Gianni hung up the phone and turned to her. "I am so sorry, Georgia, but we must go."

"Now?"

"Now. My clients are waiting for us and we are already late." He ran his fingertips over her neck, kissing the hollow of her throat. "I promise I'll make it up to you." Still wearing his jeans, he climbed out of bed and walked to the bathroom.

"I'll hold you to that!" she called after him.

"Over here, Gianni," a round man with stumpy arms and a wobbly double chin called as they entered the Lazzaro's fine-dining restaurant.

Gianni steered Georgia to the corner table where two men in sport coats and open-collared shirts sat. A burgundy carpet with gold fleurs-de-lis covered the floor, and an ornate chandelier dripping with crystals hung from the ceiling. Waiters in white dinner jackets circulated with silver-plated serving trays. One of the men stood as they approached the table, and he and Gianni kissed on both cheeks. He pulled back a clunky gold chair and gestured for Georgia to sit.

"You must be Georgia. Please, sit. I am Luigi Monserno, general manager of the Palazzo Lazzaro." Luigi had tiny eyes and sandy brown hair that he wore in a comb-over. He introduced Georgia to Mervi, his assistant, who carried a yellow legal pad and jotted notes while his boss spoke. "We hear that Claudia Cavalli brought you all the way from New York to open Trattoria Dia."

"Something like that," Georgia answered.

"You must be a great chef."

She smiled. "Well—"

"She's the best," Gianni interjected. He threw his arm around her shoulder and drew her into his chest. "Truly the best."

"How do you like Italy?" Luigi asked.

"Amazing food, wine, countryside, people, what's not to like?"

Luigi chuckled. "Good to hear."

"And this is a lovely hotel, Luigi."

"I'm glad you think so, that's important."

"It is?"

"Would you like some wine, Georgia?" Gianni picked up an empty bottle, which stood next to a carafe filled with red wine. "A 1990 Solaia. From your private cellar, Luigi?"

Luigi nodded, and Gianni filled Georgia's glass and then his own. "Now this is wine," Gianni said. "An Antinori masterpiece. Hints of mint, berry, a touch of lead pencil." He stuck his nose in the glass and inhaled deeply.

"Why don't we get right to the point, Georgia," Luigi said. "Otherwise our friend Gianni will bore us with his wine wisdom all night."

"Sure," she said. "What point is that?"

"We'd like to hire you as our head chef here at the Palazzo Lazzaro."

"You would?" She looked at Gianni, who was studiously chewing his wine. "Why?"

Luigi gestured to the half-full dining room. "We were once not only the finest hotel in Sicily, but the finest restaurant in the region. Now, as you can see, people go elsewhere."

"Right, but—"

"With a new chef, one with your skills and talent, we could again be the best restaurant in all of Sicily. And opening Trattoria Dia gives you the experience, the credibility, the name to run an Italian restaurant. The publicity alone—"

"It's perfect for you," Gianni interrupted. He'd finally swallowed his first taste.

"How are you involved with this, Gianni?" She sipped the wine. "Wow. This really is delicious."

"I'm partnering with Luigi and an investment group to buy out the hotel. As an owner I'll be here all the time. We'll be able to be together. Plus, I know you are an amazing chef. I have tasted your specials, remember?" He winked.

Luigi laughed. "Sounds like you're more interested in the chef than the restaurant, Gianni."

Georgia's face burned behind her wineglass and she tried not to smile.

"Tell her what you're offering," the assistant said. It was the first time he'd opened his mouth all evening.

"Money, of course. An apartment here in the hotel. Carte blanche with the menu—you won't even have to think about food costs. A staff of your choosing. A complete renovation of the dining room and the kitchen, under your direction. However, all this will take time, which is why we ask for a two-year commitment."

Composing her thoughts, Georgia took another sip of wine. "This is a very attractive offer, Luigi. It's extremely generous and extremely flattering, but it would be a huge move for me. I'll really need to think about it."

"Of course. Take as much time as you need."

"Thank you for understanding. And since Gianni and I just arrived, I'm a little tired. I'm afraid I won't be the best dinner companion. How about sending up a bottle of wine, maybe one of these"—she pointed to the carafe—"and a plate of something to nibble to our suite?"

"Of course." Luigi summoned a waiter.

Georgia stood and the three men followed suit. "Shall we, Gianni?"

He sucked the last drop of wine from his glass and they left the restaurant. "I can't believe you got Luigi to part with another Solaia," he said under his breath. "You really are amazing." They stepped onto the elevator, and when the doors closed, he picked up her hands. "Are you really not sure about the job or are you playing hard to catch? It's a great offer, Georgia."

"It is a great offer. But I wasn't planning on staying in Italy after opening Dia, and definitely not for two years . . ." Her voice trailed off. "I'm not sure what to do."

When they reached their suite, a room service cart holding bottles of wine and water and several covered dishes was parked in the sitting room. The breakfast table had been set with silver, napkins, glasses, even a pair of candles.

"Luigi sure works fast," said Georgia.

"So do I." In one motion Gianni swooped her up, carried her into the bedroom, and dropped her onto the bed. Before she could open her eyes, he'd removed all her clothing and was wriggling out of his own. He kicked off his black briefs and climbed on top of her, running his hands down the length of her body. He stopped for a second to put on a condom, then rolled back on top of her.

"You're so beautiful, Georgia," he said, attempting to run his fingers through her hair. He gave up and began smoothing it instead.

Georgia closed her eyes and smiled dreamily. "And you, Gianni, are well worth the wait."

He kissed her eyelids and began working his way down with his mouth, first her chin, then the hollow of her throat, her breasts, the swell of her belly. She pulled him up to her lips and they kissed, long and hard, before he slid back down. Finally, it was going to happen: no more minds changed, no phone calls, no interruptions of any sort, just pure, unadulterated sex with a gorgeous Italian who clearly knew his way around a king-size bed. Georgia wrapped her fingers in his curls, sighing happily. She closed her eyes and concentrated on what his skin felt like, what his lips felt like, what his body felt like pressing into hers. Then she thought about what she felt like, then she stopped thinking altogether.

Afterward, Gianni fell on top of her, kissed her lips, and flopped back on his pillow. "That was amazing."

"It was," she said, her eyes still closed.

"And you are incredible," he mumbled, kissing her hair.

"You are too." She nestled into the crook of his arm. "But you definitely don't work fast."

"And that is a good thing?"

"A very good thing."

Thirty seconds later he was snoring. Too excited to sleep, Georgia extracted herself from his grasp and walked into the bathroom, trying to stifle the silly grin on her face. She'd done it. She'd had sex with someone who wasn't Glenn. It had been even better than she'd hoped, without a glimmer of the awkwardness she'd feared. She sat down on the toilet and forced out a splash of pee—there was no way she'd risk a urinary tract infection after sex like that.

She wrapped herself in the Pratesi robe hanging on the door and moved to the sitting room, where she sipped wine, ate caponata and arancini, and laughed out loud while watching a *Saturday Night Live* rerun, which was much funnier in dubbed Italian. By the time she slipped under the covers next to her still-snoring bedmate, she'd decided that eating, drinking, and laughing—alone—in a luxurious Sicilian hotel room after having terrific sex with a gorgeous Italian wine geek was not the worst way to pass an evening. Whether it was the best way to pass two years of evenings, she wasn't so sure.

Limpid water lapped at her legs, and Georgia wriggled her toes in the silky sand beneath her feet. If she squinted hard enough, she swore she could make out the African coast shimmering in the distance—Tunisia? Algeria? She swished her hands through the water, startling a school of yellow fish who darted past her knee. A cerulean sky loomed above her, a blanket of white-sand beach stretched behind her. The scene had all the trappings of a Harlequin novel: the exotic Sicilian locale, the deserted beach, the bikini-clad heroine. All that was missing was the hunky stud who would stride out of the water Fabio-style, pecs rippling, long hair cascading down his back.

Instead, Mervi, his face smeared with sunscreen, a straw hat pulled low over his ears, sat perched on an oversize towel, his zinc-coated nose stuck in a self-help book. Since Gianni and Luigi had a meeting with the hotel investment group, Luigi had offered Georgia Mervi's chauffeuring services. He suggested an outing to the Vendicari Nature Preserve, an unspoiled stretch of coastline a few hours away, and she was soon riding shotgun in a lime-green Smart car emblazoned with the hotel's logo. The spellbinding scenery—olive and orange groves, craggy coast, lush greenery—had more than made up for the less-than-luxe ride.

"So, Georgia," Mervi said, walking up behind her, "are you seriously considering this job offer?"

"I am. I'd be crazy not to, don't you think?"

He shrugged.

"The chance to create an amazing restaurant, plenty of money, an apartment—"

"With maid service," he threw in.

"With maid service," she repeated. "How could I *not* seriously consider it?" In addition to all the perks Luigi had mentioned, there was also the chance to check out of her New York life and check into beautiful, tranquil Taormina. Throw in a sexy winery owner who rocked in bed, and the offer was almost too good to refuse. Except for one thing: she *liked* her New York life. Not all of it, but big, substantial chunks of it—Central Park, her friends, sushi, poppy seed bagels, the *New York Times,* Sunday-afternoon shopping trips, supersize iced coffees . . . and Sally, sweet, sweet Sally. The obvious thing missing from the picture was the gorgeous guy. But she'd been around long enough to know that not all summer romances translated into lasting relationships. Sometimes a fling was just meant to be a fling—fun and carefree and fleeting.

Mervi dangled his foot in the water. "It's freezing. I'm not going in." He returned to his towel and his book, smearing extra sunscreen across his bald chest.

Georgia took a few steps forward so that the water barely covered her knees. Grammy would scoff at her tentativeness. She used to dive into Silver Lake's icy waters—chilly even at the tail end of August—without so much as dipping in a toe first. Good for the heart, she'd say as she emerged from the lake, her torpedoed bosom leading the way, her chartreuse skirt-suit circling her thighs.

Even after Grampy's early death forced her into single motherhood, Grammy never lost her zest for life. As she told it, she could have remarried in a heartbeat. There'd been plenty of suitors—including the town doctor—but that would have been the easy way. Instead she devoted herself to building her bakery from scratch, working seven days a week so she could provide for Dorothy, her only child. By the time Georgia was born she was ready to throw in her rolling pin. She'd missed out on raising Dorothy, but in Georgia she saw her second chance, and she was determined not to miss a thing. If you want to be happy, Grammy always said, stay true to yourself and work hard enough so that you never have to ask what-if.

A batch of wispy clouds passed over the sun, and Georgia felt goose bumps rise on her arms. The ocean and the sky were almost the same color, and she stared at the horizon trying to determine where they met. Her future was out there somewhere. She reached her hands overhead, clapped her palms together, and dove headfirst into the salty sea.

Georgia slid the key card through the lock and pushed open the hotel room door. "Gianni? Hello?"

The only sound was the hum of the air conditioner, which she swore she'd shut off before leaving for Vendicari that morning. Mother Earth did not approve of running the AC all day, especially when no one was home, so she turned it off to make up for wasted energy. She kicked off her sandals and flopped onto the bed, noticing a tiny vase of white freesia propping up a cream-colored envelope on the night table. The envelope was addressed to *Signora Giorgia Grigio,* her name translated into Italian, which sounded much prettier to her American ears.

"Dear Georgia," she read aloud. "I will be back at five to take you to my friend's winery. Dress is relaxed. Until then, Gianni."

Leaning back into the pillows, she tried to envision her life as the head chef at the Palazzo Lazzaro and the girlfriend of the hotel's owner—because there was no way Gianni would have her as one and not the other. In the early stages, when she was first settling in, she could imagine a succession of dinners and winery visits and alfresco lunches and nonstop sex. Then later, when they moved from planning to execution, she'd start working around the clock and he'd start wondering what happened to the up-for-anything girl who used to jump him every chance she got and who now dropped like a brick the second she got to bed. Which begged a bigger question: Did she want to dedicate two years of her life to opening someone else's restaurant? Or did she want to go back to New York and do it for herself?

A quick glance at the clock cut short her introspection. She'd have just enough time to rinse off and choose her best "relaxed" outfit, which she interpreted as a sundress and sandals. She stepped out of her clothes and into the shower, wondering if providing a dress code was a Gianni thing or an Italian thing—and thinking probably a bit of both.

The sun pushed down from above, relentless even in the early evening. Mount Etna, snowcapped and mammoth, loomed in the background. Every once in a while, a hot wind rustled the vines, a reminder of the legendary *scirocco* that blew into Sicily from the Sahara, bringing with it swirls of dust and sand. Georgia and Gianni walked down a row of vines plump with purple grapes. Her brow was damp with sweat, and her hair, shellacked with product, was scraped back in a bun—the frizz factor in these conditions was off the charts.

"Isn't this place amazing?" Gianni said.

"It is." The drive from Taormina alone—through sunbaked hills, chestnut groves, the remains of a centuries-old town carved from lava—was worth the trip to Gianni's friend's winery, which sprawled across the southern slope of the volcano.

"And so are you." He leaned over and kissed her lips.

She smiled. Cheesy lines rolled off his tongue so effortlessly they were actually somewhat charming. With anyone else, she wouldn't be so charitable.

Gianni plucked a grape from a vine and crushed it between his thumb and forefinger. "See this?" He showed her the smashed flesh. "It's Nerello Mascalese, native to Etna. It's almost ready to be picked. *La vendemmia* will begin soon."

The Italian wine harvest kicked off in Sicily, then continued up the boot, hitting Puglia, Campania, and Tuscany, among other regions, not stopping until it passed through Veneto, Piedmont, and Trentino–Alto Adige, Italy's northernmost wine-producing province. Celebrations honoring the mighty grape abounded during the harvest, and it was nearly impossible not to run across a festival somewhere.

"Next year, we'll come here for *la vendemmia*. After the first day of picking, everyone goes back to the cantina and we eat a huge feast and have a great party. The real work doesn't begin until the next day . . . when we're back at the Lazzaro." He sucked the grape into his mouth and licked the juice from his fingers. "What do you think?"

An image of Lucille Ball, barefoot and stomping grapes at an Italian vineyard, popped into Georgia's head. Grammy had adored *I Love Lucy,* and Georgia remembered watching that hilarious episode in Grammy's den. She laughed out loud.

"Can I take that as a yes?"

"I was just remembering a funny TV show I used to watch with my grandmother."

He studied her for a moment, looking peeved with her non-answer before offering his hand. "Come, let's go have a drink."

They walked toward the main house, crunching over dirt so rocky and dry it was a wonder anything grew there at all. The rose-hued villa was designed in the baroque style, complete with Juliet balconies, arched windows, and heavy wooden doors. A double staircase, perfect for making dramatic exits, led to a terrace overlooking the vineyard.

They followed a winding path to a patio nestled against the side of the house. A pergola blanketed with violet bougainvillea ran overhead, and a couple of café tables and chairs offered respite from the sun. A wet bar with a fridge and small cooktop was tucked into the corner next to an arched door.

"My friend Ilario said to make ourselves comfortable." Gianni opened the fridge and pulled out bottles of sparkling water and white wine. "It's too hot for red, so let's have a glass of this." He looked at the bottle and frowned. "Not my favorite, but don't tell Ilario."

While he poured the wine, Georgia poked around the fridge, finding a wedge of pecorino siciliano, a package of crackers, and a jar of fat, green olives, an impromptu antipasto plate. She arranged the food on a cutting board sitting next to the sink and set it on the table.

"A toast," Gianni said, holding up his glass. "To you."

"And to you. I can't thank you enough for bringing me here. I've seen so much of Sicily I feel like I've been here for three nights instead of one. I just wish we didn't have to leave tomorrow."

"You'll be back, Georgia. As soon as you finish up at Dia, you'll be back at the Lazzaro." There wasn't a trace of doubt in his voice.

She cut a piece of cheese and put it on a cracker, which was cold from the fridge. "I don't know, Gianni. I've been doing some thinking—"

"Don't." He leaned across the table and rested his finger on her lips. "Don't say anything now unless it is yes. Otherwise, don't think about anything until we're back in San Casciano. We have this whole place to ourselves tonight. Let's make the most of it."

He was right. There'd be plenty of time to think about things the next day, or the next, or even the next. It was her last night in Sicily and she was with an amazing guy in a magical place and she wasn't about to screw it up by *thinking*. "Okay."

"Now," he said, rising from the table, "would you like to see the tasting room?"

"I would love to see the tasting room." She took his hand and they walked into the house.

The last of Dia's customers were still straggling out of the restaurant when Georgia and Gianni pulled up to the villa sometime after midnight. After a whirlwind weekend and a full day of traveling, the only thing Georgia wanted to do was crawl into bed and stay there for a week—and if Gianni wanted to join her, all the better. But since he was jetting off to spend the rest of Ferragosto with his family in Puglia, and her presence was required at the Dia kitchen first thing in the morning, the most she could hope for was a solid six hours . . . alone.

"So when do you get back?" Georgia asked.

"In a week." He ran the back of his hand down her cheek. "I wish you could come with me."

"Bruno would kill me. And if he didn't, Effie would. But it does sound nice."

"As nice as moving to Taormina?"

"Gianni," she began, but he rested his finger on her lips to stop her.

"When I get back," he said.

She nodded. "Thank you for a wonderful weekend."

"Thank you for being a wonderful woman."

They kissed good-bye, and she grabbed her tote bag from the backseat and walked into the villa.

Chapter Sixteen

Chien wiggled his rump in greeting as Georgia entered the Dia dining room, and she knelt down to give him a scratch. As the de facto mascot, Chien roamed the restaurant premises like a king patrolling his castle. In New York, a dog in the kitchen was a surefire route to a nasty health-code violation and a guaranteed shutdown. In San Casciano, the health inspector handed Chien scraps of his veal chop under the table while polishing off his third glass of Barolo, compliments of the house.

Bursts of laughter sounded from the kitchen, which could only mean that Claudia was back. Like every other Italian, she celebrated Ferragosto by going on holiday, though hers had been shorter than the typical two weeks. She'd left Bruno in charge, which had been fine with Georgia.

She walked into the kitchen, where Bruno, Tonio, and a bunch of the newer staff members were huddled around Claudia, who read aloud from a magazine splayed on the kitchen table. She said something Georgia couldn't decipher, and the group responded with a smattering of applause.

"Hi, Claudia!" Georgia called.

Claudia looked up and grinned. Her cheeks were flushed, her eyes bright. In the last few days she'd sprouted a minibump, and it protruded slightly from underneath her swingy black shirt. "Georgia!" she said. "Come listen to this."

"What is it?" Georgia asked, Chien at her heels. After Claudia, Georgia was his favorite person. And with Sally an ocean away, he offered the doggy love she craved.

"*Taste* magazine," she said happily. "The story's running in the current issue. They sent us these." She pointed to a stack of magazines in front of the fridge.

Georgia picked one up and began flipping through it. "Page?"

"One hundred eleven," Bruno answered. "But check the cover first."

She closed the magazine and held it at arm's length. A collage of images from Tuscany and beyond graced the cover of the all-Italian issue. In the top left quadrant a pine farmhouse table was laid out with a single place setting and a smorgasbord of Dia's best (and most photogenic) dishes. "The Little Trattoria That Could," read the cover line.

"Wow," Georgia said. A lovely plate of sole e luna, which didn't exist when the cover was shot, had been Photoshopped into the picture and sat smack in the middle of the table. "This looks beautiful."

The story was reported and filed before Dia had opened its doors, so long ago that everyone had almost forgotten about it. Its publishing date was timed to coincide with Tuscany's official high season, which had hit. San Casciano, along with every other town that boasted at least one church and one café, was abuzz with tourists. Even without a gushing *Taste* cover story, Dia was a tough reservation. Now, scoring a table would be like scoring tickets for the next unannounced Stones show at the Beacon Theater.

Georgia pored over the magazine's slick pages, her lips moving as she read, barely breathing until she was done. Claudia was depicted as the sexy-but-saintly gourmand who was single-handedly revolutionizing Tuscan cuisine, an Italian Alice Waters with a sprinkling of Gina Lollobrigida and a dash of Mother Teresa. The recipe for sole e luna, reworked for home cooks, was featured in a sidebar under the heading "The Dish That Doesn't Miss." American sous-chef Georgia Gray, cocreator of Dia's dish, merited one full sentence and one artfully blurred photo.

Georgia giggled at the image of herself traversing the kitchen holding a platter of painstakingly arranged vegetables. At least an hour had gone into choosing those veggies and then arranging, spraying, and rearranging them in all their unblemished beauty. Aside from her hair, which the shoot stylist insisted she wear down, Georgia was virtually unrecognizable. But her friends back home would know her 'do anywhere.

Exhaling loudly, she closed the magazine and said a silent thank-you to Ganesh. That one little sentence, along with the recipe credit, would help to erase the Marco debacle from the culinary world's collective memory. Everyone knew a chef was only as good as her last review. Though not exactly a review, and not exactly about Georgia, it was close enough.

"This is amazing," Georgia said. "Really amazing."

"Way to go, boss," Bruno said. Only he, Claudia, and Georgia remained in the kitchen; the others had streamed out clutching magazines, jabbering into their cell phones in rapid-fire Italian.

"Way to go is right," Georgia said. "Congratulations, Claudia. I can't think of anyone who deserves this more than you."

"What about you two? I couldn't have done it without you. Without any of you, but you two especially." She took their hands in hers and squeezed.

"I should go find Elena. She's going to be very excited about this." Bruno wiggled his eyebrows lasciviously. "There's no telling what might happen."

Claudia laughed. "As long as you're in the kitchen this afternoon, I don't care what you do." She walked over to the massive fridge and rolled open the freezer, rummaging around before selecting a nondescript white container.

"I think I'll look for Effie and Vanessa," Georgia said, falling into step behind Bruno.

"Actually, Georgia, if you don't mind sticking around, I'd like to talk to you." She set the container on the counter and pulled a demitasse spoon from a drawer.

"Sure."

As the squeak of Bruno's rubber clogs receded down the hallway, Claudia turned to her protégé. "Gelato? Sergio brings it to me from Vivoli. *Stracciatella,* my favorite. I'm afraid it's true what they say about pregnancy and gelato."

"No, thanks. Maybe later."

Claudia held up the miniature spoon. "I fool myself into believing that if I use a small spoon, I won't eat as much. Of course, it doesn't work, but who am I to point that out to myself?"

Georgia laughed.

"So how was Sicily?"

"Sicily was great. It's so beautiful. The bougainvillea, the citrus trees, the ocean, that air—it's the perfect mix of salty and sweet."

"And Gianni?"

"He's good," Georgia said vaguely. "How was your holiday? And how's everything with the baby?"

"Our holiday was great. Too short, of course. And the baby is wonderful. I'm convinced it's a girl. All my dreams are pink: pink frosting on cake, pink tulips, a pink lawn mower! We did a sonogram and saw her fingers and her toes. Sergio almost passed out." Her shoulders shook with laughter. "Men can be such big babies."

"Do you mind if I ask you something, Claudia?"

"Anything."

"In the beginning of the summer, you told me you didn't need a child or a husband, that the restaurants were your babies. What made you change your mind?"

"The restaurants are my babies. And when I didn't think I could have one of my own, they were enough. But when I least expected it, life intervened."

"What do you mean?"

"I gave up hope, accepted that I wasn't meant to be a mother, really accepted it, and I moved forward with my own life." Claudia shrugged. "At forty-two, what choice did I have? And then when I wasn't even paying attention, somewhere between the plaster walls peeling and the HVAC system crashing, I realized I was late. Very late."

Georgia had heard this sometimes happened with women who'd given up on fertility drugs and resigned themselves to child-free lives. They'd stop shooting the hormones and start craving pickles and bacon and milk shakes—all at the same time.

"I also realized how badly I wanted a baby. How happy I am to have the chance to become a mother. And how happy I am to do it with Sergio." She raised a perfectly shaped eyebrow. "As cooks we can always depend on our *mise en place*. Our *mise* is neat, ordered, constant. But life isn't neat and it isn't ordered. It moves and shifts and *changes*. And just when we think we have everything in its place, it moves again. Sometimes in ways we understand, sometimes in ways we don't." She shrugged. "But we trust anyway."

A chef's *mise*—all the herbs, oils, fine dices, towels, and anything else she might need to cook her way through a shift in a professional kitchen—was at her fingertips, shift after shift, night after night. It was reliable, steadfast. Life, as Claudia said, was not. Just when you thought you had everything figured out, just when everything seemed to be in its place, something came along and turned it upside down and you had to start all over again. Sometimes it was unpleasant. And sometimes it was wonderful.

"To tell you the truth," Claudia continued, "I would be fine without getting married. But Sergio, he's more traditional. He thinks she deserves married parents. So I'll do it for him . . . and for her too. Or him—there I go again!" She wagged a finger at herself.

The scent of lemon, fresh, clean, and faint when Georgia had first entered the kitchen, had grown stronger as they spoke, and it now filled the room. Georgia walked to the oven, flipped on the light, and peered through the glass door. A golden cake ballooned from a circle pan.

"Delizia di Sorrento," Claudia said. "I make it with Meyer lemons and eat it like it's bread. Another craving." She turned to Georgia. "Now it's my turn to ask a question."

"Okay."

"I hear you're considering working at the Palazzo Lazzaro with Gianni."

"I am, sort of, I guess. Okay, yes, I'm considering it. It's an incredible offer. Money, prestige, a fabulous location, a not-at-all-bad-looking guy . . . I'd be a fool not to consider it."

"Sounds *fantastico,* Georgia. It really does. But is it what you want?" Claudia held her hand to her heart. "Is it what you want here?"

Georgia placed her hands on the counter and stared at

them; the ruddy skin, slightly crepey from constant washings, the short, unpolished nails. A faint scar snaked its way around her index finger, a souvenir from her first knife-skills class at the Culinary Institute. Working-girl hands, Glenn had called them, right before slipping that sparkling ring onto her finger. Grammy's hands, she thought, clasping them together. She had her grandmother's hair and her grandmother's hands.

"I want my own restaurant. That's what I want." Though Georgia had been saying these words for years, it was the first time she believed she would make it happen. The job offer at the Palazzo Lazzaro, with all its glittering accompaniments, had given her confidence the final boost it needed. If she was good enough to run Gianni's restaurant, she was good enough to run her own. Opening her own restaurant, in her own city, was what she needed to do for herself and for her life before she could share it with anyone else.

Claudia grabbed a pair of pot holders from a hook on the wall and slid the cake from the oven. "It almost smells better than it tastes." She placed it on the stovetop, leaning over to inhale its aroma, a satisfied smile on her face.

She looked up at Georgia. "You'll have that restaurant if you want it badly enough. You have the skills, you have the creativity, and if you really want it here"—Claudia touched her heart again—"and here"—she touched her head—"you'll find the discipline to make it happen. It won't be easy. Nothing worthwhile ever is. But you can make it work."

"I know I can. I'm not sure how, but I'll figure it out." Georgia walked to the cutlery drawer and pulled out a spoon. "I think I'll have some of that gelato now."

Claudia handed her the container, which had been sitting out on the counter and was filled with slushy vanilla gelato laced with dark-chocolate shavings. Georgia dipped the spoon, not a demitasse, but a tablespoon, into the ice cream, a smile spreading across her face as she took her first bite. It was worth it.

"Ciao, bella!" Wearing jeans, a checked shirt, and those black Adidas soccer shoes all the cool guys had worn in high school, Gianni strolled across the field to meet Georgia, who waited for him by the abandoned well halfway between Dia and his winery. It was the exact spot where she'd first noticed him, and like then, he had a cell phone attached to his ear. Also like then, he looked amazing.

She wished she could say the same about herself. Patting the back of her head where her hair was gathered in a sloppy bun that felt suspiciously like a robin's nest intertwined with cotton balls, she realized that a quick glance in the mirror before dashing out of the restaurant would have been a wise idea. But she had only a sliver of time between dinner prep and the start of her shift, and she knew if she put off saying what she had to say, she could very well end up not saying it at all. Messy hair it was.

"Ciao, Gianni," she said as he walked up. She went to kiss his cheek, but he turned her face to his and, cupping it in his hands, kissed her lips. Then he did it again. She kissed him back, a flicker of doubt jolting through her. Was she out of her mind? A part of her said yes, but it was the part she wasn't supposed to listen to.

"How was Puglia?" she asked. "And your family?"

"It was great, but I missed you. My mama can't wait to meet you. It's all she talked about." He grinned. "So, I guess you have something important to tell me." He wiggled his eyebrows as her belly slowly sank. Despite their conversation in Sicily, he had no idea what was coming.

"I do have something important to tell you. Very important."

She cleared her throat. "It's really hard for me to say this, and I hate when people say that, but it's true. So I'm just going to say it."

His grin disappeared.

"I can't accept the job at the Lazzaro. When I finish at Dia, I'm going back to New York to open my own restaurant."

Crossing his arms across his chest, he stared first at the ground, then off in the distance where a brood of hens pecked at the dirt for worms. When he finally looked at her, it wasn't sadness or hurt or disappointment that she saw. It was anger.

"That is a mistake, Georgia. A big mistake."

"I—"

"We are offering you the opportunity of your life. You will not find a better situation ever. If you aren't able to see that, then you don't deserve to work at the Lazzaro."

"I do see that, Gianni, and I really appreciate all that you're offering. I do. But I don't want another job. I want my own restaurant."

"Your own restaurant? Why? So you can be one more chef feeding your own, big ego? Isn't that—how do you call it—a cliché?"

She swallowed. "I don't think I'm a cliché. I want to do something—"

"And what makes you think you're qualified to run your own restaurant? Do you know how hard it is? Do you know how many fail?"

"Of course I do, Gianni. But I believe in myself. And other people do too. People like Claudia. And people like you." She reached out for his hand, but he snatched it away.

"I'm not so sure I do anymore." He stared at her for a second before pulling his shades from his chest pocket and sliding them on. He opened his mouth as if to say something, then closed it and walked off, nearly kicking an unlucky hen who crossed his path.

"Gianni!" she called out. "Please don't leave like this."

But if he'd heard her, he pretended not to. He was already gone.

Chapter Seventeen

There was no way Georgia would face her parents alone. Not ever if she could help it, and especially not that night. So she stood outside Collina Verde, squinting in the early-evening sun, waiting for Vanessa to pick her up. The trees were thinning, a chill was in the air. September had arrived, and summer's shelf life was about to expire.

As far back as Georgia could remember, the end of summer had filled her with dread. Not the grown-up kind that causes sleepless nights and stomachaches, but a childlike belief that nothing held by fall's cooler, shorter days could ever eclipse the lazy thrills of summer. Grammy closed the Silver Lake cabin, Georgia returned to her parents, and the door on summer's carefree casualness slammed shut. But the September she went off to college, a seismic shift occurred: instead of returning home, she *left* home, in all likelihood for good. The dread lifted like a beribboned balloon disappearing into the sky. Driving the brand-new-to-her tan Toyota Camry, a combined graduation gift from her parents and Grammy, she pulled out of the driveway and waved good-bye. That year she worshipped at the altar of autumn. Never before had the leaves beneath her feet felt so crunchy. Never had the nights felt crisper or looked more star-filled. Fall became her favorite season.

While she waited for Vanessa, she found herself once again dreading the onset of autumn. Not because of the cooling air, or the thinning trees or the petals strewn across the ground, but because, just as it had all those years ago, it announced her parents' reentrance into her life and with that the end of a summer adventure. That "trip to the Continent" her dad had e-mailed her about so long ago had arrived. Soon she'd be back in New York recounting her summer saga to Clem and Lo, and all of it, the restaurant, the people—Claudia, Vanessa, Effie, Bruno, Sergio, Gianni—even Gianni—would be reduced to sepia-toned memories.

The little Peugeot pulled up and Georgia climbed into the passenger seat.

"Ready?" Vanessa asked before rolling out.

"Sure," Georgia lied.

Vanessa steered the car over ruts and rocks, loose pebbles and dirt, away from Dia and San Casciano. In Tuscany, one was never too far from an empty country road, and soon not another car was in sight. Early evening became twilight, that gray-green hour when objects are reduced to shapes, and the countryside filled with elongated triangles, rectangles, and ovals, soft and fuzzy like a pastel painting. Clutching a tissue-size scrap of paper on which she had scrawled directions, Georgia sat stiffly in the passenger seat.

"Tell me again why we're going to this restaurant?" Vanessa said through clenched teeth, her hands gripping the wheel. "Could your parents have picked a more out-of-the-way place?"

"It's close to their hotel, and the front-desk person recommended it."

"Are you kidding? Their daughter is a chef at the Claudia Cavalli restaurant on the cover of *Taste* magazine, and they rely on a bellhop for a recommendation?"

"Desk clerk. And that's my mother for you." Georgia shrugged.

"Can't wait to meet her." Vanessa shifted the car into neutral and grabbed the directions from Georgia's lap. "We were supposed to go left at that fork back there. Some copilot you are."

"Sorry," Georgia said absentmindedly. "I didn't realize it was a fork. Anyway, Effie said it was a good restaurant."

"I'm sure it is." Vanessa threw the car into reverse and zigzagged back to the fork. "But that's not the point, is it?"

At last a hand-painted wooden sign announced the restaurant. Vanessa tore down a gravelly road that morphed into a minuscule parking lot, slamming on the brakes in a spot near the entrance.

Georgia climbed out of the car and shut the door behind her. "Wish me luck, Vee."

"You're not really nervous, are you?" Vanessa whispered as they stepped carefully up the dark walkway. "They're your parents."

"Easy for you to say. You don't know my parents. Or more specifically, my mother. This will be the first time I've seen them since—"

Georgia stopped midsentence, sick of sounding like a broken record when it came to her broken engagement. She'd sworn never to talk about that or her firing again, at least until she returned to native soil. Vanessa had already been schooled on steering the conversation elsewhere the moment either topic arose.

They walked into the restaurant. With its worn honey-maple tables and chairs, floral cotton curtains, brick-red walls, and a fire burning in the stone hearth, the place oozed charm. The kitchen's wood-burning oven infused it with an earthy smell, and the pierced-tin sconces and matching chandeliers emitted a soft glow.

"Let's hear it for the bellhop's recommendation," Vanessa said. "Smells good, looks good, even has nice lighting."

While they needed no help on the food front, Italian restaurateurs could stand to learn a thing or two about restaurant design from the New World, especially when it came to lighting. Fluorescent overheads frequently glared in otherwise cozy trattorias, making food look pallid and diners positively pasty.

"Georgia!" a male voice bellowed. A bespectacled, bearded man stood up at a table in the far corner of the restaurant. "Over here, Georgia!" Hal waved his hands over his head.

"My dad," Georgia said to Vanessa, waving back. The girls made their way through the crowd of English-speaking diners.

Hal edged in front of the table to greet his daughter. Wearing pleated, forest green cords, clunky leather lace-ups, and a tweed sport coat, he couldn't have looked more professorial if he tried. He held his arms open as Georgia approached and engulfed her in a bear hug.

"Hi, Dad." She wrapped her arms around his neck and buried her head in his chest. Sometimes it took someone standing right in front of you to make you realize you had missed them.

"It's good to see you, George." He held her out at arm's length. "You look wonderful. Just wonderful."

"Thanks." Georgia beamed. "You do too. A little more salt in the pepper, maybe, but good." She elbowed him in the ribs.

"What'd you expect? I've been worried about you!"

"Where's Mom?" She looked around the restaurant.

"*Buona sera*, Georgia!" Dorothy sang out behind her. Georgia barely recognized her mother. Gone were the chunky tribal jewelry, the shapeless shirts, the flowing palazzo pants. In their place were a peach skirt that hit at the knee, a silk blouse, and a strand of oversize pearls. Her straight gray hair, which usually hung past her shoulders, had been cut into a chin-length bob and colored a silvery blond.

"Mom, did you just get a makeover or something? What's with the Barbara Bush thing?"

Dorothy grimaced. "It's too much, isn't it? I knew I looked like a Red Stater." She turned to Hal. "I should have worn my clogs."

"You look fabulous, dear," Hal said.

Dorothy took her daughter's hands. "You're the one who looks fabulous, Georgia. You're so thin!"

"Oh, for God's sakes, Dorothy. Of course she's thin! She's always been thin!" Hal turned to Vanessa. "Nice to meet you, by the way. Please call me Hal."

Vanessa grinned and shook his hand. "Nice to meet you, Hal. I've heard so much about you."

"Mom, this is my friend Vanessa. She's here for moral support."

"Oh, come now, Georgia. We're your parents. What kind of support do you need?" Dorothy asked.

"The liquid kind, for one." Georgia took the seat next to her dad and flagged down the waiter. "Campari rocks," she told him.

"Make that two," Vanessa said.

"Oh, is that the chic thing to order?" Dorothy asked. "Then I'll have one too."

"It's going to be a long night," Georgia whispered under her breath.

The waiter placed a family-style dish of tiramisù in the center of the table, and Georgia's eyes lit up like a kid who'd just had her braces removed on Halloween night. It was her favorite dessert, and since Claudia banned it from all her restaurants ("Too sweet! Too fluffy!"), she'd barely eaten it all summer long.

"Cappuccini?" the waiter sniffed, catering to their American-ness. Italians were as likely to drink coffee with milk after a meal as they were to jump from their tables, strip down to their Skivvies, and start humming the theme song from *Rocky*.

"Decaf," Dorothy said. She'd just returned from the restroom and smelled like smoke. "*S'il vous plaît.*"

"*Per favore,* Mom," Georgia said. "*S'il vous plaît* is French."

"At least I'm trying," Dorothy said. "Can you give me credit for trying?"

Georgia did have to give her mother props. Somehow, she'd managed to get through apps and entrées without once mentioning Glenn, Grammy, or Georgia's job prospects. The three smoke breaks had probably helped, but still.

The waiter retreated to fetch her decaf cappuccino, seeming somewhat disappointed that the others would take their coffee Italian-style, after dessert, without milk.

"So, Georgia," Dorothy said, "if you're done picking on me, your father and I would like to talk to you." The vein under her left eye fluttered almost imperceptibly. This did not bode well.

"Leave me out of this one, Dot," Hal said. "I'll do my own talking."

"Dorothy, did you happen to buy that beautiful bag in Florence?" Vanessa pointed to the Kelly bag knockoff slung across the back of Dorothy's chair. "I've been looking for a gift for my mother and that bag would be perfect."

"What? This? Oh, yes. At a wonderful store on via di San Niccolò," Dorothy gushed. "Normally I don't even like shopping, but you Italians just design everything so well. There's even a compartment for my cell phone." She flipped open the boxy bag. "So clever."

Hal grabbed Georgia's hand. "Don't mind your mother, George. You know how she can get sometimes."

"How's that, Hal?" Dorothy asked.

"Pushy?" Georgia offered. "Overbearing yet somehow oddly uninterested in anyone but yourself?"

Dorothy looked as if a Vespa-riding thief had just sped off into the night with her clever new bag tucked under his arm. "That's just mean, Georgia. Aren't I here now? Helping you pick up the pieces of your shattered life?"

Vanessa coughed. "So, Dorothy, that street where you got your bag is in the Oltrarno?"

"Thanks, Vanessa, but I can handle this." Georgia set down her fork and folded her hands on the table. "Let's see, Mom. Yes, I was dumped by my coke-snorting ex; yes, I was fired from my job; and, yes, I was humiliated in the city's number one newspaper."

"Number one?" Hal said. "No way. Number three, tops."

"Whatever." Georgia took a swig of Dolcetto d'Alba. "I was left with an apartment I could barely afford in a city where I couldn't get hired and couldn't even show my face. And yet"— she sipped from her nearly empty wineglass—"and yet here I am in San Casciano, where I have not only helped open one of the most successful restaurants in Tuscany, but I have been offered an incredible job by a wine fanatic with whom I have had incredible sex." No need to mention the part about Gianni never talking—let alone sleeping—with her again.

"Speaking of wine, would anyone like more?" Vanessa asked, holding the bottle in her hand.

"Let me finish, Vanessa. And"—Georgia glanced at her

glass—"actually, yes, thank you, I would like more." She turned back to Dorothy. "And I turned him down. I said no. Now I'm going back to New York where I intend to open my own restaurant because that's what I want to do. More than anything else, that's what I want to do."

Georgia sat back in her chair. "So, as you can see, my life isn't shattered. Even without a job or fiancé to go home to, *I'm* not shattered. I have plans, Mom, big plans."

Dorothy was speechless. Hal drummed his fingers on the table, and Vanessa stared at the back of the waiter's head with such intensity she could have drilled two perfect, eyeball-size holes straight through his skull.

"Wow, Georgia," Hal said at last. "Your own restaurant. Wonderful. Well, good for you. I'm sure it will be the best restaurant in all of New York."

"I think I need to go to the restroom," Dorothy said, her face ashen.

"Oh, Mom, just smoke here. No one will care."

Dorothy shook her head.

Vanessa's telepathic trick worked, and the waiter appeared with the espressos. His presence shifted the tension just enough to open a doggy-size door on conversation.

"I didn't know Glenn was a cocaine addict, Georgia. Not until you told me on the phone that you, that he, that the two of you had ended things," Dorothy said. "I certainly wouldn't have encouraged you to be with him if I'd known."

"All you cared about was that he was a lawyer. He could have been a Republican and you wouldn't have cared."

"I don't know about that." In Dorothy's mind, few things were worse than being aligned with the party that had produced George W. Bush *and* Sarah Palin.

"Who cares about the job, but how did I lose the ever-wonderful lawyer Glenn? Why'd you want to marry me off so badly?"

Dorothy stared at the few embers still glowing in the fireplace. It was late; the restaurant had cleared out. Their server stood by the kitchen furiously punching numbers into his cell phone, turning every once in a while to give his last, lingering table a dirty look. Dorothy pushed back her chair. "I need a cigarette," she said, standing up.

"Mom, smoke at the table. No one will care."

"Oh, what the hell." She sat back down, pulled out a pack of American Spirits, and lit one, blowing smoke out of the side of her mouth. "Believe it or not, Georgia, I wanted you to marry Glenn because I wanted you to be happy. Marrying your father was the best thing I ever did. I thought, I hoped, you'd be as happy being married as I've always been. It sounds crazy as I say it, but it's true."

Georgia studied her mother. Her cool-blue eyes, slightly hooded, were fixed on Hal's, and her fingers, unadorned, save for a thin gold band on her left ring finger, instinctively found his. With their elbows touching, their hands clasped, her parents were aligned, as they'd always been. "Why didn't you tell me this at Uncle Paul's? Instead of telling me how much you hate my job and how Grammy forced you to work, you should have told me this."

"It's no secret that cooking isn't the career I'd have chosen for you."

Georgia smiled thinly. "No, it isn't, Mom, and we definitely don't need to get into it again."

"But it's what you've chosen and that's what matters."

Georgia's mouth dropped. She stared at her mother without saying a word until she felt Vanessa's shoe on her shin. "Oh," she managed.

Dorothy dragged on her cigarette and looked at the waiter, who was glaring at them. "Hal, I think we should settle up. The waiter looks anxious."

"Why don't you continue, Dot," Hal said. "This is important."

She took a deep breath and nodded. "As for my mother, well, you know my relationship with her was never all that strong. It wasn't terrible, but we weren't particularly close. We told each other what we needed to and that was it. I didn't even know her well enough to know she didn't like tai chi." Dorothy suddenly looked so sad Georgia thought her mother might cry.

"Mom—"

"Let me finish. And our relationship, mine and yours, has never been very strong either. I was too busy working and too busy being in love to be the kind of mother I knew you wanted. So you turned to my mother and she turned to you, and in each other you both found what you needed." Dorothy tapped her cigarette on the saucer. "Much as I hated to admit it, hate to admit it, I was jealous of your relationship. Jealous of what you had with each other."

"But Grammy and I would have welcomed you anytime you wanted to be with us."

"I know that now. But back then it wasn't so clear." Dorothy paused. "I'm sorry, Georgia. I'm sorry I didn't figure this all out a long time ago."

Georgia was silent. Never in her whole life could she remember her mother apologizing. Not when she accidentally flushed Goldie the Goldfish—the only pet Georgia was ever allowed—down the toilet, not when she forgot to attend the final round of the county spelling bee, in which Georgia took second place. Maybe, Georgia thought, her mother really did want her to be happy. Maybe, in her own odd way, she always had.

"Okay, Mom. I accept your apology."

Hal removed his glasses and dabbed at his eyes with a handkerchief.

"Come on, Dad, please don't cry."

"I'm not crying, George, I have something in my eye. For what it's worth, I'm sorry too." He held out his hand and Georgia squeezed it.

"Oh, and, Georgia," Dorothy said, "there is one more thing."

"There always is. Go ahead, Mom."

"I'm thrilled you're having incredible sex. Life is far too short to have anything but. Never, ever settle for anything even remotely less."

Vanessa sat dumbstruck, her water glass poised at her lips.

"And that," Hal said, laughter erupting from his belly, "is one of the reasons I love your mother."

Chapter Eighteen

The last of Dia's customers ambled out and Claudia closed the door behind them. *"Finalmente,"* she said. "I thought they'd never leave."

Tonio turned on his iPod the second the door clicked shut and Italian pop music filled the restaurant. "Tonight we listen to my all-Italian playlist in honor of Georgia's last night in Italy."

"Even I can't argue with that," said Effie. "As long as there's no Paola e Chiara."

Bruno entered the dining room holding a tray of champagne flutes. "Since we kicked off the summer with Bellini at the friends-and-family party, I thought we'd end it the same way." He walked around the room doling out drinks, and by the time he reached Georgia, only two were left. *"Perfetto,"* he said as they clinked glasses. "One for you and one for me."

The entire staff had turned out to wish Georgia *buon viaggio,* even Sergio, who had spent much of the summer tending to Claudia's other restaurants. The only person missing was Gianni, who'd politely declined Effie's invitation. According to Effie, Gianni had been nursing his broken heart in the arms of his beautiful blond cousin. Georgia pretended it didn't matter, but of course it did.

At midnight, Vanessa brought out a tiramisù cake covered in whipped-cream frosting that read WE'LL MISS YOU GEORGIA! in red and blue script.

"Tiramisù?" Georgia said, turning to Claudia. "I'm shocked!"

"It's my latest craving," she admitted sheepishly. "I blame the *bambina*."

Sergio passed out cordials of Brachetto, the sparkling dessert wine traditionally drunk at Tuscan weddings, and the perfect pairing with tiramisù, and when everyone held a glass, Claudia signaled Tonio to turn off the music.

"*Buona sera,* everyone," she called. "I will be brief, I promise, and then we can all get back to this delicious tiramisù."

"We've heard that before!" shouted Elena, who had been enjoying her Bellinis a bit too much.

Claudia laughed. "Then let me get right to it. To our wonderful friend Georgia. Without you, this little trattoria would not be the big success that it is. Not only are you a talented and dedicated chef, but your presence has brightened our kitchen . . . though not so much in the early days."

Everyone laughed, especially Georgia. "Here, here!" yelled Bruno.

"I wish you the best of luck with your restaurant in New York, with your *life* in New York"—Claudia fixed her eyes on Georgia's—"and I have no doubt that you will be tremendously successful with both."

Blinking back tears, Georgia blew her a kiss.

"And finally, you should know that there will always be a place for you here in San Casciano." Claudia grinned. "But don't come back until you've opened your own restaurant—or nearly died trying."

Amid a chorus of "To Georgia," the two friends hugged. "I'll never be able to thank you enough for all you've done for me," said Georgia.

Claudia placed her hands on Georgia's shoulders. "You'll never need to."

Sergio walked up behind Claudia and rested his hands on her belly, which was still small enough to camouflage with the tent dresses she'd been living in all summer. "So you're really doing it?" he asked Georgia. "You're really going back to crazy New York City?"

"I'm really going. Back to my crazy city."

Georgia ran up the hill in the hazy morning sunshine, past the sign for the Tomba Etrusca, nearing the spot where she had wiped out, taking a bite-size chunk out of her shoulder and a bigger bite out of her ego. The roosters had woken her this morning for the last time, and she didn't want to waste a single minute.

In a few hours Vanessa would drop her at Amerigo Vespucci airport, where she'd hop a plane for JFK. Her Italian adventure was over. She knew she'd see her friends again—Effie swore he'd come work for her as soon as she opened her own place, and Vanessa, Dia's freshly minted sous-chef, promised she'd be there for the opening party. Even Bruno and Elena were planning a trip to the States, though they weren't sure whether they'd hit New York or Miami. For some reason, Italians loved Florida.

Before the road elbowed, Georgia slowed to a walk (she was no dummy), stopping as soon as she reached the olive grove. It looked much prettier from an upright position than it had while lying horizontally with a mouth full of dirt. She'd been practicing in the shower all summer, but this was the moment that mattered. She smacked her lips together a few times, pressed her upper teeth into her bottom lip, blew through her teeth, and let out a full-blown, Italian-style whistle. The *capo della polizia* himself couldn't have done a better job.

A car horn tooted behind her. With a triumphant smile, she turned around to wave it past, but it pulled up next to her, and when the window rolled down, Gianni stuck out his hand.

"Georgia," he said, taking off his sunglasses. "You're leaving."

"In a few hours. What are you doing here?"

"Claudia told me you'd be here." He put the car in park and climbed out, squinting against the brightening sun. "I didn't want you to leave without saying good-bye."

"I'm glad you found me."

A crow cawed overhead, casting a small shadow on the ground before screeching to a stop in a tree near them. Gianni glanced at the bird, then back at Georgia.

"I'm sorry about the way things ended. I'm not used to hearing what I don't want to hear, or not getting what I want." He looked off into the olive grove. "I acted like a big bambino."

"Yeah, you sort of did."

"I still think you're making a mistake, that the best thing for you is to go to the Lazzaro . . . with me. But I know you're doing what you have to do." He tapped his heart, summing up five minutes of conversation in one small gesture. "I can't be mad at you for that."

"It wasn't an easy decision, Gianni. And the hardest part about it was you." She looked down at the ground. "Seeing how you believed in me helped me believe in myself—and not just as a chef. I owe you a lot, Gianni."

"You don't owe me anything." He picked up her hands and they stood like that for a moment without saying anything.

"Oh," he said, breaking the silence. "I almost forgot. I have something for you." He walked around to the passenger side of the car and opened the door, picking up a bottle from the seat. "Drink it on opening night," he said, handing it to her.

She looked at the label. "A 1990 Solaia, just like the one we had—"

"In Taormina."

"An Antinori masterpiece, if I remember correctly."

"You must have had a good teacher."

"I did. Thanks, Gianni. For this"—she held up the bottle—"and for everything else." She kissed him good-bye, once on each cheek, and once more on his delicious lips.

He got into the car and started the engine. *"Arrivederci, Georgia, e buona fortuna."* The car rolled forward a few feet, then stopped. He leaned his head out the window. "Georgia?"

"Yes?"

"Don't forget about your friends in San Casciano when you become a famous New York City restaurateur."

"Never. I'll never forget any of you." She grinned, and though it was not at all the moment for it, pushed her teeth against her lower lip and let loose one final earsplitting whistle.

Chapter Nineteen

Georgia arrived back on home turf to zero fanfare. No WELCOME BACK signs, no waving friends, no fiancé bearing flowers. It was as if she'd returned from an overnight business trip to Cleveland or Detroit. This being New York, where no one picked up anyone at La Guardia, let alone Kennedy, she hadn't expected much. But she'd e-mailed her details to Clem and Lo, just in case.

The view from the duct-taped backseat of the yellow cab was just as it'd been when she left five months earlier: boxy buildings lining the Van Wyck, colorless sky overhead, standard-issue air freshener dangling from the rearview. SUVs holding two passengers, sometimes just a solitary driver, blasted by, their horns honking at the slightest hint of an improper lane change. Jangly Indian (or was it Pakistani?) music blared from the front seat, and Georgia felt her grip on San Casciano—her friends, the restaurant, the sights, the smells, the food—slipping. It was hard to believe that just yesterday Vanessa had escorted her to the airport, stuffing vacuum-packed bricks of pecorino and Piave into her suitcase.

The cab deposited her at her apartment, and a doorman she didn't recognize watched, refusing to budge from the entry vestibule, as she unloaded her bags onto the sidewalk.

"You subletting from Mark and Tom?" he asked after she stumbled through the door in a rush of nylon, leather, and canvas bags, breathlessly announcing her apartment number.

Georgia looked at him blankly, unable to remember the name of Clem's brother or his buddy, who'd been her summer tenants. "No," she said, flustered. "It's my apartment. I was away, but now I'm back. For good, I think." She smiled even though she didn't feel like it.

"Those guys were cool." The doorman stuck out his pointy, goateed chin. "Too bad they're gone."

"Yeah. I don't suppose you want to help me with my bags?"

A deliveryman balancing a pizza box on one hand arrived at the door. The doorman eyed the piece of paper taped to the top of the box, then looked at Georgia's bags. "Sorry. Gotta buzz 15D and tell them their food is here." He shrugged and turned his back on her, leaving her to struggle to the elevator alone.

The eighth floor smelled like a dive bar, pre-smoking-ban. A cloud of wispy smoke hung in the air, and the wallpaper, a nondescript stripe installed just before she left for Italy, had already yellowed. Taking her first wary step back into her New York life, she turned the key in the lock, holding her breath.

The apartment was spotless. Clem must have insisted her brother hire a cleaning lady, since college boys weren't exactly famous for their scouring prowess. She dumped her bags in the living room and toured her apartment like a prospective buyer, checking out the kitchen, the bedroom, the bathroom, at last coming to rest in front of the picture window. A tugboat sputtered up the East River, passing under the Queensboro Bridge, where the lights had flickered on for the evening. She was home.

A sleek-haired girl chomped into her cell phone, cupping her hand over her mouth, while two chairs down, a pudgy man with silvery pouches under each eye, and a knit cap pulled down to the tops of unruly gray eyebrows, glared at her.

"I think cell phones should be banned from all restaurants, don't you?" the man said loudly, turning to Georgia, the third and final diner sharing Pain Quotidien's communal table that mid-October afternoon.

She had carefully chosen her seat, far enough away so that she wouldn't be forced into conversation with anyone, yet off the main traffic loop that ran through the restaurant to avoid being bonked on the head by a laptop or a lapdog. She'd seen it happen.

She offered a noncommittal shrug before turning back to the pocket-size notebook on the table in front of her. On a fresh sheet of paper she'd written the words *Pros* and *Cons*. A list. She was still master of The List.

"What does *this* mean?" The man mimicked Georgia's gesture, except that his lips turned into a sneer.

She sighed. "It means I don't really care about it right now, okay?"

"Fine." He stuck his fork into the seaweed salad on his plate, then jabbed it into his mouth. A string of *hijiki* clung to the corner of his lips, and ginger dressing dripped down his chin. Georgia looked away.

"Here ya go, dear." The server, a freckle-faced boy who didn't look a day over twenty-two and was way too young to call anyone dear, set down a sandwich and a mug of green tea on the table in front of her. Since returning from Italy she'd had a hard time stomaching American coffee, agreeing with the Italians that more often than not it was burnt, bitter, or bland. Her head raged from the lack of caffeine; green tea was no match for her four-espresso-a-day habit. The cell-phone hater eye-balled Georgia's food, then quickly buried his head back in his own.

"Thanks," Georgia said, taking a bite of the fig-and-ricotta sandwich.

She edged the plate aside and picked up her pen, a graceful Elsa Peretti that was, of course, a gift from Glenn. After endless vacillating, she'd concluded that—engagement ring excluded—it was okay to keep the gifts Glenn had given her in their relationship. With seven years' worth of birthdays, Valentine's Days, Christmases, and the odd guilt-induced "just because" gift under her belt, the bounty was impressive. A few days earlier she'd collected every last bag, belt, or boot he'd gifted her, making a pile in the center of her living room. Blood presents, Clem had scoffed, eyeing a buttery Balenciaga bag. Lo was quick to point out that if Georgia ever fell on hard times, she could sell off the booty at Michael's, the consignment store where Lo unloaded her wardrobe at the end of each season. For all her griping about her upper-crustiness, Lo was as dedicated a shopper as any Park Avenue princess.

The Tuscan Oven, Georgia wrote above *Pros* and *Cons,* drawing a line smack down the center of the page. Her only chance to draw a paycheck in the foreseeable future. Her hand automatically slid to the column on the right; it was always easier to start with cons.

1. *Humiliating*
2. *Location, location, location*
3. *What if someone I know eats there?*

4. *What if Glenn hears I work there?*
5. *What if Marco hears I work there?*
6. *Will people think I work at the Olive Garden?*

She crossed out numbers 3, 4, and 5, rationalizing that they really belonged to number one: humiliating. And 6 was just petty, so she slashed a line through that too. That left her with a respectable two cons. On to the pros.

1. *It's a job*
2. *It pays*

And that, she thought, was all there was to it. After nearly two weeks of making calls, talking to everyone she knew, even, mortifyingly, responding to a couple postings on Craigslist, she needed cash. Though all were quick to congratulate her on the *Taste* article, to ooh and aah as she regaled them with tales of Tuscany, to ask about the famous Claudia Cavalli, and then, finally, to raise an eyebrow and whisper, so tell us what really happened at Marco, as if they were her closest confidant, no one offered up a job. They'd either just hired someone or were scaling back, going in a different direction, didn't have the right job, the money, the need, the fill in the blank. With her bank account dwindling as fast as her confidence, she actually considered calling up Gianni and telling him she wanted the job at the Lazzaro after all. She also considered moving back in with her folks. For a nanosecond.

Enter Effie. Good old Effie, who even a whole ocean away still managed to come to her rescue. His uncle Aldo, a big-time businessman in Bari, had a grade-school pal who owned a restaurant in New York. A couple times a year the guy jet-setted into the city and liked to have a place where he could entertain his lady friends and throw his name around. If she was interested, Uncle Aldo would hook it up. She was interested.

The Tuscan Oven, Georgia discovered, was a bi-level tourist trap at Rockefeller Center where murals of the Italian countryside covered the walls, shiny chandeliers dripped with clusters of faux-Murano grapes and olives, and Adam, Eve, and various fig-leaf-covered people frolicked with Bacchus across the dining room's domed ceiling. When Georgia arrived for her interview with Daniel, the GM, he had only one question: when would she like to start? Oh, and could she please name the shifts she'd prefer. Clearly, Uncle Aldo had clout.

"*Buon giorno,* Georgia!" Clem strode into Pain Quotidien, breezing by the hostess and plunking down her bag on a chair between Georgia and the cell-phone hater. Her ginger hair swished at her shoulders and a fringe of bangs fell into her eyes. She wore maroon leggings, a slouchy sweater, and a pair of tall riding boots, which, she'd tell anyone who'd listen, she was wearing way before they became chic. She bent down and kissed Georgia's cheek. "I'm still not used to having you back. I can't believe we get to meet for coffee again." She frowned at Georgia's green tea. "C'mon, George. You can't have a coffee date with tea, especially that naked green stuff."

"Get over it, Clem." Georgia smiled. Coffee dates with Clem and Lo and extended walks with Sally were the biggest things going on in her life.

"Oh, pardon me. I forgot that you're now a coffee connoisseur." Clem turned to the server. "Excuse me? Large pot of *American* coffee, please. And cream, if you have it. Doesn't that just turn your tummy, Georgia?"

"Actually, it kinda does." She sipped her tea.

"What's this about?" Clem grabbed the notebook. "The Tuscan Oven? You have got to be kidding me."

"Not kidding."

"Georgia, are you insane? Four words, my friend: Rock-efeller. Center. Holidays. Upcoming. Need I say more?"

"No one will hire me, and my rent doesn't take care of itself. I need a job."

"But I thought you were finally going to make your move, fi-nally do it." Clem swigged a sip of coffee and wrinkled her nose. "This coffee does taste sort of crappy."

"Do what?" Lo slid into the seat next to Clem, removed her paisley-patterned shawl, and draped it over the back of her chair. Her black hair hung in ropy, dreadlike chunks, completing the boho-chic look she was currently cultivating. The coif had probably set her back three hundred bucks at her chichi Madi-son Avenue salon.

"Open her own place, for God's sake," Clem said. "Hasn't that always been the plan, Georgia? Especially now that you're—"

"Essentially unemployable?" Georgia said. "Unless you count the Tuscan Oven, which you, Clem, obviously don't."

"She can't just open her own place, Clem. She needs back-ing. A lot of it," said Lo.

"What about your dad?" Clem asked Lo. "He's got more than enough to go around."

"Yeah, right. My dad would never invest in someone who's friends with *me*."

"True." Clem sighed, turning to Georgia. "You really need the money? I mean, you really need a job?"

"Um, yes. You do realize we're talking about me, Georgia, and not Lo, right?"

Clem rolled her eyes. "What about the money from Grammy?"

"Almost gone. Besides, I need to cook. I love to cook."

"So throw a dinner party."

"Funny. Besides, working on the business plan, walks with Sally, and coffee dates with you two aren't cutting it. No offense, guys." Especially since "working on the business plan" had been limited to checking out spaces she couldn't afford and fantasizing about turning away Mercedes Sante and Marco on opening night. She'd started to think the right partner might help get the restaurant off the ground, but so far the list of potential candidates hovered at zero.

"Tea dates," Clem said. "I think I'm quitting coffee too."

"Hey, how is Sally?" Lo asked. "And did you see Glenn when he dropped her off?"

"No, the lame-o had his *cousin* do the drop-off," Clem snorted.

"Sally's amazing, as always. And believe me, I'm glad I didn't have to see him."

"I'm sure. How awkward, especially since—" Lo cut herself off. "Where is the waiter? I want a tea too."

"Since what, Lo?" Georgia asked.

"Since you haven't seen him for so long?"

"Since what, Lo?" Georgia repeated.

"Oh, Jesus, Lo, just tell her. She's going to find out soon enough anyway." Clem flagged down the waiter. "Two more green teas. And you better send over a chocolate bombe too."

"I'm not really sure how to say this." Lo took a deep breath. "Glenn is engaged. To Lila Fowler."

"How do you know?" Georgia asked.

"I ran into Mrs. Fowler at Doubles. I'm sorry, George."

"Does Lila Fowler have a dog?" Georgia pictured the cockapoo sitting next to Sals on the beach in Bridgehampton. *Her new best friend,* Glenn had written.

"*That's* the first thing you want to know?" Clem asked.

"I'm not sure," Lo answered. "But I can find out."

"Forget it." Georgia tucked her head into her chest. Her black cardigan pouched out at precisely the wrong place, making her belly appear even bigger than it was. A shiver ran down her neck and she hunched her shoulders against the chill. "I don't love him anymore," she said without lifting her gaze. "I haven't loved him in a long time."

"We know," said Clem.

"We know," said Lo.

"But still," Georgia said.

The server brought over the teas and the chocolate dessert. He looked at Clem, who pointed to Georgia. "I guess this is for you, dear." Clem slid the notebook out of the way, and he placed the oozing orb in front of Georgia. "Enjoy it."

Georgia smiled wanly, her eyes still resting on her pouchy sweater, expanding and retracting with each breath. But still.

Chapter Twenty

The giant snowflake flickered over Fifty-seventh Street and Fifth Avenue, the commercial crossroads of the world for the holiday season if not the whole year through. The streets were thick with cabs, the sidewalks clogged with tourists speaking languages as far-flung as Ukrainian and the slightly closer-to-home dialect known as Brooklynese. Bergdorf's street-level windows overflowed with one-of-a-kind treasures and so much sartorial splendor one could only dream. Across the street, Tiffany was knee-deep in tourists ogling the important jewels on the ground floor before shuffling off to four to buy key rings, a charm, or maybe an egg-size picture frame. Down the avenue, Salvation Army workers collected Christmas cheer for the less fortunate, ringing their bells in front of St. Patrick's, Saks, and the trumpeting angels at Rockefeller Center. All roads led to the tree: a ninety-foot Norwegian spruce covered in blue lights, a five-pointed star perched atop its highest branch. Holiday season in New York was in full swing.

Like any schooled New Yorker, Georgia avoided the tourist-rich stretch of Fifth Avenue from Thanksgiving straight through the New Year. The lone exception to this ironclad rule had been her and Glenn's annual pilgrimage to behold the tree. The tradition began innocently enough one clear December evening after drinks at the Four Seasons, a couple of those ghastly green apple martinis that had enjoyed a fleeting moment of fame in watering holes across the city. Glenn suggested a walk, and arms linked, they strolled down the avenue, pausing at each overdecorated window and picking out gifts they'd never buy for everyone they knew. Rock Center was almost deserted, and they held hands and gazed at the tree, forgetting for the moment how cheesy it all was. The next year they repeated the tradition, even sitting on the same uncomfortable barstools. The only difference was the champagne that filled their flutes, a necessary upgrade.

This year, she'd skip the trip. First, there was the Glenn-is-engaged-to-someone-else issue. Second, she now passed the tree twice a day, once on her way to the Tuscan Oven and once on her way from the Tuscan Oven. She'd started as head chef in the middle of October and now, two months in, was fairly cozy in her new position. The job was virtually stress-free: absentee boss, no chance of getting reviewed, customers who barely spoke English. The more comfortable she got, the harder it was to start working on her own restaurant. Plus, she rationalized, everyone knew that nothing was ever accomplished over the holidays. The question of a partner gnawed at her, but she pushed it aside. Her grand plans would wait until the new year, which, Claudia's astrologer would surely confirm, was a much more auspicious time to start a new venture anyway.

Wearing a chunky knit hat pulled low over her head, a trim down coat, and jeans tucked into knee-high boots, Georgia arrived at the Oven. Snow was forecast for later in the evening, and the city eagerly awaited the first flakes of the season to fall. The door blew shut behind her, letting out a little squeal. If the wind kept up, the snowstorm would become a blizzard and the restaurant would be dead. Even tourists knew how to order takeout. She walked under the distressed-brick archway into the dining room, heading for her locker.

"Georgia!" a voice called out. "Ciao, Georgia!"

Georgia whipped her head around, her eyes landing on a man sitting at the Oven's primo corner table. He tossed an espresso cup in his left hand as if it were a Super Ball. "Yes?"

"Luca Santini," he said, rising from his chair and placing the cup on the table, rim-side down. The top two buttons of his shirt were open, revealing a tuft of shiny chest fluff. His hair was the color of tarnished silver, but he had a full head of it, and he wore it to his collar, parted in the middle, no bangs. He looked like a man who'd been told so many times he looked decades younger than his sixty-plus years that he now believed it. He was dressed like a thirty-year-old investment banker out for a night at the Boom Boom Room.

Georgia stared at him blankly. "Hello. So nice to meet you." She held out her hand.

"I own this restaurant," Luca said, staring at her outstretched hand without taking it. "Now does the name ring the bell?" He cocked his head slightly and puffed out his lower lip in a gesture Georgia would soon learn to imitate perfectly.

"Oh, Luca, Mr. Santini, I'm so sorry." Georgia smiled. "My friend Effie has told me so much about you."

Luca cocked his head again. He stared at the hand hovering so close to his and, after what seemed like an eternity, grabbed it between his own puffy paws and squeezed. Hard. "Call me Luca. Please have a seat." He pulled out a chair.

Georgia settled stiffly into the chair, flexing the fingers of her right hand under the table. The imprint of his ring was embossed on her finger, and Georgia glanced at the mondo diamond shining on her new boss's pinkie. She tried to remember what Effie had said about Luca and if the word *godfather* played a part in the conversation.

"You made a big impression on that boy, Effie. Aldo, his uncle Aldo, my friend Aldo, says all he talks about is coming to New York to work for you."

"For me? Oh, you mean here, at the Tuscan Oven."

"Of course here. Where else would I mean?"

Georgia shrugged. "So what brings you to town? Holiday shopping? Business? Broadway?"

"Oh, a little of this, a little of that. Mostly I'm interested in meeting you."

"Me?"

The GM had told Georgia that she'd probably never even lay eyes on Luca, who blew through the restaurant with a bevy of blondes every month or so and cared more about replenishing his private wine stash than the state of the restaurant.

"Since you've started, I hear the food has really improved. Tickets are up, food costs down. All in, what, two months? You've been here two months, yes?"

"Yes. I started in the middle of October." In two weeks it would be Christmas.

"So, tell me what you've done. What you're doing here at the Tuscan Oven."

"Sure, Luca. You mean with the food?"

"Unless you've painted us some new frescoes I haven't seen yet, yes, I mean with the food." He picked up the espresso cup and tossed it in the air again.

"Well, the recipes are good, basic recipes. They just needed some TLC. A little, um, updating, a little more attention paid to the execution, to presentation, and especially to the bottom line.

There's a lot that's been going to waste that doesn't need to go to waste."

Saving money was always a safe topic with restaurant owners. No one wanted to lose money. An owner could hate the food, the decor, the service, but when it came to saving money, everyone was game.

"The recipes are my nonna's recipes. Handed down from her nonna, and her nonna's nonna. We didn't always live in Bari. If you think they need updating, you go right ahead. But they've been making Santinis happy—and fat—for generations." He patted his belly and smiled, looking, Georgia thought, not exactly like a shark, but certainly sharklike.

"Have you sampled any of the dishes since I came on board, Mr. San—I mean, Luca?"

"Not yet. I'll be in for dinner tonight with some friends. Ten of us. I'll let you know what we think. For now I just wanted to meet you, the Georgia everyone talks about."

"'The Georgia everyone talks about.' I'm not sure if that's good or bad."

"I'll let you know after tonight." Luca's cell phone rang, and the espresso cup crashed to the terra-cotta floor. He didn't even blink. *"Pronto,"* he shouted into the phone. He put it down and turned back to Georgia. "I'm taking this call. Thank you, Georgia."

Georgia collected her hat and gloves from the chair and walked through the dining room as nonchalantly as she could. If Luca Santini didn't positively love her food, she was out, Uncle Aldo or no Uncle Aldo.

Pablo, an elegant Spaniard and career waiter, returned to the kitchen and stood in front of Georgia. He was the only waiter who served Luca, and according to Oven lore, he'd once been

forced to cancel his annual trip to Madrid when Luca made a
last-minute trip to New York.

"Well?" she asked.

Pablo straightened his tied bow tie—no clip-ons for him—
and cleared his throat. "Too soon to tell. I'll let you know."

Georgia paced around the Oven's clumsily configured
kitchen, trying not to bump the line cooks. The antipasto and
pasta courses—funghi con polenta, zuppa di ceci, and a Neapol-
itan timbale that had taken forever to prep—had been cleared
from Luca's table, and the waiters had marched into the dining
room single file, bearing plates of crispy pollo alla capricciosa,
tender arista di maiale, and rich sogliola alla fiorentina.

Daniel, the GM, stuck his head into the kitchen. "Georgia,
a word."

The kitchen ground to a halt. Though the staff didn't care
what happened to Georgia, they certainly wanted to know what
happened.

"A word," Daniel repeated. "Out there. With Luca."

"You're kidding."

Daniel shrugged. "Powder your nose. You're a little shiny."

"I don't carry powder with me in the kitchen, Daniel."

"You do carry lipstick, I hope?"

Georgia fished in her pocket for her lip gloss and swiped it
across her lips. She straightened her chef's coat and patted her
hair down, guessing the frizz factor was a semicontained six. "Of
course I carry lip gloss, Daniel." She strode out into the dining
room, her stomach suddenly queasy with déjà vu. Huggy Henderson had asked to see her that last night at Marco. The next
day Bernard fired her. Table visits were not Georgia's thing.

Luca stood as she approached. His party consisted of a
handful of bottle blondes and two men who looked like carbon
copies of their host, only huskier.

"Georgia," he said. "The food was wonderful. And the timbale. I haven't had one in ages. It was as good as my nonna's." He kissed his fingertips.

"Thanks, Luca. I'm so glad you enjoyed it."

His guests murmured their approval. Georgia had the feeling they could have eaten shoe leather and if Luca said it was the best dish he ever had, they would agree, even as they attempted to dislodge bits of charred leather from between their veneered teeth.

"I'll walk you back to the kitchen." He took her elbow and steered her to the bar instead. "Drink?"

"I don't know if that's a good idea. It's sort of not very professional of me to sit at the bar and drink during shift."

"You think you're going to get fired?"

"I guess not. Good point."

"John," Luca said to the bartender. "Two glasses of the Lafite Rothschild. The '82 you've been decanting for me."

"An '82?" Georgia said. "I thought those didn't even exist anymore."

"They don't."

The bartender placed the decanter on the bar and poured the wine into voluminous Yeoward crystal glasses, reserved strictly for Luca's use. Luca picked up his glass.

"Your friends won't mind that you've left them?" Georgia asked.

"Are you kidding me? Free food, free wine? They're in heaven, and now that I'm not there, they can actually relax. For some reason I make people nervous." Luca held up his palms and shrugged. "Do I make you nervous, Georgia?" He cocked his head and pursed his lips.

Georgia considered the question. "Actually, not so much." It was the truth. She'd worked with much, much worse.

Luca looked slightly disappointed.

"But I can see how you could," she hastily added. "You know, make someone else nervous."

Luca chuckled, then held up his glass. *"Salut."* He took a sip. "I have a question for you, Georgia."

"Shoot." After her first sip of the sublime Bordeaux, she hoped he had at least a couple glasses' worth of questions.

"Why are you wasting your talent here? Of course I'm glad you're here, don't get me wrong. But this restaurant, my restaurant, as long as the food is decent, it will make money. The tourists will always come to Rockefeller Center, and they'll always need a place to eat, a place to splurge when they tire of that Til Friday place."

"T.G.I. Friday's." Georgia drank more wine.

"I don't need a superstar chef. Which, I think it's safe to say, you are on your way to becoming."

"You do?"

"I do. But the question is, Georgia, do you?"

"Superstar? I'm not so sure. I don't see myself with an empire of restaurants, my name in Page Six or on the food blogs, or forcing customers to eat fifteen-course prix fixe dinners, but I do—"

Luca glanced at her empty glass. "More wine?"

"Just a splash." Emboldened by the alcohol, she saw her chance. "Look, I may as well be honest with you, Luca. I do intend to open my own place. And hopefully a few more after that. It's still in the early planning phase, so not anytime really soon. I'm looking for space—"

Luca cut her off. "You have a business plan?"

"Sure," Georgia lied. If a few scratches in a notebook counted, then, sure, she had a business plan.

"I'm going back to Bari at the end of the week. Get me a

copy of your business plan. I like the way you cook. I like the way you talk. Who knows? Maybe we'll be able to do some business together."

"Wow, that'd be—"

"No promises. But I'm always interested in young talent. Youth, talent, and drive are a killer combination. Not to be fucked with, you know what I mean?"

"I guess so," Georgia lied again.

"And now I must get back to my guests. I'll leave the wine for you to enjoy, which I see you do." He motioned to her empty glass and winked. "And don't forget to get me that plan."

Georgia emptied the last of the Lafite into her glass and surveyed the nearly empty dining room. One good thing about working at the Oven was that it cleared out early. A much better thing about working at the Oven was having a boss who might be interested in backing her first solo venture, an extremely wealthy boss who wasn't in the country often. The best investors had deep, deep pockets and lived far enough away that unannounced drop-ins were unlikely. Luca qualified on both counts. Now all she needed to do was produce a kick-ass business plan.

"In five freaking days," Georgia muttered into her wineglass.

"What was that?" the bartender asked.

"Can I have a Pellegrino, please?"

Though she'd never even read a business plan, let alone written one, she was pretty sure they were chock-full of spreadsheets, endless rows of numbers that somehow painted a picture of a business's success. A culinary whiz she might be, a computer whiz, not so much. She couldn't even say for sure that her Mac had Excel.

"Double espresso too, John," Georgia added. "Actually, make it a triple." Her green tea days were over.

$\mathcal{A}$ trio of tree gawkers wearing matching pom-pom hats climbed out of a taxi, and Georgia slid into the backseat before the cabbie had a chance to flip on the VACANT sign.

"Barnes and Noble, Sixty-sixth and Columbus," she said.

If she was going to turn around a business plan in five days, she'd need serious help. As her dad preached, when in doubt, make a list. And when that doesn't work, buy a book. Better still, he'd add, index finger shooting straight to the sky, borrow one from the library. But even her frugal father would have to agree that writing a business plan from scratch, complete with a P&L and cash-flow analysis, terms with which Georgia had only become acquainted after googling *business plan*, warranted an actual purchase.

Coming up with a concept wasn't a problem. Georgia was full of concepts, some good, some bad, some so bad they were actually good. She and Clem had passed many an evening riffing on the next unpublished-numbered hot spot—one that would be written up in the gossips, host a few fashion-week parties, maybe even throw up a velvet rope before being relegated bridge-and-tunnel and slipping into oblivion. But that wasn't what she had in mind for her own place.

Her concept, if it could be called that, was to create the restaurant where she always wanted to eat. The idea was deceptively simple: a stylish, unpretentious space with eighty or so seats; a small, seasonal, market-driven menu, largely American with a Mediterranean influence; nightly specials that ran slightly more experimental; knockout desserts; attentive, friendly service; a well-edited, well-priced wine list; an upbeat, good-time vibe. It sounded like a million other places that had come and gone, and a million more that were barely hanging on, but success was in the execution and the details, and those, Georgia was confident, she could handle.

The challenge was selling this nonconcept concept to Luca. Which was why she was hurtling up Sixth Avenue, unbelted, in a yellow cab helmed by a turbaned driver shouting into his mouthpiece and occasionally throwing his hands up in the air, leaving the cab to steer itself. The traffic gods were on her side, and she made it to the bookstore not only alive but in nine minutes flat, which had to be some sort of record. The store was open until midnight and bustling with business; either New Yorkers were convinced that books really did make the best holiday gifts, or a lot of people were in need of a lot of help that night.

"Excuse me," Georgia said to the skinny guy with sallow skin and a picked-out Afro behind the information desk. In the pre-Netflix era he would have worked at an independent video store. "Where is the *Dummies* series?"

He looked at her blankly.

"You know," Georgia said impatiently, "those big yellow books? The ones that teach us dummies how to do things like build model airplanes or French-braid our hair?"

"Oh, yeah. Third floor, back of the store."

"Thanks." She spun around and charged up the escalator, her veins pumping with caffeine. Her first coffee in months, make that her first *three* coffees in months, had hopped her up like a contestant on *The Amazing Race*. She was so focused on securing her prize, a newly revised and expanded version of *Business Plans for Dummies,* she almost didn't hear her name being called.

"Georgia!" the same male voice called out again.

She grabbed the escalator's handrail and turned around carefully, so as not to lose her footing. There, descending the down escalator as she ascended the up, a red scarf wrapped around his neck, a bunch of books under his arm, was Bernard.

"Wait for me up there," he shouted before stepping off the escalator and onto the ground floor. "I just need to pay for these."

"Okay," she mouthed, forcing her lips into a smile.

Since returning to the city, she'd managed to avoid bumping into anyone from her Marco days, mostly by sticking to the terminally unhip twenty-block stretch between the Oven and her apartment. The thought of seeing Marco filled her with almost as much dread as the thought of seeing the newly affianced (again) Glenn. She couldn't face either of them until she had something to show for herself other than her Rock Center employee badge. But Bernard would be okay. A Michael Cunningham novel was prominently displayed on the Staff Picks table, and she thumbed through a copy without registering a word.

"Georgia." Bernard put his hand on her back.

"Hey, Bernard. How are you?" Despite the easy smile, her voice was tight. After Ricky, he was the best of the Marco bunch, but he was still the one who fired her over smoked salmon, runny eggs, and all-you-can-drink Krug.

"How long have you been back?" he asked.

"A few months." He looked different, younger. "What happened to your specs?"

"Oh." He tapped his fingers on his bare temple. "Contacts."

"You look good." She paused a moment, then blurted, "I work at the Tuscan Oven. Just so you know."

"I heard something like that. How do you like it?"

"It's not bad. I get to leave early. And it's at Rock Center, so there's the tree." She frowned. "Which gets annoying, actually."

"I imagine it would," he said, chuckling. "At least it's a job."

"True. What about you? How are things?"

"Me? Things are, well, things are okay. You heard that Marco shut down? In the middle of the summer. Business really plummeted after the . . ." Bernard cleared his throat and stared at the industrial carpet beneath their feet.

"It's okay, Bernard, you can say it. The review. Business plummeted, I fled the country. All because of the review."

"You didn't have to."

"I know. I could have worked sauté at that pit on the Upper West Side your friend owns. Or gone to Boston to work for Pierre du Mont. So many options, so little time." She smiled, officially letting him off the hook.

"So how was Italy?" he asked, his voice perking up a bit. "And the famous Claudia Cavalli?"

"Italy and Claudia were fantastic. Really, really great. I learned a lot. It was an amazing experience."

"I'm glad to hear it."

"Thanks." Neither of them said anything. "So," Georgia said to break the silence, "what are you doing lurking around Barnes and Noble at midnight anyway?"

"This and that. I just got off work, actually, and decided to get a jump on my Christmas shopping." He held up his shopping bag.

"You're working around here? Where?"

"That pit on the Upper West Side my friend owns. I manage it."

"Oh." Georgia felt her face redden. "I didn't mean anything bad by that. I'm sure it's great, it's just, you know, it's not the most chef-friendly neighborhood. But I'm sure your restaurant is totally different." She swallowed. "Right?"

"Actually, Georgia, no, it's not different. It sucks. But it pays."

"I know how that goes," Georgia said, unable to feel the schadenfreude she felt was her due. Unlike Marco, who should have been skinned, skewered, and thrown on the barbie, Bernard was a good guy and was great at his job. He deserved better. "Remember, you're talking to the girl who works at the *second*-most popular restaurant at Rockefeller Center."

"And what is the girl who works at the second-most popular Rock Center restaurant doing here? I know you don't live around here."

"I'm on my way to the third floor and I have"—she checked her watch—"thirteen minutes before the store closes to find some very important books. Want to join me?" If he'd told her he was working with David Chang or Keith McNally or Daniel Boulud, she wouldn't have asked. But he ran a neighborhood joint with off-brand food on the Upper West Side. He also had a superhuman knowledge of the inner workings of many of New York's top restaurants. So she asked.

"Why not?" he said. "I have nowhere important to be tomorrow. I'd love to join you."

An hour later Georgia and Bernard were ensconced in a ripped-red-vinyl booth at the F&A, a dive bar a block from the bookstore. A half-full pitcher of Bud sat between them. Georgia refilled Bernard's glass.

"So let me get this straight," Bernard said. "You have five days to write an entire business plan for your boss, who lives in Bari, may or may not be connected, and wants to back your restaurant even though it means you'd leave the Oven?"

"Yes."

"And you haven't started the plan yet?"

"Not officially. I mean, I have notes. I have the idea. I've even seen a few spaces that could work. I've done some groundwork, just not much number crunching." She burped. "Excuse me."

"Have you ever read a business plan?"

"No."

"But that doesn't worry you?"

"Of course it worries me. That's why I just bought an entire library on how to write one." She dumped the Barnes & Noble bag on the table. In addition to the *Dummies* book, she'd bought three more. "These ought to do the trick."

"I hate to burst your bubble, Georgia—"

"Please. There's nothing you can say to me that could be worse than 'You're fired.'"

"How about 'You're crazy'? There's no way you're going to crank out an entire business plan, a good one, with real numbers, in five days."

"Well, I have to at least try." Georgia stood. "Do you want fries? I want fries."

"Nah." Bernard shook his head and flipped open one of the books. "Had my fill of grease before I ran into you," he said without lifting his eyes from the book. "Back at that pit I manage."

Georgia laughed. "Not gonna let me live that one down, are you?"

"Not likely."

At the jukebox a twentysomething guy wearing a White

Stripes T-shirt over a ratty thermal studied his musical choices. A foursome drinking bottles of Brooklyn Lager stood around the pool table while a petite girl with dangly earrings broke, smashing the cue ball with a satisfying thwack. Georgia bellied up to the bar, taking a seat as the bartender shouted her order to the one-man kitchen. Outside, snow had started to fall. The first few bars of "Let It Bleed" sounded, and the guy at the jukebox strummed his air guitar à la Keith Richards. Georgia hummed along, feeling the effects of the Bud mingling with the espresso. The jukebox guy primped and preened around the pool table, forsaking Keith for the flashier Mick. " 'Well, we all need someone we can lean on,' " he sang, his lips contorted into a puffy pout.

Bernard sat at the table, poring over the *Dummies* book, completely oblivious of his surroundings. Only Bernard could read a book like that in a bar like this, Georgia thought. The bartender deposited the greasy basket of fries on the bar, and Georgia looked at the basket, then at the bartender, then at Bernard, her eyes widening. Only Bernard. She swiveled her stool all the way around so she was facing him. His head rested on one hand and he jotted something down in the book with the other. She grabbed the basket and raced back to the table.

"I have a crazy idea, Bernard." The fries sat in her outstretched hands like an offering.

"Really." He popped a fry into his mouth. "Shoot."

She slid into the booth next to him. "So here's the thing. In Tuscany, I learned, well, I learned a lot. But the most important thing I learned, other than it's okay to be alone, I mean, alone as in no fiancé, no boyfriend, no lover—"

"I get it. Alone. Go on."

"Is that it's okay to ask for help. You know? I learned to rely on my coworkers, my colleagues, my boss, for help. Teamwork,

Bernard. That's what it's all about, at least what it should be about. Are you with me?"

"Teamwork. I'm with you." Bernard stifled a smile, which Georgia ignored.

"So, the restaurant. My restaurant. It doesn't need to be just my restaurant. It can be, well, for example, it can be our restaurant. We can do it together, B."

"Georgia—"

"Wait, let me finish. You owe it to me to listen."

He nodded. "Okay."

"You're the best GM I've ever worked with. And I like you. You're smart, you're organized, you're so, *so,* together. And I, well, I'm a good chef. A damn good chef. You said so yourself. And I have a potential backer. But I can't do it alone, and now I realize that's fine. I don't need to do it alone because I ran into you at midnight at Barnes and Noble and you have nowhere important to be tomorrow."

Georgia took a deep breath. "So I'm asking you, Bernard, what I'm asking is, do you want to be my partner? Do you want to open a restaurant with me?"

"I do," he said calmly.

"You do?"

"I do."

"Seriously?"

"Seriously. You are a damn good chef. And I'm a damn good manager. We make a great team, as I seem to recall someone saying. And, I have a business plan. Or part of a business plan."

"The spreadsheet part?" Georgia asked.

"The spreadsheet part. With real, quantifiable numbers."

"Holy shit."

"Yes. Holy shit." Bernard picked up his glass and handed Georgia hers. "To our restaurant."

"To our restaurant."

They clinked glasses and sipped the lukewarm Bud.

"Now let's get to work," Bernard said, rising from the table. "I can't bear to work at that pit much longer."

He tucked the empty pitcher under his arm, picked up their glasses, and dropped them off at the bar, returning with two tall Coca-Colas.

"I guess you mean business," Georgia said.

"I do."

"That's good. Because so do I."

When they left the F&A at quarter of three that morning, the city had been transformed. Snow blanketed the sidewalk, the street, the parked cars, swirling from the darkened sky above, dancing in the swaths of light issuing from streetlamps and the occasional slow-moving headlight. Tomorrow's rush hour would render the winter wonderland a dull gray, but for the moment the city was pure and clean as a new beginning. Georgia's notebook was filled with notes, full sentences and fragments, some marked by double exclamation points, others less sure of themselves. Tomorrow she would transcribe these half-drunken scrawlings into a cohesive proposal, Bernard would tweak the numbers to fit their concept, and they would have the first draft of something resembling a business plan. They were on their way.

"Four days?" Clem asked. "You turned this around in four days?" She held a half-inch-thick, spiral-bound business plan in her hands. The back cover was chocolate brown, the front a rich cream, with brown lettering spelling out *GB Restaurants, LLC* ("May as well be optimistic," Georgia had said about adding the *s* to their company name).

"Impressive," Clem continued. "I love the colors."

Georgia smiled. Bernard had wanted to go the lime-green/tangerine-orange route, but Georgia vetoed, citing Luca's tastes as more da Vinci than Haring. Besides, that palette was as played out as the tuna tartar app.

"So how much sleep have you had?" Lo asked.

"Um, none?"

"Wow. You don't even have bags," Lo said.

"Paula Dorf concealer. Buy the stock. The stuff is amazing."

The three friends sat in Lo's spacious Upper East Side living room, eating sushi and waiting for Bernard. As soon as he arrived, he and Georgia would practice their pitch on Lo and Clem in preparation for their sit-down the next day with Luca. Luca scheduled his meetings at the Oven according to course, with the most important timed to the entrée. Georgia and Bernard had scored the aperitivo-and-antipasto slot, thirty minutes of swilling Cynar and eating cured meats. If all went well, Luca would NetJet back to Bari with the idea for a brand-new business bobbing in his head.

"So how's it going? I mean, with Bernard? Do you want to kill him yet?" Clem dipped her toro into the soy sauce. "Sushi Seki has the best toro in the city," she announced, popping the piece into her mouth. "Mercury be damned."

"At fifteen bucks a pop it better be the best," Lo said.

"Good thing your dad has an account there," Clem said. "Otherwise you'd be broke."

"Good thing for you too." Lo pointed her chopsticks at Clem's mouth.

"It's only been four days," Georgia said. "If I wanted to kill him already, we'd be in trouble." The truth was, Georgia loved working with Bernard. He was on top of everything, funny, upbeat, and sharp as her chef's knife. At three o'clock in the morning his charms curdled a bit, but then whose didn't? Four bleary-eyed all-nighters later even Brad Pitt would begin to grate.

The buzzer sounded and Lo propped open the front door for Bernard before picking up the intercom. Georgia sipped her sake.

"You can't drink," Clem said.

"What do you mean?"

"Are you going to drink before you pitch Luca Santini? I don't think so." She swiped Georgia's ceramic sake cup from the coffee table.

"Are you kidding me? The man drinks 1982 Lafite Rothschild like water. Trust me, we'll be drinking."

" 'Eighty-two?" Bernard said as he walked in the living room. "I thought those were impossible to come by."

"They are," said Georgia. "And hi."

Bernard exchanged kisses with Clem and Lo.

"Are you still mad at me?" he asked Lo.

"Mad?" said Lo.

"I seem to remember you were pretty pissed off at Georgia's send-off party. I hope I'm forgiven."

"You will be if you help Georgia open her restaurant."

Bernard didn't say anything, but his ears flamed pink. Georgia had discovered that when he was upset or embarrassed, the tips of his ears turned hot pink. Her face turned red, his ears went flamingo. Hopefully both partners would remain pale as paper during the meeting. If Luca smelled any weakness, he'd pounce.

"It's not my restaurant," Georgia corrected Lo. "It's ours. Mine and Bernard's. Or it will be if we nail this pitch."

"Sorry, I wasn't thinking." Lo held out a pair of chopsticks for Bernard.

"No worries," he said, popping a piece of toro. "Sushi Seki?"

Lo nodded.

"We should get started," Bernard said. "We need at least a few hours of sleep before the meeting."

"See?" Georgia swung her arm around his shoulder. "That's why I love my business partner. He's *all*-business."

Two hours later, Georgia and Bernard left Lo's apartment, their bellies fat with fish, their brains bursting with numbers and key phrases. Clem followed them out, and they rode down the elevator together. Lo and Clem agreed the two had, after a half-dozen attempts, finally nailed it. If they could remember to speak clearly (Georgia), kill the *um*s and *you know*s (Georgia again), and the *in other words* (Bernard), they could present a killer pitch in fifteen minutes, which, according to their bible, *Business Plan for Dummies,* was about all the time they'd have. Just a quarter hour to knock the cashmere socks right off Luca Santini's feet.

Clem flagged the first cab she saw and headed down to the Perry Street Towers where she was dog-sitting. "Knock 'em dead, guys!" she shouted from the cab's open window. "You're gonna be great!" She pumped her gloved fist into the bitter air as the cab lurched away.

"You think we will be?" Georgia asked. She pulled her hat low on her head and yanked up her hood. Since the snowstorm, the temperature had hovered in the teens, making it impossible for any snow to melt. Mini-mountains of gray mush piled at street corners, and the curbs were covered with snow cleared from sidewalks.

"Be what?" Bernard asked. His red scarf was wrapped around his face, and a matching red hat covered his ears. Smoke wisped from his mouth.

"Great. Do you think we'll be great?"

The doorman waved from inside the lobby, and Georgia motioned for him to turn on the taxi light.

"I think you'll be great," Bernard said. "I think I'll be fair to middling."

"Funny," Georgia said as a cab pulled up. "Want me to drop you at the train?"

"Nah, the cold air will do me good."

"Whatever you say, partner. I'll see you at the Oven tomorrow. Twelve thirty sharp. Do not be late."

"You're kidding, right? When have you ever known me to be late?"

"Never. Good night, Bernard."

She climbed into the toasty cab and settled in for the short ride home. The streets were desolate. Nights like these were made for soup dumplings, General Tso's chicken, and a good bad movie on demand. For snuggling under the covers in a ratty T-shirt and sweats with a husband, a fiancé, a boyfriend, or, in Georgia's case, a big yellow mutt with bad breath. Much as she adored Sals, it was these kinds of nights that made her miss Glenn. Two months in the city without any type of male companionship could make a girl lonely. But those girls, she reminded herself, didn't have dogs like Sally, or friends like Clem and Lo, or business partners like Bernard. They didn't have a restaurant in the works, a dream about to take off.

Chapter Twenty-two

$\mathcal{G}$eorgia paced in the Oven's tiny basement locker room, her sliver-heeled boots clicking across the scuffed vinyl tiles. She glanced at her wristwatch and frowned. In the two years she'd known him, Bernard had never been late. Their meeting with Luca was scheduled to begin in fifteen minutes, and not only was there no sign of her partner, but calls to his cell went straight to voice mail. Since Bernard equated punctuality with godliness and was at least seven minutes early for everything, this was deeply disturbing.

Upstairs in the dining room, Luca was probably polishing off his third espresso, perfectly timed to coincide with the end of his first meeting, a number-crunching session with his accountant. Georgia and Bernard were up third, right behind the waste management contractor, a disagreeable man from New Jersey with stale breath you could smell across the table. That one, Luca's assistant assured her, would be brief.

"He went to the john. You just bought yourself ten minutes," the assistant, an unfriendly guy who wore a permanent sneer, called into the locker room, his voice tinny over the intercom.

"But you better hope your friend gets here soon." He'd reluctantly agreed to give Georgia updates on Luca's progress.

"I know," Georgia said into the intercom. "Believe me, I know."

The thought of pitching Luca without Bernard to cut in, interject, and flat-out take over when talk moved from concept (her deal) to money (his) made her head and, strangely, her feet hurt. Or maybe that was just the four-inch-high Louboutins pinching the bunion on her left foot. A Barneys warehouse score, the boots were so uncomfortable they'd only seen sidewalk on two other occasions: an impromptu expense-account lunch at Le Bernardin with Glenn because his VIP client stood him up (clearly the client had never tasted Eric Ripert's food), and her interview at Marco, with Marco. Not the most auspicious history, but Lo insisted killer heels were a must when asking someone to part with large sums of money. Then she wrapped a Pucci scarf around Georgia's neck, declaring it added just the right amount of Italian flash. "He's from Bari," Lo said over Georgia's protests. "He'll love it." Though Georgia thought the scarf was more Midwestern flight attendant than Sophia Loren, she'd dutifully tied it that morning precisely the way Lo had shown her.

For the eleventh time, Georgia punched redial on her cell, and Bernard's voice, maddeningly polite, exceedingly casual, instructed her to leave a message. The scarf felt like a noose around her neck, tightening with each message she left. "Where are you, where are you, where are you?" she said quietly, lest anyone be lurking outside the locker room. No need to advertise that her partner had ditched her.

She closed the phone and picked up the top business plan from the pile she'd stacked on the metal folding chair, the lone piece of furniture in the room. This was her personal plan, the one that contained her notes, critical phrases, ideas, things she couldn't forget to say. "Okay," she whispered, flipping through the plan. "You can do this, Georgia. You can do this." The cheat sheet stuck under the front cover fluttered to the floor, and before she had a chance to pick it up, the assistant's voice rattled across the intercom.

"Georgia, you're up."

"But the meeting isn't even supposed to start for"—she looked at her watch again—"two minutes. And you promised me ten on top of that. Can't you stall?"

"No can do. Sorry. He sent the last guy packing early."

"But my partner isn't here." Her feet and temples throbbed in unison.

"Yeah, well, Luca's schedule is tight. There are five people after you, and the car is taking him to Teterboro at four. You want me to cancel?"

"No, don't cancel. I'm coming up."

She grabbed the business plans from the chair and ran as fast as her four-inch heels would allow, then realized her cheat sheet was floundering on the locker room floor. Hesitating for just a second—could she do it without Bernard and without the cheat sheet? Answer: no way—she ran back to the locker room, snatched up the flimsy piece of paper, and flew up the stairs two at a time.

Pablo placed a plate of buffalo mozzarella, oven-roasted tomatoes, and basil pesto before Georgia, dipping his bald head slightly.

"Thanks, Pablo," she said.

He flashed a quick wink, then disappeared. Before becoming a waiter, he was a majordomo for some zillionaire who docked his pay anytime their eyes met. Out of financial necessity he learned to make himself invisible and could now clear an entire four-top without anyone's noticing he'd been there.

"You like insalata caprese," Luca said.

Georgia couldn't tell by his inflection if it was a question or a statement, so she nodded. "Who doesn't." It was true. Even the snootiest of chefs, the foodiest of foodies, liked a good caprese. A bad caprese was another story.

"I happen to love insalata caprese. But these tomatoes, I'm not so crazy about. Your change, yes?" He poked a tomato distastefully and puffed out his lip.

"Um, yes, it is my change. Winter's tough on tomatoes. Cherries taste like newspaper pulp, the beefsteaks are the size of walnuts, and the Israeli hydroponics, while lovely to look at, have zero flavor. Roasting the plums makes them rich and earthy, attractive, and the customers really seem to—"

"You have something you want to talk to me about?" He stabbed his fork into the tomato, watching the juice drip onto the mozzarella.

"I do, Luca. It's about my and my partner's idea—"

He held up his hand without looking at her, seeming to collect his thoughts for a second. "Partner? I don't see a partner at this table. I don't see anyone at this table but you and me." He made a show of staring at the two empty chairs kitty-corner to him.

"Unfortunately, he was held up and couldn't make it, but I'm sure I can explain everything—"

"Held up? You mean with a gun?" This time he looked at her.

"No, not with a gun. I mean, he was held up—"

"Because that would have been a good excuse. There's not much you can do when someone's sticking a gun up your nose, you know what I mean?"

"Yeah, I think so, but, no, no guns, just a family emergency. Some family, um, issue."

"Mmm. That's too bad."

"But as I said, I'm sure—"

"Because where I come from, if you have a partner, the partner is supposed to show up. Maybe it's different here, but that's the way I do business. I'm not all that comfortable with the partner who doesn't show up." He shrugged his shoulders.

Georgia swallowed; Luca was a bigger son of a bitch than she'd realized. She folded her hands on the table, took a breath, and leaned forward. "Luca, I understand that this might look a bit odd, but I assure you my partner is one hundred percent dedicated to this project. Once you hear about it, I think you'll be as excited as we are."

Luca crossed his knife and fork and dropped the utensils onto his picked-over plate, branding the *caprese* with a gigantic *X. Eat at your own peril!* the dish seemed to scream. He rested his chin on manicured hands and narrowed his eyes. Twin rings, thick as washers and dusted with diamonds, encased girlish pinkies, strangely hairless considering the fluff around his neck. Georgia hadn't noticed the matching rings earlier, just the one that had dented her pinkie.

"Go on," he said.

She took a sip of water and cleared her throat. "Our idea is to open an eighty-seat restaurant on the Upper East Side. As head chef, I'll run the kitchen. My partner will run the front of the house. Between us, we have over twenty years of experience in New York City restaurants, as well as experience in Italy and France."

"Upper East Side? Why not the West Village? I thought all the hot restaurants were downtown."

"The West Village is oversaturated. It doesn't need another food-driven, quietly stylish restaurant where you're guaranteed a good meal and a good time. But aside from the three- and four-star culinary havens, the Upper East Side has nothing but frat-boy joints, red-sauce Italians, and overpriced bring-the-parents-as-long-as-they're-paying places with mediocre food. There's a void." She folded her hands on the table in front of her. "And a need."

Her confidence, absent all morning, started to rebound. Maybe it was her hair, which she'd glimpsed in the rococo mirror behind Luca's head, registering an unheard-of frizz factor of one. (Pro blowout, plus newly purchased silk pillowcase, plus frigid temps equaled insanely smooth hair.) Maybe it was her feet, which had finally stopped hurting. Or maybe it was because she suddenly knew that—with or without Bernard—she could ace the pitch.

Pablo arrived at the table with a pair of Luca's Yeoward glasses and a bottle of Col d'Orcia Brunello, which he held out for Luca's inspection. She wondered if this was the usual drill or if the wine signaled she'd passed some sort of test. Pablo eased the cork out of the bottle and handed it to Luca, who pocketed it, then nodded his head, apparently deciding tasting was superfluous.

"Enjoy," Pablo said after he finished pouring glasses for both of them.

"Go on, Georgia," Luca said, swirling the wine in his glass.

So she did. She started with the food, describing a light summer dinner of parchment-baked orata in a *pistou* of baby vegetables, Israeli couscous, basil and heirloom-tomato salad, and lemon-rosemary gelato; and a hearty winter dinner of butternut squash and apple risotto, braised lamb shanks, smashed fingerling potatoes and wilted collard greens, and warm banana-and-chocolate bread pudding, so he'd see she wasn't a one-season chef. She talked menu strategy, so he'd see she knew her way around food costs. She talked about the wine list, naming off-the-beaten-path producers to appeal to the oenophile in him, and the short but steep list of house drinks, designed to fatten both the cocks-and-apps crew and the bottom line. She talked about giving uptown a chance to dine in the hood and downtown a reason to risk nosebleeds uptown. The furrowed brow slowly relaxed, the throbbing vein slashed across his forehead quieted, the jangly foot rested. He liked what he was hearing.

Emboldened, she walked him through the restaurant, beginning with the cast-bronze door handle under the portal window, the arrangement of pear blossoms by the hostess stand, the random-width pine flooring reclaimed from an old barn in Columbia County, the hand-rubbed-maple bar. Luca squinted his eyes, staring at some faraway place, so Georgia continued, moving on to the gauzy drapes and crisp linen napkins on farmhouse tables.

Nerves and nonstop talking had made her mouth dry as a mohair sweater, and she took a tiny sip of wine. The silence sliced through Luca's reverie like a mandoline, and he flicked his hand in the air angrily, either swatting a nonexistent fly or signaling her to continue. She quickly jumped back in with her favorite part of cooking, the smells that would infuse the restaurant from open to close. Nutty olive oil, zesty herbs, briny oysters, lusty chocolate, pungent cheese, crisp greens, fresh citrus, bracing vinegar. Luca's nose slowly stretched skyward as his eyelids drooped.

Before she could talk herself out of it, she slipped into finances, telling him how much they'd need and the breakdown between hard and soft costs, why the HVAC system was such a huge and necessary expense, justifying the need for a Pacojet. She continued with how much to allot for rent, key money, monthly payroll expenses, and time frames for the planning and design and construction phases, including change orders. Then she hit the piece that made Luca's eyes go wide: how much money he could expect to make in one, three, and five years. All this with less than ten *ums*.

"I guess you're telling me your place won't be a tax write-off, huh?" Luca said, smiling at last.

"Definitely not. We intend to make money, and we know we can." Out of the corner of her eye, Georgia noticed Luca's assistant waving frantically.

Luca kept smiling, but his brow wrinkled. "That's some talk from someone who's never run her own business." He rapped his fingers on the table. "There are no guarantees, in business or in life. That's a lesson we all discover at some point. Only the truly lucky won't."

"I think I've already learned this on both fronts, Luca."

"Because you got fired once or twice? Had your heart broken a couple times? I hope you're right, Georgia, and God bless you if you are." He stood up. "Looks like my assistant is going to have a heart attack if I don't end this meeting right now. I've already kept the councilman waiting for"—he glanced at his Piaget—"eighteen minutes, just three shy of rude."

She thanked him for his time and handed him two business plans. He cocked his head almost imperceptibly, and his assistant strode over and removed the documents, glaring at Georgia just slightly.

"Too bad your partner didn't show." Luca pursed his lips and stared at her.

"Well, I'm sure he—"

"Let me ask you something. How wedded are you to this partner who can't even bother showing up for a meeting?"

She swallowed hard. "Really, seriously wedded. Till-death-do-us-part wedded."

Luca continued staring at her without speaking. "That's too bad. Hard to invest in a place when you don't know the whole management team."

"I'm sure we can arrange something."

But the councilman was already on his way over with outstretched hands and open wallet, and Luca's attention had moved elsewhere. As she walked out of the dining room, she couldn't help but wonder if she should kill Bernard, or if someone else had taken care of it for her.

The cell phone jittered across the table like a june bug, the polished marble top sending it skittering to the floor. Georgia picked it up and glared at the number showing.

"Don't think so," she said under her breath. But then again, she had to know. She flipped it open, holding it a few inches from her lips. "Where the hell are you? Let me rephrase that: Where the hell *were* you?"

Two tables down, a pair of blue-haired lady lunchers raised their penciled-in eyebrows at each other. "Such anger," one of them said while the other shook her head disapprovingly.

Georgia covered the phone with her hand. "Excuse me, ladies. Boy problems."

The women smiled sympathetically, their rouged cheeks flushing. Who hadn't been there.

"I am finally getting off the fucking F train," said Bernard. "I have been underground, in a tunnel. For four. Fucking. Hours."

Georgia twirled a curl around her index finger. "I know I'm supposed to be sympathetic and all, but may I ask why you didn't take a cab?"

"I couldn't find one, Georgia. I looked, but I couldn't find one. I have *never* had a problem on the subway. I allowed myself *two hours* to get to the Oven. It normally takes twenty-five minutes to get to midtown. The train broke down. People were fainting, screaming about terrorists, it was mass hysteria."

"Mmhmm." Georgia bit into one of three dark chocolate truffles lolling on the plate in front of her. After the meeting, she'd fled the restaurant without so much as grabbing her coat. She'd needed air. Air and chocolate, and in that order. An arctic blast smacked her face as soon as she hit the sidewalk, and with the air part covered, she headed straight to Saks, the closest she could get to killer chocolate and cappuccino in four-inch heels and a flimsy shirt.

The province of social shoppers the city over, the eighth-floor chocolate bar was the kind of place where she could easily run into people she'd rather avoid, like her creepy freshman-year roommate, or Lo's snooty younger sister, or, worst of all, Glenn's mother. Fortunately, none of the above were in attendance, and Georgia had gratefully sunk into the first seat she saw.

"I know you're furious, but please just tell me where you are. I need to hear what happened," Bernard said.

"Saks, eighth floor. And you're lucky I'm even speaking to you."

"Was it that bad?"

"That's for me to know and you to find out if you play your cards right."

The waiter stopped at Georgia's table just as she polished off the last truffle, a strange curry flavor she didn't care for. She ordered four more truffles and a double macchiato. All things considered, she'd done well. More than well. She barely referenced her cheat sheet and answered every trick question Luca posed. If she were the Bari godfather, she'd invest.

Two truffles later, a beleaguered Bernard walked into the café. His face was ashen, his red tie askew, his eyes puffy.

"Have you been crying, Bernard?" Even if the answer was

yes, Georgia's sympathy for her no-show, cheapskate partner would still stagnate in the low-to-nonexistent range.

"No, Georgia, I have not been crying. I have spent the past four hours in a toilet paper roll with one hundred of my now closest friends, many of whom don't bother to bathe or brush their teeth. Ever. Do you expect me to walk in looking fresh from a shave and a haircut at Paul Mole?"

"Have a chocolate."

"Only if it's laced." He fell into the chair across from her, prompting the ladies to cluck. "With strychnine."

"He's cute," one of them whispered from behind peach fingernails.

Georgia smiled.

"What was that?" Bernard asked, raking his fingers through his pouffy hair. It had probably looked good when he'd left the house five hours earlier.

"Nothing," she said. "So."

"Tell me. Please."

And she did, beginning with the double drama of his not showing up and the meeting starting early, then Luca mistakenly thinking Bernard had been held up by a gunman and actually seeming excited about it.

"Great," Bernard said. "He'd rather I get shot than pitch him?"

"Possibly." Georgia sipped her espresso. "Actually, yes, I think he would have been happy if you'd been shot."

She told him what she'd said about the food, the menu, the specials, the wine, the look and feel, the vibe. And how she'd handled the finances, juggling numbers and spewing them out like a regular Wharton-degreed, Wall Street whiz. As she spoke, her eyebrows danced, her hands whirred, her fingers stabbed the air. By the time her story reached its climax she had to grab the chair's armrests just to keep from jumping out of it.

"Sounds terrific, Georgia."

"Well, yeah, it was, until the end." She sighed, her ebullience evaporating.

"What happened then?"

"He said it was too bad he hadn't met my partner. He said he didn't know how he could invest without meeting the entire management team."

"So I'll fly to Bari or something," Bernard said, flipping his fork into the air and watching it crash onto Georgia's truffle-filled plate.

"That's what I told him."

"You did? And what'd he say?"

"He didn't. The meeting was over." She felt flat, like a half-drunk bottle of champagne forgotten in the fridge, a celebration that never quite got off the ground. She'd had Luca, she knew she had. The meeting started on a prickly note, but as soon as she mentioned her orata, his taste buds kicked in. By the time she'd moved on to finances, he was there, envisioning himself at the restaurant's primo table, swirling a glass of Vietti Barolo, surrounded by the usual bevy of blondes, only these girls were younger, prettier, blonder than the current crew. When she told him how much they anticipated the restaurant would gross, Luca's eyes boinged out of their sockets, hanging there for a second before ka-chinging back into place. If his assistant had suddenly shuffled over with an attaché case stuffed with unmarked Benjamins, Georgia would barely have batted an eye. Alas, no briefcase materialized, no deal was struck. Instead, the meeting ended with a whimper, the recollection that half the management team was missing and the dreaded promise to be in touch.

The only thing to do, she told Bernard, was to hope he'd call, and if he didn't, to wait enough time before calling him. And to start looking for alternative investors.

"What time is he leaving?" Bernard asked.

"Four." She looked at her watch. "Fifteen minutes."

He grabbed Georgia's macchiato, draining it in one gulp, jumped up from his chair, and sprinted out of the café, knocking into a display of holiday chocolates. "Keep your cell phone on!" he shouted right before pitching onto the escalator.

"Where are you going?" she yelled. But he was already gone, the top of his head disappearing into the sea of shoppers.

The ladies looked at her, their mouths agape. This was more excitement than they'd seen in months.

"Men," Georgia said to them, shrugging her shoulders. She flagged down the waiter and ordered a replacement macchiato.

"Can't live with 'em," one of the ladies said.

"Can't live without their credit cards," the other finished. They erupted into throaty laughter.

"Georgia Gray?" Carrying multiple shopping bags in one hand and a crimson Birkin in the other was none other than Huggy Henderson. A cashmere cape, decorated with a jewel-encrusted brooch, was draped over her shoulders.

Smiling, Georgia stood to greet her. "Huggy. It's good to see you."

"You too, dear. The last time I saw you, you were cooking at that Marco restaurant downtown. After that review, I think it's safe to assume you've moved on?" Huggy rested her bags on the ground. "Mind if I take a seat? My feet are killing me."

"Please do." Georgia sat down, her eyes resting on Huggy's croc pumps, which would set her back at least a month's rent. "I left Marco a long time ago."

"Left?"

"Was fired."

"There's nothing shameful in being fired, Georgia. Don't you let anyone tell you there is." Huggy removed her cape. "And what are you doing here? I don't see any shopping bags."

"No, no shopping for me. I just finished a meeting and was craving chocolate." She looked at Huggy fiddling with the Chanel scarf at her neck, her nails the perfect shade of shell pink. For the first time in her life, Georgia understood what it meant to have a lightbulb go off in her brain. "Actually, this might interest you. I'm opening a restaurant. I was meeting with an investor."

"How brilliant! Please let me know when you open. Do you have my card?" She unlatched her bag and pulled out a leather card case. "I'll send all my friends."

"Thanks, Huggy. Actually, we're still raising money. I have a great partner, and we have a great business plan, if you—"

"Waiter!" Huggy called suddenly. "Truffles. Six of them. All dark. And a black coffee. Large." She turned to Georgia. "Did you know that dark chocolate helps you lose weight? Not milk, not white, just dark. Especially around the tummy. It's absolutely true."

"No, I didn't hear that," Georgia said. "So, we're looking for investors now. The idea is to open an eighty-seat, market-driven restaurant on the Upper East Side—"

Huggy turned to her. "Are you telling me this because you think I might be interested or because you think I might be an investor?"

Georgia sipped her espresso. "Hopefully both?"

"Sadly, I'm in no position to invest in anything, dear. Larry and I, well, let's just say that *sociopath* made off with most of our money, just as he did with everyone else's. That greedy . . ." Huggy bit her lip.

Georgia glanced at Huggy's plump shopping bags. "Oh."

"This is the first time I've been shopping all season. Everything else I'm wearing is at least a year old, the bag is almost five." She cupped her hand over her mouth. "But it's true what they say about Hermès. Worth every penny."

Georgia tried to smile.

"Don't look so crestfallen, Georgia. All is not lost, it never is. You do remember my son, Andrew?"

Of course she remembered Andrew: the golden voice, the soulful eyes . . . the stunning girlfriend.

"Andrew's a venture capitalist. He invests in small businesses, usually tech companies, but he's dabbled in the odd off-Broadway show or nightclub. I happen to have his card." Huggy pulled out a different leather card case and handed over Andrew Henderson's card. "I'll tell him to expect your call."

"Thanks, Huggy. I appreciate your help."

"Of course. Now I'm afraid I must go. I'm late for my training session at Brownings."

"What about your truffles?"

"Take them home with you." Huggy stood up and swung her cape over her shoulders. "Because the truth is, dear, the best thing for the tummy is really no food at all."

Hot water spilled from the spout, bubbling when it hit the eucalyptus bath salts sprinkled in the tub. The tiny bathroom quickly grew steamy and saunalike, and the scent of the lime, basil, and mandarin candle Georgia had bought at Saks filled the air. Her hair was piled on top of her head in a messy bun and a sticky clay mask covered her face. A month-old *US* magazine, a glass of ice water, and the phone rested on the floor between the tub and Sally, who had stretched out on the bath mat and was intensely gnawing her paw. Georgia couldn't risk missing a call from Bernard.

She settled into the bath and gingerly leaned back onto the cool porcelain, relieved she'd arranged for the sous-chef to cover her shift at the Oven. She'd correctly predicted that after sweating rivers in front of Luca at the pitch meeting, the last place she'd want to be was sweating rivers in his kitchen during dinner rush. When she'd gone back to the Oven after Saks to retrieve her coat, Pablo met her at the door, coat in hand. Though he was too discreet to ask any questions about the meeting, he did mention something about Bernard sprinting down the street in what looked like a high-speed chase. Of what, he didn't know, nor could he say for sure whether Bernard was the chaser or the chased. Whichever it was, it didn't sound good.

The bathwater started to cool, and she pushed down on the drain release with her big toe and leaned forward to blast the hot. A good, long soak was just what she needed. When the phone rang, she pounced on it and it slid from her soapy hands, bouncing off the tile floor.

"Georgia." It was her mother.

The door on her relationship with Dorothy had creaked open in San Casciano, and Georgia didn't want to be the one to kick it shut. Still, she always had to be wary with Dorothy, and she braced herself for her mother's usual line of questioning—dagger-sharp, double-edged, and designed to make her only daughter feel like dirt—to begin.

Strangely, it didn't. Sure, she grilled Georgia about the meeting, but she actually seemed interested in her responses. So while Georgia spilled out her story in a rush of run-on sentences and mangled clauses, Dorothy did the unthinkable: she listened.

"Well, Georgia," she said when her daughter had finished, "from where I sit, it sounds like you aced the pitch. Even if Luca doesn't come through with the financing, you should be proud of yourself for a job well done."

Georgia was shocked into silence. *Aced? Proud? A job well done?* Was this the same woman who'd accused her thirteen-year-old daughter of plagiarizing the Harriet Tubman report that won the eighth-grade essay contest?

"Thanks, Mom," she said at last. "I guess I am sort of proud. But I need the money. I really want the restaurant."

"If the restaurant is what you want, you'll get the restaurant. Maybe not from this Luca guy, but you'll get the money somehow."

"I hope so."

"Oh, and by the way, your father and I will be in New York in a few weeks, early January. We're coming for the opera, *Rigoletto,* on Saturday night. Unfortunately, it's sold out, otherwise I'd offer you a ticket."

"That's fine, Mom, I'll probably have to work anyway."

"But we'd love to see you for dinner that Friday."

"Okay."

"Your place?"

Georgia was silent for a second. "Sure, Mom, my place sounds great."

They hung up the phone when Dorothy sparked up a cigarette. As Georgia now understood, she drove Dorothy to smoke just as Dorothy drove her to eat. Maybe they were more alike than she realized.

With her toes beginning to prune, she climbed out of the tub and slipped on her robe. The buzzer sounded. Unannounced visitors were as common as rent-controlled apartments and as welcome as bedbugs. She padded to the intercom, leaving liquid footprints in her wake.

"I been buzzing you for ten minutes. Your boyfriend's on his way." It was the unfriendly doorman, whose name she still didn't know.

"My boyfriend?"

"Yeah. He'll be there in a sec."

Before she'd hung up, there was a knock at the door. Her stomach dropped. Please, she prayed to any God who would listen, not Glenn. Not now. Not ever again.

"Georgia! Open the door!"

Bernard. She'd called his cell a dozen times since leaving Saks and had heard nothing back. Despite her most Zen-like intentions, the incommunicado thing was infuriating her.

"Georgia, come on. I can hear you fuming."

She opened the door and stared at him, her hands resolutely on her hips.

"Wow. Green's your color, George."

"What?"

"Brings out your eyes."

"What are you talking about? And how about answering your phone for a change? I've left you a million messages."

Bernard stifled a smile and pointed to her face. She drew a hand to her cheek, still tacky from the green clay mask.

"Oh, please," she said. "As if you've never seen a girl in a mask."

"Georgia, you could wear a hockey mask for all I'd care right now."

"Why's that?"

"Am I allowed in? Or do I have to report from your smoky hallway?" He waved a hand under his wrinkled nose.

She turned without saying anything and he followed her into the living room.

"This better be good," Georgia said, tightening the belt on her robe and sitting on the chair, the very one on which she'd sat when Glenn dumped her. If Bernard's story ended badly, it was going straight to Goodwill.

"Oh, it is," Bernard said. "Just listen."

He'd left Saks and hightailed it to the Oven, hoping to catch even two minutes with Luca. Had he not got stuck behind side-by-side double strollers for an entire block, he might have stood a chance. Instead, he arrived at the restaurant seconds after Luca's car picked him up, according to his assistant, who was even more obnoxious when his boss wasn't around. Bernard explained who he was and pressed him for the name of the car-service company, but the assistant feigned ignorance. Fortunately, the coat-check girl knew the name of the car company and had seen a black Mercedes S500 with tinted windows cart away her boss just moments earlier.

Georgia's eyes widened. This *was* good.

Bernard hit the street where, for the first time in his life, he hallelujahed the rush-hour traffic. Cars crept forward, horns blasted, the occasional one-finger salute was raised and returned. To get to Teterboro, Luca would have to take the Lincoln Tunnel, and Bernard plotted out the most sensible route: down Fifth to Forty-second. When he realized he was as likely to hail a cab as he was a helicopter, he started running. Fast. By the time he got to Forty-second Street, he could barely breathe. Which is when he spotted the tinted-windowed black Mercedes pulling a cool pick-and-roll onto Forty-second. A bicycle taxi rolled to a stop next to Bernard, and he knew what he had to do. He climbed in, pushing out the teenaged couple snuggling under the faux-fur throw, placating them with a pair of twenties. Ride like fucking Lance Armstrong, he told the driver. The little pedicab, powered by quads of steel, closed in on the hulking Mercedes. The car stopped at a yellow light, and the pedicab rode up alongside it, victorious. Bernard tossed the driver a bill he hoped was a twenty but later discovered was a hundred, and rapped on the Mercedes's back window. Nothing. He rapped again, holding up the business plan he'd stuck halfway down his pants for safekeeping when he began his pursuit. The window inched down.

"Hello, Mr. Santini. I'm Bernard Lambert, Georgia Gray's partner. If I can just have a few moments of your time—"

"Who?" a man's voice growled.

"Bernard. Georgia's partner." He held up the business plan, smiling as charmingly as he could muster after hijacking a pedicab. *Grand-mère* would not have approved.

"Bernard Lambert? You're French?"

"Yes!" The light was about to turn green, and Bernard was pretty sure he'd get mowed down by the pissed-off driver of the van behind him, who looked none too pleased at having been cut off by a bicycle taxi.

"*Est-ce que tu parles français?*" Luca asked.

"*Oui!*" Bernard shouted. The light turned. He was a dead man.

Miraculously the door opened. "Get in," Luca said in French. "And tell me about your restaurant."

Bernard rode with Luca all the way to Teterboro. He spoke, in French only, at Luca's insistence, for the duration of the fifty-five-minute drive. Luca didn't look at him or nod his head or give any indication that he so much as heard a word Bernard said. So he kept talking. First he talked about the restaurant, then he talked about himself, and when he'd exhausted that seemingly inexhaustible subject, he talked about Georgia. By the time they pulled up to the jet center, his tongue was so swollen he could barely close his jaw around it.

"Your really think this will work?" Luca asked as he stepped out of the car.

"*Oui*" was all Bernard could say.

"You've got your money," Luca said, reverting to English. "All but a hundred grand. That needs to come from management. It's gotta hurt your pocket if you lose. Go to your friends, the National Bank of Mom, a fucking loan shark for all I care. But get the hundred grand and you'll get your restaurant."

Bernard ended his story and looked at Georgia, whose green face was frozen, the mask having finally dried. "Did you hear me, Kermit? We got the money."

"Oh. My. God." Georgia sprang from her chair. "We got the money. We got the money. Bernard, we got the money." She grabbed his hands and pulled him up from the couch. "We got the money!"

They bounced up and down together, holding hands like toddlers on a trampoline. Sally joined the celebration, barking her approval.

"Wait a minute," Georgia said, dropping his hands. "We have to come up with a *hundred* grand? How are we going to get a hundred grand?"

"I have no idea."

Georgia fell onto the couch. "Shit."

Bernard plopped down next to her. "*Merde,*" he said. "The word is *merde.*"

Chapter Twenty-three

$\mathcal{T}$he skinny guy with the scraggly soul patch and dirty white jeans pawed through the loot covering Georgia's dining table, a Chippendale knockoff that had belonged to Grammy. Dorothy had no need for repros in her authentically midcentury modern home, so the table had passed to Georgia. She loved its scratches and scars, the pale rings where Grammy's mugs of tea had rested, the gash where Georgia had dropped a rolling pin—and nearly crushed her pinkie—during one of their annual Christmas-cookie baking marathons.

"Not this, maybe this, definitely not this, ooh, I love this." The guy, called Lemming, smiled twitchily at Georgia, who looked away.

Her entire relationship with Glenn was strewn out across the table, seven years of highs, lows, and in-betweens reduced to a pile of merch; a romance that almost ended in marriage for sale to the highest bidder. The whole scene was slightly unsavory, beginning with the ratlike Lemming rifling through things that had actually touched her skin and ending with the (hopefully huge) check he would write to scoop it all up in his Nike duffel.

Lo swore she'd do better selling directly to Lemming than going to one of the established consignment stores, plus she'd get the money right away. Since Georgia's entire future now rested on securing a fast fifty grand (providing Bernard covered his half), she cast aside her moral doubts about the whole ordeal and set up the appointment with Lemming.

"This is great." He held up a red cashmere sweater decorated with a black skull-and-crossbones to his emaciated frame. "I might keep it for myself."

"You definitely should." Georgia had worn the sweater twice, the last time to a Halloween show at the Bowery Ballroom, where some drunk guy had spilled a beer on her. Later, a falafel-hummus-and-tabbouleh pita exploded as she bit into it, sending green and orange bits all over her—and the sweater. He was welcome to it.

Lemming flung the sweater to the floor and fluttered his fingers over her jewelry, which Lo had neatly arranged into separate but equally glittering groupings of earrings and necklaces. As a chef, Georgia never wore anything beyond sleeves or gloves on her arms or hands, which meant no bracelets, watches, or rings, until *the* ring.

"Me&Ro?" Lemming held up giant gold hoops dripping with fringe and tiny ruby beads.

"Aren't they amazing?" Lo gushed.

Georgia had insisted her friend attend the sell-off, as much for her support as for comments like these, which would surely bump up the final take.

"Vintage Me&Ro," she continued. "My sister threatened to buy her whole collection, but I insisted you had first dibs, Lemming."

Georgia choked back a laugh. *Vintage* Me&Ro? The earrings were a whopping seven years old, a Valentine's Day gift. At the time she hadn't even heard of Me&Ro. When Lo told her how much the gift from her then brand-new beau had cost, Georgia's eyes bugged out of her head. She couldn't fathom spending that much on earrings. Dinner at Taillevent, yes. But a pair of earrings?

"They're in good condition," Lemming said. "And they're stamped. I'll give you three."

"Okay," Lo said. "If that's the best you can do." She turned so that Lemming couldn't see her and pumped her fist. Georgia was quickly learning that in the consignment game getting less than a third of the item's original value was cause for celebration.

By the time Lemming had gone through the entire collection, the tally on his antiquated counting machine reached $3,500. The seven years she'd spent with Glenn were worth, monetarily speaking, the cost of a spiffy new spring wardrobe.

Finally Lemming left (though not, alas, before using her bathroom), and Georgia shut and bolted the door behind him. She fanned the cash in her hands, thirty-five crisp hundred-dollar bills. "Just think," she said to Lo, "only forty-six thousand five hundred to go."

Sandwiched between a fancy boutique and a fancier jewelry store in Madison's high-rent shopping district, the Viand Coffee Shop was the quintessential New York greasy spoon. The clientele was a mixed bag of conspicuous consumers, students on Christmas break, construction workers, and Georgia, who was wedged into a booth fit for a large child. Space was, naturally, at a premium. Dabbing at the beads of perspiration on her forehead, she ordered a Diet Coke with lemon and waited for Andrew Henderson, her boot tapping on the vinyl floor.

After Bernard told her about the hundred grand, she'd pulled out Andrew's card and punched his number into her cell, scared that if she waited any longer, she'd talk herself out of calling him at all. It was hard enough to call a guy on whom she'd insta-crushed after thirty seconds of small talk, harder still since he had a girlfriend, and hardest since she was calling to ask for money . . . *his* money. But she'd done it (leaving a message with only one *um*), and ten days later, just when she'd written Andrew Henderson off, he called back. He'd be happy to meet her, he said, and could she possibly do it in, say, an hour at his favorite coffee shop? Within forty-five minutes she'd exchanged pj's and slippers for jeans and booties (with a reasonable two-inch heel), run ten city blocks, and claimed Viand's back booth. She'd just finished sucking down her soda when Andrew walked to her table.

"Georgia," he said, a smile spreading across his face. "How are you?"

She looked up into his deep brown eyes, feeling for a second as if she were on a first date and really wishing she were. Except that she'd have suggested a different venue, and the last and only other time she'd met Andrew he'd been kissing a beautiful woman. "Hi, Andrew. How are you?"

"Great. Happy belated holidays." He slid into the demi-booth opposite hers, still smiling. "If you haven't been here before, the turkey is amazing. Fresh roasted."

They placed their orders—a turkey club and another Diet Coke for Georgia and an open-faced hot turkey and Coke for Andrew. He shared a funny story about the holidays, Henderson-style (more mandatory merrymaking than could possibly be healthy), and asked about hers (two surprisingly pleasant nights with her parents for Christmas, mellow dinner party at Lo's for New Year's) before resting his elbows on the table and clearing his throat.

"Why don't you tell me about your restaurant?" he said.

Taking a deep breath, she launched into her three-minute, highlights-only pitch. She'd flesh out the details over turkey. Andrew listened intently, waiting until she'd finished.

"It sounds great, Georgia. But before we get into the nitty-gritty, I want to be up-front with you. We've gotten hammered lately, and the only terms we'll agree to in a project like yours is an ownership stake. Unfortunately that's nonnegotiable."

She frowned. "That's a bit of a problem. We're not selling a stake, we're looking for a straight loan. It's more an investment in us, or in me, since you don't really know Bernard, although you don't really know me either. Sorry to waste your time with this." She looked for the waiter. "I'll cancel my order. I know you're busy."

"No, no, no. Don't do that. Just because we can't do business together doesn't mean we can't eat lunch together, does it? A girl's gotta eat, right?"

She nodded.

"Then let's eat together. The turkey really is good, and I'm buying. What could be better for a cash-starved entrepreneur?"

Georgia laughed. "Okay, but only to try this terrific turkey. And because I never turn down a free lunch."

By the time they finished eating, Georgia was not altogether convinced she *hadn't* been on a first date. Andrew was charming and funny and smart and, she could swear, even a little flirtatious. They walked out of the restaurant, pausing on the street to say good-bye. Georgia thanked him for lunch.

"It was fun," Andrew said. "And I think your restaurant is going to kill."

"Thanks. I hope you're right."

"So," he said, stuffing his hands in his coat pockets, "botched business deal aside, do you think I could call you sometime?"

"Yeah, sure," Georgia said slowly. "But don't you have a girl-friend?"

"No. What makes you say that?"

"That night I met you at Marco there was a woman who joined your table. I saw her kiss you. And you definitely kissed back."

"Watching me pretty closely, huh?"

Georgia felt her face get hot. "Not really, I just happened to turn at the exact moment she kissed you."

"I'm kidding. That was Lisa, a short-lived and extremely *ex* girlfriend. I haven't dated anyone in a while."

Georgia's belly swirled like a lava lamp. She knew she wasn't supposed to get all fluttery about Andrew not having a girlfriend *and* wanting to call her, but sometimes these things couldn't be helped. "Okay. Call me."

"Count on it."

The table was set with Grammy's silver, hemp napkins, and plain white dishes Georgia had scooped up for a dollar each at a restaurant-supply store on Bowery. A cheese plate filled with her favorites—Mt. Tam, Humboldt Fog, Époisses, Rogue River blue—sat on the coffee table, while a bottle of champagne and several Pellegrinos chilled in the fridge. Two bottles (you never knew) of a delicious Saint Julien Bordeaux were at the ready; one was already decanting. She placed three soup shooters on the table before answering the door, Sally at her heels.

"Georgia!" Hal said, his arms outstretched. "It's wonderful to see you. And hello to you, Sally." He reached down and scratched between her ears.

"Hi, Dad, hi, Mom." Georgia hugged them both. "Come on in."

"We brought champagne," Dorothy trilled, waving a bottle. "And flowers."

Georgia hung their coats and seated them on the couch, where Sally planted herself at their feet. Dorothy's silvery blond bob had grown out and faded back to its natural gray. Chunky turquoise-and-silver earrings and a billowy sweater-pant combo, much more in keeping with her hippie style, replaced the pearls and peach suit she'd worn in Italy.

"Help yourself to some cheese, and these"—Georgia pointed to a square platter—"are smoked salmon, chive, crème fraîche, and Asian pear rolls, and these"—she pointed to a second platter—"are foie gras toast points with fig gelée."

"Interesting," said Dorothy. "How . . . unusual."

"What's this?" Hal asked, picking up one of three cordials filled with soup.

"That's a black-trumpet-mushroom velouté. It's very rich." The food was fussier than her usual, but it was the first time her parents had come to dinner. It was a big night.

As she walked into the kitchen to find a vase, Georgia couldn't resist stealing a glance at her mom, who was sampling an hors d'oeuvre. "Try one, Hal," Georgia heard her whisper. "It's delicious."

He slurped down the soup. "This is terrific too."

Georgia brought out the flowers and some flutes and opened the champagne her parents had brought, a Billecart-Salmon rosé that trumped the Moët chilling in her fridge, a leftover from Lo's New Year's party. Georgia had splurged on wine and food and couldn't afford to splurge on everything.

"Tell us about the restaurant," Dorothy said, popping another salmon roll into her mouth.

So Georgia told them about Luca and how he'd agreed to provide all the capital they needed, *if* she and Bernard came up with a hundred grand of their own money to invest. Her parents exchanged looks.

"And where are you with that?" Hal asked.

"And why didn't you tell us before?" Dorothy asked.

"Well, I sold off all the gifts Glenn ever gave me for a couple thousand, and if I liquidate my bank account, I'll have a couple more. I just had a fruitless meeting with a really cool venture capitalist who can't invest, and now Bernard and I are sort of at a dead end. I'm thinking about selling those Berkshire Hathaway shares Grammy left me. And I didn't say anything because I was hoping to tell you once I'd raised all the money. I wanted you to see I was serious and that I could do it."

"We know you're serious," said Dorothy.

"And we know you can do it, honey," her father added.

"Thanks, guys. I appreciate that." Georgia stood. "Are you ready for dinner? I just need a couple minutes in the kitchen to finish up."

Her parents seated themselves at the dining table and a few minutes later Georgia brought out cumin-scented rack of lamb with herbed couscous and haricot vert. "We'll have salad after the main course."

"How Italian," said Dorothy.

Georgia poured their wine, then filled her own glass, which she promptly raised.

"Mom, Dad, thanks for coming to dinner. It's nice to cook for you."

"Thank you for having us," Dorothy said, cutting into her lamb. "The food so far has been marvelous, Georgia. I have to admit it sounds a little exotic, but you really make it work."

"This lamb is delicious," Hal agreed. "The best I've ever had."

By the time Georgia cleared their salad plates they'd killed a bottle of wine, which "paired perfectly" with the lamb, according to Hal. Good thing she had backup.

When she returned to the table with a second carafe, her

parents, whose heads had been bent together in conversation, looked up. "Your father and I have something to tell you," Dorothy announced while Georgia refilled their glasses.

Hal nodded encouragingly.

"We've decided to give you some money, the money we'd planned to contribute to your wedding. We'd like it to go to your restaurant instead."

Georgia's mouth dropped. "Really?"

"And," her mother continued, "we're also giving you the money we'd intended to give as a wedding gift. For your restaurant."

"Thirty thousand dollars," Hal said.

"Are you serious? Thirty thousand?"

He nodded. "Getting married is a momentous event in anyone's life. But following your dream, making it happen, that's—"

"Extraordinary," Dorothy finished.

Georgia was silent for a moment. When she spoke, her throat clenched a little. "Thank you. You have no idea how much this means to me. I'll pay you back as soon as I can, I promise."

"No, you won't," said Hal. "This is a gift, Georgia."

Long after they'd finished dessert, they sat around the dining table—Grammy's dining table—talking. They talked about the memoir Dorothy's book group had just read, and about the newest instructor to join Hal's department, and about the color they would paint the house in the spring, low-VOC of course. They talked about their old neighbor Mrs. Hadley, and about how much they all loved Florence and about why Georgia would never want to be a contestant on *Top Chef*. When they'd left, Georgia flopped onto the couch, pulling Sally up with her. Thirty. Freaking. Grand. From her parents.

Petal leapt onto Clem's lap and wiggled his rump against her merino sweater, his sharp claws pulling at her pricey Wolford tights.

Clem scratched his head and smiled, feigning delight at the little pug's annoying antics. Petal was Clem's best dog-sitting charge, not only because his owner was nice, generous, and frequently out of town, but because they lived in a palatial apartment in the Dakota. Putting up with the pug was a small price to pay for digs like these.

Georgia stifled a laugh as Clem tried unsuccessfully to shove Petal off her lap. The housekeeper had seated them in the living room, where they waited for the lady of the house, an über-successful businesswoman not much older than they. Georgia checked out the sweeping views of Central Park visible through the side-by-side picture windows, wondering how it would feel to own a place as grand as this.

Less than a year had passed since she'd last sat in the Bordeaux-colored living room, lamenting the lousy state of her life to Clem. Thankfully, much had changed since that depressing day. She was on the verge of opening her own, still-nameless restaurant. She was single and reasonably okay with it. Though she'd be thrilled to go on a date with Andrew Henderson, between scrambling for money and searching for a space, she didn't have the time, or the inclination, to worry about not being half of a couple. Instead she focused on being all of herself. The restaurant, *her* restaurant, was happening.

"So tell me her deal again?" she whispered.

"Makeup mogul. Runs Lime Cosmetics, that behemoth that owns every brand you've ever heard of. She's supersharp, single, really funny, and likes a good meal. I mentioned I had a friend opening a restaurant, and she said she'd always wanted to invest in one."

"But, it's not investing in a restaurant, it's investing in—"

"You, I know. I told her the deal. She's still interested. Who knows, maybe she'll back number two and you can dump the godfather."

"Clem," said a lilting voice with a gracious Southern twang. "So good to see you, and I hope I haven't kept you waiting long." Charlotte Troy, a tall, fortyish woman, crossed the living room, her dark blond curls hitting her shoulders. She wore slim black trousers, a fitted black jacket, and diamond studs. Her lips were that perfect red that's impossible to find and even more impossible to pull off, and her skin was flawless alabaster, unblemished by even a single freckle. No wonder the *Daily* dubbed her the Lipstick Queen.

She and Clem hugged, then she extended her hand to Georgia. "I'm Charlotte. And you must be Georgia. Clem's told me so much about you. Did she happen to mention that I'm a Georgia girl myself?"

"No, she didn't. I've actually never been there, but it's where my parents met, so I guess they decided—"

"Her parents met at a Dead show in Atlanta," Clem interjected. "Isn't that hilarious?"

Georgia smiled through clenched teeth. Charlotte Troy looked as if she'd grown up dancing in cotillions and sailing in regattas. She did not seem as if she'd be entertained by trippy tales of Dead shows.

"Really?" Charlotte said, drawing the word out to three syllables. "I spent a summer on Dead Tour myself, if you can believe that. My boyfriend and I bought an old VW bus and caught something like twenty-five shows." She flashed a peace sign.

"See?" Clem said to Georgia. "I told you she was cool."

"So," Charlotte continued, "Clem says you're looking for a small investment for your restaurant. Why don't you tell me some more about it." She pulled up a chair next to Georgia and sat down. Petal hopped onto Charlotte's lap, abandoning Clem for his full-time mom.

"First," Georgia began, "I should make clear that I'm not selling ownership in the restaurant. My partner and I have already raised the majority of the money from a single investor. What we need now is a hundred thousand dollars of our own to contribute. So I'm looking for a loan, really, that I'll pay back in full, with accrued interest, five points above prime, to be repaid year two, fourth quarter."

Though Clem had listened to Georgia and Bernard's pitch a dozen times, she'd never heard Georgia utter anything even remotely financial. Bernard talked dollars, Georgia talked concept. Clem cleared her throat, covering her mouth with an upwardly pointing thumb.

"And how much of that hundred do you already have?" Charlotte asked.

"Thirty and change."

"So you're looking for seventy."

"Yes," Georgia said. Bernard was chasing a few money leads, but she might as well go for it. "I brought a copy of the business plan, so you can flip through it when you have some free time. And really quickly, so you know why I'm qualified to run my own restaurant, I was head chef at Marco, a pretty popular spot downtown, and I also worked—"

"I know Marco," Charlotte said stiffly.

"Marco the restaurant? Or Marco the man?" Judging by Charlotte's downturned mouth and crossed arms, Georgia could guess.

"Unfortunately, both."

"Yeah," said Georgia. "Me too."

"Let's just say that reading that half-star review was a gleeful moment for me. I'm not normally a vengeful person, but . . ." Charlotte held up her hand. "I'm sorry you got stuck in that, Georgia. Clem told me Marco tried to screw the reviewer's teenaged daughter and that she decided to screw the restaurant in return."

"She did, did she?" Georgia stared at Clem, who fidgeted in her chair, refusing to meet her friend's eye. "That's sort of on the down-low, Charlotte. I'd hate for anyone to think I'm spreading rumors because Marco fired me." Clem and Lo were the only people Georgia had told the whole sordid story to. Even Dorothy and Hal, her new best friends, didn't know.

"Of course," said Charlotte. "Anyway, it's over and done with. I heard Marco decamped to D.C. That town is perfect for him."

"Believe it or not, the best thing that happened to me was getting fired from Marco." And getting dumped by her fiancé, Georgia could easily have added. If those two things hadn't happened, she'd still be stuck in a life that looked too good, from the outside, to give up. Without anything or anyone tying her to New York, she'd taken a risk and ventured to Italy, alone, setting in motion the chain of events that led right to this very moment in Charlotte Troy's lovely living room.

The housekeeper walked into the room. "Charlotte, Lucy's up. Do you want me to bring her in?"

"Oh, sure. We're pretty much done here anyway, but I'd love for Georgia to meet her. Lucy and Clem are already old friends."

Georgia smiled. "I'd love to meet her. Mine's waiting for me at home. Her name's Sally."

Manhattan dog owners took pampering their pets to another level entirely, but having the housekeeper bring in the dog after her nap instead of letting her walk in on her own seemed extreme. She probably took Lucy to the doggy day spa too.

Charlotte's brow wrinkled slightly, but she didn't say anything. Clem hugged her sides, her face turning red as the Bordeaux walls.

"Here she is," said the housekeeper, who had tiptoed back in. "Little Lucy." She handed a bundle wrapped in a light pink blanket to Charlotte.

"My perfect baby," Charlotte cooed. "I missed you so much. Mommy missed her little angel." She cradled the bundle in her arms and turned her body so that Georgia could see a tiny baby with a shock of black hair swaddled in the blanket.

"Oh," Georgia said. "A *baby*. Lucy's a baby. I thought she was, I mean, I don't know why, but I just assumed she was another dog." Georgia's face got hot, and closing her eyes, she prayed it didn't match Clem's.

"Because I'm not married?" said Charlotte. "Lots of people are surprised. But I never saw being single as a reason not to have a child. Better to be raised in a happy home with one parent than in an unhappy home with two."

Georgia nodded. "You're right. Lucy's lucky to have you." A successful businesswoman, a successful, *new* mother, and she had to be—flawless skin or not—at least forty-one. Clem was right; Charlotte *was* cool.

"I'm the lucky one, really. Single mothers aren't exactly welcomed with open arms in Saigon. It was more red tape than you can imagine, but worth every ounce of frustration to finally hold my daughter in my arms."

Clem, who'd never met a misty moment she didn't love, stared wistfully at mother and child, a dreamy smile on her lips. For all her toughness, she was as sappy as a pine tree.

"Georgia, why don't you leave the business plan for me and I'll have my lawyer look it over," Charlotte said. "But count on the seventy. And we can revisit the payback after you open."

A smile spread slowly across Georgia's face as those words sank in. "That's terrific, Charlotte. Really, really terrific." She was opening her own place. Correction. She and Bernard were opening *their* own place. She had to call him. She had to call her real-tor. That old laundromat on Sixty-seventh Street would be perfect. She had to call Ricky. Start staffing immediately. She had to call her old purveyors, even the waste-management guy. She had to call the architect, the construction manager. She had to . . .

Charlotte stood up to walk her guests to the door, propping Lucy on her shoulder. "If all goes well, it might make more sense for me to reinvest in your next venture. I'm much more interested in growth opportunities than I am in fixed ventures with limited returns. As it seems you are too."

"I am." Georgia clapped her hands together, feeling a rush of adrenaline or endorphins, like the kick of drinking the first half glass of really good champagne.

Charlotte Troy, single woman, cosmetic mogul, MoMA trustee, party-page fixture, onetime Deadhead, had adopted a baby girl from Vietnam at age forty-one. Claudia Cavalli got engaged and pregnant at forty-two, all the while presiding over several hugely successful restaurants. Georgia was thirty-three. There was plenty of time to open her restaurant, open another, and another, meet her man, fall hopelessly in love, and start a family. Or not. But there were options. Lots and lots of options.

Happy hour had just started, and Georgia rushed to claim a booth while Clem hightailed it to the bar. In a city of $22 drinks, two-for-ones were too good to pass up, and the F&A quickly filled with a motley crew of college kids, young advertis-ing types, out-of-work actors, and the slightly grizzled middle-aged men who drank for sport.

From her perch in the booth, Georgia spied Bernard's sig-nature red-scarf, navy-peacoat combo, and she waved him over, watching him fight his way through the crowd, the smile never leaving his face.

"Georgia," he said when he reached her. "You did it."

"No, Bernard, *we* did it."

Lo arrived, looking chic and out of place in over-the-knee leather boots, leggings, and a fur chubby. Having given up her dreams of becoming the next Norah Jones, she'd taken a job with a fashion PR firm and was dressing the part with a vengeance. "Can I ask why we're celebrating raising a bazillion dollars in this sketchy dive bar?"

"Because," Georgia said, "this is where Bernard and I decided to partner, and where we scratched out what became the basis for our business plan. We owe a lot to the good old F and A."

Clem walked over carefully, sliding a tray with two pitchers of beer and four glasses onto the table.

"Two pitchers?" Bernard asked.

"It's two for one, and I, for one, am not dealing with that crowd again. Push over, George." Clem slid into the booth and poured four foamy beers. "So how about our girl?" she said, raising a glass in Georgia's direction.

"How about our restaurant?" Georgia said.

The four friends knocked their glasses together.

"I hate to bring up a sore subject," Lo said, "but what about a name? Have you guys come up with anything yet?"

"We've come up with a million names. It's just that they all suck," said Bernard. "It needs to mean something. It can't be the address or some slick-sounding one-syllable word or some kooky animal we love."

Georgia had been carrying her notebook with her everywhere, in case inspiration struck while on the subway, waiting on line at Citarella, or getting her toes polished, but the perfect name had so far eluded her. Bernard was right. It needed to mean something, but it also had to sound interesting and comfortable and be easy to read and pronounce.

"Anyway, we have the money. That's the important thing. The name will come." Bernard sipped his beer.

"I still can't believe Luca Santini came through with all that money," Lo said. "He must really be rolling in it."

"You know, I honestly believe that if I didn't speak French, he wouldn't have. Thank God for my grandmother. She moved in with us when my grandfather died and refused to learn English. The only way I could talk to her was in French."

"Who'd have thunk the Bari godfather would be such a Francophile?" Clem said.

Georgia considered Bernard's words. "I'd never have become a chef if it weren't for my grandmother. I practically grew up in her kitchen." Georgia was silent for a second, then looked at Bernard. "Grandmas are the link, Bernard. Without our grandmas we wouldn't be here."

"Would that be such a bad thing?" Lo asked, looking over her shoulder at a ZZ Top clone who'd just belched up the state of New Jersey.

"I mean we wouldn't be opening our restaurant if it weren't for our grandmothers, Lo."

It was true. Without Grammy, there was no way Georgia would have been sitting at the F&A with her business partner and best friends drinking bad beer and trying to come up with a name for the restaurant she'd dreamed of opening since baking her first gingerbread girl.

"No offense, George, but *Grandma the Restaurant* is hardly going to pack 'em in," said Clem.

"*Bubbe? Gammy? Gams? Dita? Mamie? Grandy? Nonna?* Help me, guys," Georgia said. "There has to be a word that means 'grandma' but doesn't sound grandmotherish."

"Nana's?" Bernard offered. "Means 'grandma,' but it's not too precious. There's also that cool dog in *Peter Pan* named Nana who took care of the kids when the parents weren't around. And it sort of rolls off the tongue."

"Nana's Kitchen?" Georgia said.

"Nana's Kitchen," Clem repeated. "I like."

"Meet me at Nana's Kitchen," Lo said. "Have you been to Nana's Kitchen? Hey, did you hear Sam Sifton gave Nana's Kitchen three stars?" She smiled. "It works."

Bernard poured another round of beers, killing the first pitcher and moving right into the second. "To Nana's Kitchen?"

"To Nana's Kitchen," Georgia said.

Chapter Twenty-four

A huge whiteboard sat on the dining table, propped up against the wall. An assortment of multicolored markers idled in a coffee mug next to it. Bernard had just returned from Staples with his latest office props, and the transformation of Georgia's apartment into Nana's Kitchen's headquarters was now officially complete.

"This whiteboard is so late-nineties new media," Georgia said.

Bernard drew a giant grid and began filling in the columns with the various and infinite tasks that needed to be accomplished before Nana's could open. Next to each task he assigned a *G* or a *B*, using a different-colored marker for each letter.

While the list grew, Georgia pulled out her notebook and began talking aloud, as much for Bernard's sake as her own. "Okay, we signed the lease last week, so check that one off. That was a big one. The graphic designer is tweaking the logo based on our comments. The architect is presenting *final final* plans tomorrow—can you give us half a check for that one?"

Bernard kept writing.

"The demolition will be done at the end of next week. Don't worry, I won't ask for a quarter check, seeing how you responded to the idea of half. Continuing to interview kitchen staff, having a major problem with the kitchen-supply store, and the bar will take way longer to fabricate than we thought; need to rethink that one. Meeting with the liquor lawyer on Friday, he says it's going to be tough to get the license. The contractor says water's not the issue, since the space was a Laundromat, but that the HVAC is going to be a bitch." She closed her notebook. "Bernard, how are we ever going to get this all done by March?"

Bernard had finally finished writing and took a step back from his color-coded masterpiece, which looked like a Damien Hirst spot painting. "How? You know how. The same way we created the business plan, raised all the money, and found the perfect space. Hard fucking work."

Georgia frowned. "I was afraid you were going to say that."

Several dozen people milled around the defunct restaurant, a midtown behemoth in a former bank that had lasted thirteen years, surviving 9/11, the economic meltdown, and three years worth of scaffolding—on either side of the entrance—before the landlord sold the building to a group of investors who were opening an H&M or a Zara, depending on whom you asked. Thirteen years was an impressive record for any city, but particularly New York, where failed restaurants were more common than off-duty lights on cabs during rainstorms. Boxes of china, flatware, linens, and stemware were piled on tables and chairs in the dining room; cases of wine were stacked on the bar; ice machines, coolers, pans, trays, and other equipment lined the kitchen. All of it was a little worse for wear, and all of it was for sale—down to the (bad) artwork on the walls. How many still lifes of bowls of fruit and dead pheasants did one restaurant need?

The owner, who stood outside smoking while potential buyers pawed through the various lots, was a friend of a friend of Bernard's, which was how it came to be that Georgia was feigning interest in a box of scuffed Ginori soup bowls, waiting for the auction to start. The object of her desire was a practically brand-new La Marzocco GB5 espresso machine, the undisputed Rolls-Royce of espresso machines. The off-the-shelf price tag was way out of their budget, but Bernard swore they could get it for a fraction of that.

Smacking his gavel on the hostess stand, the auctioneer kicked off the action with a lot of racks. Georgia checked her phone for a message from Bernard, who was meeting with the contractor at Nana's. The millwork had just been installed, including a work-around for the insanely expensive and nearly impossible to fabricate bar, and Bernard was inspecting the result. Despite his less than perfect vision, nothing got by Bernard. No message, no text. He was probably embroiled in an argument about the bar's patina.

At last the auctioneer moved on to the big-ticket items, starting with an eight-burner Garland range. The Marzocco was up next. Georgia made her way to the front of the room and pulled the paddle from her bag, gripping the handle so tightly her knuckles turned white. It was her first auction. Still, the chances of its magically floating upward seemed slim, and she had to laugh at herself. At five hundred bucks she placed her first bid, surprised by how empowering it was to wield that flimsy paddle. She raised it again at nine and again at fourteen. By two grand, only two bidders remained: someone in back the auctioneer referred to as "the man with the dark black hair," and Georgia, "the curly girl up front." At four grand she turned around to check out her competition, but most of the light fixtures had already been sold and she could barely see him. At forty-five hundred she started to sweat. She couldn't go any higher than five, half the value of a new Marzocco. Luckily, the guy dropped out in the next round and the espresso machine was Georgia's for the "low, low price of forty-seven hundred dollars." Bang.

"I let you have it," said a voice behind her as the auctioneer moved on to the next lot.

She turned around. "Marco. I had no idea—"

"Yeah, I figured. How've you been, Georgia?" He licked his lips and fixed them in a pout. His skin was so bronze he'd either just returned from South Beach or a session at Portofino Sun Tanning.

"Great. Good. Opening a restaurant."

"Figured that too. Congratulations." He jangled the keys in his pocket, then ran a hand through his black hair, which was now a shade beyond shoe polish. Anything to hide the gray.

"Thanks. What are you doing here? I thought you were in D.C."

"Nah, that town sucks. It's all politics and nerds. Boring with a capital *B*. I'm opening up a place in Jersey. It's gonna be great."

"I'll bet," Georgia said. "Well, sorry about the Marzocco."

"No biggie. I'll buy a new one. Money's not a problem. Anyway, the used ones break down all the time."

"Right." Georgia stifled a laugh. He hadn't changed a bit.

A burly guy in a plaid jacket wheeled out the espresso machine on a dolly. "Where do you want this?" he asked Georgia.

"My friend will be out front with a car in a second. You can leave it here for now, thanks."

The guy turned to Marco. "What about you? I got all those plates and pots and pans and forks and knives and all that other shit you bought. Where do you want it?"

Marco glared at him. "I was bidding for a friend. You'll have to ask him, since it's not mine."

"I don't care who it belongs to. I just gotta get it outta here. Let me know when you find your friend." The guy walked away.

"Where the hell is he?" Marco muttered, scoping out the restaurant over Georgia's head.

She peered out the window, where Bernard had just pulled up, double-parking the van he'd borrowed for the day. After dropping off the Marzocco at their restaurant, they had a bunch of smaller equipment to pick up on Bowery, which would save on delivery charges. Every dollar helped. "I don't know where your friend is, but mine's out front. It was good to see you, Marco. Good luck with the new place."

"Yeah, you too. Good luck with your new toy."

Georgia walked outside to greet Bernard while Marco took off, presumably to look for his pal.

"Who were you talking to?" Bernard asked.

"Marco."

"*The* Marco?"

"*The* Marco."

"What's he doing back in New York? What happened to D.C.?"

"My guess is that Marco was too slimy even for D.C. He's opening a place in Jersey, and I beat him out on the Marzocco. He also cleaned out the whole restaurant, even the flatware, and then pretended none of it was his. I'd say our old boss is not in a good way."

Bernard chuckled. "Awww, poor Marco."

"I can't believe I'm saying this, but I sort of feel bad for him. Two years ago he was on top of the world. Now he's scrounging for chipped china. What if that happens to us, B?"

"Not a fucking chance." Bernard pulled open the van's doors. "And can you honestly feel bad for a guy who calls you 'the chef-ette'?"

Georgia shook her head. "Not so bad, I guess."

"Good. Now where's the Marzocco? We have places to go."

The guy rolled the dolly onto the sidewalk. "This your friend?" he asked, gesturing to Bernard.

"Yeah. And he's also my partner." Georgia squeezed his arm. "Thank God for that."

Standing outside the Oven, wearing a wool hat pulled low, leather gloves pulled high, and a knee-length coat, Georgia hopped from boot to boot, trying to keep warm and to settle her nerves. She had a date. For the first time in her post-Glenn New York City life, she had a date. And he was eight minutes late. Normally, this wouldn't faze her. But since it was already eleven o'clock, and her days now routinely began at dawn, the clock was ticking.

"Georgia," a voice said behind her. A lovely voice.

She pivoted on her toes, and Andrew Henderson stood before her. As promised, he'd called, she'd called back, and they'd embarked on a game of phone tag so endless it could have become an urban legend. Finally, a few nights back, they'd connected; she couldn't remember who'd called whom. What mattered was that they were here, together.

"Andrew. It's great to see you." Wearing her four-inch-high Louboutins—her lucky Lous, Lo christened them after Luca came through with the money—she and Andrew were just about the same height. They simultaneously bent in for the kiss, bonked foreheads a bit, and she got a whiff of his shaving cream, the drugstore kind that came in a peppermint-striped aerosol can. She liked it.

"You too." He wore a thick, navy blue duffel coat and jeans and looked as if he'd stepped out of a Kennedy family photo. This was not a bad thing.

jenny nelson

"So where are we going?" she asked. Midtown at eleven was not exactly teeming with options.

"I thought we'd stay here," he said, looking around him.

"Here?"

He pointed to the ice rink below, which looked slightly forlorn now that the tree was gone. A few die-hard skaters stumbled around the rink, but with the windchill at ten degrees, and without the tree looming overhead, the romance was gone. Even tourists thought the rink looked plain old cold.

"You want to go ice-skating? Now?"

He nodded. "Why not? We've got an hour before it closes."

"Ice-skating," Georgia said, realizing how little she actually knew about Andrew. "At Rock Center. Is this a typical date for you?"

Andrew laughed. "Don't worry, Georgia, I'm not some freaky Ice Capades fanatic. You've been in a restaurant all day, and when you weren't physically in a restaurant you were thinking about restaurants, so that pretty much rules out going to a restaurant. Besides, it's eleven o'clock, it's a school night, and the rink is right here. What do you say?"

"All right. I guess I'm game."

While Britney or some other deposed pop princess sang breathlessly about broken hearts and broken promises, Georgia and Andrew lurched onto the ice. Their ugly brown rental skates were as sharp as soupspoons, and within minutes Andrew's feet flew out from underneath him and he landed smack on his butt. He pulled himself up while Georgia tried to look sympathetic.

"This wasn't my idea," she reminded him. "But it is sorta fun."

On their first painfully slow loop, they skated single file, heads down, hands clutching the rail. Between the boppy music and the slippy ice, there wasn't much room for conversation, beyond the occasional "I haven't been on ice skates in ages" or (mostly from him) "Oh, shit." During the second, slightly less sluggish loop, Georgia dared venture away from the rail and next to her date, and they started talking, beginning with a topic they both knew: his mother. Andrew quickly put the kibosh on that one, and they moved on to another topic they both knew: restaurants, namely hers. By the fourth, still-speedier loop they'd covered favorite movies (his, *The Sting*; hers, *To Kill a Mockingbird*); first real job (his, runner at the New York Stock Exchange; hers, garde-manger at Simon Says); last relationship (his, the aforementioned Lisa; hers, Glenn); favorite thing to do on a rainy Sunday (both: matinee, followed by an overpriced late-afternoon lunch). On the fifth-and-fastest-yet loop, he took her glove in his, and they skated hand in hand without saying a word . . . for a whopping twenty feet, when the loudspeaker announced that the rink was closing.

"I guess our Tai Babilonia–Randy Gardner moment is over," Georgia said.

They returned their skates and walked side by side to a nearly empty Fifth Avenue. Having reached that slightly awkward point of the date where they could either share a cab or go their separate ways, they both peered up the avenue, looking for the vacant taxi(s) that would determine their fate.

"Hmmm," said Andrew. "Doesn't look like there are any cabs."

"No. I guess we could—"

"Walk?"

"Sure," she said, glancing down at her Louboutins.

Andrew held out his hand, and Georgia slipped hers into his, instantly forgetting about her pinched feet. He took her other hand and they stood looking at each other for a second or two before he leaned forward and kissed her, softly, on the lips. When they pulled away, they grinned that first-kiss grin at each other, the one that says "I like kissing you and I think I might really like kissing you." She pulled him toward her and they kissed again, and this one was long and warm, and she felt that pinging in her belly, and she knew that she could absolutely learn to love kissing Andrew. He cleared his throat and looked down so she wouldn't see the smile playing out on his face, but she did, and she knew he was thinking the same thing.

"So," Andrew said, grinning, and this time looking directly at her. "Shall we?" He held out his arm.

"Yes. Let's."

"Want to take Fifth?"

"Nope," she said. "I'm over Fifth. Let's go Park."

They walked slowly despite the frosty air, coming to a complete stop at every crosswalk. With the streets almost empty, their chances of getting mowed down by an irate driver seemed slim, but after the Sally incident Georgia wasn't taking any chances. Besides, it was the best walk she could remember taking. They turned onto her block, stopping shy of her building's awning, so they could say good-bye without an audience. Within seconds, they were kissing.

"You know, I'm glad you didn't invest," Georgia said when they finally broke their embrace.

"So am I."

Georgia raised an eyebrow.

"Not because I don't think you'll be a smash success. But if I had, I couldn't be here. And I'd rather be here."

"Me too. And if you play your cards right, you may get an invite to our opening party."

An elegantly dressed white-haired couple approached the building, and Andrew stepped aside to let them pass. The man motioned with his hand to his head, as if to tip the hat that wasn't there.

"So," Andrew said. "I really had a great time tonight, Georgia."

"I did too."

He reached out and touched her cheek. "I'll call you."

"Good. I'll count on it."

He kissed her once more, then headed uptown for the seven-block walk to his apartment.

This year, instead of a preholiday jaunt down Fifth, Georgia had taken a postholiday stroll up Park. It was too soon to say whether it was a new tradition in the making, or just new. But she'd find out.

"We got it!" Bernard blew into Georgia's apartment, pumping both fists in the air.

"Got what?" Poised with a pink marker in her hand, Georgia crouched by one of the many whiteboards with which she and Sally now shared their apartment. She turned to look at her partner. "And why are you acting like you're at a Black Sabbath concert?"

"Robert from JAM just called." Bernard paused to catch his breath. "We got the C of O!"

They'd been waiting for the certificate of occupancy, the series of licenses that would allow them to open Nana's Kitchen, for weeks. The puzzle was complete.

"We got it? Oh, Bernard, that's fantastic!" Georgia leaped up and threw her arms around his neck. Bernard's hands encircled her waist and they jumped up and down until they were both breathless, Sally barking at their heels.

When they stopped hopping, Bernard gazed down at Georgia, whose hands had slid to his chest. She dropped her arms to her sides and took a step backward.

"So now what, B?"

He pointed to the five whiteboards leaning against the wall, lined up like cars in a train. Though he'd never cop to being superstitious, he refused to erase anything once it had been checked off, afraid it would somehow undo the action. He bought a fresh whiteboard every time they ran out of space. Though she indulged him this pricey quirk, she stopped short of allowing him to hammer into her walls and hang them like paintings.

"Would you like to do the honors?" Bernard asked.

"I'll let you. These boards are much more your thing."

Bernard knelt by the last one, where only one square of a dozen remained blank. He rummaged through the mug of markers until he found the one he wanted. "Here it is," he said, popping the top of the cherry red marker. He drew the final check with a flourish. "Checkmate."

"I can't believe it. We're really opening."

"Yes, we really are."

"What do we do now?" Georgia bent down and scratched Sally's ears. "I suddenly feel like I need to go for a run, or do a cartwheel or dunk my head in the East River or—"

"Drink vodka and eat caviar at Petrossian?"

"Exactly. That's exactly what I need to do."

Chapter Twenty-five

Bernard lit the final votive and blew out the match in his hand. "There."

Standing with her back against the bar, Georgia directed an appraising eye around the room. After three go-rounds, the walls were finally the perfect color: a burnt sienna that cast a warm glow during daylight hours and grew cozier as the sun went down. The walnut floor, reclaimed from an old farmhouse in upstate New York, had needed nothing more than tung oil to bring out its natural patina. Diaphanous drapes covered floor-to-ceiling windows; on warmer days they would be pulled back, the windows thrown open, and a handful of tables set upon the small bluestone patio next to the entrance. A huge antique mirror backed the bird's-eye maple bar, and custom built-ins along the wall housed simple stem- and glassware.

In the center of the room a vintage Murano chandelier was ablaze with tiny white lights. Bouquets of calla lilies, kumquats, and eucalyptus leaves in burlap-covered vases were placed around the room alongside glass votives wrapped with twine. On the buffet table, servers set platters of grilled vegetables, cheeses of all shapes and sizes, various pestos and spreads, trays of cured meats, and plates of multihued, bite-size canapés. The only thing missing were the tables, chairs, and barstools, which still hadn't arrived from the mill in North Carolina. Ever industrious, Bernard arranged for an acquaintance who ran a banquet-supply company to drop off a slew of ballroom chairs and tables in exchange for an invite to the opening party. If the furniture didn't show in two days, there'd be trouble, but for now all was okay.

"It does look great, doesn't it?" Georgia said happily. She turned to her partner. "And so, I must say, do you. Very natty, Bernard. Must be the French in you."

Bernard wore a navy velvet jacket and a red-and-blue silk tie with slim trousers. Though quintessentially American, he'd inherited the Frenchman's flair for dressing (in addition to his love of red wine and punk rock—Georgia had yet to meet a French guy who wasn't fanatical about both).

"And you," he said, "look even lovelier than our restaurant."

Her hair was pulled back and tied at the neck with a simple black ribbon, frizz factor a barely there two. Wavy curls framed her face, which, save for a few coats of black mascara and a swipe of red lipstick (*the* red lipstick, courtesy of Charlotte Troy), was bare. She wore a sleeveless *melanzana* dress that nipped in slightly at the waist and strappy black sandals. Cabochon amethyst earrings (borrowed from Lo, of course) dangled from her ears, and a ring with a jade stone carved into an elephant's head, her old pal Ganesh, sat on her left ring finger. A gift from Lo and Clem to celebrate the opening, it was only the second ring she'd worn since graduating culinary school, and it fit a whole lot better than its predecessor.

"We did it, B. We really did it."

"We sure did. To us, a good team."

The four months between Georgia and Bernard's random run-in at Barnes & Noble and the opening party had been packed with as much drama, cuticle biting, and curl pulling as a *Falcon Crest* rerun. Would they get the money? Would they get the additional money? The space? The staff? The certificate of occupancy? The liquor license? Their quest seemed endless, but it had ended in the right place, in the right way, and even, Georgia thought, at the right time.

"Good? Look at this place." Georgia gestured to the restaurant with an open palm. "Don't you mean *great*?"

"You're right. To us, a *great* team."

Absent any drinks, they bumped fists, laughing as they recalled the first time they'd exchanged those words. The night Mercedes Sante reviewed Marco seemed like a lifetime ago; it was hard to imagine that not even a year had passed. There was no telling what might have happened had the restaurant got the three forks it was due, but one thing seemed certain: it couldn't beat opening Nana's Kitchen.

In a few minutes, the party would start. Guests would arrive, hors d'oeuvres would be nibbled, drinks consumed in rapid succession. A cleanup crew would roll in shortly before midnight, sweeping up all traces of the party so that at the next day's mandatory staff meeting, the restaurant, if not the staff, would be well scrubbed and well rested. A week later, Nana's would officially open its doors and anyone who'd wondered if redemption was possible after a crushing, half-fork review could find out for themselves.

"Yoo-hoo!" Clem shouted as she walked in the door. "George, you were right. I never thought I'd notice a door handle, but it's really beautiful."

"See?" Georgia said to Bernard, who had balked at the price the Vermont metalworker charged for a simple door handle. "I told you. It's all in the details."

"Right." Bernard nodded his head while staring at her. "It's all in the details."

Lo arrived next. "This place looks amazing. I can't believe that just four months ago it was the home of the Suds 'N Buds Laundromat."

The head server peered out from the kitchen. "Do you want us to start passing?"

Georgia and Bernard looked at each other and then back at him. "Ten minutes," they said in unison.

Clem frowned. "It's sorta creepy how in sync you two are."

Dorothy and Hal walked in before Georgia could respond, and she ran over to her parents.

"I'm so glad you got here before everyone arrived," she said. "How's the hotel? I hope it's okay. They said they'd upgrade your room. Did you get the flowers and fruit basket—"

"The hotel is wonderful. And they're really giving us the VIP treatment. It's good to have a daughter who's a famous chef!" Dorothy wore a royal blue raw-silk tunic over flowing black pants, and a double strand of chunky lapis beads hung down to her belly.

Hal hugged his daughter tight. "It's good to have a daughter who's *you*, Georgia." He kissed the top of her head. "We're so proud of you."

"Thanks, Dad, and Mom. For the money, for believing in me, for your support over the last few months. You've really been great." Georgia felt her eyes welling, then remembered the two coats of black mascara she'd applied.

"I wish Grammy were here to see you," her mother said.

"Georgia! Ciao, bellissima!"

Georgia turned in time to see Vanessa charging over with outstretched arms. Her brown hair was braided and wrapped around her head Heidi-style.

"Vanessa! I'm so glad to see you. I can't believe you came all the way from San Casciano for this." Georgia grabbed Vanessa's hands and kissed her on both cheeks.

"I wouldn't miss it for anything. Everyone at Dia says to tell you *in bocca al lupo*—that means 'good luck.' Effie's still mad that Claudia wouldn't let him leave, but since she had the baby, she needs all the help she can get. She's so in love with little Bianca we barely ever see her. Here, the latest picture." Vanessa whipped out a black-and-white photo of a wispy-haired baby in a onesie.

"She's beautiful. A perfect mixture of both her parents." Georgia had Skyped with Claudia a few days earlier, but Bianca had been sleeping. She fingered the photo in her hand before returning it.

Vanessa walked off to get a bite and a drink and was immediately intercepted by Dorothy and Hal, delighted to see someone they'd met "on the Continent."

"Who's your friend, Chef? She is *smoking*." Wearing a white chef's coat, khaki cargo pants, and Crocs, Ricky walked up next to his boss. Persuading him to leave his job at the three-hundred-seat pan-Asian palace where he'd worked since Marco's demise hadn't been too tough, especially when she and Bernard revealed how he fit into their plans. Executive sous-chef today, chef de cuisine and part owner of restaurant number two tomorrow, was how they'd put it. Having already said he'd take a job at Mickey D's if it meant working with Georgia again, he hadn't needed any more convincing.

Once Ricky was on board, the rest of the kitchen staff had fallen into place. Several Marco alums were joined by some fresh faces, including a plucky Culinary Institute grad named Alice who reminded Georgia a bit of herself. The front-of-the-house staff had been assembled almost as quickly, but didn't include any Marco vets.

"My smoking friend, who doesn't smoke, by the way, is Vanessa," Georgia said to Ricky. "She just arrived from Italy. You should go meet her. I bet you guys would get along great."

"Everything's under control in the kitchen, so if you're cool with it, don't mind if I do." Ricky was running the kitchen, allowing Georgia her one chance to relax in the restaurant before the official open. He picked up two drinks from a passing tray, tossed his hair, and made his way through the crowd to Vanessa.

In under twenty minutes, the restaurant had filled with all the people Georgia would ever want to see, and a whole bunch she had never before seen, who she assumed were Bernard's half of the invite list. They'd agreed not to include industry types unless they were real friends, but it looked as if a few had snuck in anyway. A high-profile restaurant opening, especially one with a juicy backstory, was not an event to miss. Free food and booze didn't hurt either. The place was jammed.

At one end of the room, Dorothy and Hal chatted with Bernard's parents, each parental package brimming with pride. At the other, Lo and a cute mystery man listened intently to Clem, no doubt telling one of her trademark "all true; swear" tales. At the bar, Vanessa and Ricky sipped their drinks and giggled. By the door, Luca Santini chatted up Charlotte Troy, an unlikely pairing if ever there were one. Everyone who'd helped bring Nana's Kitchen to life—architects, designers, various contractors, attorneys, and purveyors—was there, along with friends of Georgia's and Bernard's from every stage of their careers. Only a handful of people who'd RSVP'd hadn't yet shown, and only one Georgia really cared about.

Date number two with Andrew had been an impromptu affair on a rainy Sunday afternoon. They started with a revival of
The African Queen, followed by raw bar and beers at Aquagrill.
He took her to her apartment in a cab and they shared kisses
number five through eight in the steamy backseat. He'd wanted
to continue on to an exhibit at the Whitney, or at least up to her
apartment, but she had a meeting with Bernard. When he jokingly asked if he'd always be number two to Nana's, or number
three behind Nana's and Bernard, she could tell he was a little
annoyed. Since then she'd been too swamped to carve out even
the two hours required for a decent date. She'd vowed to never
again sacrifice herself for the sake of being a pair, but she really
hoped Andrew would be there when she surfaced. And she
really, really hoped he'd show for the party.

The door shut behind another batch of newly arrived guests.
Acoustical tiles hidden in the ceiling kept the noise to a boisterous buzz, and the strains of Wilco were just barely audible on
the ACS sound system. Bernard may not have been able to appreciate a hand-cast door pull, but a six-pack of Harman Kardon
speakers was another matter entirely.

"Georgia," said that unmistakable voice. "Sorry I'm late."

She looked up at Andrew Henderson, cutting a dashing
Darcy-esque figure in a dark gray suit, crisp white shirt, and
maroon tie.

"Andrew, I'm so glad you made it. I was just wondering if you
had forgotten."

"Forgotten? Hendersons never forget." Huggy Henderson,
wearing nickel-size diamonds clipped to her ears, stepped out
from behind her son, grabbed Georgia's shoulders, and kissed
her cheek. "You look gorgeous. And this room, my God. Who did
the flowers? They are so fabulously understated."

"Huggy, it's good to see you. I'm so glad you came."

"Larry is here somewhere—you haven't seen him, have you? Before I rush off to rescue my husband and leave you to my son, let me say congratulations. I knew from the moment I met you that you were destined for great things. That Marco place was just too tacky for you." Huggy squeezed her arm. "Excuse me, dear. And don't forget to get me the name of your florist."

"She's something," Georgia said when Huggy was out of earshot.

"She is, but I'm more interested in you right now." Andrew's lips curved into a smile. "You pulled it off, Georgia."

"You know, I'm still not sure how, but I think we did."

"What are the chances we can squeeze in our third date before you open your next restaurant?"

"I'd say very good. It may have to be a six a.m. power breakfast at the Regency or midnight churros, but if you'll bear with me for a while, it will get better, I promise."

Andrew picked up a flute of prosecco from a server passing by and raised it in Georgia's direction. "I think I can do that."

Vanessa and Ricky walked over, and Georgia made introductions all around.

"He's so cute," Vanessa said under her breath.

"Oh, no, you don't," Georgia said, shaking her head. "Those were the exact words you said about Gianni."

"First of all," said Vanessa, "Gianni *is* cute. But Andrew's cuter. And second of all, I wasn't talking about Andrew."

"Oh." Georgia cast a quick glance in Ricky's direction. "I see."

Ricky looked at Georgia and grinned. Clem and Lo joined the group and after introductions bent their heads together conspiratorially.

"Who's that guy you were talking to earlier?" Georgia asked her friends.

"Oh, that's Brian," said Clem. "I hope you don't mind that I invited him."

"Are you kidding?" said Georgia. "Of course not. Who is he?"

"Just this guy I've sort of been dating," Clem said.

"What? Why didn't you tell me?"

"You had other things on your mind, George. And I didn't want to tell anyone about him until, well, you know."

Georgia played dumb. "Until what?"

"The third date. I wanted to get beyond that damn third date."

"And did you?" Lo asked. "Get past it?"

"Date number five, baby. Right here at Nana's Kitchen." Clem held out her hands, palms up, and Lo and Georgia each slapped one.

"Right here at Nana's Kitchen," Georgia said. "I like the way that sounds." She looked around the room, a smile spreading across her face. Next week she would turn thirty-four, right there at Nana's Kitchen. She wasn't married, as she thought she'd be, she didn't have a baby, or one on the way, as she thought she might, she didn't even have a serious boyfriend, as she'd always had, but she was exactly where she wanted to be. Right there at Nana's Kitchen.

Acknowledgments

Heartfelt thanks to Stephanie Lehmann, my patient and determined agent; everyone at Elaine Koster; my astute editor Kathy Sagan; Jen Bergstrom, Louise Burke, Jessica Webb, and the wonderful team at Gallery Books. For their invaluable insights into the magical world of restaurants, thank you to Sandra Ardito (for her lightning-fast responses), Jimmy Zankel, and Mike Howell. Peter Marcus, Melissa Chapnick, Jason Carreiro, Jenny Swift, and Susan Breen offered much-needed encouragement early on, and the New York Public Library, the Millbrook Free Library, and Starbucks provided a place to plug in my laptop. My oldest and dearest pals Anne Krumme, Sarah Dillon, Chrissy Drabek, and Merri Hahn never tired of talking about "the book," and Yuliya Livchak took care of things on the home front so I could get out and write.

I feel blessed to have such an amazing family, starting with my parents, Carol Nelson and Jay Nelson, whose love, support, and encouragement have been constants in my life (plus, they make me laugh), and a sister, Steffie Nelson, whose advice and taste I trust implicitly (and who also makes me laugh). My daughters, Flora and Ava Elghanayan, are the two coolest girls I know; their enthusiasm, curiosity, creativity, and empathy are traits I try to emulate every day. My multilingual mother-in-law, Shoshana Gol, gladly translated everything I needed into Italian. Finally, my husband, Warren Elghanayan, who quietly and persistently urged me on, patiently talked me through plot points and character development (frequently while we were huffing up hills on our mountain bikes), and bucked me up—as he always does—when I felt as if I were writing this book for myself. My love and gratitude are immeasurable.

Georgia's Kitchen

jenny nelson

INTRODUCTION

Georgia Gray's life seems close to perfect; she's head chef at a trendy New York restaurant, recently engaged to her handsome lawyer boyfriend, and on the verge of getting a career-making three-fork review from one of the city's toughest critics. But when her sleazy boss makes a disastrous decision, Georgia finds herself trying to hang on to her credibility as a chef while her personal life crumbles.

Suddenly unemployed and unengaged, Georgia picks herself up, packs her bags, and moves to Tuscany, where she helps her mentor, a renowned chef, open a new trattoria. The breathtaking scenery and delectable food help clear her head, the success of Trattoria Dia rebuilds her confidence, and romance with a sexy vineyard owner helps heal her heart. But Georgia realizes she can't stay in Italy forever, and when the summer ends, she returns home to the city she loves, determined to make good on her dream and open her very own restaurant.

QUESTIONS AND TOPICS FOR DISCUSSION

1. The novel begins and ends in New York, yet Georgia has been on "a long journey with more twists and kinks than her hair after a hot summer day at the beach." (p. 172) Compare the early version of Georgia with the woman she is by the end of the novel. Do you feel she has changed? In what ways?

2. After Georgia confronts Glenn about his cocaine use, he leaves her, first temporarily, and then for good. What might have happened if he hadn't broken up with her? Would she have left him?

3. At Georgia's urging, Glenn quits doing coke and cleans up his act. While she is clearly the catalyst for his change, a drug-free Glenn decides that he doesn't want to marry her. Have you ever helped someone through a difficult time only to find that your relationship suffered or changed as a result?

4. Georgia's best friend Clem says, ". . . no one knows what will make them truly happy until they find it." (p. 100) Do you agree with this statement? Support your argument using other characters from the novel, or even examples from your own life.

5. Though we never meet Grammy, she is an important character in the novel and, in many ways, Georgia's role model. Discuss Georgia's relationship with Grammy versus her relationship with Dorothy. Is a grandmother-granddaughter relationship sometimes easier to navigate than a mother-daughter relationship? Why or why not?

6. Dorothy and Georgia's relationship isn't an easy one, to say the least. From what do you think the tension stems? Are Dorothy's expectations for her daughter fair? Do they take into account the

kind of person Georgia is or the kind of person Dorothy wishes Georgia were? Conversely, is Georgia too hard on Dorothy? Does she expect too much from her mother?

7. According to Georgia, neither Clem nor Lo will ever "get what it felt like to grow up in a household where you were a third wheel to your parents" (p. 99) the way that Georgia does. "Her parents were like two teenagers in love, even after almost thirty-five years of marriage." (p. 50) How does her parents' tight relationship affect Georgia? How does it shape her relationships with men? Has your parents' relationship had an impact on your own relationships?

8. When Georgia first meets Sergio, he says, "We used to care more about family. Friends. Life. Now we care about success. Money." (p. 126) How true do you find this statement? How true is it in regard to Claudia? In regard to the other characters in the book?

9. Claudia tells Georgia to "Stop looking for what you don't have, and start seeing what you do." (p. 151) Do you think Georgia has learned how to do this by the end of the book? Is this something that people often forget to do in their daily lives? Can you think of an instance where that advice helped (or could have helped) you?

10. *Georgia's Kitchen* has a cast of strong, supporting female characters. Think about all the different women who influence Georgia's life. What does Georgia learn from each of these women at various points throughout the novel? What do you think they learn from her? Think about the women who play important roles in your own life. What have you learned from them?

11. Georgia has three significant romances over the course of the book: Glenn, Gianni, and Andrew. Discuss the impact each rela-

tionship, and each man, has on her and the choices she makes. Which of these men do you think is best suited for Georgia?

12. The title of the novel is *Georgia's Kitchen*. Discuss the significance in relation to the story. What does Georgia learn in the kitchen? Out of the kitchen? Why is it so important for her to have her own kitchen in her own restaurant?

13. Perhaps the most important lesson Georgia learns is that while "it's okay to be alone . . . it's okay to ask for help." (p. 254) Do you think she would have succeeded in opening Nana's Kitchen without Bernard as her partner? Is her success any less meaningful because she shares it with Bernard? Have you ever had to choose between doing something on your own or asking for help in your own life?

14. At the end of the novel, Georgia reflects that even without a husband or a baby ". . . she was exactly where she wanted to be. Right there at Nana's Kitchen." (p. 319) Does Georgia's happiness resonate with you? Does working hard to achieve a goal make the end result more meaningful? Is there something you've worked hard to accomplish in your own life that made you feel the way Georgia does about Nana's Kitchen?

ENHANCE YOUR BOOK CLUB

1. Georgia is determined to create Trattoria Dia's signature dish and, with a little help from Bruno, she succeeds. Have a book club banquet by asking each member to create their own signature dish and bring it to the gathering.

2. Tuscany and Sicily are important settings in *Georgia's Kitchen*. Have each member do some research on either place and share what they discover with the group.

3. If *Georgia's Kitchen* were made into a movie, whom would you cast?

A CONVERSATION WITH JENNY NELSON

What inspired you to write *Georgia's Kitchen*?

I've always been fascinated by the inner workings of restaurants and the people who make them tick. It's amazing how a calm, well-run dining room reflects none of the craziness and drama taking place in the cramped, hot kitchen, just inches away. As my ideas about Georgia and the book's overall themes began to crystallize, I knew that she had to be a chef. I could visualize her in the kitchen, see how she would act, react, carry herself. No other career encapsulated who she was in the same way.

What was the general experience of writing a novel like for you?

I started writing *Georgia's Kitchen* as a stay-at-home mom. What began as a short story morphed into a first chapter (completely different from the one in the book) and when I was about fifty pages in, I knew that I wouldn't stop until I'd completed a novel. It was thrilling to see those pages mounting, and even more thrilling when I started getting positive feedback, because for a while I was really writing in a vacuum, not sure whether anything I'd written was any good. Once I'd completed it, I found my agent and soon after sold the book. I'm still amazed at how things unfolded.

You really bring your settings to life, be it the beauty of San Casciano, the rush of New York City, or the heat inside a top restaurant's kitchen. You currently live in New York, but have you spent a significant amount of time in Italy? Did you need to do much research for the settings of your book—other than eat great Italian food?

I'm lucky to have spent a good bit of time in Italy, all over, really, but mainly in Tuscany. My husband and I were married in Fiesole, at a villa that once belonged to Dante Alighieri (if this feels familiar it's because Georgia reflects on a wedding she and Glenn attended that sounds suspiciously like ours). In addition to relying on my own experiences, I did a lot of research on Tuscany and Sicily—on the architecture, the landscape and, obviously, the food and wine. As for food, New York is filled with incredible Italian restaurants, and I make it a point to eat at as many as possible, which is no great hardship! My mother-in-law, who grew up in Milan and still spends a lot of time there, was able to help with all the Italian translations.

There are great descriptions of meal preparations in the book. Do you cook? What was the inspiration for the signature dish Georgia creates for Trattoria Dia?

I love to cook, but with twin six-year-old daughters, sometimes it's more about getting dinner on the table than preparing a fabulous new recipe I've discovered. Luckily, they're both good eaters and will try just about anything, so I do get to be a little more experimental at times. Italian food is my absolute favorite to make—I love how forgiving it is, and how it all begins with good, basic ingredients. As for the signature dish, I wanted it to be vegetarian, and because I would happily eat risotto for the rest of my life, I thought it'd be fun to come up with something that was a riff on a traditional risotto.

You provide a lot of detail about each character's sense of style, as well as passing references to various designer clothing and accessories (such as the scene where Clem and Lo are talking about different types of jeans). As you wrote, did you find that the way you visualized the outward appearance of each character reflected a lot about their personalities?

Absolutely. I had a lot of fun figuring out how each character would look and what he or she would choose to wear. Often, when I was creating a character, I would see them for the first time and know exactly what kind of shoes they would wear, how they'd want their jeans to fit, how they'd style their hair, if they'd wear makeup or jewelry.

Who are your writing influences and what are you currently reading?

I read anything and everything. I just finished *Wolf Hall* (I'm obsessed with the Tudors), loved *The Help, Olive Kitteridge,* and *Unaccustomed Earth*—Jhumpa Lahiri is one of my favorite writers. I also love the classics—*The Great Gatsby, The House of Mirth,* and anything by Jane Austen. I'll pick up pretty much any novel or collection of stories, but nonfiction is a harder sell for me.

Many authors find that their characters are extensions of themselves, in one way or another. Do you find that to be true? Are any of the characters in *Georgia's Kitchen* based on people you know?

None of the characters are pure extensions of anyone I know. This isn't to say that certain characters don't borrow traits or characteristics from people I know, but that's really the extent of it. I did enjoy throwing in elements from my own life (such as the wedding) or the name of the bar where Georgia and Bernard decide to partner (the F&A, named for the way it sounds and also for my daughters Flora and Ava), but you'd have to read really closely and know me really well to pick up on most of these!

The complicated relationship between Georgia and her parents is central to the development of the novel, and a theme that most people can relate to. What made you decide to write a character that was closer to her grandmother than her mother? Was it based on personal experience?

Because I have great relationships with both of my parents, I thought it would be interesting to explore a parent/child dynamic that was fraught with tension and disappointment. So often the intentions are good, as I believe Georgia's, Dorothy's, and Hal's are, and yet actions and words can easily undermine these good intentions. Having had two wonderful grandmothers, both of whom lived well into their nineties, I know how important grandmotherly love can be for a kid, even as she grows older. Most grandparents don't have to do a lot of the heavy lifting associated with raising their grandkids, so they're free to do nothing but love them. From my experience, unconditional love from a grandparent really is unconditional. I'm also intrigued by the idea of a less-than-stellar mother becoming a terrific grandmother.

One of the most significant ideas in the book is learning how to see what you do have, instead of dwelling on what you don't have. Is that a mantra you live by?
I wish I could unhesitatingly say yes, but like Georgia, I'm still learning.

Are you planning to return to Nana's Kitchen and this cast of characters in your next book, or do you feel like Georgia's story is finished? If so, where do you think you'll go next?
I don't think Georgia's story is finished by any means, and I'd love to pay her a visit after Nana's Kitchen opens to see how things are panning out. Is the restaurant the smash success she hopes it will be? Is she still with Andrew? Does she get her own Food Network show? Will she get pregnant? Married? Open a second place? Return to Italy? The possibilities are endless, but writing a sequel is a ways off. Right now I'm working on a novel about a woman whose world is turned upside down when her husband is convicted of a white-collar crime that sends him to jail. Forced to give up her moneyed New York lifestyle, she moves to the country where she falls in with a very different crowd and starts raising goats. Like *Georgia's Kitchen*, it's got a food motif running through it, though in a very different way, and love, family, and self-discovery are important themes.